AN UNHOLY RITUAL

Now Faran turned away from him and went to the nearest mortuary slab, where the first victim he had uncovered lay, his withered face peering up from the ripped winding sheets. He set the Chalice and its precious cargo down on the slab and pulled off the second of his leather gauntlets. Underneath his hands were dead white, the veins showing as black. He dipped his index finger into the Chalice, brought up a bead of blood and placed it on the dead man's tongue. The corpse's body suddenly arched, as if it had been struck by a bolt of energy. Golon leapt back, surprised. The body spasmed again, then came to rest once more on the slab. Faran peered down at it, a small smile twitching at the corner of his mouth. Even Golon stepped a little closer, fascinated by what he saw. A blue vein began to throb in the man's neck, once, twice, building up to the slow pulse of the dead: four in a minute.

"He will wake soon," Faran said. He gestured to Golon to move on to the next slab. He pointed to the dagger, which was still in Golon's hand. "Cut them open, every one of them."

The sorcerer approached, holding a sleeve of his cloak to his mouth, the other the obsidian knife. He awkwardly forced open the corpse's rigidly set jaw. . . .

OLIVER JOHNSON'S
THE LIGHTBRINGER TRILOGY:

THE FORGING OF THE SHADOWS

THE NATIONS OF THE NIGHT

THE LAST STAR AT DAWN

Book Three of
The Lightbringer Trilogy

THE
LAST STAR
AT DAWN

Oliver Johnson

A ROC BOOK

ROC
Published by New American Library, a division of
Penguin Putnam Inc., 375 Hudson Street,
New York, New York 10014, U.S.A.
Penguin Books Ltd, 27 Wrights Lane,
London W8 5TZ, England
Penguin Books Australia Ltd,
Ringwood, Victoria, Australia
Penguin Books Canada Ltd, 10 Alcorn Avenue,
Toronto, Ontario, Canada M4V 3B2
Penguin Books (N.Z.) Ltd, 182–190 Wairau Road,
Auckland 10, New Zealand

Penguin Books Ltd, Registered Offices:
Harmondsworth, Middlesex, England

Published by Roc, an imprint of New American Library,
a division of Penguin Putnam Inc.

First Roc trade paperback printing, November 1999
First Roc paperback printing, April 2001
10 9 8 7 6 5 4 3 2 1

For my brother, Peter

Iskiard

The Iron Gates

GREAT ICE LAKE

Scalprock   Maligar
The Black Mines

The Tournament Plain

The Lake of Lorn
Lorn
LORN
Astragal

Shandering Plain

THE LAND OF CLOUDS   THE NATIONS OF THE NIGHT

Goda   Segron   The Palisades
Height

The Old Father   THRULLAND

THE   Forgeholm   Thrull
ASTARDIAN
SEA   The Fire   The Niasseh
Mountains   Range   Valeda
Superstition
Mountain   Bardun   ATTAR

GALASTRA   SURRENLAND   OSSIA

Imblewick   Perricod   Nush   Tiré Gand

The Dragon's   The Dry River
Back   Morgar   Gorvost   The Inland Sea

SRAIM DESERT

Wizard's   HANGAR PARANG
Tower

Leagues
0   50   100

The Last Star at Dawn

CHAPTER ONE

Sunset in the Tower

He wakes me, the young scribe who I can no longer see. I have slept away the afternoon and it is evening. I was far away, dreaming of the lands that stretch away below this tower; the lands I travelled through in my youth.

But now I am awake, I become the Abbot of Forgeholm once more. I rise from my chair. There, through my gummed eyes, I see an orange glow: the sun is setting over the Fire Mountains. I raise my palms to it and give the scribe the evening's blessing. *"May our lord Reh find Galadrian's golden thread in the night's labyrinth. May his sun barge fly across the heavens: may its rays shine on you, friend Kereb."*

My mind is not on the words. Dreams of the past still haunt me. Tonight Kereb and I will finish the final chapters. Time has come full circle—in my end is my beginning: this story began in this tower. Now it will end here too.

I was twelve when I first came to this place, carried half-dead from the temple below to these heights where everything beneath, the monastery and its people and the mountain and the passes, seem miniatures of another world, far removed. For many years my only companions were this worm-eaten desk, these dusty alembics and retorts, this narrow cot and the three books that my master Manichee gave me before he died.

They stand propped on the mantel over the fire-blackened hearth, catching the light of the setting sun—in that exact same place where I placed them when my time came to leave.

All those lands that I visited in my youth are described in one of the books: Thrulland, Surrenland, the Nations of the Night, Ossia, Attar and the Land of the Lost City, Iskiard.

But my travelling days are over—it is the other two books that draw me to them. They have remained unopened since the day I returned forty years ago, though every evening I take them down and touch their covers—as I do now.

The first book is dedicated to my God: Reh, Lord of the Flame and the Reborn Sun. The *Book of Light.* I hold it close to my eyes; its tarnished silver edgings, and the lapis lazuli set into the four corners of the ancient leather cover, catch the beams of the falling sun and blaze with a blue-white light: the color of magic. Every evening I hold it like this— I do it not from devotion to my God but knowing every evening that *she* used to do this: silently praying, holding the book up to the westering sun.

Now I pick up the smallest of the three books. I feel its leather-bound boards: I remember its color: that of the soot-blackened mantel on which it has lain all these years. My fingers tingle, as if I held a living, breathing thing. From within I feel a barely discernible pulse: it is the pulse of magic, my friend.

All my craft lies in it: no thicker than a thumb; no longer than a hand, its leather worn and warped by fire and water and the hands of a hundred adepts that lived before me, Manichee the last. His words of farewell echo: "Learn it well. For in it is every form of pyromancy known to the Flame. With it you will summon fire even from wind and ice, and bring lightning from the heavens." Oh, master, I did so, and smote our enemies.

I replace the books. Kereb is silent. He is anxious to get

on with the evening's business—the dictation of my history of the Wars of the Flame and the Worm. He has no reason to love me. I do not pay his way, or have a rich living in my gift. It is the High Priest in far-off Perricod who has sent him here, has ordered him to share my exile, when once he expected greater things. Together we endure our sentence. Mine is for life, his perhaps will end when our work, this history, is finished.

And tonight it will be, if Reh and my memory allow.

So Kereb sits with pen and ink, ready, maintaining the charade of diligence when he and I know we might spare him the pains of his labor. Do they think I am deaf as well as blind? Do I not hear after each night's dictation the horse's hooves clattering in the cobbled yard, the shouts of the rider, the heavy gates groaning open? And in the silence of the night the sound of the hooves echoing back up the pass, off each crag, over each hairpin. I follow the rider in my mind's eye: five days and nights, all the way to Perricod, post after post, until he stands at the gateway of the temple.

Only the High Priest knows what happens to my words. Perhaps he reads them, a rueful smile upon his face, as he sees only the ranting of a heretic and a fornicator. Perhaps that is what I am. But also I am a heretic and fornicator who tells the truth: a truth too dangerous for him.

And yet, tonight I will begin as I do every evening: I will speak to the shadows. Pretend that someone else but the High Priest will read these words; tomorrow, or the next day, or in a thousand years . . .

I take a deep breath. There is a particular smell in the air: it is that time when the flowers that grow up the side of the tower begin to close; their scent drifts away like a faint memory.

The sunbeams have gone. I remember how a mellow violet hue sits upon the mountains on evenings like this, and how the lizards bask on the warm rocks that hold the last of the afternoon's heat. The heather will come in a month or two. Heather! We never dreamed of such a thing in the cold years of my boyhood. The flowers of even that most hardy plant would not bud in the year-long cold, the absence of the sun.

Below I hear voices and laughter in the refectory. I can picture the scene. A yellow light blazes from the kitchen windows and doors, like golden fire. The acolytes are sweating over the pots. Over the clatter I hear a verse of a bawdy country song. Once more they have been at the cider that the farmers bring up from the orchards on the plains far below.

But the laughter doesn't displease me. I have made an oath: let the laughter continue. Never again will the fear and the beatings return to Forgeholm. Though I am Abbot, I am a man as well.

It is now properly night: all the world is covered in shadows, just like it was forty years ago, when the darkness covered the sun and the earth even during the day.

Until *she* came and relit the sun. The day returned and once more Reh showed his face to her, the Lightbringer.

In my early years when I first lived in this tower, Reh's return would have meant everything to me, everything that I lived or cared for; for was I not a priest of the Flame and the Reborn Sun? But listen, scribe: now I am old: gone are the certainties—if only I could return to the sweet and certain prejudices of youth, not flinching at anything—even the blood sacrifices and burnings—whatever was prescribed in that self-same book, the *Book of Light* that sits upon the mantel—for in those certainties is the only happiness.

But now I have no certainties—apart from what lives in my heart. Believe me, Kereb, I have seen the original of the *Book of Light*—it is dust; I have met the ghost of Marizian the Mage, he who wrote it—he wanders not in paradise but in the damned region of Shades. And as for Reh? I have traveled through the heart of the sun and found the sun that burns in my heart. *That* is all that matters: the light within. Let it burn for the transitory moment that we have on this earth—let it burn in the fleeting laughter of those novices in the kitchen below, in the brief colours of a wildflower, the fugitive cry of a bird in the sky: for all that burns within eventually consumes itself and dies.

But now I need that fire again, however dimmed. The darkness of the mind, in which the thoughts of old age are entombed, grows deeper as the night, the time of Iss, draws on. Old evils stir like ghosts in my memory, just out of sight.

Though the war is won and Iss' cities and temples razed, the enemy is never dead, but merely sleeps. Where there are underground places—vaults and catacombs, even the grave itself—he waits, like a coiled serpent, the Worm that eats its own tall until time is no more. O children of Reh, be wakeful.

Now, Kereb, let us begin.

My name? You know it by now if my words are known. And if they are not, then my name is dead along with my words. But I will speak it one last time. It is Urthred of Ravenspur, priest of Flame.

Once I had a face that no man or woman could look upon. Yet with it I found love. Now I, like the sun, have turned full circle: now I have an old man's face, a face that the young despise, and once more I am alone. In my beginning was my end. Sunrise and sunset; light and dark: the world has turned through them again and again. Yet the greater darkness has averted and only one remains for me, the darkness of the end.

Before it comes, I will speak, though I speak only to shadows.

Let this tale, the last of Thalassa, begin . . .

CHAPTER TWO

The Coming of the
Bare-Backed King

Thrull. The fourth day of winter. Mist comes as night falls.

The demon, Nekron, is a hundred yards long, carried by a thousand feet, a horned skull head, his skin a million dully glittering obsidian scales. He slides between the houses, his body slithering from side to side, toppling gable ends and supporting walls. He leaves a glistening track behind. Now each height and depth bears the silver trail of his passing, so in the moonlight penetrating the mist, the granite-cliffed city looks as if silver thread had been wound round and round its sides.

The demon's time on earth is short. Already, steer-sized slabs of viscous skin slough off, the great maw gapes and sinks to the ground, scraping slowly along it, bone and teeth breaking away.

The demon climbs: up to the temple square, his thousand legs more and more sluggish, ranks of them collapsing under his weight. But at last he is upon the summit of that cursed city. In a rage his tail thrashes into the bases of the two temple pyramids of Iss and Reh, toppling walls, fracturing their bases. The pyramids crumble, masonry breaks off their sides and falls over the cliffs, toppling slowly down onto the houses of the lower town in a dusty avalanche.

Nekron dissolves into a vast lake of his own green acid; the bubbling liquid burns downward, searing through the stones of the temple square, scorching a vast crater in the summit, percolating down into the catacombs below, burning holes through the many levels of the underworld, even to the Silver River a mile beneath.

Below one of the ruined crags, a human hand pokes out of the rubble: the skin a mottled blue and chalk white, the edge of the cloak sleeve visible: purple and brown. The colours of the God of Darkness—Iss. The man's soul is with his master. A leather-bound book has fallen from his dead hand. The Holy Book of Iss: the Book of Worms. And on the open page, this is written: *On the fourth day of winter Thrull will be destroyed.*

The cold wind blows over the marshes. The pages of the book start to turn, over and over, nearly faster than the eye can see: a date, a sigil, a drawing, a kaleidoscope of wormy lines, are momentarily glimpsed. Then it comes to rest on the very last page, where the vellum is yellowed and the lines of ink are smudged and faint, but where this prophecy is still legible.

In the year after the coming of Nekron—Iss' enemy and Reh's hope, the Lightbringer, will pass into the land of Shades and there she will die, and the light of the sun will die with her. Lord Iss will come from the stars and establish a kingdom upon this earth. And all shall praise him, the Dark Prince, who shall reign forever in the eternal darkness.

The winter passes. No spring or summer comes. The earth is frozen, the sun hidden. The time of darkness is beginning.

All through the winter the blizzards howled in from the Fire Mountains. Many leagues to the south of Thrull stood Perricod, ancient capital of Surrenland, in the great horseshoe loop of the River Donzel, its towers and grey battlements rising above a wasteland of snow. It was a city once dedicated to Reh, but now its ruler, Lord Sam, was dead and its walls stood unguarded to any who might brave the winter wasteland to come to it.

This evening, three months after the destruction of Thrull, the shortest day of the year was ending prematurely. Just after noon the sky had darkened, and the starving wolf packs that roamed outside the city walls started to howl.

Inside the city only one inn remained open of all the dozens that had once done a brisk trade with farmers, soldiers, and merchants. It was called the Gryphon's Head, a ramshackle hostelry hard by the northern gates. This evening there was no throng in its common room and the fire within had burned low, giving light but no heat. There was no food save horse meat nor wine save the vinegary lees of the vintage before the great freeze.

The few remaining guests whispered to one another: falling silent every time a blast of wind rattled the door. The afternoon grew darker and darker. The guests had much to discuss. Vampires were already abroad in the city and rumour had it that an army of the undead was marching from Tiré Gand; that this very night they would arrive and the thousand-year rule of Reh in Perricod would finally be at an end.

The city was lost anyway: plague and famine had come to it months before. Worse, the bitterness of the winter and the absence of the sun could only mean one thing. Surely this was the beginning of the final night of man, when the sun disappeared forever and Lord Iss returned to earth?

The patrons of the inn shook their heads gloomily, but there was a certain expedience in their gathering here: even though they were not enthusiasts of the Dark God and his doctrines, they went under his protection: the outside of the inn's door was chalked with the symbol of the Worm, the serpent consuming its own tail, signaling that all those gathered gave themselves to Iss' guardianship.

Outside, huddled figures scurried down the streets in the premature darkness, leaping over the frozen races of the open sewers, avoiding passing under the eaves of houses where spear-shaped icicles hung ready to fall, skirting the piles of the dead, their stiff limbs pointing from the carrion heaps at every street corner like the stiff boughs of trees.

A tramp of feet and presently a column of men dressed in the Dark God's purple and brown robes appeared. The acolytes of the Worm. Fierce-looking, sallow-complexioned, shaven-headed thugs, their faces covered with boils from lack of sleep and poor nutrition. Each was armed with a thick stave three inches across, four feet long, a serpent head carved upon its end. At their belts they carried pouches filled with soot. They drove the few malingering townsfolk from their path with blows and snarls.

They passed the inn, and plunged into the jumbled labyrinth of streets, seeking the houses of the unconverted that had no serpent symbol, striking each unmarked door with the staves, the sound putting those therein in mind of the six hammer strokes of doom predicted in the holy books: the hammer strokes that would announce the end of the world.

And after the noise of the staves died away, the acolytes cried out to those in the houses to hear the words of the dark scripture: how the sun would not rise again after this night.

And many of the people who heard their words, who in better times, when the Temple of Reh had been strong, had warmed their hands at the execution pyres of such heretics, looked out their mullioned windows at the sky as dark as a coal scuttle and believed that, indeed, the evening of that endless night had come. Meekly they donned their darkest clothes and left their houses, heads bowed low in shame, to follow the procession of shaven-headed acolytes through the city to the Temple of Iss.

But those who refused to open their doors or shouted curses back were singled out for a worse fate. The acolytes reached into their pouches and pressed their soot-covered palms onto their doors, leaving a mark—the black hand. Later, when the night was darkest, the undead would come, as they came every evening, digging through the cellars of the marked houses, or climbing through the windows, taking all those they could find.

Now as darkness settled the wolf packs closed in, as they did at every dusk, surrounding the northern gates; not daring to enter the city, for the scent of their enemy, man, was still thick in the air but knowing their time would come soon. Their howling was as high and persistent as the noise of the keening wind.

But then they fell silent. The wind died too. A sudden mist appeared in the streets. The acolytes froze, their heads cocked to one side, listening.

At first the only sound was the hissing of snow particles gently blowing down the frozen streets. Then came the sound of a horse's hooves on the metalled road that led to the north over the frozen fields.

Gradually the rider emerged from the gloom of the evening, mounted on a grey gelding. He rode into the northern gatehouse of the city: there were no guards left to challenge him. The horse's shoes rang off the cobbles and echoed as he passed through the archway and into the grey streets of Perricod.

The patrons of the Gryphon's Head gathered curiously at the windows and stared at him as he rode by. He was the first man who had been down the northern road in months. But there was no sign he had spurred his horse through the wolf packs, or that he was now unduly concerned by the growing dark or the savage cries of the acolytes echoing about the streets. He rode easily, rolling gently on the swaying back of his mount, a born horseman. He had no saddle or harness but rode bareback, as if horse and rider were one whole, not needing the usual accoutrements of control to find one equal understanding. He rested one hand on the horse's withers, the only gesture towards balance or mastery. He was covered from head to foot in a cloak of grey wolf fur, rimed with ice and hoarfrost from the driving blizzard. The cloak spread down to the hindquarters of the horse and over its flanks. On its hood the head of a wolf stood with jaws agape baring yellow teeth and eyes that gleamed with malignant life.

Under the wolf's-head cape the rider's eyes were nearly as fierce as those of the dead creature. He rode down the street in the direction the acolytes had gone, and was soon swallowed by the shadows of the houses that leaned over horse and rider, the sound of the hooves muffled in the snowdrifts.

For several months horse and rider had wandered the wilderness south of the Fire Mountains. The rider's name was Fazad Falarn. He was only thirteen and a half. A noble by birth, but from the age of five he had been a slave. But now only a faint vestige of boyhood and none of slavery remained on him. His face was burned nut-brown by the cutting wind. A hard intelligence played around his eyes; the skin surrounding them seemed prematurely lined. There was no vulnerability in his look.

He rode on slowly through the streets, paying no heed to the buildings that overarched his way, not stopping to inspect the inns or shops, which were boarded shut in any case. The long months of travel had taught him that a man must always seem to know where he is going in a strange city, even if he doesn't.

The horse carried him into the southern part of the town. Then it snorted, great puffs of vapour billowing from its nostrils, and it whinnied quietly. Fazad sensed it too: danger ahead. A now-familiar smell of burning. Then he saw four or five figures fleeing a house. Through its mullioned windows and diamond-shaped panes he saw a ruddy orange glow. A fire, raging; he felt the blast of its heat. Looters.

Another lawless town. He had seen many.

He rode on, not looking back. Then the crowded streets of the old town fell away, and he saw through the murk of snow and dusk an open place in front. Trees like black skeletons lurched out of the mist. He was in a park. This must be the area he was looking for: the nobles' quarter. Snow cloaked everything, but he sensed he was in a broad avenue leading to the southern walls, where the meander of the encircling river formed a great bend. The horse's hooves sounded on broad paving stones. This must be the way to Lord Sain's palace. His long journey was nearly over.

A sudden gap in the snowfall and now he saw it, half a mile in front standing on a small knoll, its wide roofs slightly upturned in tiled waves, pagodas on its three eaves tops, its worked stone walls and wooden doors and window frames blackened by fire.

He uttered a word, and the horse came to a halt. The rider stared at the ruins for several moments, then sighed and wearily nudged his mount forward again.

Now he concentrated on either side of the avenue. Here there were lesser mansions, giving off a desolate, long-abandoned air. As be passed by them he heard the ghosts of children cry with laughter, the gentle calls of their dead mothers, the shouts of spirit men. The dead spoke and he heard: he was no stranger to them, had been with them all his life.

The darkness was now almost absolute though it was but late afternoon. He searched for signs of life in the dark houses; a light, or a plume of smoke from a chimney. Nothing.

But dark figures lurked outside the deep gateways of the abandoned mansions. Their purple and brown robes were almost indistinguishable from the shadows. The servants of Iss were here already. His eyes fixed on the snow and ancient lichen frontages over their heads, the carved coats of arms of the nobility could still be discerned on the architraves of the gate's facades. But he saw no lights, no possible welcome in the dead windows of the mansions. Every now and again he would murmur to the horse and it would slow. On each occasion his master stared hard at the faded heraldic designs in the near dark. Then each time, with a slight click of his tongue, and no other command, the horse set off again.

Eventually he came to a gloomy mansion, in the lee of the fire-gutted palace of Lord Sain. Dark poplars reached up to the darkening sky from its park. Its entrance was shadowed by a grey stone cornice supported by tapering pillars.

He squinted again and saw carved on the stone architrave the sign of a sun and a bushel of corn. He murmured and the horse came to a halt and he dismounted stiffly, staring at the iron-studded wooden door, barely visible in the shadows under the overhanging porch. There was a black handprint on one of the panels.

One of the Iss acolytes had been observing his halting approach down the avenue from some ruins across the street. His name was Tarant—a sallow-faced, hollow-eyed young man. He had travelled to Perricod from his home city, Tiré Gand in Ossia. At first the rider had been too far away in the dusk to make out any details, but the cloak and the ghostly whiteness of the horse had given both a sinister appearance and he had quailed at approaching them.

But he was desperate. Three nights already on the freezing streets, and not one soul converted and brought to the dark halls of Iss! His master, a gruff fellow from the Mother Temple in Tiré Gand, had no patience with those who did not pull their weight. Tonight he had been told to bring in a convert or he would be sent back to Tiré Gand, through the wolf-inhabited wasteland: not an attractive prospect.

As the rider dismounted, Tarant now saw that, under the voluminous cloak, this new arrival was no more than a strip; a weakling perhaps. Tarant mustered his courage and stepped out into the street and approached him, a dog-eared copy of the *Book of Worms* under one arm.

"Sir . . ." he began but got no further as Fazad whipped round at the sound of his voice. His face under the wolf cape was revealed in the faint gloom. A nervous, triumphant smile twitched on Tarant's face. The rider seemed but a boy: easy meat. He took another step forward, but then he locked eyes with the child and stopped. Strangely the boy's brown eyes were hard and empty of fear, lupine, as if indeed he had been lent kinship with the wolves by the cloak he wore.

The acolyte swallowed hard, seeking for words. A child was but a child after all, could be brought round by persuasion. He took yet another step nearer. "That's a fine horse for one so young," he said, making to pet the gelding's mane.

The horse's nostrils twitched and suddenly it reared, threatening the acolyte with its hooves.

The Ossian backed away, "Whoa," he said, trying to shield his body with the massive tome in his arms. Fazad held up his hand—the horse instantly calmed, its front legs returning to the ground.

The boy's eyes never left the acolyte's. "What do you want?" he asked. His voice was high, but only with youth, not fear.

"Just to talk," the acolyte replied, his eyes nervously darting from rider to horse and back again. He remembered his mentor's words: there were no easy converts, even babes in arms might at first resist the doctrines of Iss, but they would eventually come to recognise the Lord of Darkness. "Master, you see how things stand," he began as persuasively as he could, waving generally at the settling darkness and the frozen street. "It is nearly night, the sun may not return on the morrow. You must think of your soul—what will happen to it in the Prince's dark midnight."

The boy stared at him, no emotion in his dark eyes. "Be sure of this: the sun will rise again," he said flatly. "Now leave me alone."

The acolyte, seeing the horse was quiet, stepped forward, grasping the sleeve of the boy's fur cloak. "Come," he whispered, "my friends are waiting, in the cellar of the house yonder." He leaned closer, so the boy could smell his breath, a strange mixture of cloves and camphor. "One bite, then eternal life will be yours!"

The boy's lips twisted in anger at the touch but before he could reply, one of the massive wooden doors of the gate at his back swung open with a bang. Boy and acolyte both turned quickly to see who had opened it. A large man stood in the entranceway. He was clad in a simple faded brown woolen tunic, his trunklike legs exposed despite the cold, his bulk silhouetted by a glowing lamp set on the floor behind him. One of the sleeves of his tunic was bunched up to the shoulder joint, showing he had lost the arm sometime in the past. He held a stout axe in the remaining arm, its edge glinting in sharp contrast to the blueing of its blade.

His dark eyes were fixed firmly on the acolyte: there was no mistaking the menace in them. Tarant began to back away.

"I've told you what would happen if you came again," the man said in a bass growl, his eyes falling on the black hand symbol on the door.

The acolyte had continued to retreat and was out in the street again. He clearly felt himself a safe distance from the one-armed man for now he risked replying: "Your door is marked, seneschal. The risen dead will be with you this night or the next . . ."

The man snarled and took another step into the street, the axe upraised. The acolyte's next words evaporated on his lips and he took to his heels, fleeing into the twilight.

CHAPTER THREE

The House
of the Iremages

Fazad's rescuer took one or two steps after the acolyte, then stopped, glaring down the road until the man had disappeared into the gloom. He was breathing heavily, his massive chest rising and falling.

After a few moments he seemed to remember the boy's presence and turned to him.

"Are you all right?" he asked. The boy merely nodded, staring at the axe. The man followed the direction of his gaze, then laughed gruffly. "Come," he said, "I mean *you* no harm, only those vermin out there." He narrowed his eyes when he saw how young Fazad was. "It's late to be out. What is your business here?"

"I am seeking Gurn, seneschal of the Iremage family."

"Then you have found he who you seek; Gurn is my name. And now you know mine, what is yours?"

"I . . . I am Fazad."

"Fazad?" Gurn repeated, his dark brow creasing, as though trying to remember where he had heard that name before.

For the first time, the boy averted his gaze, seeming unsure of how he should say what had to be said next; as if it had been too long since he had last spoken anything, and the words, so often rehearsed in his mind, would not come out.

"Well, boy," Gurn prompted.

Fazad swallowed, mustering courage, then turned back to the seneschal. "Is it true that your lord, Artan Iremage, swore an oath with Count Falarn of Thrull, to eternally protect each other's honour and blood, even in death?"

The giant's ruddy face suddenly lost colour and his dark brow knotted; he was suddenly suspicious. "You speak strange words of introduction, lad. But it's true: such an oath was indeed made on the walls of Thrull before the great battle."

"And is Lord Artan still alive?"

Gurn shook his head. Now it was his turn to swallow hard. "No, he is dead: I alone of all the hearth servants returned to this house."

The boy regarded him solemnly. "Then you are the last man alive who can fulfil Artan's pledge."

Gurn's frown deepened. "Tell me: who are you, how do you know of this oath?"

The boy straightened. "I am Fazad, the son of Count Falarn. Sold into slavery after the battle of Thrull; now I am free once more."

"You have escaped? From where?"

"From that selfsame place of which you spoke—Thrull."

"Thrull? But it is three hundred leagues away."

Fazad looked away, down the long avenue back into the centre of the city and beyond, to the frozen countryside, in the direction of the Fire Mountains and Thrull beyond them. "Aye—three hundred leagues," he replied. "And you ask yourself: how could I, but a boy, survive the cold, the snows, the wolves? And sometimes I ask myself the same question." He paused, turning once more to stare at Gurn as if sizing up the older man. "Do you believe in magic, seneschal?"

"Magic? Another strange question." Now Gurn looked away. "Perhaps once I believed," he said softly. "I believed until that day on Thrull field when our battalions were mown down like sheaths and the vampires leapt from their graves and our sorcerers stood uselessly by. After that I don't know what I believe in." He pointed behind him at the armorial carvings. "Except in this house and the honour of its family."

Fazad turned and patted Cloud on the withers. "Three things have brought me safely here over the Fire Mountains, through the forests of Bardun and over the plains of Surrenland. Cloud here is the first. Do you recognise his name?"

Gurn shook his head.

"This is Baron Illgill's mount."

"Illgill?" the seneschal repeated as if in a dream. At his master's name, Cloud whinnied slightly and stepped forward through the snow and snuffled at Gurn's tunic. The seneschal stared wonderingly at the grey gelding that looked back at him with soulful brown eyes, not unlike his rider's; eyes full of a lambent half-human, half-animal intelligence.

"He is no normal mount, but has lived, generation after generation, in the Illgills' palace in Thrull. He speaks to me, and I to him. He has carried me through all the dangers, brought me here, where he knew there were friends," the boy continued.

"This story is strange; but strangely true also," Gurn answered. "But you spoke of two other things that have brought you here."

Fazad nodded. "The second is fate: fate and half-remembered words that my father told me on the day of that battle that ended his life, for even when the soldiers of Iss sold me into slavery and I served as a lowly pot boy, those words came into my mind, like an echo."

"What words were these?"

"He told me of the blood oath between our families and that if anything were to happen to him I was to come here, to Perricod, and seek out the sign of the bushel and the sun."

"You found the sign, but you knew my name too. How is that?"

The boy was silent for a moment. "Magic again—for as

I rode through the city it was as if I saw it as it was eight years ago, before the battle of the marshes. The sun shining, the streets full of people, all those who now are dead. I heard their voices. And then I saw you, as you were then, younger, and the children cried out to you as you walked the streets, and I heard them call you Gurn, seneschal of the Iremage clan, and then I saw your dream self pass into this house and I snapped back, and once more it was cold and dark, but there on the lintel, I saw the sun and the corn sign and knew I was safe."

Gurn's face paled as if indeed a shadow of his old self had brushed by him. He looked from the boy to the shadows that were closing tight all around. "This seems like it will be a long tale." He patted Fazad on the shoulder. "I believe who you say you are. Tonight and always the blood oath holds between the Iremages and the Falarns. Come inside." He thrust the axe into his belt and with his other hand pushed open the other double door leading into the mansion. "Lead your horse in here."

"Cloud needs no leading," Fazad answered. "He understands speech as well as you or I." He jerked his head and with a little whinny, the horse walked in. The seneschal shook his head in wonder, then gestured for Fazad to proceed him, bolting the gates behind them. They now stood in a small cobbled courtyard open to the darkening sky and covered with a thin layer of snow, a stable block to one side. The seneschal pushed open the stable door and Cloud docilely entered followed by the two humans.

After the bitter cold outside the stable was warm and redolent of new-mown hay. An old nag stood tethered in one of the stalls, eyeing them curiously as they entered.

"This is Wildfire," Gurn said, stroking the horse. "She brought me back from Thrull." The seneschal filled a manger with some straw from a hamper overhead, then threw a blanket over Cloud's back and dexterously buckled it under the horse's belly with his one hand.

When he saw the horse was comfortable he turned to Fazad. "Come, now: Cloud is seen to, you need food and

warmth yourself." Despite the wolf's-fur cloak, the boy's
lips were blue and he was shivering from the cold.

He took Fazad by the arm and helped him back through
the courtyard to where two steps led up to a massive stone
doorway. The door stood ajar and yellow lamplight flickered
from within. When they'd entered, the seneschal thrust the
door shut and bolted it behind them.

Fazad found himself in a great stone hall with rusted suits
of armour on stands on either side and arms arranged in intricate patterned circles on the bare stone walls. Gurn led
Fazad through to the right to a room heaped with broken furniture, partially draped with dust sheets. A fire blazed in the
hearth and a pot containing gruel rested warming on the
hearthstone.

Gurn pointed to a rough trestle and the boy shrugged off
the fur cloak, which fell about his ankles. Now that he was
inside the house and the cloak had been removed he somehow looked less feral, less wild—a frail, trembling child.
Gurn offered Fazad some of the gruel and he watched as the
boy ate greedily. "Now," he said when Fazad was finished,
"tell me of your journey."

The boy wiped his lips with the back of his hand. "It's a
long story."

The seneschal pointed at the dark skies outside the windows. "Neither of us is going anywhere. It is night, and no
one wanders the streets of Perricod, as they did in better
times. None that is but the cursed worshippers of Iss."

"And the undead?"

Gurn nodded heavily. "They as well. But we are safe
here. Tell your story."

So Fazad began. He told how after the battle of Thrull he
had been enslaved and sold to an innkeeper. How seven
years later one dark night, as dark and as vampire-haunted
as this in Perricod, Jayal Illgill, long thought dead, had appeared like a ghost at the inn where Fazad was enslaved.
The haunted young man—his fate seeming to hang off him
like a shroud—seeking for something.

How Jayal had confronted him and told him never to forget his noble lineage. How that night for the first time it was as if Fazad had woken from a long dream and felt shame for his condition and hatred for those who had enslaved him. How his father's words had come back to him, telling him to go to Perricod, and he'd sworn that once more he would be a Falarn. How Jayal had entrusted Cloud to his care.

After Jayal had gone, he thought that his humdrum existence would reassert itself. Yet that night was to hold even stranger things in store. The fires blazing in the city; the Creature of the Spike breaking its shackles and flying off into the night; the demon, as high as the battlements, rising up from Marizian's tomb, destroying everything in its way. And then the undead bursting into the inn, falling on the living. It was here then he had run to the stables and taken Cloud.

In the end the horse had saved him, taking him through the vampire-haunted streets of Thrull until the gates were thrown open at dawn and they rode through the hordes of Dead in Life and out onto the causeway over the marshes. But even then strange things had happened: the weird light that glowed briefly from the top of the pyramid of skulls at dawn and the comet that rose from it into the sky: an omen, perhaps, that the followers of Reh were not forgotten. Afterwards, Fazad and Cloud had ridden all day down the causeway over the marshes, and up into the mountains until the city was far below.

How then horse and rider had turned and had seen the temples of Reh and Iss falling in an avalanche of pulverised stone down the sides of the granite mountain. The end of Thrull. Afterwards, they rode on through devastation all the way to Perricod.

He finished. Gurn's face had a faraway look as if he still followed the comet into the satin night of the sky and heard nothing else. But then he stood abruptly. "This is news! Faran Gaton's city is destroyed; he too perhaps. Maybe the slaughter of the battle was not in vain." He took in a great breath, his chest stretching the seams of his tunic: then he exhaled, very slowly. "Aye, great news. Our blood is redeemed." He pointed at the empty sleeve of his tunic. "Perhaps this too."

"You lost it in the battle?"

"Yes," he replied, staring abstractedly once more.

"Tell me of the battle," Fazad asked, suddenly eager, boyish. "I speak as though I remember that day, but it is really nothing more than a blur."

Gurn eyed him for a long minute, then glanced at the sinister cloak lying on the floor. The boy had spoken of three things that had brought him here. Cloud and Count Falarn's words were two. He began to suspect that this outlandish garment would be the third. But, whatever the mystery of the cloak, he sensed that it would not be easily teased from the boy. He decided to give him breathing space and talk first.

"Very well. I will tell you of the battle." He stood and began to pace the room restlessly.

"We arrived in Thrull a day before Faran Gaton's armies. That night we saw the corpse lights burn on the marshes and we knew that they were burying the undead in front of their battle lines. We feasted in your father's palace; we feasted but we were weary after the long march and a little afraid— we had seen the size of Faran Gaton's army. So dinner was a cheerless event, which ended early. The next morning, just as the sun rose, we marched with the Falarns onto the marsh. And there we drew up, our battle lines next to each other's . . ."

Gurn paused, his eyes falling on the fire as if conjuring up the spirits of the dead in their flames. "We were on the left wing. For a while neither we nor the Ossians advanced, but merely stood, exchanging arrow fire. One or two men fell, and I could see my soldiers trembling, barely holding the line where we had been ordered to stand motionless. But then, ignoring the hail of fire, my master rode out and spoke with your father. And both men threw their heads back and laughed, the sun glinted on their armour and their plumes, and they saluted each other with their lances and rode back.

A brave sight, and all the soldiers cheered, thinking that with men like those victory must be ours.

"Where a moment before we had been rigid in fear we now turned to our fellows in the line. Tongues wagged, jokes were cracked, bets were made, who would take the first blood, that sort of thing. They were so young my men— they thought death could never touch them." He turned and fixed Fazad with an avid stare. "But it did—took them like reaped corn, and their voices are heard no more."

"Go on," the boy urged, leaning forward eagerly.

Gurn sighed. "It is not good that a boy hears these words, but tell you I must, for a son must hear how his father passed from the world." Again his eyes took on a faraway, abstracted look. "The first charge went badly for us. The mud slowed us. Their archers filled the air with sorcerous arrows that cut us down. Some said that Illgill fell, his horse shot from under him. Faran's army began to advance, pushing the centre and right back and back, only we who stood on the left wing held. We were swiftly cut off, the Ossians pouring across our front and flank. And there our own battle began.

"The day drew on, an inch gained, an inch lost. I remember the setting sun, low on the Fire Mountains in the west, a fiery ball, sending orange lances through the spears of our ranks. Then we began to move forward and our lances threw shadows like the spokes of the wheel, circling over the faces of my comrades: shadow and fire, shadow and fire . . .

"The night came and the buried undead sprang howling from their graves. Faran's van advanced ever closer to our centre, but then I saw your father, Count Falarn, gesturing to my master, pointing. Faran Gaton must have forgotten about our little battle on the wing, he was eager to be in for the kill. For there in the light of the corpse pyres we saw Faran's palanquin, a thing of black lacquer and silver armour, shaped like a serpent borne on four carrying poles, four men to each pole, labouring under its armoured weight.

"A hundred yards, no more, an arrow shot, but all our arrows were spent, and between us were our attackers, two lines of the Mourners of Lethe. Aptly named, like all the battalions of Tiré Gand. Many a widow did they make weep that day. As one we all saw this was our last chance, the last chance for the Flame.

"And then my master gave the signal and I raised a horn to my lips, the same I still keep in that old chest over there"—he pointed to a dusty trunk in a corner—"and I blew it and we charged, with one mind and one voice. We carved through the lines of Faran's men, right to the palanquin. Not many of us still lived, but I stumbled on, my axe ready, eyes only for the black curtains covering the litter."

Gurn stopped abruptly, right at the end of his pacing of the long room, his back to Fazad, then swirled melodramatically, a fierce look on his face. No doubt he did not consciously wish to scare the child but his expression was spine-chilling.

"The curtains burst open, and he was there: Faran Gaton Nekron.

"He stepped down, a dark-bladed sword in his hand. His palanquin-bearers lay slain on either side, and he had no guards left. I stood alone in front of him, my axe came up. There was a mad blood lust in my heart. Vampires cannot die, I knew, but I would cleave his head from his neck, let him seek it about the field, kicked like a ball hither and thither. But then my eyes caught his, even as my axe swung: suddenly the blood lust was gone . . ." He threw out his single arm as if trying to steady himself, his eyes clenched shut. "Instead, dizziness, and a sense of falling. Mesmerism. His eyes were like a whirlpool. I was sucked in, deeper and deeper into the vortex, my axe was stayed, half lifted above my head, and his sword came round like a scythe, through my arm: I saw it happen as if it happened to another. The arm fell to the ground, the sword deflected off my cuirass. I stared at the stump, but no blood came, for the blade must have been sorcerous, cauterizing as it cut. I stared at the wound, and then at Faran. It was as if I stared into the mouth of Hel, a long and depthless drop, then I fainted quite away."

His voice moderated, no doubt suddenly realising the terrifying effect his words had had on the boy, "My men were loyal, and though I would have had them save themselves, those around me snatched up my body even as our lines broke and the slaughter deepened. They carried me back to the surgeons' tents, but the bone menders had fled. So they joined the retreat, and fighting every inch, brought me back down the causeway, back to the Fire Mountains."

"And what of my father?" Fazad asked.

Gurn turned away, shaking his head. "He fell leading that charge, surrounded by Faran's personal guards. He died a brave man. A hero—if only the Flame had more men like him."

The answer seemed to satisfy Fazad: he stared mistily down the room, a gleam of pride in his eyes.

Gurn continued, "I alone of this household returned to Perricod."

His hand went up to the stump where his arm used to be. "And now? Now when the vampires are out in the streets, I feel them in this wound. And Faran Gaton's face swims in front of my eyes and I curse myself for a weak-willed fool that didn't strike in the seconds that I had. Oh, for that time again. Let the God and ghosts of the Iremages and Falarns forgive me!"

He sighed, shaking his head. "I have guarded the house these last seven years, not knowing why, for no Iremage will ever return." He stared moodily at the fire. "Perhaps it is for the honour of the thing that first I kept the looters away, now even when the winter clouds cover the sky and it seems eternal night has come, and with it Iss and his devilspawn—yet honourable actions are never empty ones: that is what my father told me, and I would tell my own son, if I had one." His eyes seemed to mist slightly.

"Maybe my trust has been repaid. You have come, and I have been able to pay a blood debt to one of my master's friends. Reh has made it so. You are welcome, Falarn's heir."

"Though I have no estates, nothing but my horse and my cloak, and all the riches of the Falarns are lost, I thank you from my heart. Wise men say the gratitude of the poor man is the most sincere," Fazad answered.

"It is very true. But before you sleep, there is one more question. You spoke of three things that brought you here. One was Cloud, the other the words of your father. What was the third?"

The boy sucked in his breath. "Haven't you guessed?" he asked, looking at the discarded wolf cloak.

Gurn studied it for a moment. The dead red eyes of the wolf gave back a sinister gleam. A shiver went up his spine. He quickly stooped and placed another log on the fire to hide his sudden fear. "It's the cloak, isn't it?"

"I will tell you how I got it, and then I will tell you what it does," Fazad said, in a voice barely above a whisper. Now it was his turn to rise and pace the room. "I rode Cloud over the Fire Mountains, we passed over the foothills of Surrenland. One day we reached the hills overlooking the city of Bardun. But a haze of smoke hung over it. The legions of Ossia had got there before us.

"I scrambled down and found a vantage point and saw the place was full of the legions of Tiré Gand—it was the Temple of Reh that was burning. I hadn't eaten for days, and I thought Bardun was my last chance. I was in despair, but knew it was death to enter the city. I found a cave in the woods. At night from my vantage point I could see the main square, all lit by torches. The inhabitants were rounded up, some were set on stakes and in the stocks, and . . ." His voice trailed off.

"The vampires came?" Gurn supplied.

Fazad nodded. "Aye: it was just like the stocks in Thrull. I heard the cries, but there was nothing I could do. For the next week I wandered about the caves, Cloud following. There I found one or two of the city folk who had escaped, and they shared their meager scraps of food with me.

"The woods were full of Ossians rounding up refugees. I fled further into the woods. I found a new cave, deep in the greensward. At first I was too frightened to enter: four dead cubs lay outside, pierced through with arrows, black fletches like those used by the legions of Tiré Gand. There was wolf spoor outside and grey wolf's hair caught on the tangled undergrowth at its entrance. Cloud whinnied and seemed afraid. But it was bitterly cold out, and I had but a thin cloak to keep out the wind. Presently I gathered my courage and left him and I entered alone and saw that another refugee had got there before me. An old crone, sitting wrapped in this very cloak in the shadows, her eyes had all the appearance of evil, yellow in colour, and I was about to flee, but she called softly. I smelled her breath when she spoke—it was sour. She told me to stay; I was safe for a while. The soldiers had just been and would not return for a day or so. Despite her strange appearance, I was tempted by her offer. I had no need to go outside again to tether Cloud, for he never strayed far from where I was. Besides my eyelids were drooping with tiredness; I sat and must have fallen asleep despite my fear.

"The old lady's voice came to me as I slept. I must leave Bardun, travel to the south, to Perricod: live to take revenge on the Worm. I must take the cloak, it would help me, without it I would die. My dreaming self protested, telling her she must keep it, she was old, she needed protection against the cold. But again and again she told me to take it. Then something disturbed my dream and I woke. Outside it was the predawn grey. There was a commotion at the cave mouth and I got to my feet and stumbled out. Cloud was jumping around as if scared by a wild animal. I soothed him but when I went back into the cave, I found the old crone was gone, the cloak lying neatly folded on the ground and at the back of the cave, something I now only saw in the dawn light: an old female she-wolf lying dead, her eyes half-eaten by maggots, killed by the same hunters who had slain the cubs outside. The cubs must have been her last litter.

"I stared at the cloak for some time, feeling its aura, its magic, but I was growing cold once more, for though it was day, the bitter wind was unrelenting. How many nights of sacrifice had there been in the city, how many vampires were there left who had not been satisfied—who had not drunk the blood of the living? Many, I suspected. Soon even more of them would move into the hills, scenting out any last refugees. Without another thought, I donned the cloak.

"At first I felt nothing.

"I approached Cloud, but he wouldn't let me anywhere near him, the scent of the cloak set his nostrils flaring and he pawed the ground. But eventually I soothed him and I mounted up and we rode, rode like the wind, out of the woods, past the burning city.

"As soon as we were in open country I heard the howls of the wolves, and then I sighted them. Their red eyes beaming in the gloom, their tongues lolling. Hungry. First there were only one or two, but then more and more. I called to Cloud and he began to canter, then to gallop, but even over the sound of the hooves I heard a panting sound and looked back. A dozen or so wolves were following. I encouraged Cloud to go faster. He was skittish, but he galloped on, quicker than ever before. The wolves ran behind.

"Eventually Cloud tired and began to slow. I looked behind fearfully, and my heart nearly stopped: more had joined the original pack and now a hundred wolves followed. Now I thought we would be ripped to shreds but the wolves had slowed too, and looked at me, their heads tilted to one side, their tongues lolling from their mouths for anything like dogs expecting a command. I was hungry and saw a farm. Maybe there would be food. I shooed the wolves then, and they skittered away, just as when you shy a stone at a pack of dogs; but they came back, a trusting look in their eyes. I dismounted, watching them nervously, for I knew I could ride no further, but they didn't approach me, merely followed when I entered the place.

"The vampires had got there first, the farmer and his family were slaughtered. But I felt no horror. No, worse, I felt a strange savage triumph at that terrible sight, and my nostrils twitched at the smell of the blood and my heart began to beat quicker. Reh help me if my mouth didn't water a little. I turned quickly from the dead and went to their larder and scavenged for food." He fixed Gurn with his soulful brown eyes. "Yes, even where blood soaked the floor, I scavenged, like an animal. Even as the wolves pulled the blood-drained corpses of the farm people to pieces I ate the dead family's bread and dried meat and the sight of the poor ruined bodies didn't touch me a whit, or rather it incited my own hunger so I ate with a barbarous appetite. And as week followed week and the cloak never left my back and more wolves followed me, the more I became one with them in my needs and instincts.

"On we rode. Strange noises echoed in my head, growls and snarls, a language I now understood, but at first hadn't. It was as if I were with the wolves, part of their pack—no, I was their leader. Their wilderness had become part of me." He glanced down at the garment lying in a heap on the flagstones, then looked up again, catching the seneschal's eye. "Do you need to hear more?"

Gurn shook his head heavily. "You have said enough. The cloak is magical. That crone was no old woman but a wolf spirit."

Fazad nodded. "Yes. It was she who passed into me, wishing revenge on those who had slaughtered her and her cubs. The spirit of the wolf still lives in it—the longer I wear it, the more I take on the attributes of the wolf: cunning and stealth, ruthlessness . . ." His voice trailed off and he stared again at the item on the floor, the flames of the fire playing over it so the eyes on its cape gave back the strange gleam once more.

"Come, child," Gurn said, "now you are safe. You no longer need that damned garment. Promise me: never wear it again."

Fazad looked at it, then back at Gurn. "It's too late. A week ago I woke in a house a few leagues north of here. We had got there at dusk and there again human corpses littered the floor and the wolves fell on them. I woke amongst the scattered bones and the feral smell of blood and fur. I was disgusted and ripped the cloak from me and ran from the house, calling to Cloud, who came trotting to me. And I mounted up and rode an hour or more. But still the wolves' voices were in my head, on and on they sounded until I stopped and turned Cloud and returned and there put on that cloak once more, for once put on, it can never be put to one side again." His voice was uncertain, wavering, as if somewhere still he had a grain of hope that one day he would escape its malign influence. He glanced nervously at the discarded garment. The glinting red eyes of the animal gleamed back with a proprietorial air.

He sat once more, wearily, his head in his hands. "Will the acolytes return?"

"Perhaps," Gurn replied. "Every night, they pass up the road hammering and shouting, but they are scared of me, for they know I don't fear them, their God, not even death itself. However, tonight I'll be cautious." He left the room and went into the flagstoned hall; Fazad stood and followed him. A bitter chill crept under the jamb of the mansion's door. Gurn listened at it, but all that could be heard was the keening of the wind and the distant crackling of the fire behind them. He turned and found Fazad staring at the armorial displays high on the wall.

"There are weapons enough for an army here," the boy said.

"Aye, if we had an army. This was once a great house, as great as the Falarns and the Illgills. But now you are the only one of those three families left alive."

"And Jayal."

"Yes, Jayal. What happened to him?"

The boy shook his head. "I never saw him again after that night."

"Then he, too, is dead."

The boy looked up almost shyly. "No, I believe he's still alive."

"Go on," Gurn said.

"When he came to the inn, Jayal had a sword, I saw it glowing even through the scabbard in the darkness of the inn's stables. All I know of magic, I have learned since I first put on that wolf cloak. But I recognised that light as magical. When I saw it first, it was as if my heart lit up with its energy."

"And?" Gurn asked, encouraging him.

"Why, anyone who carries such a weapon is too strong to die," Fazad answered with wide-eyed ingenuousness.

Gurn chuckled mournfully. "Fazad, I have seen so many who thought the same thing: warriors who believed that a fire-forged amulet would avert the blades of their enemies. Sorcerers who conjured spells and threw energy fields about them thinking that arrows wouldn't pierce them. But each and every one of them is dead, for magic cannot avert steel and muscle for long."

Fazad shook his head. "Not this sword. This was no useless talisman. Its power was alive, of older times . . ."

"Perhaps, perhaps . . ." Gurn said, leading Fazad back into the firelit room from the hall. His look was not unkindly. "Who can tell? What I want to know is why he risked returning to the city, into the heart of his enemies? Surely he knew it to be suicidal?"

"He asked for a woman at the inn: Thalassa Eaglestone. He had no joy from the patrons. What's more he attracted unwonted attention to himself. He saw that my master would betray him. I showed him the way over the roofs and that was the last I saw of him."

Gurn nodded his head. "If I remember, this Thalassa was his betrothed. Perhaps that explains it. When you are older, you'll understand that love can drag a man into places he shouldn't be . . ." He clenched his single fist, shaking his head. "But I don't think he would have come for her alone. I'd wager he came back with another purpose as well. He must have been seeking the baron, his father. Even in Perricod people say the baron is alive, that he fled to the north, there to gather strength in the Flame's cause in the dark times."

He gestured at the shadowed rafters above their heads. "What darker times than these? We need the baron now as Iss' eternal night beckons—he was the only lord capable of rallying each ruler to his cause. Now is a time of prophecy:

on one hand, the Worm tells us how black midnight will last forever; on the other, the priests of Reh how the Second Dawn is not far away. Which will prevail? I do not know: we can only pray, pray that the baron if he's still alive will return from the north at the head of an army. Otherwise I know what will happen in this city soon: you have seen it yourself in Thrull. The vampires grow and grow in number. And the same I hear happens all throughout the western world."

"What is to be done?" Fazad asked.

The older man stood in silence for a while. There was something charismatic about this strange boy. An aura, whether granted by the wolf cloak, or through some natural factor of his birth, gave him even at the age of thirteen an air of command, an allure. For the first time in seven years, seven years in which, if he was honest with himself, his spirit had quietly festered in this place, a place now no better than a memorial to his dead lord, he found that his heart was beating a little faster, the palm of his single hand slightly damp with sweat as his thoughts raced.

Perhaps the Flame was not dead yet: friends could be rallied to the cause, a movement started against the worshippers of Iss. After all, no one out there had yet heard the welcome news that Thrull was destroyed, Faran Gaton's power base broken . . .

He looked up: his own mounting excitement had not spread to his guest—Fazad's eyes had begun to droop, exhausted from the journey and his long tale. But Gurn's thoughts raced on. He paced up and down the room until he had made his decision, and when he had made it, he involuntarily clapped his hand on his thigh, making Fazad start from his doze and look at Gurn with blurry eyes.

"That horse of your must have another journey," the seneschal said. "You see how it is in this city; the legions of Tiré Gand are moving south and will soon appear and there is no army of the Flame to oppose them. Imagine, Perricod will fall in a single day when it has resisted Iss for a thousand years and a hundred sieges! But the day has come. The Flame will die in this city—we must leave."

"But there is nowhere else in this world to go—Surrenland is the last country free of the Worm," Fazad said, dropping his tired eyes sadly once more.

But Gurn shook his head. "You're right: there is nowhere on this continent, but the Flame still burns over the seas. There is still Galastra."

"Where is that?"

"It lies over the Astardian Sea. I have beard that the queen of that land, Zalia, is a friend of the Flame." Gurn continued, "She lost her husband in the war. Tomorrow we will set out. The journey will be hard: a hundred leagues: first the wolf packs, then the great Forest of Darvish, then the ocean, but we must get the news of Faran's destruction to her."

Fazad might have hoped that this final proclamation would be the cue for going to bed, for in truth he could barely keep his eyes open for tiredness, but Gurn had other things in mind. He went to the old oak chest that stood in a dusty corner of the room. From it he pulled a white silk banner and an ivory horn, the same he had blown before that forlorn charge at Thrull seven years before. This he tucked at his belt. Then he unfurled the banner, holding it high in his single hand. It was ripped and crudely stitched back together, a golden salamander on a white field, surrounded by the bushel and sun motif that Fazad had seen on the architrave outside the mansion. The boy could only imagine the one-armed man struggling over many nights to repair it, holding the twine in his teeth and the needle in his hand.

"The Iremage flag," Gurn announced. "My master would want us to take it, the White Rose enfold him, to where the Flame still burns." As his words faded, he looked at Fazad expectantly and found that the boy's lids were closed and he was fast asleep on the settle. Gently, the older man lifted the boy's legs onto the bench so he lay flat, and under his head he placed the bundled wolf cloak as a pillow and over him, as he might once have covered the honoured dead of Thrull field, he draped the tattered banner, now the symbol of his reborn hope.

CHAPTER FOUR

To the Astardian Sea

They rose before dawn the next day. Fazad handed
Gurn the Iremage banner and then retrieved the wolf
cloak from the floor, where it had fallen. Gurn
thought to protest, but for the moment held his tongue. The
cloak had protected Fazad from the wolves outside. Today
they would need its powers again.

After a hasty breakfast they carried their supplies out to
the stables. Outside, the world was shrouded in a bleak twilight; the northern wind had died and the snow finally
stopped; a sinister silence reigned over the city. The thick
mist that had descended the night before still blanketed the
sun, cutting out the little light that might have been expected
on this midwinter's day.

They led the horses out of the mansion, and Gurn locked
the doors. He looked wistfully at his master's property, turning the large brass key in his hands as if memorising the moment. Perhaps this was the last time he would ever be here.

Then they heard a new sound filtering through the stagnant air.

The muffled sound of armour and mailed boots, a large
formation, moving towards them. Soldiers. Strangely there
were no voices, no shouted commands. Then another sound
came through the drifting fog. A sound that no soldier who

had been on Thrull field could ever forget. Bone horns. As hollow as death sounding from every corner of the foggy city. The undead legions of Tiré Gand had entered the city during the night. More bone horns echoed from every quarter: Perricod was lost.

A dark mass, the front of a column, appeared in the grey murk advancing down the avenue towards Lord Sain's palace.

Fazad and Gurn hesitated no longer, but mounted hurriedly and spurred their horses off in the opposite direction. Within minutes they had skirted the ruins of the palace and had reached the second gate in the southwest of the city. Here a massive arched bridge crossed the wide reaches of the River Donzel. They rode through the bridge guardhouse and out onto the highest arch of the bridge. They reined in and looked back the way they had come. Above the undulating mist they saw the tops of standards advancing down the wide avenue, gilded skulls bobbing atop the poles. The ensigns of a whole legion of six thousand men. Over the tramp of boots came the muffled sound of a single set of horse's hooves clattering over the frozen cobblestones.

The seneschal's face was deathly white. "I saw those standards on Thrull field. The Drinkers of the Viaticum. They came from their graves when the sun went down. Undead, veterans of a thousand wars."

"But the sun shines!" Fazad said, pointing to the pale disc fighting through the overcast.

"It shines, but doesn't penetrate the fog," Gurn answered. "Come," he said urgently, "before they scent our blood on the air."

Fazad shivered, and Cloud, sensing his master's thoughts, turned and lengthened his stride, his hooves clattering on the flagstones of the bridge. Soon they reached the ice-covered water meadows on the other side, the stalactites on the branches of the willows like frozen waterfalls. They hastened over the ice, through an abandoned village and onwards over its fields, to the metalled road that now turned westward.

They rode on for several hours through the winter waste-land. From a mile or two behind they could hear the moan of the legion's cow horns: the Drinkers of the Viaticum had followed them over the bridge. Were they following the two fugitives? Or did their purpose lie to the west, over the Astardian Sea? Had they been sent to destroy Galastra?

Strangely, there was no sign of the wolf packs. They seemed to have vanished into the mist. The day progressed: now they had to spell their horses, especially Gurn's ancient nag, whose pace grew ever slower. The undead closed the gap. The rider they had heard in Perricod seemed to scout in front of the column. From time to time they heard the solitary horse's hooves behind them, ringing on the road surface.

Three or four times the bone cow horns rang out again; yet never to signal a rest: each time it seemed a signal for their pursuers to lengthen their strides. Each time Fazad muttered to Cloud to hurry, but Gurn's mount was fading fast.

By late afternoon, the sun had still not appeared. They guessed that the legion was only a few hundred yards in the mist behind. Both Gurn and Fazad were nodding with tiredness despite their terror. Finally, the seneschal had to dismount and lead his horse. But the long ride had taken its toll. Soon Wildfire sank to her knees and couldn't be encouraged back up, though Gurn pulled lustily on her bridle. The sound of the advancing legion came closer. He left her where she lay and mounted up behind Fazad.

All that day and that night and into the next morning the pursuit continued. Cloud rode on unfatigued, even by his twin burden, but the undead behind also needed no sleep or rest.

Both riders were exhausted, Gurn only keeping his seat by clumsily holding on to Fazad's wolfskin cape with his one hand, and Fazad by lacing his hands round Cloud's withers. But even the gelding's pace slowed noticeably as the day continued.

Gurn broke the long hours of silence. "Boy," he said.

Fazad had been nodding, but now came wide awake. He looked back.

"We are too slow. They are catching us." He slid from the horse's back. "Take Cloud—the forest I told you about is ahead: hide in it. When the danger is past go on to Galastra. May Reh be with you."

Cloud had pulled up the moment Gurn had slipped off his back. He pawed the stones of the road surface impatiently as he scented the undead getting closer. Fazad looked down at the older man from the horse's back. "You forget—I am a Falarn—we have a blood oath with the Iremages. We don't abandon our friends."

"Why should two die? Go, I beg you, it is nearly night, their strength increases with the darkness. Tonight they will catch us."

"Come, mount up," Fazad said, offering a hand, his voice stern, belying his tender age. With a groan, Gurn hauled himself back, his eyes gluey and almost shut. Fazad hurriedly urged Cloud forward again, but the horse needed no encouragement, and the short break seemed to have given him renewed energy.

They continued in a trance as the light leached away from the white shroud of fog surrounding them. But then Cloud halted abruptly, jarring both of them awake.

"Why have you stopped?" Gurn asked from behind. Fazad didn't answer. Gurn peered past him: through the mist he saw the boles of oak trees and their bare branches dripping with condensation.

Darvish Forest. It stretched from this point all the way to the coast. In better times he and his master had hunted in it. But there was no safety from the undead in its depths. Even if the sun was to miraculously return, the shade of its trees would shelter the vampires. The pursuit would continue.

Fazad slipped from Cloud's back. "They are waiting for us," he said, his voice quivering with excitement, or so it seemed to the weary seneschal.

"Who?" he asked.

The boy merely gestured at the tree line. Then Gurn saw

something he hadn't noticed at first: movement, in the shadows of the trees. At first it was as if he saw a layer of grey
smoke nearly indistinguishable from the mist, close to the
ground writhing in and out of the boles of the trees. He
thought his eyes were playing tricks; it was as if the ground
had become a moving, living entity. Then he saw what it
was.

Wolves, hundreds if not thousands. So thick as to cause
this mirage of coursing grey smoke. They were strangely
silent, the noise of their rough fur against the bark of the
trees the only sound. His blood turned to ice. Fazad took a
few steps forward, a strange growl coming from the back of
his throat. His face was transformed, stretched into a strange
grin, his arms outstretched.

"What are you doing, boy?" Gurn whispered.

Fazad heard him. He stopped and looked back up at him,
the dead eyes on the wolf cape glinting in the dying yellow
light filtering from the western sky and through the trees.
"These are our friends, seneschal. You are safe. They will
obey me." As if in answer to his statement there came the
first protracted howl from the dark woods.

Fazad advanced on the line of wolves in the shadows of
the trees, both arms raised. The howling of the wolves grew
and grew as he neared and Gurn watched impotently. The
boy was deluded, he thought he was invincible—instead,
surely he would be ripped to pieces.

Then a sound from behind—hooves on the road. Cloud
executed a half turn towards the noise. Coming out of the
mist was a solitary rider, on a white mount, not so much a
horse as a ghostly apparition, its bones sticking out of its rib
cage that lay open and decayed on its flanks. The rider wore
white armour, not the white of purity, but the grey chalk-
white of a corpse, its great helm open, revealing a shrivelled
mummified face in which yellow teeth smiled from beneath
empty eye and nose sockets.

Cloud whinnied, backing from the terrible apparition.
Gurn glimpsed Fazad by the trees, arms still raised. Then
several wolves broke from the shadows, their tongues

lolling from their mouths, picking up acceleration. Cloud reared, and Gurn had to desperately cling to his mane to keep his seat.

Then the wolves were past him, snarling, arrowing towards the skeletal rider. The undead rider yanked on his rein and with a twitch of his stirrups the skeletal horse turned and disappeared into the mists, pursued by the loping wolves. There came a mild gust, the fog billowed, thickening, blanketing the scene. The sound of hooves and the howling of the wolves was silenced.

Gurn urged Cloud forward towards the wood, where he found Fazad waiting alone. The remainder of the wolves had melted back into the shadows, but Gurn saw a thousand eyes glowing in the near darkness. He turned back to Fazad.

"You see, seneschal," the boy said, "the wolves are our friends."

"Your friends, maybe," Gurn answered, "but not mine."

"We will have need of them again before this journey is finished."

"Perhaps," Gurn grunted. He eyed the dark forest. Weeks of journey lay ahead, and at any moment these creatures could turn against them. But what lay behind? The Drinkers of the Viaticum. "Let them come, but keep them at a distance."

A small smile on Fazad's lips, the first Gurn had ever seen.

"I promise," he said. Then he mounted up again and they entered the forest.

If winter in Perricod had been bleak, the depths of Darvish were even more so. League after league the grey boughs of leafless trees and their skeletal branches. How unlike the autumn when Gurn had come here with his master, Artan, for the wild boar. He remembered how their chargers had churned up the first fallen acorns on the ground; how the changing leaves had charged the glades with bronze and gold, how the woods had been full of the muted light and the sweet melancholy of the dying year.

They rode on for several days, following the highway to

the west, camping at night in the foresters' abandoned villages. It was as if the rest of humanity had simply vanished: there was no sign of the woodsmen and the charcoal burners that Gurn remembered from his previous visits, who had once lived in the settlements. For the moment they heard no more of the bone horns of the pursuing legion. At night the wolves ringed their campsite, but as Fazad had promised, none approached closely.

Each night it was the same as they lay down in one of the abandoned village huts: the howling of the wolves, rising and falling through the frozen clearing. Gurn tried to sleep in front of the spluttering fires of damp green wood that was all to be found in village after village, but he was too anxious, the howling of the wolves seemed to come closer and closer as the nights wore on. But Fazad slept, wrapped in the wolf cloak, his face contorted into a strange rictus, emitting the occasional grunt or snarl. Gurn realized the boy was far away in his dreams, in the surrounding forest, with his brethren. But Gurn himself only dozed fitfully until the sun had once more risen and instilled the grey freezing mist with a pearly light.

Then Fazad would stir and the fierce look would drop away like a mask and he would look about him in surprise, as if not recognising where he was, what these rough-hewn wooden walls and crude pieces of furniture were. Many a time, as Gurn prepared their modest breakfast of oats and water, he would speak of how he had ranged the woods in his dreams with the wolves. And how far down the highway to the east he had heard the boots of the undead legion marching onwards through the night. Gurn never answered him, thinking that to speak would be to encourage him, wondering how long he or the boy could continue like this without going mad.

Thus they rode on, for two weeks or more. The road, the foresters' villages and the mist so unvarying that it seemed they remained still while a barely changing scenery of overhanging trees passed by.

One night they made their camp in a clearing occupied

only by a solitary wooden hut, its walls greened with moss, inside its few sticks of furniture festooned with spiderwebs. It was that time of evening when Fazad would habitually slip into his troubled sleep. Their conversation had dried up a long time before, but this evening Gurn, though he had lived a virtual hermit in the Iremage house for the past seven years, felt he would go mad if he didn't talk.

There had never been glass in the windows in this crude hut, but the shutters were open despite the bitter cold. Gurn looked out at the dark trees surrounding the clearing, white wisps of mist played in and out of them. He sensed the glowing eyes of the wolves watching them. Though many of them roamed the forest, there were always a hundred or more ringing their nightly camp.

The boy's eyes were closing with fatigue. Soon he would be in his dreamworld with the wolves again, slipping even farther from humanity. Even as Gurn watched him, the desolate howling of the wolves began. Gurn saw Fazad's eyes open a crack at the sound, and got to his feet quickly.

"They are not of the sun, boy—these wolves. Only Reh gives light and reason to our lives. They are a darker force— of the world which has no form or shape, merely instinct. You must give up the cloak, Fazad, before it's too late."

The boy's eyes were fixed on him—he seemed to have his attention.

"I am no holy man, it is true," Gurn went on hurriedly. "But I know that Reh inspirited every living thing with a seed of fire which blooms or dies according to the light one brings to one's life."

"My nursery teacher told me these things," Fazad said, his eyes once again remote, distant.

"Then she taught you well," Gurn replied. "I'm worried about you—worried that that cloak will snuff out the light in you and you will become like them, a thing of the darkness."

Fazad hung his head. "Perhaps you're right—perhaps it's already too late for me. But the darkness came to Thrull and only desperate remedies saved me. The same in Bardun.

When darkness covers the world, you need darkness inside you to survive."

Gurn nodded slowly. "Yes, strange things happen in this darkness: perhaps it is the eve of eternal night. But we must still have faith: Reh's prophecies tell us this. Why there is even a prophecy concerning this self-same forest."

"Darvish? Tell me of it." Now he had Fazad's undivided attention.

"When I came here with my master we used to sit after the hunt on nights like this, and the foresters used to tell tales, and one of them was taken from the *Book of Light*, of the faery folk that live invisibly in the woods. Creatures made of ethereal flame invisible to mortal eye, so spiritlike that only the complete absence of light that will come at the end of time or the darkness on a moonless night makes them visible."

"Elves live here?" Fazad asked eagerly, sleep now totally forgotten.

"So the foresters said, and even these humble folk had studied the *Book of Light* closer than I, a seneschal. Somewhere in the far depths of these woods, where mortal has never trod, there is a fair city made entirely of blond wood that glows like gold, and there their palaces are raised on stilts and buttresses of ever-growing roots that lift them high towards the stars. And under an emerald canopy of leaves they hold court. Yet they cannot be seen by humankind, save once a month when the night is utterly moonless: then the mortal eye can just pick them out like a faint chalk mark in the dark."

"And what happens to those who see them?" Fazad asked.

"Ah, the elves' attitude to mankind is ambivalent. For once they were men like us, but over the ages we have become more corrupt and made of clay, and they have transmuted away from the corruptible body until they have become creatures of pure light. Many a forester have I spoken to who told me tales, some of fortune, some of mischief that these invisible spirits caused, of men led home on a night like this, full of a creeping fog, when wild animals were tracking them and they had given up hope of seeing their loved ones again. But other times they spoke of how after they had glimpsed the faery folk in the dark glens of a moonless night, the next morning they would find the earth disturbed where a man had buried his gold, and his few savings all gone, or his wife stark dead in their bed when the night before she had got into it in the best of health, and other such calamities."

He paused. "Now, I have never seen these creatures myself, but these last two weeks as I have lain awake, too scared to shut my eyes, I have thought of them often, the spirits of the woods. And it has put me in mind of the prophecies in the *Book of Light*, the prophecies that started all this darkness and these wars between the Worm and the Flame. Believe me, boy, for though we both have seen bad times, worse times are to come, when the light will be dead, no dawn will come."

The boy nodded. "Aye, there were Iss acolytes who came to the inn in Thrull and spoke of it."

Gurn fixed him with an earnest stare. "A world without the sun. Can you imagine it? But it is written in the *Book of Light* that the darkness will bring two things. First the faery folk I have spoken of will become visible and they will help mankind. Secondly the one they speak of as the Lightbringer will come and rescue us from the darkness."

"The Lightbringer?"

"Aye, she—for the book refers to her as a woman—will save the world, make the sun shine once more."

He looked about him, as if in that dank and dismal spot he hoped that the spirits would reveal themselves prematurely and grant them some light. But the fire had burned lower and lower as he had spoken and only gloom and a deathly chill surrounded them.

Suddenly he no longer felt like talking and he was very tired. His spirit was sapped from the long journey, this talk of endless night. Perhaps this was the despair into which man would slip at that terrible hour? Soon they retired for the night, the older man's head full of dreams of the elven folk.

After that night it took another two weeks to reach the sea. Each morning the last few days Fazad woke him with the same alarming news. Once more he had strayed with the wolves and seen how the Drinkers of the Viaticum had lengthened their pace, no longer stopping at sunrise but marching on through the daylight hours, still protected by the mist and the shade of the trees. Soon they were so close that Gurn and Fazad didn't halt but rode on through the night: once more the bone horns echoed through the forest and they heard the faint thunder of the legion's boots behind them. They clung to Cloud, desperate to stay awake.

Towards the evening of the next day, they both felt a faint breeze from in front. Not the dead decaying air of the forest but a strong gust carrying with it the tang of the sea air. The fog that had blanketed them ever since Perricod rolled away in a bank and they saw a silver gleam at the end of the tunnel cut in the forest. Light—open air. They blinked in the unaccustomed radiance, then hurried forward, warmed by the weak beams and the knowledge that at least until night had fallen the light would protect them from their pursuers.

Then, in front of them, they saw the sea irradiated by the sinking sun, a blazing silver light. The Astardian Sea. But unlike any sea that Gurn had ever seen (for Fazad had never seen the ocean in his life) here there was no constant restless movement of waves: all was static, frozen. Each wave was caught in motion and held there in an iron grip, corrugation after iron corrugation, racing to the west. From here the sea stretched away around the world broken only by the island of Galastra. Far over the horizon, according to some, was the edge of the world over which the ocean poured in an endless waterfall.

It was said that Galastra was sometimes visible from Surren's cliffs. But all that could be seen as sunset fell was the pink light struggling with the rolling slate-grey sky. Snow squalls hurried from the north like fleeing figures, grey arms stretching from sea to the sky.

Perhaps Gurn's already faint hopes evaporated when he saw that Galastra was invisible. Where was the island? If his optimism had caused him hitherto to underestimate the distance from the shore to the island, now reality led him to overcompensate so it appeared in his mind's eye not ten leagues, but half a world away—where the ocean dropped into the abyss at the edge of the world.

But the endless expanse of ocean seemed to have an enlivening effect on the boy who sat astride his mount, his brown eyes alive with a curious fire reflecting the pink of the setting sun.

He turned and looked back: the fringes of the Forest of Darvish. Its edge ran like a black wave to left and right, the road a dead chalky white in the dying light plunged into the forest's heart.

"Let's go," Gurn said, anxious to be away. Fazad merely nodded and instantly, without any visible encouragement, Cloud moved forward and began making his way down the steep switchback to the beach: a little way off they could see a small fishing village.

After their descent, they stopped on the pebble strand and stared over the wilderness of frozen waves, which loomed in front of them, so much more intimidating now they were at sea level. They followed the road that ran along the top of the strand into the village. They passed long-abandoned nets hung up to dry on frames; now they were frozen like spiderwebs. In the village shutters creaked in the wind, but no one moved and in the tiny harbor the boats were crushed in the ice, their hulls smashed, icicles hanging from their broken masts. The place had been abandoned a long time before.

"Where have the people gone?" Fazad asked, staring at the melancholy scene.

"They have done as we must do," Gurn replied. "Taken to the ice. It can only be two days' march to Galastra—if the ice is sound."

"And if not?"

Gurn didn't favor his young companion with a reply. Instead he peered down the beach back to the path from the cliffs. A black stream of wolves now poured down it. Some hesitated when they reached the beach, making phantom runs at the frozen waves, then balking and fleeing back, as if the waves were still liquid breakers, but others, their bodies pressed low, their ears pinned back, began to pour across the ice.

"Look," Fazad said, "they're leading us."

"Then let's follow," Gurn said wearily. His limbs ached and he felt his eyes drooping with tiredness but it was nearly dark and the Drinkers of the Viaticum would any moment appear at the head of the cliffs.

"Come, Cloud," Fazad whispered, running his hand through the horse's mane, and as always, without the encouragement of spur, stirrup or bridle, the horse began picking his way delicately down the beach until his hoofed feet touched the ice, skidding slightly, his legs splaying. He regained his balance, but the surface was like glass. They both dismounted. A whipping gale was now throwing a blizzard of ice into their eyes, and the only indication of their direction lay in the carmine stain of the setting sun through the storm clouds and the dark line of wolves running straight towards it.

"Come," said Fazad, offering his arm to the seneschal, "my brethren will bring us safe to Galastra."

Then, armed only with faith, he led them out into the wilderness of ice . . .

CHAPTER FIVE

The Last Sanctuary of the Flame

Galastra was a bleak granite island, standing where no land deserved to be, where wind contended with tide right at the shelf of the ocean before it plunged into the illimitable depths. Most of its interior was taken up by a barren mountain range called the Dragon's Back. The capital was Imblewick, a large port city on the sheltered east coast.

Apart from the products of the small copper mines hidden in the high fells, Galastra had no natural resources: instead, over the centuries, it had relied on those of other lands. Its fleets had carried the arable produce of the north to the south, the precious stones of the south to the east, the timbers of the east back to Galastra, where they had been planed and bent over flames and hammered into thwarts and the thwarts hammered together into hulls: every year the fleet of Galastra had grown and grown and its ships had controlled the oceans of all the known world.

Eight years before, the king of Galastra, Larchamon, had pledged his fleet to the service of the Flame against the armies of the Worm. It had been destroyed attempting to outflank Faran Gaton's advancing columns in the Inland Sea when a demon-created storm had sent its two hundred ships to the bottom. With them went ten thousand marines and sailors, and the country's king, Larchamon, with his treasury.

The king left behind a widow, Queen Zalia, and some fifty ships that had been in Imblewick that ill-fated day.

Ten leagues of the world's roughest seas separated Galastra from the mainland. Ancient prophecies in the *Book of Light* spoke of how only when the sea became solid ground would Galastra be lost to the Worm, for the undead would never willingly cross open water. And in all history only a few of them had come, hidden aboard ships. Fanatics, prepared to risk the Flame for spreading their disease in the virgin territory. Most had been captured and burned immediately, in autos-de-fé in Imblewick's central square. Others had started brief reigns of terror, and midnight hunts over the roofs and in the sewers, but their end had also been on the execution pyre.

And each time, after the terror had gone, the ancient soothsayers had come forth and once more reminded the people how they would be safe until the sea became solid ground and the people had looked out at the spume-filled wilderness of the ocean and known that would never be and had rejoiced in the power of Reh.

But that had been before the big freeze that had turned the waters of the harbour to glue and then to ice, and crushed the remaining fifty ships of the fleet until they were no more than shattered planks and cordage, held up by their mooring lines. Before the frost had taken each successive wave and arrested it in midmotion, before the sea as far as the horizon was a succession of frozen breakers.

With the ice, the flow of grain and other foodstuffs from the southern wheat fields had ceased, and the pinch of hunger was felt in every household in the grim granite city. The population waited, starving and desperate, looking at the ice, watching for the armies of the Worm.

There had always been travellers in Imblewick's harbour area, merchants and sailors, and some were stranded by the great freeze. But as the months passed new faces were seen in the foreigners' quarter by the docks.

It was said they came from across the frozen sea at night, the vanguard of the god Iss, worshippers of the Prince of Darkness. As darkness fell they left their hiding places and went out in the streets. They wore no robes to betray their allegiance, though they stood in conspiratorial huddles, on the cobblestones, whispering in the frozen alleyways, sour-faced men, spat at and cursed by the population hurrying home through the freezing city.

Here, just as in Thrull and Perricod, it had begun.

Such was the animosity shown towards these strangers that it was difficult to believe any of the townsfolk would fall to their persuasion, yet many remembered the words of the soothsayers, of how when the sea became solid ground it was only a matter of time before not only the armies of the Worm would come, but also Iss' endless night. Each evening more and more thronged the strangers' numbers.

After the death of her husband, Larchamon's widow, Zalia, had retired to the grim fortress at the top of the granite mount overlooking Imblewick. In that somber city one feature glowed like a beacon even in the gloomiest evening. From above the grey machicolations and the slates of the steeply pitched roofs of the keep a slender white marble tower rose into the air—many was the sea captain in the past who had made his landfall navigating by the White Tower of Imblewick.

And in that White Tower overlooking the grey sea of ice the queen had retired to mourn. There she gathered as her only companions fellow widows of the war and a few wise men and soothsayers. She had not been seen in the council chambers since the tragedy, abandoning the government of the isle to the few generals who had returned from the war.

One of these had now come to prominence, and he had been named governor, a man called Rutha Hunish, whose decrees were absolute law, whose personal guard ruled the city with a fist of iron.

Now the islanders' only contact with their monarch came when one of the soothsayers would every month come down from the White Tower and from a balcony proclaim to the populace what they had seen the future to hold for Galastra.

The last time a soothsayer had appeared was two months before. He had spoken of terrible signs in the heavens: Orion embraced in the sickle moon; a dreadful portent: the Hunter embraced by mutability. An omen that their enemies, the un-dead hordes from Ossia, would be coming soon, over the ice, and Galastra's warrior nation would be enfolded by death forever. Since him, no soothsayer had been seen. Now only a handful of the townspeople dressed in rags and moth-eaten furs gathered in the cutting wind in the hope that a wise man would appear again, this time with better news.

On an evening two days after Gurn and Fazad had left the Surren coast, a lone watchman kept his vigil on the city walls overlooking the harbour. The battlements were cov-ered by a thick black hoarfrost and deserted: only one lone watch fire burnt at the top of the round tower that dominated the main gate. The frozen sea stretched away to the invisible shores of Surrenland. Firewood was at a premium in the bit-ter weather. As they did every day some of the townspeople had passed through the gate pulling ice sleds out to the bro-ken hulks of the fleet. The day had been punctuated by the sound of axes biting into wood. Later they returned dragging the cut timbers of the once mighty Galastrian fleet behind them on their sleds. The guards let them pass. Even they pil-laged wreckage from the harbour for firewood. No one else had entered or left the city all day. An hour ago the great double gates had been pushed to. Now only one man was left on the battlements and all was silent save the whistling of the wind.

The watcher had an iron brazier full of the same salvaged wood blazing by his side; its flames did a little to take away the biting sting of the wind. His eyes ached from the un-remitting icy blast from the north and the effort of searching for movement on the far horizon in the dying light of the day. Each of the snow squalls hurrying towards the city might conceal an enemy at its heart.

Then, as he began to think that soon it would be too dark and he could give up his vigil, he saw movement, way out beyond where the granite breakwater had once protected the harbour from the seas. He peered forward: whatever it had been was gone again. Five minutes passed. Now in the gap between the eastern cliff and the tip of the breakwater he saw what he had seen before.

A single horse and rider, led by a second man. Behind, in the grey wilderness of ice, he saw something new: it might have been a dark wave, fanning out a mile across, as if the sea had unfrozen and cast up a single dark ripple, rolling slowly in his direction. He blinked his eyes against the drifting snow, then it was gone—perhaps it had been merely another of the racing squall lines.

The guard had a brass trumpet lying against the frozen parapet: he had been ordered to sound it at the approach of anyone or anything from the east. But now he hesitated: surely his sergeant had meant for him to blow it only at the approach of an army, not that of only two men and a horse? Yet he was a soldier: orders were orders, to be inflexibly obeyed. He pulled aside the wool cloth protecting his face and held the mouthpiece to his lips, cursing as the frozen metal glued to the tender skin, ripping it—he tasted his own blood. No sound but the sound of his own breath came from the instrument, a bolus of ice was frozen in its inner tubes, and he threw it down in exasperation. He stared anxiously forward again, wondering what he should do. The strangers were closer, in the harbour, approaching the first wreck in the outer roads. They were hurrying in front of another black squall that pursued them like a demon from the east.

The guard scurried down the stone steps to the postern, shouting as he passed the heavy iron-studded oak door of the guardhouse. But no answer came: no doubt the men inside were drunk or asleep in the warm fug of their quarters.

He pulled open the iron spy hole set into the postern: it gave a view of the wharf and the deserted harbour. The two men were closer, picking their way between the frozen hulks of the fleet, ducking under the anchor chains with their necklaces of icicles. Then they disappeared from sight as they dipped beneath the line of the near harbour wall. They were heading towards the ramp leading up to the dockside. A few moments afterwards they reappeared, the horse struggling for purchase on the icy cobblestones of the ramp up to the quay. Both the man who led the horse and its rider had their heads bowed against the fierce wind. They struggled on until they came up to the great double gates of Imblewick, unconscious, or so it seemed, of the guard inspecting them from the spy hole.

The guard saw how one of the sleeves of the man leading the horse hung loose. He had a grizzled pepper and salt beard, his face showed the grey fatigue of long travel.

The rider was bareback. His head and his whole body were wrapped in wolf furs. He now sat very erect, whereas when the guard had first spotted them he had been slouched. It was as if he had suddenly been wakened by the appearance of the city walls in front of him. He turned his head from right to left, surveying the defences in front. He, too, seemed oblivious of the face staring at him from the hatch a few feet away. He turned in its direction and the guard saw under the fringe of his cloak a boy's face, his cheeks blue from the cold.

The horse whinnied, as if challenging those hidden behind the gates to give them admittance.

The noise finally stirred the guard. "Who comes there?" he yelled, his weak voice almost lost in the mounting wind from the north. Both men flinched at the sudden noise, as if slapped in the face.

"Is this Imblewick?" the older man shouted back over the whine of the wind.

"Aye, it is," the guard responded gruffly. "Where have you come from?"

The man didn't answer immediately but turned and stared back over the deepening gloom of the ice sea as if trying to pick out the place from which they had departed: as if he needed to see it to believe they had actually come from a spot so far from here. He turned eventually and spoke again, in a whisper that the guard barely heard. "From Surrenland."

"Surrenland? But the coast is ten leagues away!"

"Aye, we have travelled two nights and two days." His head sagged with weariness and the guard had to press his ear against the spy hole to hear him. "Yesterday I thought we must have passed Galastra, were heading further and further into the middle of the ocean, would reach the place where the ice gives way to the sea, at the edge of the world. And there we would drown. Reh be thanked it didn't happen. For, as the light died in the west this evening, I saw the White Tower of Imblewick gleaming like a beacon two miles off, and I knew we were safe."

The guard by now had rallied his wits. "Wait here, I'll fetch my sergeant," he said.

Gurn's face split into a wry grin. "There is nowhere we can go, soldier. But hurry, the wind is cold and will grow colder yet when it is dark."

The spy hole was thrust shut. Fazad had played no part in the exchange, but had throughout looked back over his shoulder at the distant breakwater where the wolves had stopped, huddling in its lee, smelling mankind, not daring to come closer while it was still light. He took in a great breath of the bitter air, his face wrinkling. "I thought you said this place was free of the Worm?"

"The last I heard," Gurn said, turning from the spy hole.

"Smell the air," Fazad commanded.

Gurn screwed up his face and did so, wrinkling his nostrils. "I smell nothing but old fish and caulking tar," he said eventually.

Fazad shook his head. "Well, *I* can smell it. Winding clothes, grave earth and mildew. The undead are already here."

Gurn sniffed again. Nothing. But more than once on their journey Fazad had proven himself possessed of a sixth sense not entirely human. "The Drinkers of the Viaticum can't have overtaken us. We've seen hide nor hair of them since Darvish."

"Not them—but others of their kind—they're here already," Fazad said fiercely.

As Fazad spoke these words the spy hole was thrust back again and a new head appeared behind it. Framed by a chain-mail hood, the new face was tanned and wrinkled like a walnut, with twinkling eyes naturally disposed to merriment. The owner of the face inspected the two men, but principally Gurn. Then his lips cracked into a smile. "The Flame preserve me—it is Gurn of the Iremage clan!"

Gurn's face screwed up as he returned the stare, then recognition dawned. "Sergeant Valence, of King Larchamon's Guard!" he exclaimed.

"The same," the soldier said. "The same as stood by you on Thrull field, even when the brown and purple were all about us."

"Aye, shoulder to shoulder, even when the lines broke . . ."

"I thought you were dead."

"I too, but it is a long story, and the cold is not a friend."

Valence turned away from the spy hole. "Quickly, open the gates," he shouted at the guards hidden within, "these are friends."

Presently the gates were pulled back on their rusty hinges and there stood the short, stocky figure of the sergeant, clad in chain-mail armour. He stepped forward and seized his friend's single hand, noticing the empty flapping sleeve as he did so. He looked from it to his old friend's face. "I saw you take that wound . . ."

"Yes, but like the lizard that leaves its tail when its enemy seizes it, so I left my arm and escaped. But that too is a long tale, to be told in front of a fire and a pot of ale."

"Both shall be yours," Valence promised. "There's truth in the saying: old soldiers never die. Come in out of the wind, you and your young friend," he said, leading Gurn black into the shelter of the postern. They passed through the gates into a wide cobbled square covered with frozen snow and slush. Inside stood six soldiers wearing the orange and red of one of the Flame legions, now much faded by wind and rain.

Beyond them the square presented a melancholy sight. Abandoned pallets and nets lay heaped on the cobbles, stray cats braved the biting wind, scavenging amongst the detritus. A brazier full of salvaged wood blazed away on the cobbles, giving light but only the illusion of heat. The tall buildings fringing the plaza were all built of the local grey granite, their gables sagging towards the square, the alleys canyonlike beyond, leading up to the dark mass of the citadel that loomed like the capsized hull of a ship cast by some monstrous wave onto the granite crags above them. Above it, like a symbol of hope, the White Tower was caught by a final ray of the sun and blazed like a beacon. Beyond it, through seething purple storm clouds, the snow-covered flanks of the Dragon's Back appeared and then were covered again as the raging winds howled over them.

Fazad muttered something to Cloud, and the gelding followed Valence and Gurn, the boy all the time looking from left to right, his face wrinkled in suspicion. The gates were closed behind them.

"How did you make your way back here after the battle?" Gurn was asking Valence, his hand outstretched to the illusory heat of the fire.

"We left the transport behind in Thrull. Then we walked over the mountains, a long journey, the men not stopping at day or night, thinking that Faran would send a pursuit. The survivors embarked on the last ship from Surrenland. When we got here the city was in ferment: an invasion fleet was expected at any time. Weeks and then months passed—nothing."

"You fled from ghosts, old friend. There was no pursuit. Faran never even came into Surrenland."

"Why?"

"Perhaps there was blood enough for the undead in Thrull, for that is where he remained," Gurn said.

"Then, friend, why have you come when you were safe in Perricod?"

"For one, Perricod is not safe. The Ossian legions got there a month ago. As for the rest"—Gurn nodded at Fazad, who was still mounted on Cloud—"let the boy tell his tale—then you'll understand."

Valence glanced at the strange boy who all this time had been silent.

The boy slowly dismounted, patting the horse on the withers, before turning again to Valence.

"Thrull is destroyed, Faran Gaton driven out."

"How do you know this?" Valence was suddenly deadly serious, a pallor under his tan.

Fazad was not put off by the sudden change of manner but returned the older man's stare. "Because I saw it with my own eyes: and since then I have travelled the lands seeking a place to bring my news where it will be received with rejoicing."

"Then you were right to come here where the Flame still burns," Valence answered.

"It burns for the moment, Sergeant, but not for long. The darkness comes."

Valence turned to Gurn, puzzled. "He means the undead, my friend," the seneschal explained. "They are in Surrenland, Perricod has fallen. Worse, a legion followed us through Darvish Forest. But surely there are none here already?"

The sergeant shook his head sadly, looking off into the darkening streets. "Ah, friend: so that is why you came? Because you thought Galastra safe? But you should know: nowhere is safe. How long is it now? A year or more. That is when the night watch first began to find the corpses in the streets, drained dry. No one knows how, but the Dead in Life are here. Overnight each man began to suspect his neighbour, even his family, no one trusts each other except in the light of the sun. Many have fled into the mountains. At night this place is a ghost city, the doors are locked and no one stirs. The Worm is everywhere—in men's minds and in their hearts. But you don't need me to tell you this, you will have seen enough of it yourself."

"They're here?"

Valence nodded. "Even here."

"How many?"

Valence shook his head. "Who can tell? It could be a dozen or a hundred or more. Now you tell me a legion follows. There are scarcely five companies to face them."

Fazad had kept silent, apparently not even listening to the interchange of the two old soldiers. But now he spoke again. "So it was in Thrull to begin with. At first there were rumours that the undead were in the catacombs, then men began to disappear, panic seized everyone and then the undead armies arrived. Where a fly lands, there maggots breed, a million strong."

Fazad's eyes had never left Valence's. "You may wonder how a mere boy can remember the events of seven years ago, but I heard enough of them afterwards when I was a slave: the boasts of our conquerors. And I have my own memories, of after the battle."

"What happened?" Valence asked, but it was clear he regretted his question the moment he had uttered it.

Too late: a wry smile broke over Fazad's face. "I have heard wise men say that the young forget. That the years heal our tender minds. It has not been so with me, Sergeant. I saw loved ones slaughtered before my eyes, others receive the bite that turns the spirit to the Life in Death. I fled with my nurse through our palace, but the undead scented us out. And so I would have died or been changed, if my nurse hadn't hidden me beneath her skirts even as they butchered her. Her blood spared me, for even the undead were so overwhelmed by its perfume that they didn't sniff me out, a living infant in her bloody rags. When the mortal soldiers of Iss found me the next morning, I was spared and sold as a slave."

The colour had once more drained from Valence's ruddy face. "You remember this, you who were so young?" he whispered.

But Fazad had fallen into a distraught reverie and so he

might have remained as the night settled and his limbs froze if Gurn hadn't broken in with an affected good humour.

"Come," he said, "let us leave these ghosts and the past behind. Faran is defeated—isn't that enough to lift our hearts? Valence, take us to the palace so we may tell the queen."

"Of course," the sergeant replied. "But be warned—the queen has not granted an audience since her husband was killed."

"Surely she will receive us, who have come all the way from Thrull and Perricod?" Gurn answered, but even his bluster was muted, affected by the sergeant's uncharacteristic gloom.

"Come then," Valence said. He led them along the side of the wall to a lean-to shack with a chimney out of which smoke billowed into the bustling wind. It was evidently the guards' barracks. He kicked the door open unceremoniously and rousted out the sleepy men inside with a few ardent curses. A small group of unshaved, bleary-eyed soldiers poured out of it, and gathered round, staring from their sergeant to the new arrivals.

"These are friends, boys," Valence said, his good humour partially recovered. "Gather your torches: we are going up to the citadel."

As they did so, Gurn placed his backpack on the ground and opened its top. From it he pulled a bolt of white embroidered silk, the Iremage banner. He unfolded it and let it flow out on the breeze. His eyes caught Valence's. "For my lord," he said solemnly. "Let it fly in a place where the Flame still burns."

"Amen to that," Valence answered, gesturing to his men to fall in behind them.

CHAPTER SIX

The White Tower of Imblewick

Fazad remounted Cloud and they set off in a column over the square and into the closely packed streets leading off it. Valence and Gurn led, the seneschal carrying the Iremage banner. Though night had fallen, the flag's pure white field glowed in the dark. At the unaccustomed tramp of boots passing through the usually silent streets, shutters opened and faces looked out. A strange spectacle they must have made: the banner, the ghostly grey mount and the boy clad all in wolf fur, proud and erect, saddleless on the horse's back.

Higher and higher they went through the grey streets until they passed out of the gloom of overhanging buildings and through another gate, untended by any guard. To the right, on a sloping ground leading up to the granite crags on which the citadel was built, Valence pointed out the grey barracks of the Galastrian army. No lights burned in them, no smoke came from the chimneys.

"Where are the guard?" Gurn asked.

"Things have changed in the last month or so," Valence replied. "Discipline has suffered."

Behind the barracks, the citadel rose up into the night mist that was settling over the island. They climbed a ramp up to an iron portcullis. The guard station beyond was a shack like that at the barracks gates, and was also unattended. All that could be seen was a courtyard beyond, and steps leading up to a monumental doorway set into a wall covered by ivy.

"No guards here either," Gurn said.

"Don't worry, I'll fetch them," Valence replied. He stepped forward and struck a steel clapper set outside the gate. The sound echoed round and round. Now they heard the curses of men stirring in the gatehouse and presently more soldiers stumbled from a doorway to their left. Though the men under Valence's command had looked disheveled, these were even worse equipped, and wore the bleary-eyed look of those who had been drinking all day. They stared stupidly at the procession in front of them before one of them recognized Valence and thought to go to the winch and raise the portcullis, which rose with protesting screeches into its housing.

Valence brushed past the drunken guards and into the courtyard beyond where Fazad dismounted. He and Gurn followed Valence up the dozen steps into a hall. The swell of voices echoed from inside and there was the glow of lantern light. The hall was some hundred feet long. A wooden gallery ran around it at the height of about twenty feet, its raftered ceiling lost in centuries of soot and the deep gloom. At its far end stood a moldering wooden throne, covered with dust. The dead king's. A barely smouldering fire made no impression on the chill. A checkered black and white marble floor ran up to the dais. On it stood some twenty of what Gurn took to be courtiers, both male and female, wearing ermine-fringed velveteen cloaks. Each wore a powdered wig and deathly white makeup that made them look like ghosts. Their clothing was cloaked in a chalky dust, as if they had stood in this place for a very long time, waiting for an audience that never came to pass. They had fallen silent the moment Valence and his group had appeared at the top of the steps.

The two groups eyed one another. The contrast could not have been more acute, the grubby soldiers and their travel-

stained guests and the faded nobility of Galastra. In the silence, one of the guards went off into the recesses of the
building. Presently he returned with two men who looked to
be servants though their black and silver doublets were
ragged and frayed.

The visitors were ushered towards benches set into the
marble walls of the audience chamber as one of the servants
went to fetch food and drink, while the other kicked in a
desultory fashion at the defunct fire. As this was going on,
more figures began slowly to appear on the balcony overlooking the hall, their faces frozen white with makeup, their
lips and eyes black, like clowns' faces, staring down at them
incuriously, like phantoms, stripped of any spark of anima-
tion: more members of the court.

Valence gestured to Gurn to lean close to him so he could
whisper, for the silence did not encourage any louder form
of communication.

"These," he said, nodding at those on the lower level,
"have waited through many an evening for the queen to appear and go into her banqueting hall. Each has a petition.
But they won't be heard. The queen is closeted with her
soothsayers."

"Then who will receive us?" Gurn asked. "Did Darent,
the commander of the Guard, survive Thrull?"

"He survived," Valence answered, "but he died of the
ague, just when the ice first came. Now Rutha Hunish of the
White Company is both governor and commander of the
army."

"Rutha Hunish?"

"Aye," Valence said, casting his eyes at the silent figures
staring down at them. "He led the White Company under Illgill. They were volunteers who joined the Galastrians on
their march across the Fire Mountains."

"Then he's not a native of Galastra?"

Valence shook his head. He leaned even closer to his old
comrade. "No one knows whence he came, though he
claims to have come from the Land of the White Clouds,
west of Surrenland."

"Claims, you say?"

Valence nodded. "Illgill had need of any friends he could muster, and didn't question Rutha Hunish's story, but there were others who did. But he fought well on Thrull field, carried his sword in the front line even when the battle was lost; some say he slew more than twenty of the Dead in Life."

Just then there came the sound of footsteps and the clash of armour at the top of the steps leading down from the gallery into the hall. Gurn turned: it was as if Valence's words had conjured the man, for at the top of them appeared a tall figure clad in silver-plated armour who by his warlike demeanour could be none other than Rutha Hunish, the fierce general of Valence's tale. His face was very pale, with an aquiline nose, the hair receding at the temples and swept back severely. Below was the black arrow head of a dense beard. His carriage was haughty, his eyes dark and flashing and two hectic spots high on his cheekbones betokened a man of a fiery temper.

Behind stood six guards armed with halberds, like their lord clad in plate armour. Unlike the motley crowd at the gates with their rusted mail, these men's armour sparkled and they had the hard look of toughened fighters.

Rutha Hunish surveyed the scene below him and instantly the slack movements of the servants ceased, even the faded courtiers who had again set up muted conversations fell silent. But Rutha Hunish's eyes were fixed on one person, and one alone. Fazad. Then with a measured step he began to descend, his eyes never leaving the boy, his guards following, rising and falling it seemed in unison with him as they came down the steps. As he descended, all those who had been sitting rose respectfully, all save Gurn.

Rutha Hunish crossed the floor, his metalled boots ringing on the marble. He halted before the boy, looking him up and down coldly. "So," he said, "what have we here? A child, clad in a wolf cloak?" He leaned forward and flicked his mailed fingers against the wolf pelts. "An outlandish garb. Speak, if you have a tale. I'm told you have crossed the ice. Perhaps from Ossia?"

If Fazad had been intimidated by the menace of the commander, he did not show it. Instead, it was as if he stood even more erect, his eyes never leaving Rutha's. "No," he replied, "not from Ossia, but from Thrull, to bring good news. We have come seeking sanctuary in your land, the last free of the Worm."

Rutha Hunish sneered. "Aye, others have come, before the ice closed the harbour and destroyed the fleet. They said the same, but I found them out: each of them was an Ossian spy. Each was a traitor, and each burned a merry jig in the flame."

Now Gurn rose from his seat where he'd remained all this time. Rutha turned to face him, his eyes resting on the empty sleeve of his tunic, then on the single hand that still held the crumpled white standard of the Iremage clan.

"I am a soldier," Gurn said, "I fought on Thrull field, left my arm behind, barely survived the day."

"More than limbs and blood were left behind that day," Rutha replied. "Our honour too. What makes you special?"

"Honour never dies," Gurn said.

"You are insolent," Rutha Hunish spat back, summoning the six guards with a flick of his head. They took a step towards him in unison, their armour chinking.

"Sire, I can vouch for this man," Valence said hastily, moving to his old friend's side.

Now Rutha directed his dark anger at him. "Save your words, Sergeant, for these two will be in the dungeons tonight; you, too, if you don't remain silent."

The guards had already laid hands on the two strangers when there came the sound of a footfall on the gallery. Everyone looked up. A man clad in white robes holding a golden staff of office stood where Rutha had stood a few moments before.

"Creaggan," went up the muttered refrain from the assembled courtiers.

"Who is he?" Gurn whispered to Valence.

"One of the queen's soothsayers," the sergeant replied.

The soothsayer's long face, though as crinkled as a

crushed ball of paper, was given a mild air by piercing blue eyes over a white beard that jutted out on a prominent chin. He regarded the scene below him for a few seconds. Then he spoke, low and sonorous. "Rutha Hunish, let the strangers come up to the White Tower: the queen would have audience with them."

The hectic spots high on Rutha's cheeks seemed to blaze even more fiercely and his lips twitched. He took a step forward, his mailed fists bunching. But then some self-control returned to him. He brought himself up short and bowed stiffly.

"The queen will be obeyed," he said through clenched teeth. He jerked his head and his guards pulled Gurn and Fazad forward towards the stairs, but Creaggan waved his staff.

"Let the strangers come alone, with the sergeant," he intoned, then without waiting to see if his orders were obeyed, as if he knew they would be, he turned his back and walked away.

Rutha Hunish watched him go with barely concealed displeasure, then turned to Gurn. "I will not forget your words. I know all those who come across the ice are traitors," he said, his lips curling, then jerked his head savagely indicating that they should follow the soothsayer. Gurn returned his gaze evenly, then mounted the steps with Fazad and Valence.

They passed through the silent ranks of courtiers ringing the gallery and saw the soothsayer waiting for them in the gloom of a dark corridor leading deeper into the castle. Without uttering a word, Creaggan turned and led off down an oak-paneled corridor, lushly carpeted and again covered with a thick layer of dust. They looked back into the audience hall. There stood Rutha Hunish, hands on hips glaring after them.

"This is good fortune," Valence said, rather too loudly, ignoring his old friend's frigid anger at Rutha Hunish's insulting words. "As I said, the queen has not admitted anyone to her presence these last seven years." But if Gurn was pleased, he was in no mood to show it. As for the boy in his wolf cloak, his eyes darted around him wildly as if he would be happier anywhere, even on the frozen seas, than in the confines of the gloomy citadel.

They walked on in silence for some twenty minutes, Creaggan leading them through a bewildering labyrinth of corridors, up and down, many oak-lined like the first with dark portraits staring down at them, others bare, chilly stone. Once they crossed a stone courtyard and they saw the diamond-bright stars shining down on them from the frozen sky.

On and on until they came to a wider courtyard that smelt faintly of horses and straw. To their left they heard a gentle whinny from what looked like a stable block. Creaggan had stopped. He pointed and addressed his first words directly to them, fixing his eyes on Fazad.

"Your horse will be brought here," he said. "He will be safe."

The boy ducked his head in what might have been a gesture towards a bow, but the soothsaver had already turned away. Across the courtyard the White Tower reared up into the stormy night sky. It was some fifty feet across and at least a hundred high. Creaggan led them down a tunnel at its ground level. There was a cylindrical opening in the floor above: a murder hole through which missiles and burning oil could be poured on those attacking in times of siege. When they reached the centre of the tower, he halted in front of a metal-studded door and turned to them. "Though this is the only way into the tower, and the gate is usually locked, it is not a prison, nor are you prisoners, despite what Rutha Hunish said. This is the queen's dwelling and her word holds sway in Galastra. You are her guests."

"But she doesn't know who we are, what our message is," Gurn replied.

"Oh, she knows. She has been expecting you. That is what she and I study: the future, what will unfold. Even your message," he said, turning to Fazad, "the queen knows its words before you have uttered them." His blue eyes glowed strangely in the lamplight and for a brief second the boy imagined that he did see in their indigo depths the shifting lakes and oceans of the future.

Creaggan turned away and drew a key from his pocket. It glowed strangely with silver light. There was no keyhole in the door—the soothsayer merely waved the key in an apparently abstract pattern in front of it, and it clicked and then groaned inwards. Behind, steps led upwards into the heart of the tower. They felt ahead a breath of warmth as they followed Creaggan into a round chamber, a stone throne at its centre on a dais. A white light blazed from each side of the chamber's alabaster walls, the light source hidden, but lending a white nimbus to all that Fazad and Gurn saw.

Ranged in a circle around the throne were an array of curious-looking individuals: like Creaggan they all had white hair, their skin pale as marble sculpture; old men and women, their faces lined and wizened with knowledge of the arts, of the supernatural: the soothsayers that Valence had mentioned. Younger women stood closely ringing the throne, but like their older counterparts, their hair too was white as snow. "Some of the widows of the war against the Worm," Valence murmured. "To a one their hair turned white on the day of their loss. It is said the Queen will not tolerate any company other than the widows and the augurs." Fazad and Gurn were too amazed by the strange glowing chamber to reply, but just stood where they were, dumbly gaping about them.

Now Creaggan waved them forward, and as the crowd parted slightly, they saw a woman sitting on the throne. She was very old, unlike her handmaids. Her wispy hair was very pale and her face was lined like the bars of the sand after the retreating tide, yet despite the shrunken flesh on her cheekbones, there was still a bright intelligence in her face, and her features broke into a pleasant smile when she saw them as if she had not always sat in this place of mourning, surrounded by widows. Her eyes sparkled, a curious colour, a deep blue mixed with brown that rendered them almost purple and depthless. She wore a golden coronet over her white hair. But she was very frail—her body seemed merely a collection of bones held together by her white samite gown that fell loosely on all sides of her on the oversized seat. Creaggan didn't have to introduce her: it was obvious who she was. Queen Zalia of Galastra.

Her smile didn't change as she inspected the two strangers and their escort. When she was finished she nodded her head slightly as if satisfied by something in their appearance before speaking. "Welcome—Gurn of the Iremage clan," she said, nodding at the seneschal. Gurn bowed, remembering Creaggan's words—they were expected.

Now she turned her attention to Fazad. "Fazad Falarn," she said, enunciating each syllable. "I have waited a long time for you to come. And as I have waited this island kingdom has sunk like the rest of the world into darkness. It will grow darker yet, but your coming will change all that. You will bring hope even in the black midnight of Iss' second coming. And you will be a king . . ."

"You call me king?" Fazad asked, the remoteness suddenly gone, his eyes confused, unsure, for the first time since Gurn had known him.

The queen didn't reply directly. "All in good time. For now both of you will be my guests. Now, go with my handmaidens. Your quarters are ready."

Instantly some of the white-haired women came forward and led the two to a set of stairs that curved upwards into the higher reaches of the tower. Gurn turned to say good-bye to his friend but Valence too had been led away and the throne room had emptied so quickly that it was now completely abandoned, as if their brief interview with the queen had been but a fatigue-induced hallucination of their travel-weary minds.

CHAPTER SEVEN

The Last of the Legion

Lost in the polar north of the earth, the city of Iskiard had been unvisited by man since the Age of Gold came to an end ten thousand years ago. Then the gods had quarreled over who should rule the earth. They fought on Shandering Plain. Afterwards Reh and Iss alone survived of their pantheon: but both were grievously wounded, and were healed only by the magic of their drinking cups: the Silver and the Black Chalices.

Over the battlefield the earth was on fire and the sky was black. Reh and Iss saw that nothing was left to rule. Above them, the stars beckoned—the stars from which they had come; the dwelling place of the demons. They mounted their steeds and rode them into the skies.

And what of the other gods who were slain at Shandering? Only Erewon, Reh's brother and God of the Moon, was carried to a grave—by his palace in the immortal land of Lorn. The others were left on the field of battle, until humans came and dragged their remains towards Iskiard. But the journey was far, the sun was hidden by a mighty blizzard of ash and snow that fell from the skies, the humans perished, still tied to the rope trains: the colossi behind were abandoned. The blizzards became ever more furious and soon Iskiard was buried forever under the snow.

But the two gods were safe. In the heavens, Reh mounted up on the chariot of the sun and drove it fiercely across the skies. And after a time his beams once more found their way through the roiling clouds that covered the earth, and once more the sun shone on mankind.

And Iss entered the gloomy portals of that planet of night and the grave, Pluto, doomed to dwell in its purple depths forever. But in that dark place he remembered the earth and how fair it was, and how he had been worshipped there, an equal of Reh. But when the earth's skies cleared, and he peered down from his star, he saw that man had forgotten him and worshipped only the light of his brother's sun chariot.

He seethed, for Reh had beaten him: not in the battle of the plain but in the battle for men's hearts. He plotted how he might win them back: for only by the power of their prayers could he return from his place of banishment. Reh would be defeated and an endless midnight would sit on the world forever. Then he would destroy humankind, every one of them, for they had forsaken him and gone to Reh. Afterwards he would dwell alone in darkness for eternity.

The centuries passed. When men slept he sent his shadow over the world, a dark mist, that penetrated every nook and every cranny, seeking for the instrument of his release. Five thousand years he searched, until one night the mist settled over Iskiard, the burying place of the gods. There he found the descendants of the priests who had waited in vain for the deities to be brought from Shandering. Amongst them was a man blessed by magic: the wizard Marizian. Iss saw how the magician, like all those who had tasted the gods' secret knowledge, lusted for more. He sent a dream, showing Marizian the Rod of the Shadows: the instrument with which the priests of that place had once opened the gates of Shades, allowing the dead gods to travel to the lands of death. And Marizian awoke, on fire with his vision and Iss' words. He went into the underworld and opened the gates. But he found no secrets: instead the spirits of the dead swarmed from it, slaying all the inhabitants of Iskiard. Marizian fled as the ghosts mounted up into the sky, and veiled the face of the sun so its light became weak and the earth began to die. And when the people saw the dying light they cursed Reh, and once more remembered the God of Darkness, Iss.

Marizian fled, taking the Rod, and also a magical sword, Dragonstooth, with which he sealed the gateway to the doomed city so no man could again approach it. He travelled to the south and founded the city of Thrull. And there he wrote the *Book of Light* and the *Book of Worms*.

Five thousand years passed. Now the first man in all that time has come to Iskiard. Only the magic of the Rod of the Shadows that he has carried from Thrull has preserved him. And of the twenty thousand men he used to command, only three remain. He is Baron Illgill of Thrull.

Eight years earlier he began the wars between the Flame and the Worm; then his armies were defeated on Thrull field and he fled with the Rod. Now he believes there is one last chance to save the world from Iss. The gates to Shades must be sealed once more. He has descended deep into the underworld under the city, seeking the gateway; he is close to the mystery but his energies are failing. Time to rest, time to regather supplies for the final push through the darkness.

The baron ordered two of his men back through the underworld to the surface. Their names were Zar Surkut and Otin. They retraced the hard-won steps of the previous weeks: each level of the underworld was a grave for one or other of their companions. But Reh smiled on them, for the chambers so dangerous on the way down were now curiously empty and quiet. They went unhindered, climbing the many levels, their lonely torchlight like a firefly in the vast underground chambers where the shadows were like the gloomy depths of an ocean bottom.

They climbed up hundred-foot-deep shafts by the frayed ropes they had left months before and across the planks they had stretched precariously over the chasms, still there against all the odds. Up and up and with each foot their hope grew. Then they saw the worked stones of the passageways in the lower reaches of Iskiard's great pyramid. There they paused, breathing hard at the foot of the final shaft to the surface. They peered up, where the first rope they had placed those months before hung down from the darkness above like a pale vine. The darkness seemed lighter above: perhaps they had arrived during the brief passage of the arctic day and it was the vestige of sunlight coming from the pyramid entrance high above them.

It was then Otin grasped Surkut's cloak. "Do you see it?" he whispered, an edge of fear in his voice.

"What?" Surkut asked, holding the torch higher, but its guttering light only served to blind them further.

"I saw a face, at the top of the shaft!" Otin hissed.

"The shaft is two hundred feet high," Surkut answered. "How could you see anything so far away?" But his voice, too, had taken on a high pitch of nervousness.

Both men's night vision was gone and they could see nothing more in the grey light high above them. They looked at one another, wondering whether to risk the final climb. Their gaunt and withered bodies told them they must. They would die of starvation if they remained here. So too would Endil and the baron left with the Rod below, waiting for them to return with the supplies.

Surkut went first, pulling himself up the rope, the fragile umbilical link to light and food. At any moment whoever or whatever it had been that Otin had glimpsed could cut it and he would die. But Otin and the other two would die as surely as him, for after this rope was gone there was no way back to the surface, no more food.

He reached the top, his limbs aching, covered with sweat: there was no one visible in the grey gloom that shone from the Hall of Ghosts. He sucked in the clean air that blew in from the pyramid entrance: cold but pure after the fetid atmosphere of the underworld. Presently Otin too hauled himself over the rim of the shaft, cursing, struggling for breath.

They rested a little while, then pushed on, exiting the pyramid into the bitter cold of the arctic day, the pale sun hidden by thick clouds, yet, to them, almost blinding. The low cloud hung over the thousand towers of the city, threatening another blizzard.

Something had changed. A strange energy hummed in the air, and there was a barely audible sound. It seemed to come from high up, where the pediments of the temples and the tops of the towers were hidden by the low cloud. Then the noise of the howling wind was blotted out by an earsplitting roar, and a score of geysers of flame bloomed like orange flowers through the grey. Suddenly a dark shadow passed over them—the cloud parted and they saw an enormous wingspan, iridescent armour and fire-spitting beak. A dragon. Now the sky was full of them. More and more passed overhead, alighting on the invisible towers high above them.

No dragons had been seen since the time of the gods. Why had they returned to the land of men? They were Reh's creatures: surely they would not harm them, the last of the Legion of Flame? But terror overcame reason. Crouching low, Surkut and Otin raced over the snow-covered courtyard, to the safety of the buildings ranged around the pyramid. Then they were inside and the screeching of the dragons barely carried to them anymore.

They recovered their breath and lit tapers and advanced into the labyrinth, finding their way to the place they had called, when they had first found it, the Hall of Life. After the darkness of the underworld, they beheld a vision: above them a vault made of crystal through which the sun, though weak, shone, its diffused rays concentrated and magnified by the prism of glass, and refracted into a thousand particles of light that danced about the chamber.

There was a still pool set in the centre of the floor, and in the alcoves surrounding it, they saw food set out on golden plates, fresh as if it had just been cooked and served. Every dainty the world had ever known: fifty different stews and roasts, warm bread, bowls of fruit, honeycombs, goblets of wine.

The Hall of Life, but also of Death.

When they had first come to the city, it had been Argon who had been the first to die, here, in this very hall. Then as now, their hunger had been terrible, and though the baron had warned them, they had fallen on the food with gusto. Minutes later Argon was vomiting blood, then he was dead. Afterwards, each time the men took a bite from one of the dishes, the survivors thought of him, and wondered if they would share his end; the magic food, however delicious it tasted, nearly choking them as they forced it down their dry throats.

Surkut and Otin worked quickly, filling their backpacks with the food that had appeared since their last visit, then wolfing down the excess, in their desperation even forgetting Argon's fate. Their hunger made them careless, made them linger longer than they should have. They froze, sensing the dimming of the light, the shadows growing at the edge of the glowing room.

The Marishader had come. Before, when they were with the baron, the light of the Rod had protected them, but now it was far below. They backed away from the pooling shadows, then fled. But more shadows waited in front in the Servants' Hall; the creatures fell on them in a swarm, dropping from the ceiling like cockroaches, flowing over the white pavement in a black cloud.

Somehow Surkut and Otin broke through the ring, knowing the creature's touch was death. They ran out into the plaza, the dragons roaring overhead, and into the great pyramid, All was quiet. The Marishader for the moment didn't follow. They inspected the exposed parts of their body: faces, necks, hands. There was a small pucker mark on Otin's neck. They both knew what it meant. This was how Nyrax had died.

Just then they heard a sound, a scuffling from the Hall of Ghosts. They stared wildly at one another and then ran to the rope and climbed as fast as they could down into the great shaft.

Their return journey began. Otin was silent; Surkut spoke of everything and anything but the mark on his friend's neck, trying to deny to himself he had ever seen it, but unable to do so.

And as they went lower and lower, every now and then they would hear a sound and turn, thrusting their torches back in the direction they had come but seeing nothing.

So they journeyed back to Baron Illgill.

They saw the light of the Rod from a long way away and hurried towards it down the brick-lined tunnel. Water fell from the ceiling like rain and they waded through an ankle-deep river. The baron was exactly where they had left him a week before, Endil standing guard. The baron looked up when he heard their steps coming down the mile-long tunnel, his eyes milky white: he had been nearly blinded by the constant fire of the Rod.

Surkut blurted out their story: the dragons, the Hall of Life, the Marishader, the feeling that they had been followed on their long journey back. Just as he finished, Otin sank to the floor, his mouth flecked with foam. His limbs began to thrash, then he lapsed into unconsciousness.

Over the next few hours, the foam spread from his mouth and covered his whole body with a fine white floss. Underneath the body wasted away to a husk, what was left trembling as the filaments hooded the shrunken eyes and nose. Then his face disappeared under the web that then hardened into the consistency of a mask. Soon his body was covered in an impenetrable cocoon of unbreakable weave.

It was then that the baron plunged the Rod into the heart of the tangled web so whatever humanity survived beneath no longer had to suffer. And afterwards, when the cocoon burst asunder? Otin would be like Nyrax; one of them, the Marishader.

The baron placed the smoking Rod in a niche a little way down the corridor. It sizzled in the falling drops of water. There was an alcove in the tunnel next to it and they buried Otin standing up, bricking the entrance with blocks fallen from the damp-rotted ceiling. Then they stared at their handiwork. It would not hold him for long when he woke.

Only three of the Legion of Flame remained. Once there

had been twenty thousand, but that had been seven years and a thousand leagues away.

The baron leaned against the damp brick wall, his head dropping to his chest with fatigue, his face, where not obscured by burns and the dark mat of his beard, a deathly white. Now as a lover who hates the lust that drives him, but cannot have the desired object far from him, he gazed at the burning Rod. It blazed as brightly now as it had ever since it had been taken from the lead casket in Thrull all those years before, and still he looked at it, as much in wonder as that day he had first seen it gleaming in the darkness of Marizian's tomb.

Its light lit the ceiling fifty feet above them and a hundred yards up and down the mile-long tunnel.

The light of the Rod of the Shadows: the human eye could not sustain staring at it for long. It was a bar of blue-white energy that seared the retina, a doorway into another world.

Nor was human flesh meant to endure it—in the baron's case it had not: he had carried it all the way from Thrull. His face and hands were blistered black, his lips were a running sore. It had even burned through the lacquer and metal of his cuirass and scorched his chest.

His throat was so inflamed by the burns that his only sustenance these last days had been water dripped into his mouth. The food from the Hall of Life that Surkut and Otin had brought no longer tempted him. All his concentration was on the Rod of the Shadows: yet the light that gave him purpose also slowly killed him.

It was written in the *Book of Light* that the Rod would heal the dying sun, and though the baron was no prophet, or wise man, he had faith in his God, the God whose mere instrument he was, who had led him to it in Thrull, and had preserved him through the countless dangers since in order for him to bring it here, its original home.

But though he had brought it this far, he knew it was not for him to use it, but the Lightbringer—she who followed. Then the resurrected sun like a golden vision would once more steal over the shadowed fields, hills and cities, and heal the world. Golden summer would come again, lifting with her warm hands the flowers, and the trees where they had sunk in sun-starved neglect. The fields would be white again with harvest. A summer light would bathe the world, the sky a cerulean blue. But he, Illgill, would never see that future. Nor would he look upon the face of Reh, the Sun, again. For him, only the light of the Rod remained,

The baron stirred and lifted his head. He saw both his companions clearly in the Rod's magical white light. But it was at Zar Surkut he stared most fixedly, thinking of the world outside and the lands that had once worshipped the Flame. All the Empire might have been conquered by the Worm from east to west, but surely not Galastra? So far from Tiré Gand, from anywhere. Surely the legions of Tiré Gand would never cross the Astardian Sea?

This hope, that the Flame still burned somewhere despite his defeat at Thrull, had sustained him during the bitter crossing of the Palisade mountains, through the Nations of the Night and to the magical Lake of Lorn. Only ten of his legion had reached Lorn. By then he had had enough of death. He had waited there, in that timeless place where all anxieties should have been assuaged. But even in an immortal land like Lorn, the baron could find no rest. He saw visions of the future unfold in the crystal chambers beneath the palace and knew he must leave.

The baron had touched the Rod to the mallet of the Man of Bronze and they had been carried through the planes as if they flew over a golden road through the darkness of the howling void. One second Lorn, then, as if the flash of light had ripped aside a veil from their mortal sight, he had suddenly beheld a vision. Iskiard, and in the instant of that vision, the cold like iron fell upon him. The Great Plaza, covered in snow, stretched away on all sides and the thousand towers reared up under the gunmetal sky. Amidst the temples and towers, the great pyramid rose into the near darkness of the short arctic day. All around the plaza the walls of the city were broken every few yards by massive round towers made of a rosy stone that glowed in the half-light, giving the illusion of vertical waves disappearing into the distance.

That had been twelve months before. Then he had hope that they, the remnants of the legion, could fight to the depths of the underworld and use the magic of the Rod to cure the sun's dying.

Hubris: that task was not for him but for those who followed. It was in the prophecies, auguries that had been told to him a hundred times by his seeress, Alanda. But he had paid her no heed. Only now, when the end approached, did he remember.

Three of the legion left, and he one of the survivors. What chance that he in that twenty thousand host should be one of the last three left alive? Infinitesimal. Every enemy lance, sword and mace should have been aimed at him on Thrull field: he had been a marked man in his red and black armour with the Illgill crest of fire-spitting salamander. It was divinity that had spared him. Divinity or a curse? A curse that had forced him to witness the end of each and every one of his men, apart from these last two, while he still lived. In his mind's eye the trail went back, over the miles of this endless land, this tundra, marking where his men had fallen, all the way back to that faraway battlefield.

Yes, Reh had not intended *him* to be the savior of the world. The Lightbringer would come. His duty was nearly done; he had only one remaining wish: to see his son, Jayal, again.

As he rested on the tunnel wall and thought of his son, his mental turmoil eased and a strange peace came over the baron. There would be rest soon. Eternal rest. just as long as it didn't come before Jayal. His son would come, he knew it. He would finish the quest the baron had given him on Thrull field: find the sword Dragonstooth and bring it to him, wherever he was in the world.

But now there wasn't much time: they were very near their destination, the place that Marizian had reached five thousand years before. The place where he had found the

Rod of the Shadows. He looked down the tunnel in the direction in which they must go—the darkness there seemed to suck him in.

Darkness, as all their days were dark, since they had entered the underworld. It might have been night or day in the world above, but he had lost track of time: it had ceased to carry meaning many days before.

Perhaps this place had never seen light, even in Marizian's time. Iskiard, the city from which the magician had fled to the south. Now they had retraced his steps and seen the trail of destruction he had left behind: in every corridor and every chamber they had passed through there had been the shoals of mummified corpses, each skull agape stretched back in a soundless scream. Their heads all pointed towards the baron and his men, showing that the danger came from below, in the direction they were going.

Now the skeins of destiny came together in a tight knot: Surkut had told him the dragons had returned to the city. Now the light would do battle with darkness.

Surkut leaned wearily against the tunnel wall, unaware of his leader's fierce scrutiny. He was a sandy-haired man, his face covered by a blond beard: he was only slight, not like those many others who had died, men it seemed hewn of a core of oak, who had fallen to their knees, their life blood spilling out. Again the baron wondered: how had fate passed by Surkut, when stronger men had fallen so easily?

But now Illgill studied him not for his physical appearance, but that imagined gleam imprisoned in the prism of his eye, that glimpse of the sun that he, the baron, would never have again.

The other six of the legion who had reached Iskiard were scattered over the levels of the underworld beneath the pyramid, in places that would never be found: vaults guarded by creatures more fearful than even the Marishader, or fallen deep into the mile-deep chasms. There would be no birds of prey to take their bones to Reh's everlasting light, or priest to cremate their bodies.

But Otin at least would have life again. He like Nyrax

would come back to them, in the dark, his face a mass of cobwebs, reborn as one of the Marishader. That was the creature's gift.

The baron stared at the loose barrier of bricks in the tunnel wall that was Otin's grave. The legion was almost gone. He picked up a flint from the floor of the passage and leaned forward, his eyes squinting, half-blinded by the light of the Rod as he scratched the names of those who had died on the brick side wall of the corridor, its face spongy from the centuries of dripping condensation. Gorven, Nyrax, Otin, Minivere, Argon and Krastil. His hands shook and when he stepped back he saw the names on the sodden wall were no better than the graffiti he had seen scrawled in the streets of Thrull by wayward boys. But it would suffice.

He turned to the two survivors: Endil and Surkut. "Let this be a mark: if my son finds Iskiard he will know that we have gone further—further into the depths, to the mystery." The two men bowed their heads. Long before they had thought him mad, but had no option but to follow him into the lands forgotten by men. But now they were beyond thought, and criticism. They merely followed blindly.

"We must go on," the baron continued, pointing down the slope of the corridor. "If you have words for your sergeant at arms, Surkut, speak them now."

The Galastrian noble raised his head to the ceiling. "Lord, none of us will see our God again. We are but clay; only the sun will give us life once more: so let it bring life to Otin at the Second Dawn."

The baron followed the direction of Surkut's stare. Even in the dazzling glare of the Rod, the vaulted brick ceiling was barely visible. The sun still shone up there, symbol of his God. Once more a shadow passed over his soul. Was it his spirit that failed now, or his dying body? He prayed: let Jayal or death come soon.

CHAPTER EIGHT

A Traveller
Through Shades

The Doppelgänger had come very far in the long journey from the Forest of Lorn to Iskiard. But his journey couldn't be measured in yards or miles, though great gulfs of space had been traversed in it. As for the duration of his trip, that too could not be measured, for to him it seemed at the same time as long as eternity and as short as the blink of an eye, for that was the nature of the plane through which he travelled, Shades. Once he had lived in that shadow world through which he passed—lived in banishment. He remembered it well, its strange timeless quality—the maddening passage of the hours. There he had suffered while his shadow, Jayal Illgill, lived in the real world. And there the Doppelgänger had been doomed to stay until Jayal one day died and then he too would have perished and faded away into a wraith and his spirit would have floated out of that place and up through its gates into the Mortal World, and there he would have joined the millions of spirits that swarmed in front of the sun.

But his banishment had ended abruptly, not by death but by the magic of the Rod. He had been brought from Shades to earth, there to dwell in Jayal's crippled body while his brother took his.

No person or spirit willingly returned to the place of his

onetime banishment, but he had. So he travelled through that zone that is the mirror image of our world, that world where our opposites dwell, the good halves of the evil, and the evil halves of the good. Vengeance had been the goad, vengeance on his twin and the priest of Flame, Urthred.

His thoughts went back to the peak of Astragal where he had fought the priest. That had been the beginning, when he had realised that without the Rod of the Shadows he would never prevail. Twice already he had been defeated by the priest's magic, the second time when he had fallen from the cliff on which they fought, wounded by the priest's fiery dart.

He had fallen far. Then had come the impact with the ground. Unconsciousness, then pain when he woke. Pain: an enemy he had made his friend, ever since he had inherited this broken body on Thrull field. Pain: sweet communion!

He thrust himself up on his intact arm. He was under a rock overhang. The moon beamed down. Astragal was above him. So, too, his enemies, but they would have to wait. First he must get the Rod of the Shadows. He had a long way to travel.

He concentrated on his pain. Was pain like fire? No fire was constant. This pain was fugitive, hurrying from one place to another: first from his broken arm then his back, then his cheek where Urthred's fire dagger had scarred his already scarred face.

His head reeled. Blackness returned, but he shrugged it off. He jerked his head forward violently, smashing his forehead into the rock face. The blood ran into his eyes. More pain came but he laughed—he was master of it. He had killed the pain in his arm, it was taken over by this new sensation, blood running into his eyes; he tasted blood, ran his tongue over his lips, drank in its coppery gall. It was good—sweet.

He walked through the forest, towards Ravenspur, where days before he had seen the portal in the Black Tarn—the portal that led to Shades.

When he had first come this way, summer green had still

clung to the trees, a soft emerald light. But now black hail wept from the sky, and the remaining leaves were withered black. Ghostly shapes soared and circled, twining like serpents around the boles, invisible to a mortal eye, but not to his. He had lived in the shadow world. These souls were as his had been before the Rod had brought him back; insubstantial, invisible to mortal eyes.

He followed their wailing trail through the woods, until at the blasted forest edge he saw in the morning light the red mountainside of Ravenspur rising up before him. From near the summit three thousand feet above the ghosts ran down the sheer slopes like a flying wall of mist. He felt the bitter coldness of their breath close by him as they passed, spewing out malediction upon the world. A hate he recognised, hate for the world from which they had been outcast.

What was this justice of the gods? Their arbitrary sentences of mankind, the fixed time span of curses, a capricious justice that mortals could never understand, meted out by unknown rulers whose edicts consigned their victims to indescribable and near endless suffering. Such victims were these ghosts, now liberated from Shades: he watched them fly onwards, to Lorn and the immortal enemies who dwelt there. How could there be human justice, when the fathers who had made this world had none? Yet that arbitrariness he had come to love, for by it he understood there was no moral order in this world, despite what doting philosophers had said in ancient times when the Golden Age was not the forgotten dream it was today.

And so where all was chaos, only his will was paramount.

The ghosts passed, yet none troubled him; revenge on the mortals who even in this dying world lived in a better state than them was what they sought. Up, up he went, seeking that place they came from: the nexus point that led to his home—Shades.

And there it finally was, below the peak, a dark lake, bubbling with the forms that came through it from that region of the damned.

He scrambled down the slope, the ghosts so thick he was half-blinded by their hurrying bodies. He didn't pause at its shore but immediately plunged into the dead chill of the waters, saw the faces materialising below him. His way was contrary to theirs. He sank into the dark water and swam through that cursed zone and into Shades.

Now he journeyed onwards—to Iskiard.

Endil stared at a tattered map: like the food they had stolen from the Hall of Life, it had been obtained by another fight and another death, months before, when they first arrived in Iskiard. It lay in a golden shrine hidden by a golden scroll case. Krastil had been unable to resist its glitter, but when he opened it, he'd found not only the scroll but a demon that had been left there. It had taken his soul in exchange for the scroll's magic.

Endil held a quill in his trembling hand: it was not just the fever that wracked him, though they all had it, caught from the stagnant water that was all there was to drink, but fear. When he, the next man after Krastil, had first unfurled the parchment vellum, it had been mostly blank, merely showing in its left-hand corner the part of the underworld they had already explored. Endil had thought no more of it, but taken it, not knowing why, angry that a worthless object had cost Krastil his life. Only when they had already descended quite deep into the underworld and become lost in one of its many labyrinths had he taken it once more from his backpack. His intention was to write a last memorial to his wife and son in far-off Thrulland in the remote chance that someone would one day come to this inaccessible place and take pity on his bones and take the letter to his family, or his descendants, so someone would know what had happened to him.

He'd unrolled the parchment, exposing it to the light of the Rod. Before his startled eyes, lines, hitherto invisible, appeared, snaking out, taking shape, covering the page like a spiderweb, tier after tier beneath the city: nine levels in all.

Those they had already passed through, and those to come.

Now, with the aid of the map, they had found their way out of the labyrinth and reached the eighth level. They were very near Marizian's mystery.

The Doppelgänger's journey ended abruptly: one instant he was in the Mirror World, the next it was as if the world had turned upside down, inside out. His vision twisted and turned as it had seven years before when the Rod had brought him back to Thrull. Now he was born again into the Mortal World, as he had been then, ripped from Shades and carried back to earth. Some were born to the fire, some to water; some of earth, some of iron. He was born of that which was not, was the opposite of life, of essence. Non essence. Shadow.

He lay on his back in a pool immersed up to his neck in a strange liquid, grey and gluelike. It brought no cold, nor heat.

He pushed himself upright and stood. The pool was shallow; he waded forward and pulled himself over, its edge. He was at the end of a long nave, two hundred yards in length though its end was veiled in grey light. Along its walls were a thousand alcoves occupied by stationary figures. He intuited that they, too, had come from the land of shadows, had found their way through the planes, as he had. They were neither alive nor dead—they merely waited for that moment that would give their existence meaning. There they stood, imprisoned like ghosts. Not he! *He* was free.

He turned—beyond the pool in that direction was a large circular chamber. He walked towards it. His wounds, those that had caused him such pain on the walk from Lorn, had now vanished, healed by the liquid. He felt reborn. All his senses were on fire. He cocked his head, detecting distant sounds. There was a large circular shaft in the floor of the chamber. A rope snaked into the gloom. He peered down— a near bottomless depth. There, far below, like a firefly, he saw a torch. He heard tinny sounds, faint voices raised in agitation, then silence. Then the rope twitched; one of the men had begun to climb.

The baron stirred. Despite his words exhorting them on-wards, the three of them had not moved, but had remained slumped near Otin's grave, unable to continue. He had been napping, dreaming. His thoughts circled back. Endil had un-furled the map and they had been looking at it, when this mysterious weariness had sealed his eyes.

The map: it showed the way onwards, there was hope. His two companions had nodded off too, exhausted. He roused them. "Come," he croaked hoarsely. "It's not far." The other two didn't reply, but began to gather their rusted equipment, their faces gaunt in the light of the Rod. The baron stared at them dumbly for a moment—blind obedi-ence, as it had been since Thrull. Yet their spirit was nearly gone.

Despite the burns, and his weakness, despite the fact that there were only three of them left, he would go on, blaze a trail into the underworld that his son could follow. He turned and walked stiffly to where the Rod blazed in the niche. He hesitated before putting out his ravaged hand. Already he felt the bone-eating rage of its fire. Behind him there was the scrape and jingle of metal armour as Endil and Surkut pushed themselves from the floor. The three eyed each other in silence.

"Let's go," the baron said, but even as the words escaped his lips, he heard it, just on the edge of sound.

"A noise," Surkut whispered, spinning round, staring into the mile of darkness of the corridor down which they had come.

The baron listened. Nothing now. What had it been? Surkut stared at him. He remembered the Galastrian's warn-ing that he and Otin had been followed through the under-world. What had they brought?

The baron turned once more to the darkness, his eyes and ears strained. Then like a distant star that only appears the longer the observer stares into the night sky, he saw a light beyond that of the Rod; a faint shining light, perhaps the light of a torch down the tunnel. How far away it was.

Then he heard the noise, like a whistle of the wind, down the length of the tunnel. Whooaeeee! Haunting. Again, like an etiolated scream, or a cry, half human nevertheless. For a moment his blood froze: had one of his dead men come to life again? Following him, even in death? He had seen the ghosts as they passed through the Hall of Mirrors: he had looked to one side and there they were—the spirits of his legion, reflected in the thousand mirrors, suddenly made visible, marching behind him in death, as they had in life. Each and every one of his men, their pale faces staring on their commander mournfully, a column without end in the receding tunnel of reflections.

But those ghosts had made no sound, no complaint. Again the noise came, slightly closer, and now the baron recognised it as a human cry distorted by the echoing walls of the tunnel.

Was it one of the Marishader? They stole the voices of their victims, luring the next prey to them before throwing their inky net over their heads.

But neither ghosts nor the Marishader needed lights; only they, humans, needed it. He pulled his sword, stiff with rust, from the scabbard, the blade barely gave back any light from its pitted surface. Its name, etched into the dull flat of the blade, mocked at him: Wormslayer. Yes, some of the undead had died by it, their acid blood scouring its blade, but never enough, never enough.

Endil's and Surkut's swords were ready too. The star came ever closer, went from pale white to yellow. They watched it as if hypnotised, saying nothing.

Now the sound rang out through the deathly silence again. They recognised it: a halloo. The baron's ears strained for any recognisable word, but the figure was too far distant. He turned to the other two: their faces reflected his own uncertainty.

"Come on," he said gruffly. "Let us see what this thing is." He advanced, finally snatching the Rod from the niche, the sweat that had suddenly appeared on the palm of his hand sizzling as he grasped the magical surface. The others were close behind, their swords at the ready, the two lights converging. Then the halloo rang out again, and this time he distinctly heard the words that followed, and with them his heart froze, for they were words he had never expected to hear again.

"Father, it is I—Jayal!"

The baron halted abruptly, his limbs numb with shock.

A voice he had not heard for seven years. It was as if his ears betrayed him, giving him what he wanted to hear. But there it was again, Jayal's voice. His son had found him!

And so he stood, speechless, as the light of the torch came on towards them. Yet with it came a growing darkness. The light of the Rod began to die, as it never had since he had taken it from the lead casket in Marizian's tomb those eight years before.

He had been about to shout back, but his words froze on his lips. His mind had comprehended before his heart had. This was not Jayal.

Death came; not his son.

Surkut and Endil stood nervously, sensing something was amiss, looking from the baron to the light, uncertain of what to do or say.

Then the figure entered the dying arc of light cast by the Rod, a bent, stooped figure, not the proud erect young man that Jayal once had been. This being's face was half turned from the failing light of the Rod.

Yes, it was him, the Doppelgänger. The thing that should have been burned, destroyed on Thrull field: why had Manichee disobeyed him? The ghost of the thing that Manichee had cast out all those years before. The sword in the figure's hand was but a mortal weapon; rusted, pitted steel, not the great blade of legend that was Dragonstooth.

But magic or not, its edge looked sharp, and he had only the dead edge of Wormslayer. The light of the Rod guttered. Now the figure threw his face into the expiring light.

"Father," he whispered. "How I have sought you, the

height and breadth of this land. Always you eluded me, but now I have found you."

"Whatever you are, don't call me father, you abomination."

"Ah, hard words," the creature simpered, "it was always thus in Thrull. Always you preferred the other voice, the voice of the milksop, the one you saved. Not me! Cast into Shades. But how you would rejoice in my works, Father. Death has followed me, just as he has followed you, and exulted in my acts. We are one and the same."

The baron shook his head. "Then let death decide which of us he champions now!" He lunged forward, cutting at the Doppelgänger's head with the sword. The creature swung his own weapon up and there came a spark as the two clashed. He stepped nimbly to one side, and stabbed forward. The baron barely reacted in time, the point passing through his tattered cloak.

"Clumsy!" the Doppelgänger needled him. "You'll have to be quicker than that."

Now Endil and Surkut moved forward. The Doppelgänger stepped away, drawing the baron after him, throwing the lantern down so it landed between them and the advancing men. It shattered on the ground, oil spilling out and creating a barrier of fire. Endil and Surkut cursed at the flames that now separated them from the baron, trying to find a way round them, but the baron half turned, his face russet in the glow. "Stay back, this is between the two of us."

The Doppelgänger laughed, high-pitched, maniacal. "Chivalry, Father! Never without it. Come on then. I will kill your puppies after you."

"If things of darkness have such, say your prayers now," Illgill snarled, slashing again. Again a parry, but the sword merely deflected a whisker past the Doppelgänger's face.

"Careful," he said, "lest you kill your son."

"I've told you I am not your father, and you are no son of mine," the baron cried, thrusting again.

Once more the Doppelgänger retreated nimbly, further into the darkness away from the pool of burning oil. The light of the Rod, still clutched in the baron's left hand, was now completely extinguished; he was gradually being sucked into the gloom away from the light of the burning oil.

"Disown me then," the Doppelgänger answered, dropping his guard, so the sword hung by his side and his chest was left exposed, the baron's sword point but three feet from it. He was suddenly very still. "Disown me and kill me." The baron's blade came back for a thrust. "Kill me and kill your son as well."

"What?" the baron exclaimed.

"Aye, you heard aright. You wonder how a stinking corpse thrust onto the carrion heaps of Thrull could live." He tilted his head back, his Adam's apple bobbing with near silent laughter, his single eye mocking Illgill. "Why? Because the one of us needs the other to live on this plane—that is what your magic unleashed. Kill me now, Baron, and kill Jayal, wherever he is. He will drop like a slaughtered heifer."

The baron's sword wavered. He saw it now. This was the curse that Manichee had warned him of. Now the decision was his. Let this abortion live or kill him and by doing so kill Jayal? Then the solution came to him. The Rod! It had separated the two. Wouldn't it banish this creature back to its plane? His eyes fell on it. But it was but dead metal in his hand, cold, suddenly drained of that magic that had blazed over the years. Was it the Doppelgänger's presence that robbed it of its power?

He never knew. For on the instant of that thought, the Doppelgänger sprang forward. His sword point smashed into the rotted area of leather linking the chain mail at Illgill's neck. The baron did not see the wound, only the geyser of blood that suddenly sprayed up in front of his face.

His mouth opened in a scream.

CHAPTER NINE

The Scream

The scream woke Urthred: he had been dreaming, and in his sleeping mind the scream sounded like the long drawn-out howl of the Fenris Wolf in the Forest of Lorn: the howl of the winter wind, growing from a whisper, to a murmur, then suddenly unloosening in full force.

His eyes snapped open, and he thrust himself upright, disoriented. He was on his sleeping mat, lying out in the open. A full moon shone down from the night sky. A black and white checquerboard of trees and snow-filled clearing was in front. His mask had come off. He snatched it up, covering his face, his heart beating wildly. Why had he taken it off? For a moment he couldn't even remember where he was. Then memory returned: Fenris had been destroyed. Lorn too. They were at the northern fringes of the forest; Garadas and his men had brought them here on sleds dragged by dog teams.

It was the howling of the sled dogs that had penetrated his sleep. Their baying echoed around the moonlit clearing, interspersed with frantic barking and the rattling of the chains with which they had been tied to the trees.

The din would have woken the very dead themselves, but it was something else that had drawn him from sleep, another, human noise. Before the baying of the dogs had even begun.

He hauled his long body to his feet, the sleeping rugs falling away, his naked chest suddenly cold. Had the noise come from inside the camp, or from outside the perimeter? He peered into the darkness. The moonlight glinted off the virgin snow that blanketed the ground, lit up the circular clearing in the pinewood, each tree perfectly etched by its silver light. The moon was waning. It was nearly dawn.

He turned to the north, to the Man of Bronze. He was at the post that he had taken at nightfall the evening before. It looked as if a statue stood upon a small rocky outcropping some fifty yards away. It was thirty feet tall, solid metal, glowing silver in the moonlight, its limbs hidden by massive greaves and vambraces. Its head swivelled slowly towards him and suddenly its eyes opened and red beams of light shone from them and he was basked in ruby light. It penetrated even his mask, half blinding him.

Urthred ducked his head: another shock, for there was a figure sitting upright on his sleeping rug. Thalassa: her fan of hair shone like copper in the ruby glow. He realised why the Man of Bronze's gaze had come in this direction—he stared not at him, but at Thalassa.

Now he remembered the previous evening. When the fires had burned down, she had come to him.

The night had been bitter cold; he had heard the footsteps, lightly crunching down on the snow, felt someone kneel, then slip under his blankets. He had barely had the courage to breathe or stir as he felt her body nestle next to him, the warmth of her so close.

Perhaps she would have slipped away before dawn, as she had on so many previous nights. He had understood why she did so. She was no longer the person she had been in Thrull. To the villagers, she was the Lightbringer, a semidivine being, above the pulls of the flesh and desire. But now all the villagers and Jayal, too, would see. And his vows of celibacy, too, would be seen as a sham.

Urthred looked around him defiantly. The villagers had

thrown off their sleeping rugs and stood, weapons raised, staring at him and Thalassa, their looks registering shock and surprise.

But in all the commotion there was one figure who was absolutely motionless. Jayal Illgill. He too stood, but unlike the others, his whole body was rigid, his face pale, staring ahead as if at something unfolding a long way in front. The sword Dragonstooth was in his hand, glowing with white fire. Even at a distance of several yards, Urthred could see how the young knight's hand trembled.

Now Urthred was certain: the first noise that had woken him had come from the young knight.

Ignoring the gaze of the villagers, Urthred pulled his cloak closer around his lanky body and strode across the clearing to Jayal's side. Thalassa rose and followed him.

Jayal's face was like a mask, only his bloodless lips twitched slightly. His look was blank, the whites of his eyes showing: there was now a touch of grey in the sky and his head was turned towards the dim outline of the hills they had seen beyond the forest's edge the evening before. His body shook convulsively. Urthred saw he was having another of the fits he had suffered ever since they had come into Lorn. Another moment when the Doppelgänger possessed his mind. Each time he had been reduced to a state of near cata-tonia, as he was now.

Urthred was unsure whether he should touch him, try to spring him out of his reverie. But it was Jayal who moved first, snapping awake, suddenly registering that the priest was standing next to him. He turned, one hand clasped to his brow, the other with the sword outstretched towards the far horizon.

"My father," he whispered through pale lips.

Urthred followed the direction in which he pointed. Nothing was visible, save the stark leafless trees, the snow and the hills beyond. "What of him? What do you see?"

"I saw him."

"It was nothing but a dream," Urthred answered, stretch-

ing out a gauntleted hand to comfort him, but Jayal shrugged
him off.

"I saw him as clearly as I see you," he insisted. "He was
in Iskiard, deep in an underworld. I was approaching him,
down a tunnel. I saw the light of the Rod, then all was darkness."

"A dream, nothing more," Urthred repeated.

Now Jayal turned and faced him. "I don't dream anymore, priest. Dreams are for those who are still part of this
world. But I live neither in this world nor the next, but with
my twin in that nether land that lies between. I see the
Shadow World when I sleep and when I wake."

He paused, his haunted eyes boring into Urthred's mask.
"You are a priest, a man of God. You have conjured dragons
of the air and walls of fire. But have you known magic like
this? Magic that steals a man's dreams and gives him another's? What is a man if his very dreams are not free?
Tonight the Doppelgänger came to me while I slept. He
showed me a vision of my father. Seven years since I last
saw him on the battlefield and then, suddenly, he was there.
He held the Rod of the Shadows, but as I watched its light
died and all was dark again."

"What does it mean?" whispered Urthred.

A grim smile puckered Jayal's mouth. "Don't you see?
He wants to make sure I hurry, go on as fast as I can to
Iskiard. He wanted me to see my father is in danger, needs
my help." He shook his head. "But however fast I go, one
thing is certain: my father is dead; I know it. The Doppelgänger has the Rod: now he controls our destinies."

Urthred turned to Thalassa, hoping she would have
words of comfort for the young Illgill, for he had none. But
she, too, was silent, her eyes downcast.

Jayal saw their silent exchange, and his lips twisted in a
sneer that might have belonged to his evil twin. "Now I see.
You are together: there is nothing you can do for me. Live,
enjoy your dreams." With that he began stumbling through
the thick snow towards the snow plains and the black line of

hills. Then suddenly he caught up short, clutching his head between his hands.

"Forgive me, friends," he said, still staring at the barely visible line of hills. "I strive for the best, but like a cancer, *his* voice enters my mind, comes through my lips. Once I was a man. I had appetites, hope. But they are gone, destroyed by the whisperings of the voice. Others have life: have love and lust, drink wine with pleasure, enjoy the laughter of friends. But those others were not born with the voice.".

He whirled on his heels in the snow, sending a geyser of powder into the air. "Don't think I have always been Jayal Illgill." He thumped his chest with his gauntleted hand. "Once this being contained our two spirits: the good and the evil. A dark voice whispered to me in my youth and drove me to dark impulses—so when the black moods fell on me I would not sing but would snarl; would not stroke but rip apart; would not drink but would spit. Everything that was opposite, that was I in those mad fits. I became only him, the Doppelgänger, and the small good that was in me was lost. Only when Manichee drove that voice away, into Shades, did I live again. But evil, once created, can't be merely sent away. The Doppelgänger will live while there is breath in this borrowed body, for substance cannot live without its shadow, and shadow without its substance. Evil owns you until you die."

Urthred could listen no more, but stepped up to him and laid a hand on his shoulder once more. "Come, my friend. Iskiard is near—and with it your cure. We'll find the Rod and banish this spectre back to Shades, and you'll live once more in peace, as you once did in Thrull before the wars."

Once more that ghostly smile played on Jayal's lips. "You don't listen priest. The Doppelgänger has the Rod, for I didn't tell you the end of my dream." A chill played up Urthred's spine. Jayal continued, "I saw it as if I was my twin, as the light of the Rod died. There were three men: one was my father, another a Hearth Knight." He paused, searching his memory. "Endil—that was his name. The other I didn't know; another soldier, a foreigner. I went towards them. I heard my voice calling for my father. He peered forward staring at my face. Oh, what faith and hope I saw there as he approached, and how I saw his suffering, his burned face and his hands too"—Jayal's voice broke with emotion—"he held them up as if he was going to touch me, comfort me as he never comforted me in life. But suddenly his face changed from joy to fear: he saw what came, not his son, but the abomination that Manichee brought back to the world. The life went from his face as if he knew it was death that came to him. Then . . ."

He halted, his face twitching. "*Then* all went dark, priest. My father is dead, his companions too. The Doppelgänger has taken the Rod." A half-strangled laugh suddenly exploded from his lips and for a moment it seemed to those ranged around the Doppelgänger's mad chuckle. He wiped some spittle from his lips, pulled back in a savage grin. Then he calmed slightly though his whole body trembled. "He has the advantage; he waits for us there, over those hills, in Iskiard. He knows we're coming, for these traitor's eyes," he cried, frantic once more, clawing at his lids with his nails, "show him where we are and what we do each day.

"He is strong, stronger than I, though these limbs are cast from the exact mold, each of his muscles fashioned as mine, except where he carries my wounds. And even though he is crippled, his body twisted, his sight impaired, yet he is stronger. Why? He is a thing of pure will: his one desire is for revenge. And I? What do I want? Honor is dead, love too. My father is gone, and I will never see the light of the sun restored. I am carried hither and thither by fate, like a cork upon the sea."

"Iskiard is not far," Urthred said. "Your father may still live: have faith."

Jayal shook his head. "Promise me something: when I am dead, take the Rod and bury it as deep as it was buried before my father dug it up; so deep that no one will ever find it, as long as the earth still lives."

"I will do that, I swear, for I know the misery it has brought the world, the curse that fell on my master,

Manichee, for using it," Urthred answered. "But let's think of more hopeful things." He pointed to the east. "See, it's nearly dawn." Slowly, the sky was lightening even more.

Thalassa looked up at the black velvet of the sky overhead where the stars still shone. One particularly glowed brightly in the southeast quadrant of the sky; there it was still dark, the star shining despite the brilliance of the setting moon, which sank low over the trees, and the rosy coming of the sun that now stippled the eastern horizon.

There was a strange serenity in her stare; her face glowed in the fading moonlight, and once more Urthred felt a strange dislocation. She was the one the prophecies called the Lightbringer. Yet she was flesh and blood and a woman too.

The scream had woken him so abruptly that the night before had been all but forgotten. But now the details came back. After she had come to his sleeping blanket, he had dared not move, or speak, but presently he heard her voice, a light breath close to his ear whispering his name, and the tickle of her falling curtain of hair on the exposed nape of his neck. He had felt the warmth of her body pressing at his back, and he had turned slowly and looked at her, her face pale in the starlight, the camp utterly still beyond.

"I'm cold," she whispered, and he could see that though she wore her white cloak, her shoulders were shaking. He had taken off his glove harnesses. Wordlessly he held up one of his mutilated hands, opening the sleeping blanket further with the other. She slipped in beside him, and he dropped the blanket over her back. She balled herself at his chest. He felt their twin heat join under the blanket, his heart beating faster and faster. Still he couldn't speak. Presently she raised her head. "Take off your mask," she whispered. She must have sensed his reluctance. "I want to see your face under the stars," she added.

He hesitated, frozen. "What do you mean?" he asked, but she pressed a finger lightly to his lips, silencing and sensual at the same time. As if mesmerized, he slowly reached up to the latches of the mask where they were attached to its leather frame, wondering if this wasn't a dream, and did as she asked, hesitating a moment before abruptly pulling it to one side.

He clenched shut his lidless eyes, as if by closing them, it would block out her sight of him. But now he felt one of her hands exploring the cruel ridges of scar tissue on his face, where his ears once had been, the hair that had begun to regrow there.

"You're healing," she said. Still he didn't reply, but he knew she spoke the truth. He had witnessed it for himself. He opened his eyes and saw that her lips were very close to his, the gentle susurration of her breath, playing on his own mouth as if breathing a healing balm upon him. The scent of her breath . . . what was it like? Like the perfume of a half-open desert flower. His mind flashed back to the Temple of Sutis, that first moment of temptation. How he had punished himself for falling to a whore's guile. How he had fought her allure, her beauty. For beauty was nothing but the beginning of the terror of what was to follow, a terror that he was just able to bear. Terror, terror of that which he could not control: something alien, yet necessary and desirable, a jewel that might be had, but only after giving up one's soul. But perhaps his soul had been forfeit even then. She had sucked it from him, like a succubus that takes the last breath of its amour, as its tongue forces apart his lips and plunges deeper and deeper to the beating rose of the heart.

As he lay upon the sleeping mat one half of him knew he must step back from the abyss. He was about to fall, deep into the darkness of that mouth, those lips so near . . . yet, before he knew it, he had leaned the inch to her lips and pressed his, those horrors of shredded flesh, gently to hers. He felt her arch forward in response. It was as if half of him witnessed the kiss from far away, detached from his parody of a body, wondering how she could kiss him, yet the other half of his consciousness was in his body, in the here and now, and he pushed forward himself, and found that his hands were on her back, on her breasts, on her thighs, and she was naked beneath her cloak, the flesh so smooth. Satin he had heard men call it, a woman's flesh, but it was no satin, for it was flesh, flesh that needed, unlike mere cloth, a heart that beat, blood that flowed to animate it.

She was pulling him, whispering something to him. A distant part of him asked: had she whispered these words to those others, the hundreds in the temple she had lain with? But the part of him that was in the here and now didn't register this other doubting voice, as if by entering her he would enter the earth and conjoin with the principle of life itself, and that was all that mattered. He rolled towards her, the fire beginning to mount, burning from his heart into his groin, and then he felt her opening to him and he was lost again, as he had been so many times before, in that darkness, forgetting in a moment of self-annihilation all the denials of his beliefs.

All this seemed but a dream to him now as he watched her in the growing light of dawn. Now she turned to him, and the expressionless goddess was suddenly gone as she smiled slightly, and in the growing dawn light he saw the sparkle in her eyes as if her mouth and lips were lit by a secret fire that only he could see. Then he knew it hadn't been a dream.

He had looked at her too long. Jayal was still there: there was a fleeting tightening of his features—was it pain, for that future he had spoken of, that Urthred and Thalassa could look forward to, but he could not? For now the Doppelgänger's voice would always blast his new-formed desires so they withered in the bud. Did he remember this secret look of Thalassa's, when it was intended only for him, long ago in Thrull? That secret look not so secret to him who had once loved her too?

Garadas and his men had stood at a distance all this time, looking on anxiously at the exchange that had taken place between Urthred and Jayal. But now Thalassa gestured to the headman, indicating that all was well.

Garadas barked a series of orders. The discipline of the last few months reasserted itself. Forty villagers had come with them through Lorn. Each knew what he must do. Instantly the men hurried off to their tasks, rekindling the burned-down fires and filling their cooking pots with the snow that lay in thick drifts in the clearings between the trees. Others went to feed the stout mountain dogs that had drawn their sledges through the forest from the Broken Hines. The animals' yelps reached a climax, their lolling pink tongues almost obscene against the thick white bristles of their fur.

Thalassa nodded at where the towering figure of the Man of Bronze stood on his lonely knoll. "Come, we have a few moments," she said, "let us speak to the Man of Bronze; see if he knows anything more of this dream of yours."

She wrapped her cloak tighter around her and strode through the snowdrifts, Urthred and Jayal trailing behind. The sun was rising slowly over the edge of the forest in front of them. Its beams ran over the snow plain, twenty miles across, to the sinister line of black hills they had seen the evening before. Now they were clearly etched in the growing light; they looked for anything like the half-buried heads of giants glaring over the plains towards them.

Though the sun now imparted faint warmth to their frozen limbs, each remembered their awakening: Urthred and Thalassa from dreams of love, Jayal from a dream of death.

CHAPTER TEN

The Duirin Hills

wo great armies, forty thousand strong, had met on
Thrull field. On one side Illgill, on the other the legions of the Undead Lord, Faran Gaton Nekron. As
the baron's army was destroyed, so, too, the legions of the
Worm that had won the day. Thrull was now lost, Faran
Gaton fled. Three alone of his mighty legions were left. The
three travelled under the ground, along an ancient subter-
ranean tunnel to the north. They too journeyed towards
Iskiard.

Faran Gaton Nekron raised his gauntleted hand, sig-
nalling a halt to the three who followed behind, the sole survivors of the horde he had brought from Tiré Gand to
subjugate the lands of the Flame. Two of the crack legion,
the Reapers of Sorrow, and his sorcerer, Golon.

He stopped not because he was weary, for weariness was
nothing to him and he had not slept in two hundred years.
He called a halt because it was important that the three who
followed kept their strength, that they were alive when he
needed them, and their blood.

That moment would be soon, for another full moon was
coming, and he must drink before that night or sink into the
second sleep from which there was no return.

Though it was dark, the perfectly round tunnel stretched

as far as his darkness-sharpened eyes could see. North, always north. Away from Lorn, away from the lord of Ravenspur.

A green algae-thickened sludge covered the floor of the tunnel. His boots were now rotted away, the remnants bound together with strips of cloth. Dampness was eating his feet, the flesh was sloughing away, but he felt no pain: the nerve endings had died two hundred years ago when he first became one of the living dead.

He stared down the tunnel as the others got their breath. The shaft was called Iken's Dike. An ancient highway of the gods. It began three hundred leagues to the south on the northern face of the Palisades in Harken's Lair, where Reh's dragons had once been stabled. Then it ran over the Plain of Ghosts, under Ravenspur, coming to the surface again on the Plain of Wolves, before dipping underground in the Forest of Lorn. This was where they had begun their journey, nearly a year before. Since then they had marched relentlessly onwards under the endless and unseen Forest of Lorn above. North were the Duirin Hills and, if legend was correct, Iskiard, the city where Marizian had come from and where the secrets of the prophecies would finally be resolved in favor of either Iss or Reh.

The tunnel had once been buried deep under the greenwood, but over the centuries erosion and the forest had worked their depredations on its structure. The roots of giant trees had broken through the roof, causing cave-ins of fallen bricks, the pale roots like dismembered arms disappearing into the darkness. Water dripped through the ruptured ceiling. During the day, stabs of light cut into the darkness of the tunnel. Light, his enemy, that would reduce him to a mist. In those places they waited for the night to come before moving on.

He had lived off the blood of the followers he had rounded up after the killing of Smiler and their flight from the Master of Ravenspur. He had found thirteen in the tunnels under Lorn. Eleven had died these last months.

His followers had had more meagre fare. The water in the

tunnel's puddles had slaked their thirst though it was sour and brackish from the ancient metals that had leached into it. And there on the damp walls of the tunnel, when Golon judged it to he evening and the sun was setting on the world outside, he muttered words from one of the God's black codicils, conjuring grey growths, mushrooms from the moldy cracks of the brickwork, mushrooms whose odor filled the tunnel with the stink of decay, but upon which he and the surviving Reapers fell hungrily, cramming the pulpy greywhite flesh into their mouths. Many were ill afterwards, wracked by stomach cramps. But Faran would not let them rest and drove them on, through the endless night of the tunnel.

He sighed. This question of blood. He breathed shallowly, trying not to take in the scent of the three men who followed: he needed to control his appetite—blood was scarce, would become more so the further from the habitations of man he went. Blood lust would drive him mad. Had he not traveled for nearly a year, and had not the drought got worse and worse, day by day?

Yes—to one such as he, one of the undead, the world in these last days before Iss' midnight was like a desert spreading wide and nearly bloodless. Even in Thrull there had not been enough blood slaves for all the Dead in Life and he himself had survived for seven years off blood-engorged leeches.

Now there were no more leeches—merely three men, three moons; then the second death, if no more blood could be found.

And if there had been no blood in Thrull where the living had long ceased to outnumber the dead, what here in this endless tunnel under these northern wastes where there was barely a living soul?

So, to drink the last precious supplies now, or wait a little while, in the hope that they would find their enemies soon? This night or perhaps the next it would be the full moon. If he was to have blood, he would need to kill one of those who followed him.

The faces of the Reapers were hidden by the skull masks of the legion on their faces. Though they were elite soldiers, they would be the first. They turned and bowed reverentially to him when they saw him staring at them: fanatics who would willingly give their life to him.

Whether to drain a man dry or just take sufficient? The first meant that he would be satisfied for a clear month after, but it also meant that the supply was gone forever, the man dead, a bloodless husk. Yet if he spared the drinking, only took enough to satisfy the craving, then the bitten man would become his subject, one of the Dead in Life. And then the subject too would need blood before the next full moon and Faran would be in a worse position than he had been in before: another demand on his limited resources, another desperate thirst to assuage, then the end of his quest. And they were so far from any blood. Yes, the metaphor was apt: as travellers in the widest desert without water.

The fourth surviving member of his party was Golon: sorcerer, summoner and demonologist. He would be the last of the three: his arts were too valuable to lose now.

Faran signalled that he was ready to move off again. Golon produced a small purple bead on a leather thong and held it out in front of him. It swayed slightly in the sorcerer's rock-steady hand and then, as if pushed by an invisible finger, swung to the south, in the direction they had come and held there in midswing. So it had been every day, ever since the Nations of the Night: each time the bead had swung in the direction of the most powerful magic near them, the sword carried by Jayal Illgill, Dragonstooth. But today something different happened. The bead held for a brief second at its apogee, and then swung dramatically in the opposite direction, to the north.

"What is happening?" Faran asked.

Golon looked up. "There's strong magic in front as well as behind."

"What is as strong as Dragonstooth? Are we near Iskiard and the Rod of the Shadows?"

Golon shook his head. "No, both are still a distance away.

This must be something else, perhaps another place where the gods left their magic."

"Let's go on," Faran commanded, his interest piqued. They passed another spot where the ceiling had caved in: the moon beamed down from above. He could see the dark boughs of the forest trees and beyond, the shining disc, newly risen. Erewon, Reh's brother. He saw tonight it would be full. He must drink now.

He snapped his fingers, not looking behind. How it was that one of the two Reapers decided it would be him who gave himself to his lord, he never knew. Perhaps they had already drawn lots for the privilege. One of the men passed him now, heading further into the gloom.

Faran followed him until they were a hundred yards from the other two. The soldier stopped and withdrew his mask. Faran's eyes locked with his. A young man, jet-black hair and curious blue eyes, like lapis lazuli. At first he thought that the Reaper might resist his mesmerism, but then those stonelike eyes became opaque and watery and Faran knew he had him under his spell, that he had become nothing more than part of his will.

Faran's lips pulled back from his teeth, and before be even knew it himself, he was at the man's neck . . .

He drained him: strong soldier's blood, tasting of sweat and iron. Faran held him, feeling each last flutter of the waning heart, feeling the strength in his own veins as the soldier's ebbed. The Reaper sunk to the floor after he'd finished, his eyelids fluttering, his face stark white. Then he was dead.

Now Faran was sated, he was like one who having murdered in a blood rage returns to the stark light of day and fancies every person's eyes are upon him, guessing his guilt. He wiped his face with his gauntlet: the leather was stained dark by the Reaper's gore. Some strange nicety made him drag the corpse into a side tunnel where it was hidden, then he called the other two. As they passed him, he saw that Golon averted his eyes.

The three travelled on, a day or two. Then Golon pro-

duced the small bead again. He dangled it in the air: once
more it pulled first in one direction and then the other, but
this time the bead did not stick on its apogee, but only
halfway through its swing.

Faran looked at him questioningly.

"Two things," Golon said. "First Dragonstooth is nearer:
Thalassa and the priest and the young Illgill are catching us:
they'll overtake us soon. But secondly, this other magic is
closer too."

"Can you tell what generates it?"

"Only one of the ancient artifacts or a demon could affect
the gem."

Just then the surviving legionary, who had scouted forward, called to them and they hurried to join him. He stood
at the entrance of a chute that fed into the side of the tunnel.
He stood on the great mound of rubble that had accumulated
at its entrance. He held his torch up and its light flared along
the shaft showing it extended a long way back.

Once more Golon held up the gem. This time the gem
jerked fiercely in his hand, almost tugging him up the shaft.

"Let's go," Faran ordered and they began to climb up the
rubble-strewn passage, leaving Iken's Dike behind them.

They climbed for a quarter of a mile. Then a space
opened up in front of them and to either side. Faran peered
around him and saw a vast chamber; in front it ended in a
cliff face scarred by rough-hewn terraces: ancient workings,
the naked rock stained orange from the minerals that had
once been mined here. The floor in between was choked
with great tangles of rusted metal, fallen from the heights in
some long-distant disaster. They picked their way through
the maze of jagged wreckage, until they emerged on the
other side, at the floor of the cliff. The terraces of the mines
reached high into the darkness so even Faran's eyes failed to
reach their heights.

He gestured for Golon to bring light and the sorcerer conjured the ball of blue flame that weeks before had lit the underworld beneath the Palisades. In its luminance they saw
beyond the darkness even more galleries rising upwards, a

thousand feet or more: it was as if they stood at the bottom of a hollowed-out mountain.

"What place is this?" Faran asked the sorcerer.

"Sire, my knowledge of the northern lands is small, but in Tiré Gand I read of a place where in ancient times the gods set their human slaves to work in the bowels of the earth. This seems to be that place."

"Does it have a name?"

"Aye, the Black Mines, under the Duirin Hills."

Faran peered up through the darkness: far away to the north, more than a thousand feet up and a mile away, at the limits of even his vision, he saw another tunnel mouth at the end of a level set high into the rock face.

"Show me where Iskiard lies," he commanded Golon. Once more the sorcerer brought out the small purple gem from the fob on his belt, and held it up. It twitched hither and thither on its leather thong, stirred by the invisible currents of magic, attracted to the strong source nearby and also now to a more distant one, the magic of the lost city of Iskiard. The sorcerer clenched shut his eyes, communing with the now-minute movements of the gemstone.

"Dragonstooth and the Man of Bronze lie behind us, but the Rod of the Shadows and Iskiard lie over there." He pointed to their right, where a large rock fall had buried one side of the cavern in a jumble of scree.

"How far is Iskiard?" Faran asked.

"The current is not strong. It is still several days' march." Golon opened his eyes and peered at the cave-in. "But the way is blocked. We must find another route to the surface."

Faran looked up at the great vault of the workings and the distant opening so far away. Somewhere up there lay daylight and all the hazards that it brought to one such as he. The blocked tunnel meant that that was the only option open to them. "We'll go up," he said, motioning for the surviving Reaper to lead the way.

They began to climb slowly up the zigzag levels of the workings, the blue ball of unearthly fire showing them the way. A hundred, then two hundred feet and then a thousand fell away, until they had reached the highest of the terraces and the tunnel mouth they had come from appeared no bigger than a dark spot in the eternal gloom far below. They stood on the topmost terrace, a rubble-covered wide ledge. Ahead a square entranceway had been carved into the rock cliff of the mountain. At a gesture from Faran, Golon sent the blue light floating down its length, revealing a winding corridor beyond. He motioned the Reaper to lead off once more. Faran followed.

He saw the walls of the corridor had been worked smooth many years before like the tunnels under Thrull. At first, there were small alcoves filled with fragments of yellow bones. He stooped and inspected them, the remains of human skeletons.

He needed more men. Iskiard lay ahead with all its dangers. Three men, even as powerful as they, would stand little chance. Had not even Marizian fled its terrors? But he had magic still, magic to raise an army. The instrument that had healed Iss himself after Shandering Plain. Magic enough to raise a mere mortal from the first sleep of death: the Black Chalice. But even its magic had limitations: these pulverized fragments were beyond reanimation.

Ahead, wide rock-cut steps led upwards. They climbed them to another level overlooking the great chamber. They were now very near its ceiling, a dizzying chasm below them falling in a vertical cliff. On the ledge a gallery ran to left and right. The one to the left ending in a metal gantry that hung over the empty drop; more than a thousand feet of darkness lay below it.

To the right another opening disappeared into the rock face. The only way on. There was a new quality to the air. Not thick and metallic as it had been lower down, but fresher with the slightest of breezes. They were nearer the surface. Once more Faran gestured for the Reaper to proceed. He entered the dark corridor, the blue light of the magical orb casting his long shadow in front of him. Another breath of air sent a layer of sand skidding past their feet, so fine it was like liquid.

The passage ascended in a slight gradient, then dog-legged to the left, the way to the right ending abruptly in an opening overlooking the cliff and the abyss. Here the Reaper halted abruptly and gestured for Faran and Golon to come up.

He stood in front of a plaster and lathe plug blocking a side passage to the right of the dog leg. A rune had been cut into the exact center of the barrier.

Golon stepped forward and peered at it in the magical light. He reached out a shaking hand and brushed away the thick layer of dust that had collected in the hollow of the carving, then withdrew it as if he had touched a snake.

"What is it?" Faran asked.

"It's the sigil of a demon." There was a faint uplift of excitement in Golon's voice. "This is the magic that the bead detected."

"Which demon?" Faran asked.

But Golon didn't answer him straightaway. He had closed his eyes, his brows furrowed, corrugating his forehead. He was silent for a few moments, then he took in a great draft of air, and apparently satisfied with his memory, he turned, a bright glitter in his eye. "Hdar, the demon of plague—he is here, alive."

The Reaper stepped back in alarm at his words, his eyes roving to left and right down the length of the corridor.

Golon laughed at the man's fear. "For the moment he is imprisoned beyond this seal." He turned to Faran. "Do you remember, lord? Hdar—the same I conjured outside the gates of Nush by the banks of the Dry River."

The scene came into Faran's mind. The march from Tiré Gand seven years before. The city that stood on their route that refused to surrender. The inhabitants' bravado had cost them dearly. That day Faran had withdrawn his army behind a line of low hills, safe from what Golon summoned. Golon had been left alone upon the pebble banks of the river beneath the city. Perhaps the people of Nush wondered what this solitary person did, sitting cross-legged upon the strand, his palms open upon his knees, looking heavenwards. But some superstitious fear must have seized them, for not one of them sallied out.

All night he labored, and not one of Faran's army alive or dead dared breast the rise and look down upon the sorcerer and the doomed city. On the horizon of the hills they saw purple lights flashing in the sky. Then at the first glimmering of dawn Golon had returned, tired and exhausted.

From his curtained catafalque Faran had given the order and the bone cow horns had sounded. The siege engines had groaned forward to the line of hills and the army's drums began beating a solemn tattoo.

But there were none to hear the drums or the bone horns in Nush. The battlements were manned only by the unmoving dead. Faran's siege ladders were thrown up, the legions scaling the walls unopposed. They found only a handful of the populace still alive, and they expired soon after. The city was left dead and empty as the legions marched on ever westwards.

Faran nodded heavily at the memory. "The people of that city did not live to see the dawn. But what does the sign mean here, where no man has lived in ten thousand years?"

Golon's bald, gnomic brow furrowed. "The gods came from the stars where the demons live. Once they were the gods' slaves. And the gods put them to work upon this world of ours, with all their attendant benefits and curses. Hdar too. What more mighty foe, he who with one exhalation can slay an army a hundred thousand strong? Yet once released a demon cannot be penned and so Hdar roamed the world slaying all he could find until he came to this place: his victims and he lie behind this door."

"He still lives? Surely each conjury has some finite term? How could he have lived so long?"

Golon shook his head. "Sometimes the summoning lives in the bodies of those he has slain. He lives on in the spores of the disease, as thistledown in their lungs waiting for the next breath, so the demon waits for the next breath to waft him about the world, killing all who breathe it in."

Faran pondered for a moment: if Golon was right, then

the bodies of those incarcerated here might be preserved, sealed from the air, lest they infect other mortals. Perhaps they still possessed enough articulation to have a use for him, just as those buried in the catacombs in Thrull had had their uses when he had first arrived at that city. A plan was developing in his mind.

He reached inside his cloak and brought out the Black Chalice, and studied its depths. So small it barely filled his hand, yet it was as if he stared into a lightless area greater than even the mine working that they had just now passed through. How could an infinity be encompassed in something so small?

Yet from this would come his last legion, the last before Iss came from the stars and took command of his armies. He would raise enough troops to defeat the last supporters of the light.

He turned to the Reaper. "Cover the mouthpiece of your mask, then break down the door," he ordered. The man made no reply: his expression was concealed by his skull mask, but he had heard every word they had said, had taken an involuntary step back from the doorway after Golon's first words. He might have been the last of Faran's army, but he approached his doom as the other twenty thousand had, without complaint. He pulled a piece of cloth from his cloak and tied it over the nose and mouth opening of his skull mask, then hefted his bronze mace, turning one of its cruel flanges so that it would strike the portal at the right angle.

"Lord—" Golon began as if to protest, but Faran stilled him with an abrupt gesture.

"Cover yourself, if you would live."

"A cloth is not enough, Hdar is strong . . ."

"Silence!" Faran roared, rounding on him even as his command echoed away over the vast abyss behind them. "Do I care for those who live? Whose souls are theirs and not Lord Iss'? You are nothing, will turn to nothing at the Last Day! Now get back."

Golon hastily shuffled away from the opening, lifting the hem of his cloak so it covered the lower part of his face.

Faran nodded at the Reaper and the soldier swung the mace; it bit into the plaster face of the opening, gouging out six inches. He swung again and again, at each stroke Golon stared in fascination—Faran had ordered no warding, no magical bonds to be prepared for the demon—they would all die. He flinched away even more, expecting the pale blue features of the death's-head demon to suddenly appear in the hole and like vapor be inhaled into the soldier's mask. Another blow: more plaster fell until a dull gleam of metal could be seen in the hole.

Faran motioned him to stop and leaned forward, pulling away some of the plaster, enlarging the hole. No demon had appeared, and Golon regained his courage slightly, tiptoeing forward to see what Faran was looking at.

The whole exposed area was covered by metal, forming an impenetrable seal. The metal looked solid enough, but just on the edge of the hole made by the Reaper, Golon saw a handle inset into the door; a piece of metal wire and a coin-sized wax seal hung from it. He could just make out the same sigil as had been stamped on the plaster of the ancient surface of the seal: the sign of Hdar, the Breath of the Plague. Whoever had buried what lay within had taken no chances.

Faran reached forward and teased the handle out of the surrounding plaster. He looked around at the other two. He could see the eyes of the Reaper behind the skull mask, filled with fear. Golon backed away again and stood in the shadows, the cloak clutched tightly to his mouth.

Faran smiled thinly, then with a jerk, he pulled the handle towards him, breaking the seal.

Instantly there came a hissing noise and the corridor filled with a freezing gray mist that rushed outwards from the edge of the door. The mist swallowed the corridor, and they were all blinded for a second, then the faint breeze caught it and wafted it away. The Reaper of Sorrow was seized by a dry hacking cough; Golon was too terrified to breathe. The mist cleared.

Faran held the door in his right hand. Nothing apart from

the plaster seal had kept it in place. He flung it to one side, and it fell in the dusty corridor with a dull clang. He peered through the slowly dissipating mist at what lay behind, then stepped over the threshold into a large chamber fifty yards square. Though the furthest extremes of it were still shrouded in white mist, its nearer walls were now visible, clad all in white marble. Row upon row of marble slabs, twenty wide and fifty deep, stretched away into the haze, and upon each was a shrouded figure, cocooned in white winding sheets. Further figures lay on shelves set into alcoves in the walls—a thousand or more. At the far end, beyond the last of the marble slabs, a raised dais swam into view, some ten feet high, upon which stood a curious wrought-iron throne—a thing of twisted columns and tapering Gothic spires.

Ignoring the prickling cold of the mist, Faran stepped up to the first of the bodies, and seizing the cloth at its head, rent it apart. A withered blue face, wrinkled like a seal's, but still recognizable as a man's, was revealed: ice frosted a half-grown beard, its eyes were closed by the puffy skin around the sockets. A single stitch had been inserted, looping from its top lip to its bottom. A ten-thousand-year-old corpse. What would it be like to be woken after ten thousand years of death, of dreamless sleep?

Faran reached down with his long tapering nails and, in one quick movement, severed the stitch holding the man's lips together. Then, bracing himself, he wrenched open the corpse's jaw with a cracking of bone. He pushed aside the tongue, white and furred like a fungal growth: behind it the man's throat was unobstructed.

"Golon!" he called. "Bring me the Chalice."

CHAPTER ELEVEN

Of Prophecy and the
Black Mines

It was going to be a clear day, Urthred saw as he followed Thalassa and Jayal up the path to the small knoll where the Man of Bronze waited for them. But though the weather was kind, there was a strange weight in his heart—was it Jayal's dream, or something else? The three of them congregated at the Talos' feet. He towered above them, his bronze armour beginning to glow in the rosy light, the silver mallet in his fist glinting like white fire. Urthred's head barely came halfway up his massive calf; the welded, plate-clad feet were twice the size of his body.

"Guardian," Thalassa called up. "You who see all things: tell us what you have seen in the night."

He stirred then, his armour creaking slightly as his metal joints broke his motionless vigil. From deep within his mighty chest there came a ratcheting sound, as gears and cogs, unused since the night before, came back into motion. He turned his head slowly and tilted it down, ruby eyes blazing two pools of light at the still-dark ground at their feet.

"I have seen, as I see many things buried however deep and however far, how the young Illgill's shadow has come to Iskiard," he announced, the voice coming almost as a thin whistle from his metal jaws and through the sealed great helm, as if he spoke quietly, not in the stentorian voice to which it was accustomed.

"Then it was a true vision?" Jayal said quietly.

"All visions are true, in that they belong utterly to the dreamer. But if this is what you dreamed I can confirm it, for through the lens of this instrument"—he lifted the mallet high to the sun—"I command all the nexus points and tunnels in time and space that have ever existed. And deep in the night I saw the gates of Shades open and your double creep forth into the cursed city."

"Is my father alive?" Jayal asked.

"Only you can answer that, for do you not see with the Doppelgänger's eyes? Are you not he, as well as Jayal Illgill? Have you not seen the murder in his heart, how he hates the Illgills and will not rest until they are all destroyed? But even my vision faded after he entered the city—I can't say what happened to your father."

"How far is it to the city?" Urthred asked.

The Man of Bronze raised his mallet so it pointed due north, to the range of low black hills at the edge of the forest. "First, the Duirin Hills—in them are the Black Mines where mortals laboured for the glory of the gods, bringing metals to the world, metals that built the cities. There, too, are the great pyramids that were built as the tiring places of the gods. Beyond the hills is a great ice plain, and beyond that another range of mountains. There is only one way through them: the Iron Gates. Marizian sealed them with the magic of Dragonstooth: only by its magic will you be able to pass through them again. Beyond lies Iskiard."

"How long will it take to reach it?"

"Without the sword? An eternity. But with it, only a few mortal days. But do not hasten in your imaginations to destinations far away. Think of today: danger is at hand, over yonder plain, in those hills."

He pointed his mallet toward them. "The vengeful dead, those slaves of which I spoke, have awoken. I see them risen from their graves in the mines, thousands of them, waiting."

"The undead?"

"Yes, those who served the God's will ten thousand years ago. Faran Gaton Nekron is there. He has arrived before you, waits for you, waits for her." His head turned to Thalassa and she was bathed in the ruby light of his eyes.

She took a step back, her hand going involuntarily to her neck where she had so recently borne the wounds of the vampire's bite. "How can he have followed us?" Jayal asked. "How does he know where we go?"

It was Urthred who answered. "He knows that in this whole world there is only one place where destiny leads us all. He saw what Thalassa and I saw, in Marizian's Orb. He knows the Rod of the Shadows is in Iskiard, that Thalassa, who he prizes over all things, will go there."

"But how has he raised an army from the dead? Surely only the living are susceptible to his bite?"

"Through the Black Chalice," the priest answered. "How many were raised through it in Thrull? Ten thousand? More? All he needs is blood."

"Aye," said the Man of Bronze. "In the times of the God, the drops of it could raise the dead like rain falling upon a field of corn. Now its powers are less, yet still, filled with the blood of the living, a draft from it could bring a man back from death, no matter how long the corpse had been cold. This is how he has raised them in the Black Mines. And now they wait for us; Faran too."

"But the sun still shines," Urthred said. "The undead cannot be stirring from the darkness yet—we still have time to cross the pass before nightfall."

"Only just. For now it's day they hold to the shadows of the mines. But as evening comes the shadows will run out from the lee of the hills, and they will be free to roam once more."

"Can we cross the pass before night?" Thalassa asked.

"If we go like the wind and nothing stays us."

"A prayer first, and then we will leave."

By now, the light had grown stronger, and through the latticework of the bare trees they saw the orange ball of the rising sun. Each of them, even the titan, lowered their heads.

"God of Light, protect your servants," Urthred intoned, yet today of all days, when danger was so near and they needed Reh's help more than ever, the words sounded hollow. The Man of Bronze's warning had struck a dark note, and even as Urthred continued with the prayer he heard the sled dogs begin to howl in the camp as if they too had picked up on the threat lying ahead of them.

"Galadrian has led you from the dark. Let your golden barge shine," he went on, his voice stronger.

"Let us rekindle your flame," Thalassa answered.

The prayers over, the three humans left the Talos and returned to the clearing. The villagers were striking camp and harnessing the sled dogs as they arrived. Some men were waxing the runners on the sleds so they would move easier over the snow. Soon the backpacks were lashed on to the sleds.

Garadas approached, already dressed in his furs and clutching his whip. He pointed at the dogs, who continued to whimper and whine. "There is something strange with the animals today," he said. "Will you bless them?"

Thalassa went to the group of dogs lying on the frozen ground. As one, they lifted their heads and stared at her, their heads cocked slightly to one side, their whimpering forgotten for the moment. She knelt before them and opened her arms as she had many times before in the last few months. On those occasions, one by one, they had got to their feet, wagging their tails, and almost shyly come forward to snuffle at her hand, then had walked away leaving another to take their place, and thus it had been until the last one had come to her.

But not today. They cowered where they lay. Garadas shouted at them, cracking his whip in the air, but still they would not stir, growling and baring their teeth.

Finally, they had to be dragged into their traces, many more precious minutes being wasted as the sun mounted higher into the sky. Finally, when all was ready, the party mounted up, and there was a crack of whips, but even then the dogs were sluggish and only when the lashes fell on their backs did they begin scrabbling at the snow, seeking purchase in the powder, before they got a grip and the heavily laden sleds began sliding forward, ever faster, the waxed runners hissing across the snow of the plain towards the Duirin Hills and Iskiard.

CHAPTER TWELVE

A Shadow on Galastra

Each day, the white-haired soothsayer Creaggan came to the guest quarters in the White Tower and commanded Fazad to come with him. The boy left the wolf cloak and Gurn behind, and was brought to Queen Zalia. From the first her interviews took a particular course: she asked him gently about his family, his childhood upbringing in Thrull, the battle and his service under Skerrib, the landlord of the Gaunt's Head.

Never once did she mention the destruction of Thrull, though this was the news that he and Gurn had expressly come to Galastra to impart. He wondered why she didn't mention it. He answered as politely as he could her innocuous questions, but inwards he seethed. Why didn't she summon her generals, order the army of Galastra to cross the ice, smash the legion that had followed them, drive the Worm from Surrenland and fall on Ossia? With a surprise attack her armies might be victorious. Now was their best chance.

But, at each session, the queen continued with her gentle questions, like a kindly aunt, oblivious to how the boy stood in front of her, nearly hopping from one foot to the other in impatience, his mouth working, desperate to speak on any other subject but those that the queen settled on. Afterwards, he was led to a dining hall where he was fed, then led by

Creaggan back to his chamber, where the soothsayer lit a candle for him and reminded him to say his prayers before departing. Sometimes Fazad cracked open the door of the chamber late at night and saw Creaggan sitting, a lamp burning at his feet, guarding his young charge.

As more and more days passed, Fazad felt some of the impatience, the tumult inside him, begin to slip away. He began to understand the method in the queen's way: as each day passed he became tamer and tamer within. The memories of the terrible journey he'd undertaken, from Thrull to Bardun to Perricod and now to here, began to vanish. Perhaps, as days passed and he no longer wore it, the influence of the wolf cloak was leaving him.

A week in, he learned to smile again. When had he smiled last? The day of the battle when he had been five? An image flashed into his mind: kissing his father good-bye on that morning. He never saw him again; his last impression of him was the rough stubble against his cheek. But with that memory came the nightmares also, visions long suppressed in his subconscious. He had watched the battle from the terrace of their house overlooking the marshes. The soldiers like miniature toys far below. The mournful cow horns blaring over the marshes, the distant cries of men and the tinny clash of arms, the orange and red lines of the baron's army, fragmented, becoming dots of colour, pushed ever backwards and then swallowed by the dark encircling half-moon of brown and purple that was the army of Tiré Gand.

Then it was as if the sound and sight had been amplified—what had been small and distant was now loud and overbearing, roaring in his ears, the fires mounting higher than the temple summits, ashes and sparks, a vision of Hel. He held the hand of his nurse, but there was no nurse, just a bloodied stump and the burning mansion, the flames rising like an orange curtain, the air full of the screams of the dying . . .

The memories came, took him like a wave. Still he stood in front of the throne, trembling. He felt a seat placed behind

him and he sat and, in her turn, the old queen finally rose for
the first time. She stepped down to him and lay a hand on
him and he looked up into her blue eyes. And there he found
comfort. Perhaps they were like the azure skies that earth
used to have when the sun was young?

"My people call you the Wolf King," Zalia said. "The
wolf preserved you on your journey. But I must drive the
creature from you, because you had become like that old
lady who gave you the cloak in Bardun: a lycanthrope."

"What is that?" he asked tentatively.

"One who changes: their minds are full of the wild, of the
hunt. Do you hear their voices, boy? When the moon waxes
full and the clouds fly in front of its face: do you feel your
throat parch and your stomach growl; does not every muscle
of your being ache to be roaming, hunting? Your body is
aflame, one huge itch. You look down: fur grows on the inside of your hands, you lift your hands to your mouth, your
incisors overbite your lip, they have grown long. Where the
human ends and the wolf begins is indistinct."

Fazad swallowed, the tears thick on his eyelashes. Had he
become like one of those? Had he worn the cloak too long?
Was it too late to be saved? His shoulders shook with un-
controllable waves of sorrow

But instantly the queen called for music, and some of the
widows took up their golden harps that stood upon stands
about the throne room. The light shone through the great
oriel windows, fractured into a hundred prismatic hues,
lighting up each and every dark spot in that place, making
all merry.

The music began. Fazad had expected a dirge, consonant
with the sorrowing widows; instead they plucked a gigue
that seemed to set the dust motes flying around the glowing
hall. Now the years appeared to fall from Zalia, and she
teased him, calling him the Bare-Backed King. She clasped
his hand and took some paces up and down the hall with
him, measuring out the steps of a dance, the courtiers clap-
ping, then joining the woman and the boy in the dance. The

sorrow lifted from him. Thrull was forgotten for the moment, as were the wolf-infested plains.

When the music finished the queen asked him to show her Cloud. The two of them and Creaggan descended to the stableyard under the White Tower. And there, as if it had been arranged beforehand by the queen, stood Cloud held by a page, the horse's breath a mist on the air, his head arched proudly, stamping his hooves impatiently on the stone of the courtyard when he saw his master coming.

Fazad went up to him and placed his hand on the horse's grey forelock. Then he stepped to one side: the horse understood and whinnied, tossing his mane, then trotting off, deviating to the left, turning in a circle, round and round, the boy at the centre of the circle.

Then Fazad mounted, and sat tall and erect: horse and rider as one. Cloud slowly advanced, lifting a fetlock in the air as if in obeisance to the queen, and the old lady's face cracked into another smile. At least they gave each other this one thing: the ability to smile. Her lonely blue eyes were alive again, just as when a ray of sun falls upon the sea and is lit with a million diamonds.

He was only thirteen, but he suddenly understood. She was so alone, he realised. Since he'd left Thrull he had seen many desperate sights: the dead plague victims filling icy ditches, starving children wailing on the breasts of their mothers, the undead roaming the countryside at night scenting out their prey. Cries of misery had been with him all through his journey, but since he had donned the wolf cloak, no pity had entered his heart. Now, though, it came, not for the thousand, thousand afflictions he had seen but for this one single old woman: her king eight years dead, no heirs. Somehow he had given her hope, had become the focus of her hope. Why?

Before he could pursue this line of thinking any further, she gestured to horse and rider and Cloud lowered his head and advanced diffidently towards her, gently hoofing the ground.

The old lady beamed at Cloud and his rider: "Yes, I

named you well—you are not the Wolf, but the Bare-Backed King."

But something was puzzling Fazad and he frowned. "That is the second time you have called me king. Why do you call me that, when I have no title, own nothing?"

The queen smiled faintly, as if at some inner joke. "Young people hate advice, but it is the old's responsibility to give it nevertheless. Possessions are nothing, child. You must be king of your heart, and then other men's hearts. Seek for what will win those hearts."

"What is that?"

"Hope. For in the end hope conquers everything. You know what the *Book of Worms* says, that darkness will descend upon this earth, and the sun will never shine again?"

Fazad nodded. "Those who follow that creed have no imagination," the queen continued, "for they think the darkness will be for a day or two and then be superseded by something else, some other state. They have no concept of eternity, never-ending, immutable eternity. And that is how long Iss will hold that darkness over this world: until everything, every spark and shoot of life is extinguished, and all is dead and barren."

She pointed at the overcast sun. "The people ask: Why lose our life when the Death in Life beckons? Though we lose our soul, our bodies will live forever! But they are not alive who turn to the Dark Prince. For there is no life in his kingdom, the kingdom of fear. Seek the light of the sun, the sun that will always burn, though now it seems to gutter. My soothsayers have seen it: the darkness will come, and the sun will not rise, but after that time the light will return—Reh's Second Dawn."

"Let the Flame make it so," Fazad replied.

The queen was very close now. She reached out and stroked Cloud's muzzle and the horse rubbed her hand. "I may not see that day," she whispered, barely audible.

Fazad was about to ask her why, but the queen went on quickly in the same undertone. "Tell me, wolf boy: did you not smell it, when you first came here?"

"The smell of the undead?" Fazad asked.

Zalia nodded solemnly. "Exactly that."

"Has the undead legion followed us into the city?"

The old lady nodded. "Perhaps. They would have come in over the ice by night, and entered the underworld by the sewer outlets in the harbour walls." She looked around, the high walls of the ramparts on one side and the palace on the other forbidding under the dun-grey sky. "But there is more."

"More?"

"Treachery, child," the queen whispered. "Forget the legion: agents of Iss are already in the city."

Fazad's eyes swept over the ring of apparently deserted buildings around the yard.

Zalia shook her head. "They're not in the citadel yet. We are alone, you and I and Creaggan."

"Why don't you muster the army? Send them into the underworld, drive them out?" he asked.

"Already their numbers are greater than ours. The army would be swallowed by the darkness, and we will need every man when the day comes and the undead swarm out onto the streets. They only wait for a signal."

She fixed him with her dazzling stare again. "You came here, thinking it safe from the Worm. But where darkness pools, there will always be the Worm. Now we have to be strong, and though you are still young, you too must be strong. Use the gifts you have: your wolf cloak has given you many things, Fazad: attributes that will help you through the days to come. But do not let its magic ensorcel you, as I saw it nearly had when you first arrived here. Remember that a human heart beats in your breast; you see with a human eye, let pity temper your anger. Even the wolf knows pity. Have you not heard how it will suckle human infants abandoned by their mothers? And do not forget how the old lady of Bardun took you in when you were nearly lost." Then she summoned Creaggan and together they exited the courtyard, leaving Fazad alone with Cloud, his head spinning with the queen's words.

The next morning he told Gurn of the interview. The two of them had been given spacious chambers in the tower, looking south from an ivy-hung casement over a deserted part of the city. A jumbled slope of ruined walls, choked with ivy and abandoned gardens, fell in stepped terraces to the roofs of the lower town and the frozen harbour. Only bats had their dwelling in this lonely place.

It was a cold clear day. A shaft of light descended from the cloud, and Fazad fancied he saw a black line far, far away on the horizon, the coast of Surrenland. Was it really that near? Why had it taken them so long to reach the island? Where had the Drinkers of the Viaticum gone? If Galastra had been their destination, surely they must be in the city by now? The people were uneasy; he could almost smell the fear emanating from the lower town. From his vantage point, he could see barely a soul moving through its apparently deserted streets.

Apart from his audiences with the queen and his talks with Gurn, Fazad spent the days on his own, reading the books that Creaggan left him; books that told of the earth's Golden Age. He found the company of anyone but Zalia and Gurn a burr in his flesh. But as the days passed Gurn was frequently absent, leaving the tower to visit Valence. The seneschal returned each day later and later, his face pinched, worried, though he said nothing to the boy. Fazad guessed he had been discussing the rumours, but he seemed reluctant to talk about them with Fazad, keeping instead to neutral topics.

Each morning, Fazad stared into the mirror in the chamber: gradually his appearance changed back to how it had been before: it had seemed that his face had been becoming angular and thin; perhaps through hunger, perhaps through the influence of the cloak. But now the yellow tinge faded from around his eyes; the tightness of his mouth, pulled into a savage grin for most of their journey, eased. In the day, he no longer heard the call of his wolf brethren in his mind. But at night, their voices still came to him, a keening higher than human hearing, as he lay restless on his bed, their voices out on the frozen sea, where they hungered, slowly dying, wondering why he had abandoned them.

The curse—or had it been a blessing?—of Bardun was lifted. But still the wolves haunted him, were in his blood. Outside on the freezing ice, he felt them expire, one by one.

For several nights he struggled, but finally it was too much for his tortured mind. He went to the balcony as Gurn slept in his own chamber and threw open the windows, calling silently for those who still lived to enter the city, to hide themselves. He felt them like a dark tide passing between the frozen hulks in the harbour, finding the sewer outlets the queen had told him about, nervously scenting the faint smell of the undead in the air.

From that night on, he heard their howling from the warehouses on the quays and on the grey outcrops of rock that overlooked the town. And each day he went to meet with the queen and expected to hear her rebuking him for bringing his brethren into the city, but each day she said nothing. At night while Gurn slept off his drinking bouts with Valence, Fazad lay awake, feeling his lips fold back and a strange low noise come out of his mouth, as if in inarticulate sympathy with his brethren's cries.

The wolf cloak hung untouched in the large dark oak closet in which he had placed it that first day. But even though the closet stood on the other side of the chamber and its doors were a solid inch thick, he still felt the wolf's dead eyes staring into his soul, telling him that Fazad could not avoid the dead spirit of the old lady of Bardun for long, that he would need her skills again soon.

Early one morning, two weeks after their arrival, he was woken by thunderous blows delivered upon the lion-head clapper of the White Tower's door. He was disoriented for a moment, as if their journey to Galastra hadn't happened, that it was the day after he entered Perricod and these were the clappers of the Iss acolytes, hammering on the door of the Iremage mansion. But then he remembered where he was— he was safe. Yet something strange was going on. Now there came the sound of footsteps outside, and whispered words, and whoever had tried to wake them was sent away. Now he heard Creaggan calling and Fazad opened the door.

"You must come now," the soothsayer said solemnly to him and to Gurn who had finally appeared from his own chamber, wiping the sleep groggily from his eyes.

"What is it?" Fazad asked.

"The general, Rutha Hunish, has summoned the court. Even strangers must come."

"What is happening?"

"Why, boy, did you not notice the moon last night? It is nearing the full."

"I saw it."

"The general has decreed that at this time every month those suspected of being Iss worshippers must be purged from the jails. They who go to their deaths today have been tried and found guilty. Today they will burn."

Gurn and Fazad dressed quickly and were led out of the tower and up onto a balcony overlooking the barracks square. Forty or more mounds of kindling, some twenty feet high, had been arranged in neat lines across it. Each had a prominent spar of wood protruding from its summit.

Around the square the balconies of the houses overlooking it groaned with spectators, as did the upper windows of the barracks. On either side the ramparts of the citadel were thronged with courtiers, the same that Gurn and Fazad had seen on the night of their arrival. They looked jealously at the strangers on the queen's balcony high above their own stations, who had been granted admittance to the White Tower, a place they were never allowed themselves.

The queen and the widows arrived with a busy fanfare of trumpets and sat on the high-backed chairs at the centre of the balcony. They wore black, as did all the spectators, black high-brimmed hats and dark capes inlaid with brown ermine. Now there came another trumpet blast and the gates of the barracks, which also served as the prison, were thrown open.

Rutha Hunish and his guard strutted out into the square, followed by a shambling line of prisoners. Some of them

were covered from head to toe in black shrouds—these were
the ones that Fazad took to be vampires. The shrouds were
to keep the sunlight off them so the public would not be
cheated of the moment of their death. Each of the prisoners
carried a cross strut behind their backs to which they were
shackled. Those not shrouded were, it appeared, ordinary
folk accused of worshipping Iss: grey-faced men, business-
men, sailors, foreign mercenaries stranded here since the ice
froze the sea—there was little to distinguish them from the
spectators apart from their prison pallor. Not one of them
yelled any defiance or pled for their lives. It was as if they
had been drugged.

Each was led to a mound of kindling. First those not
shrouded were carried to the top of the pyres by pairs of
burly guards who lifted them and their cross struts bodily
over the wood uprights.

The prisoners began to struggle then, but with their arms
pinioned behind their backs and the uprights holding them
fast, they had no way of escaping.

Then the pyres were lit. The prisoners began to cry out
when the first black smoke eddied up from below. Then
their feet began to kick until the sheer heat of the inferno lit
their leggings and they were enveloped in flame. There they
burned, their limbs kicking in agony as they spun round and
round the wooden spars.

Fazad looked away until each and every one of the first
series of pyres had been lit. All morning until midday they
sat on the balcony covered by white ashes and a fatty patina
deposited by the burning corpses. Despite the raging fires,
they shivered in the biting cold, for they were too high up on
the walls to benefit from their heat.

Just before each lighting, Rutha Hunish would turn his
eyes up to the ramparts and bow. Perhaps he looked up to
show his obedience to the queen, but all day she sat on her
throne, her face a deathly white, her eyes closed shut, so the
gesture was wasted. But though Rutha Hunish was some
fifty yards away Fazad felt the stare fall on him. He shiv-

ered. A shiver not of fear, but as if hackles of fur rose on his back, as if answering a silent challenge in the captain's stare.

When the first prisoners had been dealt with, they moved on to the shrouded ones. The shrouds were attached by string sashes that the guards whipped away. In the weak midday sun those who watched caught a brief glimpse of human forms before the rays struck them and the figures beneath disintegrated into a thick oily mist and drifted sluggishly away in the cold breeze. One or two of the prisoners survived their unveilings and they were led away back to the barracks, whether to be pardoned or brought out at the next auto-da-fé neither Fazad nor Gurn knew or cared to ask, so sickened were they by the spectacle. Now the cold wind that blew down from the Dragon's Back strengthened, sending cinders and sparks roaring over the square from the pyres. The courtiers retreated back to their halls and the queen left the balcony with her sombre handmaids, looking neither to left nor right. That day Fazad was not summoned to her presence.

It was exactly two weeks after their arrival. That night he found sleeping difficult. Next door he heard Gurn's powerful snores. Fazad tossed and turned on his bed, between sleep and waking. He rose again, lighting a taper, staring into the mirror. The night of the full moon: the time of the month when the vampires most felt the need for blood.

He sat on a chair, willing himself to keep awake. Outside, the wolves were curiously silent, as quiet as they had been since he had summoned them to the city. His eyes fell on the door of the closet where the wolf cloak hung. It was as if an invisible pulse beat there in time with his own heart. His body ached, every nerve ending telling him to go to the cloak, put it on.

He must have dozed, then slipped into a deep sleep . . .

Suddenly he was wide awake again. He sat bolt upright in the chair. The lantern had gone out. The moonlight streamed in through the mullioned casement in diamond patterns. His body was covered in sweat.

The wolf's song: from every compass point: from the

high fells to the north, from the cliffs to the west, and the low beaches to the east, from the ice-covered sea and from every corner of the town itself. Their howl was rising like a symphony to the moon, stronger and stronger. Their baying seemed to reverberate like a tuning fork in an inner part of his soul. A warning: they were warning all who would listen, but only he understood.

Was this the night the queen had predicted? Was it the time the Worm had been waiting for? Though the lantern had long gone out, he saw the light set outside the door, the light that Creaggan sometimes placed there. He was safe.

The howling did not stop. He rose and saw that Gurn's door was open and his bed was empty. A chill went through him: the seneschal had been taken! He hesitated no longer— but strode to the wardrobe, his hands clutching the brass handle. He had fought the temptation for two weeks, but now he wrenched it open without a second thought.

The red eyes of the dead wolf stared back from the shadows. Once more Fazad was back in the cave above Bardun with the old lady's eyes burning into his soul. Her words came into his mind. He must have revenge on all Ossians. He felt the change begin, the tightening of his skin over his face. He lunged forward and ripped the cloak from its hook. Its pungent smell filled his nostrils. Once more the darkness was on him, the racing blood, the scent of the hunt, the feeling of lithesome speed, a ferocity that sung in his blood. He was as he had been back in Darvish Forest: his senses almost unbearably acute, his sight, his hearing, his smell . . .

Then he scented it on the air just as he had that evening of their arrival in Imblewick: mildew and grave cerements. The merest whiff, sitting on the bitterly cold air, They were here, somewhere in the citadel. The vampires.

He went to the door and listened. Was that the creak of a distant floorboard? The sound died. The tower was silent once more. He twisted the latch handle. Outside Creaggan's lantern burned on the floor. But there was no sign of the magician. He sniffed the air again, He smelt Gurn. A heavy scent, sweat and leather armour, liniment. He had passed down this way a few minutes before. Fazad followed the trail down a corridor to a wooden door. It led to a set of crooked stone steps set into the southern side of the White Tower. The side that overlooked the ruins and overgrown gardens. He went down them, a little scared of its lightlessness and the thick cobwebs that fell over his face. He followed Gurn's scent and that of the vampires, commingled with the smell of the frost and the frozen night air. Finally he was at the first level of the tower. His eyes made out an arched window overlooking the ruins. He saw the silhouette of a leafless tree against the moon. A dark figure was crouched there looking out.

The wolf cape lent him stealth as well as perception and he silently glided closer and closer to the figure. A vampire or Gurn? Fazad took another step forward, but he must have made the slightest sound, for as he discerned the telltale empty sleeve hanging down from his cloak, Gurn whirled round, a dagger flashing in the moonlight.

"It's me, Fazad!" the boy hissed. The dagger halted an inch from his throat. There was a wild look in Gurn's eyes; the whites showed and perspiration ran from his temples down the side of his face.

Finally he seemed to recover some of his composure. "In Reh's name, don't creep up on me like that!" he hissed, reversing the knife and pushing the boy back into the deep shadows cast by the moon. He glanced nervously out of the archway and Fazad followed the direction of his gaze. Beyond, in the ruins he had noticed from his bedroom balcony, he saw an old burial ground, ancient grave plots all marked by three circular stones of diminishing size placed one on top of the other. He had puzzled over them until Gurn had told them they were the symbol of Iss, the stones crudely representing the articulations of the Worm.

The graveyard had always been deserted before, but now he saw figures moving in it, at work with spades and hoes: one of the headstones had been moved to one side. As Fazad watched, he saw a man clad in dark robes come from the shadows. He donned the ornate skull mask of a priest, then descended into the open grave.

Boy and man crept forward. The base of the tower was slightly elevated, and they could look down. A corpse, no more than leathery skin and yellow bone, lay in the ground, its arms crossed on its rib cage, its skull grinning up at the priest, who now leaned down and with an incantation appeared to kiss the skull on the mouth. A ghostly blue exhalation issued from the priest's mouth and was sucked into the skull: it was as if a flare had been lit within, and the skull glowed an intense mauve. Fazad saw the skeletal hands twitch, the skeleton begin to half rise out of its shallow grave. The priest muttered something and the corpse slowly reclined back into the earth. Then the priest rose and gestured at the men ranged around and they quickly shovelled the earth back into the hole again, then faded back into the shadows of the ruins overhung with ivy. Within seconds the graveyard was as empty as it had been during the day.

"What are they doing?" Fazad asked.

"Reanimating corpses. When the time comes, it will be like Thrull field—the dead springing from the earth," Gurn answered grimly.

"But when will the day come?"

Gurn shrugged. "We are not prophets, boy. That secret is locked somewhere in the *Book of Light* and the *Book of Worm*—it is not for us to figure it."

"We must tell the queen what we have seen."

Gurn nodded solemnly. "Tomorrow. She is locked in her part of the tower, and Creaggan is nowhere to be found."

"What of Rutha Hunish and the guard?"

Gurn faced him. "Who is charged with protecting the citadel?" he asked. Fazad was about to reply, but Gurn anticipated him. "Rutha Hunish, that is who. Tonight the wolves would have woken the dead. They roam the thoroughfares. Would not any other commander call out the guard and drive them away? But no call has come, the guard remain in their barracks. Was he afraid what the soldiers

would discover after the wolves had gone? There are probably scenes like this all over Imblewick."

"He is a traitor?"

"Remember, boy, I fought at Thrull. Even during the battle the tales of his exploits against the Worm were passed up
and down our lines to give our soldiers courage. And after
the defeat he led the survivors back here. Then there are the
executions. Surely he wouldn't destroy his own kind?
Surely he is beyond suspicion?" Gurn shook his head. "But
Valence and others I have spoken to disagree. They think he
is a traitor, and all he does is a subterfuge for a day, not yet
come, when he will raise the dead and undead and take the
city."

"Yet he is not one of the Dead in Life. We have seen him
in the light of the sun."

"Not all those who follow Iss are vampires. A vampire's
bite will enslave the victim to its dominant, a fate that Rutha
Hunish would never accept, for he is too proud. There is
only one instrument that confers what they call everlasting
life without thraldom to another."

"What is that?"

"The Black Chalice—the cursed instrument that Faran
brought with him from Tiré Gand to populate the western
world with the living dead. That is what Rutha Hunish waits
for." He muttered an imprecation under his breath. "The executions were just a sham, to lure the last of the garrison into
their sottish ways. Every day when I have been with Valence
I have seen it—their ill discipline growing and growing.
Soon only those who dwell in the queen's tower will oppose
Rutha Hunish and his cohorts: the soothsayers and us."

They returned their gaze to the graveyard. All was silent
now, the wolves quiet once more.

"Tomorrow we will see, boy," Gurn said. "When the
queen has been warned. Tomorrow we will see what mea-
sures we can take." They crept back up the stairs of the
tower as silently as they could. Outside the room the lantern
still burned, the sorcerer's seat was still empty.

CHAPTER THIRTEEN

The Black Mines

Far under the Duirin Hills, Golon handed the Black Chalice to Faran and then stepped back, his cloak pressed to his mouth to keep out the invisible spores of disease that he imagined were milling about the underground chamber. The white mist that had filled the room had nearly gone; only a few wisps twisted up from hidden vents in the floor and drifted towards the door like escaping ghosts, but he knew the demon's breath was all around him.

The blue light shone at the centre of the room, turning the white winding sheets of the corpses a mauve grey. Faran strode to the slab where they had exposed the first of the corpses. He turned and gestured to the last surviving Reaper. The soldier left his position by the door and approached, his skull mask white from plaster dust so he looked even more an embodiment of a walking death.

But it was for his life, and his coursing blood, that Faran wanted him: blood that would give life to the thousands who lay on the mortuary slabs waiting for resurrection.

Faran studied the Black Chalice. It was difficult to imagine that a god should have sipped from an object so mundane. It was no greater than an alehouse pot, with curved lips and a heavy waist; its weight suggested that it was made of lead, but in reality he knew it must be some metal long forgotten to man, its black surface inscribed with dark runes more ancient than learning or human memory.

Faran gestured for Golon to begin. The sorcerer kept his cloak closely pressed to his mouth and joined the other two at the centre of the chamber. He produced a small phial from his pouch and handed it to the man: the final viaticum, Lethe in vapour form. The soldier threw back his mask, unscrewed the cap and sucked deep into his nostrils. His face went slack, the phial fell from his hand and smashed on the floor, then his knees gave way.

Golon caught him in his arms before he fell. He felt for a pulse but only got the barest murmur of a beat. The man now inhabited a stage halfway between life and death.

Now Faran too stooped over him, taking his legs and indicating that the sorcerer should take the other end of his body. Together they lifted the Reaper onto a vacant mortuary slab. Then Golon drew a sharp obsidian knife from his belt and held up the man's limp hand. He nodded to Faran, who held the Chalice at the ready. Then he slashed down on the man's wrist. At first it seemed only that a pale pink lip appeared on the white flesh, but then as red paint welling through a field of white varnish, the blood blossomed.

And so it began. They laboured for many hours, he and Faran, until the man had given up his blood, drop by drop into the Black Chalice, Golon kneading the flesh around the wound as assiduously as a farmer the teat of a cow. The Reaper had slipped slowly into a deeper and deeper coma and at the last, after many hours, the blood from the wound had slowed, then the ooze from the wound ceased altogether. But even then Faran was not satisfied and seizing the Reaper's mace, with several mighty blows smashed the man's ribcage and ripped out his heart. He gripped it fiercely between his leather gauntlets, squeezing the blood into the Black Chalice, his face contorted in a look of maniacal ferocity.

Then Faran threw the heart to one side and stared into the receptacle. No bigger than any ordinary drinking cup, yet each gallon of the Reaper's blood had disappeared into it, as if within it there was an invisible well. Just one drop, a precious drop, could revive the dead. The black metal seemed unremarkable, save at its edges where the blood touched it: there the metal seethed like acid. A heavy odour, a coppery gall, emanated from it. He plucked off one of his mail-studded gauntlets and dropped it to the floor, then tipped the cup to his pale purple lips and took a draft.

Golon watched him, his mouth and nose once more swathed with the cloak, glad that his master was intent on the Chalice and not on him, for if he had glanced up at the sorcerer, he might have seen the look on his face, the look Golon knew he had worn ever since he had given Faran the drinking cup. A look of anger and of resentment: just a single draft, like the one Faran took now, and he would have immortal life.

Faran had given the boon of the Life in Death so freely to others less deserving. But not to him. Perhaps he withheld it because he knew it was the only gift that Golon desired, the only thing that would keep him loyal. Or maybe he had simply forgotten his promise.

The injustice burned more and more in Golon's mind, until it was like a raging fire that consumed all other thoughts. Whose conjuries had won victory for Faran seven years before? And after the victory? Even the dead buried in the catacombs under the Temple of Iss, those dull burghers who had no doubt only paid lip service to Iss during their lives, whose real interests had never gone beyond a groat of tin tacks or a bushel of horse feed, they with no scintilla of magic or redemption in their dead veins, had been given the precious drops, been brought back to life by the Chalice, had been granted immortality. Even the traitor who had followed Reh but had turned to Iss, the turncoat, the High Priest Varash, had been rewarded on the very first day he had prostrated himself to Faran.

Yet he, he who had unleashed demons in the van of his lord's army, still went without. What justice was there here? The treacherous thoughts, like an unscratchable itch, tormented him.

Perhaps Faran intuited them, for he lowered the Chalice abruptly and whirled upon Golon. His face hooded, murder-

ous, his lips dyed purple with blood, his eyes like black
stones. The sorcerer stepped back as his eyes met Faran's:
each was like a whirlpool into which he was sucked. Mesmerism. His mind reeled and he fought to keep from fainting.

Faran's gaze penetrated to the centre of his being, as if it
corkscrewed down a dark tunnel right into his soul. Dis-
tantly he heard his master's warning: "Remember—nothing
is hidden from me."

With that Faran relinquished his gaze and Golon was free
again. That was his lord's power, with which he controlled all
those who came into contact with him. How many times had
Golon sunk into that deep well? How many times had Faran
read what was in his mind? What gave the undead this power
over the living? Was it desire, a desire that so outweighed
human need that it was undeniable to those who lived?

Faran went to the mortuary slab where the first victim
they had uncovered lay, his withered face peering up from
the ripped winding sheets. He set the Chalice and its precious cargo down on the slab and pulled off the second of
his leather gauntlets. Underneath, his hands were dead
white, the veins showing as black. He dipped his index finger into the Chalice, brought up a bead of blood and placed
it on the dead man's tongue.

The corpse's body suddenly arched, as if it had been
struck by a bolt of energy. It spasmed again, almost bending
double, the skull cracking back onto the marble slab. Golon
leapt back, surprised by the intensity of the reaction. Faran
peered down at the corpse, a small smile twitching at the
corner of his mouth. Now Golon regained his courage and
crept a little closer, fascinated by what he saw, forgetting
the threat of the plague. He saw a blue vein begin to throb
in the man's neck, once, twice, building up to the slow
pulse of the dead: four in a minute.

"He will wake soon," Faran said. He gestured to Golon to
move on to the next slab, and pointed to the dagger that was
still in Golon's hand. "Cut them open; every one of them,"
he commanded.

The sorcerer approached, holding a sleeve of his cloak to

his mouth, the obsidian knife in his other hand. But once more he had to relinquish the cloak, once more he could almost taste the corrupt air, the spores of disease spreading from his throat and nose to his lungs. He awkwardly forced open the corpse's rigidly set jaw: a blast of fetid air as pungent as mud dredged from a pond bottom nearly overwhelmed him.

Faran dipped his finger into the Chalice and brought out a swimming bead of blood. He stooped over the corpse like an alchemist bent over his alembic with a pipette and dropped it with great care down the purple windpipe. A faint hissing sound, again like acid, then the corpse's chest rose and a rattle came from its throat, followed by what might have been the intake of breath. The corpse's chest rose again slowly, and its eyes fought to break through the centuries of gum and dust that plugged them.

Faran smiled as he watched the creature's movements. To him, it was like a birth. His plan was working. He turned on Golon, who stared on with equal horror and fascination. "Prepare the others," he ordered.

The sorcerer started out of his reverie and went to the next corpse, cutting open the winding sheets around its head and slitting the thread sealing its mouth. For many hours he passed down the line of the ancients, always one or two ahead of Faran, who followed after like a dark vulture, repeating over and again the procedure. The repetition dulled Golon's anxiety, put him into a kind of trance. His head swam with fatigue; he began to hallucinate as he bent over each corpse that it was not the blank eyes of the dead miners into which he stared but once more Faran's dark gaze.

Behind him he heard a rustling, a stirring, at first no louder than a cockroach nest disturbed, but soon it became louder, a continuous noise, like surf. But Golon didn't look around to investigate as he went about his task, passing from one slab to another like a blind man, his jaw tucked into his chest in a futile attempt not to breathe too deeply of the atmosphere.

But when he reached the end of the last row and there were no more corpses, he turned. His blue magical light still burned over the vast chamber. The breath in his throat, al-

ready shallow, stopped completely when he saw the scale of
what they had done. On every slab there was movement. In
their white winding sheets, the writhing, waking bodies
looked if anything like wriggling grey worms.

He pushed the sleeve of his cloak back into his mouth.
He felt empty inside. This then was the end, or at least the
beginning of the end. Not like his six brothers, killed by
their own conjuries, but dead by one that had been made ten
thousand years before.

The air was full of death. He knew he would soon be
dead, as dead as these poor unfortunates had been a scant
hour before. And knowing the essence of Hdar he knew the
death would be agonizing: black growths blossoming in the
secret damp places of his body; his groin, his armpits,
spreading to his torso and his limbs, and his internal organs.

And if that was so, then there was only one help. A small
sip of the Black Chalice could save him, as it had saved
these others for the Death in Life. At the last, when Faran
saw he must lose him, would he not offer him the cup? Perhaps he would. Perhaps he had read Golon's treacherous
thoughts. A chill went up the sorcerer's spine. He was impotent. His fate in the hands of another man, though in his
hands he controlled the very emissaries of the gods, the
demons. If he died, where then would be his life, his hours
of study? His self-sacrifice? His denial of pleasure? Lost in
the darkness, dust, a waste.

But Faran was oblivious to him now as he always had
been; he stood over the last slab, his hands clenched together
around the Chalice, his dark eyes burning. Then he seemed
to come back to his senses. He turned slowly to Golon. He
gestured up and down the lines of bodies. "Cut them loose,"
he commanded. The mesmerism of his eyes once more
made Golon giddy, the room began to rock from side to side.
Unconsciously he obeyed.

More hours passed as he retraced his steps—staggering,
like a drunkard, clumsy with weariness, cutting the dead out
of the winding sheets that imprisoned them. Now he saw
their naked yellow flesh, like ill-cured vellum, their hair

grown long, even in death, their sour smell, their eyes hard and black like stones, sunken into their heads. Some snatched at him, and he had to jerk away quickly; others rose, looking neither to right nor left, breathing hard, like men who had run many miles, their faces pallid, discoloured by mottled purple patches of the plague on their cheeks. The noise sounded like one breath, the air had a strange odour: old leather-bound books, curdled milk, mingled with the whiff of decay.

When all was done, he retreated quickly to the dais at the end of the chamber and stared in horror at the tableau in front of him. It was the furthest he could be from the revenants without actually leaving the room. Though he had longed for the Life in Death, now, not for the first time, he wondered if theirs was indeed such a happy state: they had died in agony. What did they think to wake thus in this place that had been their prison?

At an unspoken command from Faran, one by one, in the order they had been released, the corpses ceased their labored breathing and turned their dark eyes on their lord. Silence. He walked to the end of the room and stood on the dais in front of Golon, and raised his hands. As one the dead leaned their heads back and emitted a dry, etiolated snarling from their throats. Slowly they lowered their bodies from the plinths that had held them for so long and shambled forward. Some fell and struggled like upended cockroaches on the floor, but most were strong, as strong as the day they had been struck down.

Faran lowered his hands, and their noise ceased. He turned to Golon. "Go—find the surface," he ordered, pointing at the shattered entranceway to the tomb.

Golon had no recollection of how he left that cursed room; his legs carried him from it without him even noticing. Outside in the corridor he took the first really deep breaths he had taken for hours. From inside the chamber he heard the moaning of the undead. Faran's new army, but he was no part of it. He was utterly alone. He was the last living person anywhere in the mines.

CHAPTER FOURTEEN

Of Dead Gods and Demons

Golon summoned the glowing ball of blue light and sent it ahead of him down the unexplored shaft in front. His heart lifted at the prospect of seeing the outside world again. He had been buried in the earth too long: first on the Silver River, then in Iken's Dike and now these Black Mines.

He climbed up through many levels of workings, past the ancient rust-covered engines of the gods, their bodies like giant beetles fallen to the ground in a shower of unarticulated sections; their former purpose only remembered by the mute army of the undead below.

At last he saw a vast cavern in front. Snakelike metal lines had been set into the floor, like the silver trails of snails on the black rock, each of them converging on the exit. What lay beyond was obscured by the unfamiliar brightness of day.

He wondered: Should he not free himself from his ungrateful master and the Dead in Life? Did he have to live every moment of his life in fear? Should he not just walk away from the mines now, hoping that the plague was not in him, walk out and travel across the snow plains and blasted forests, back to the south, to Tiré Gand? And if he lived to cross those six hundred leagues, would anyone remember him? It was eight years since he had left that city. What would his welcome be like?

But he wouldn't care even if they had forgotten him: would welcome it in fact. No longer would he be importuned every hour of every day by people needing his skill. He would return to his lonely tower on the edge of Gibbet Moor, far above the city, where the ravens circled the grey uplands. No longer would he dabble with the summoning of demons, demons like Nekron and Hdar. He would not be destroyed like his six brothers had been destroyed.

If only it was not too late already—if he did not have the plague. If he didn't he would rejoice, forget about the Chalice, live out his mortal days and die peacefully. And before he died, in his will he would ask for his body not to be buried but to be burned like the followers of Reh. Then he could never be brought back from the damp grave or the cold slab by another greedy master—not for him that bleak awakening that he had just witnessed, the howling chorus of the undead, their intellects erased, their one imperative the getting of the blood that would keep them in that state forever. No one ever would have such a handle on him again. The mind—its sanctity—this was the most precious thing. There in his old tower he would be happy until the end of his natural days.

He shook his head. Impossible thoughts. Once set on the road of magic, man could not step off it so lightly. He had come too far, discovery and knowledge like twin stars beckoning him forth into the darkness from which there was no return.

He was a prisoner, he realised, always had been. Since that night when he had been led in a procession of servants from his upland tower down to Faran's gloomy palace overlooking the River Furx in Tiré Gand. It had been almost dawn when he arrived and was ushered into the windowless room, lit with some flickering torches on the damp-stained walls—Faran sat on a wooden throne, in front of him a table on which was an elaborately carved, worm-eaten box.

Faran's gaze had settled on him and it was then he first felt his master's power. And only when Faran was satisfied that he was fully in that power, did the Undead Lord gesture for him to approach. Slowly he had raised the lid of the box and Golon had taken a sharp intake of breath, for inside was the Worm's most holy relic: the Black Chalice. Faran had promised that one day he would drink from it. How his heart had beaten with hope. To cheat the fate of his six dead brothers, to live forever!

But the day of that release had never come. It was as if Faran had forgotten his promise, or willfully ignored it; perhaps he disdained Golon for so readily falling in with his plans.

The sorcerer went forward into the daylight, drawing in a deep draft of fresh air. Snow lay banked at the entrance. He stepped out into a white world of grey clouds and slate-black rock.

The entrance to the mine stood on a ledge a thousand feet above a mountain pass. He remembered the names of the hills between which the ancient road to Iskiard passed: Scalprock and Maligar. This must be the side of Scalprock. It was exposed to a cutting wind that blew in from the icy steppes. The pass below was covered in snow A deep groove ran down its centre: the line of the road, hidden by the snow. He followed its course to the south. It dipped into a ravine, then reemerged below the fractured grey shale cliffs that skirted the hills. The ground eased out into a flat icy plain and in the far distance, he saw the dark edge of a forest. Lorn. He had last seen it days before, the day when they had murdered the Master's servant, Smiler, then fled his retribution.

That had been a hundred leagues away. Then a dark cloud had hung over the forest. But now it was gone; the sky to the south was empty, grey and featureless, a pearl-grey winter sky. Perhaps the Master, too, had gone, back to Shades.

He brought the purple gem from his fob again and dangled it in the air by its leather string. It twitched to the south, drawn by the invisible magnetism of magic as it had been in the tunnel. Yes, the sword and the Talos were there. But a contrary tugging came from the opposite direction, from the north. He turned. The Rod of the Shadows—in Iskiard.

He stared toward the lost city. A steep slope led down to another snow-covered plain, a mile or more away and a thousand feet below. It was absolutely smooth, and he guessed the snow must conceal a lake.

At the base of the cliffs stood three granite pyramids, arranged in an asymmetrical pattern: the furthest from his viewpoint was the largest, the second slightly smaller and the third, nearest one, the smallest, so the foreshortening gave him a curious feeling of altered perspective, as if the horizon bent upwards rather than down. Perhaps whoever had built them had meant them to be viewed thus, so that from this pass neither one nor the other seemed to have precedence but all appeared the same size. The pyramids were enclosed by the ruins of high walls. Covered causeways ran from each of them over the rocky foreshore and into the lake to wharves. Sailing ships were moored by icy covered hawsers at each one, their rigging dripping with a thick icing of stalactites.

He found some steps buried in the snow and carefully cleared a foothold on each. Then he climbed slowly down to the road and followed it to the ruined temple complex. It was bitterly cold, the cold merely adding to the general air of abandonment that hung over the ruins. The pyramids loomed overhead, higher and higher the nearer he got. He stopped at the first ruined wall and saw words in the script of the Tongue of the Worm written on a large tablet set into the ancient brick. He read carefully, struggling over some of the words of the language he had studied so long ago in Tiré Gand.

The inscription told him of the history of this place. How Reh and Iss had decided to end their arguments once and for all upon Shandering Plain. The gods knew it was the end of their time and that many would die. So it was decreed that the dead should be taken to Iskiard. The Black Mines were a staging post. Here, in these pyramids, their bodies would be dressed before they were taken over the lake to Iskiard. And there in the underworld the gates of Shades would be opened by the Rod of the Shadows and they would pass into the Shadow World forever. Three funeral barges waited here. That belonging to Reh was called the *Windhover,* and Iss' was the *Dark Ship.* The one for the use of the other gods had no name.

In the end neither Reh nor Iss had died, for both were

saved by the drafts of the Silver Chalice and the Black Chalice. They had left this world that they had devastated with their fire and now dwelt in the stars.

Golon wandered until he came to steps leading into the maze of covered walkways. It was dark within, but with a snap of his fingers the blue light flared slowly into life once more. He walked for half an hour, down broader and broader covered ways, until he came into a vast dome-shaped atrium, dominated by a massive slab positioned right at its centre. The circular walls were divided into elliptical panels tapering towards the opening above his head. On each was painted a vast mural. Hybrid creatures, perhaps a human's idea of a god, half human, half bird, or toad or serpent or star or moon. Beneath this stylised art, set in niches under each of the paintings, were twelve stone thrones: the number of the ancient pantheon of the gods.

Three broad corridors led off from the atrium towards the three pyramids and wharves.

The first corridor had the Flame sigil of Reh carved over its entrance, the second the Worm devouring its tail, the sign of Iss, and the third the symbols of the rest of the gods: the moon of Erewon, the star of Arcos and many more.

The wind gusted again outside, an eddy finding its way into the hall. A desolate howl echoed down the corridor from the direction of the third pyramid: with it came a strange scent, acrid, chemical. Surely the corpse of a god lay there, only an arrow flight away. Perhaps the howl was the weeping of a servant who had survived these ten thousand years.

Who was this third god? Unnamed he seemed even more terrible. Golon's natural curiosity began to build. He had brought demons from the stars, but he had never looked on a god, even a dead one. He entered the passage. Now, a quarter of a mile away at the entrance to the pyramid, he could see a ghostly grey light flickering on and off. He got closer until he was fifty yards away and the opening loomed large in front of him. He squinted against the light that now was quite bright. In the afterimage of the flickering he saw a wall of grey and mottled green beyond the entrance to the pyramid and in it, a pale oval covered with a tracery of blue veins and a fringe of delicate dark hairs. As he stood, wondering what it could be, the dome shuddered and he saw that it was a giant eye, the eye of a god. The grey-green wall was the God's cheek. He heard a stentorian breathing, and then he realised. The God was still alive!

Just as this thought came to him, the eye blinked open and regarded him. For the split second he stood looking into the eye of the God, he saw a million things imprinted there on its retina: the fires of the final battle as high as the skies, the dead falling like mown corn, the screams of agony, the God's long journey to this place, his endless waiting. When Golon could see no more, he turned on his heels and fled.

He arrived back in the domed hall and skidded to a halt, looking back fearfully. All was quiet again. Surely the God couldn't follow? If he could, why hadn't he left this place aeons ago? His breathing settled. He turned to the corridor dedicated to Reh and sent the blue flare down it. The sloping rampway was painted: faded images of flat figures drawn in the ancient style, dense calligraphy underneath, but not in a tongue he knew: it was the same script he remembered from Marizian's tomb in Thrull, the language of the Flame. The series of pictures showed a funeral procession, a white-haired corpse being carried down to the lake and across it to a city on the other side. He saw a picture of a ship like the ones he had seen outside.

Reh, unlike the other God, was gone from this earth. Golon decided that he would explore further. He took a couple of steps towards the entrance but then there came a tingling down his spine and his hairs stood up on end. He sensed the buzzing of the invisible current of magic. He searched for it and found it, a pulsing ganglion of knotted energy over the portal, again just like in Marizian's tomb. A warding of fire. Anyone passing under it would be incinerated. He eyed it for a moment, wondering whether to dispel it as he had done the magical barrier in Thrull. But he was weary, his energies were low.

He walked to the next entrance. Inscribed on the architrave

was the symbol of the serpent eating its own tail. Iss. Again a warding. One of interment. Whoever tried to pass through this gate would find themselves buried alive in a grave deep beneath the earth. This was magic he knew well: the secret knots that bound the spell were not hidden from him. He reached into the ganglion of energy with his mind, finding its secret point. The spell fell away as if it had never existed.

He sent the flare down this corridor too. It was a mirror image of that of Reh, another series of faded reliefs, this time showing the serpent loaded on a funeral barque and taken over the lake towards Iskiard to be buried in Shades. But this scene of interment had never happened: Iss had escaped the earth. His barge had not been used.

Golon followed the rampway downwards. At the end of it, wan sunlight filtered in from between stone columns. Beyond be could see the dark, hoar-covered hull of a ship. Now he was closer he saw that its hull was not wood, but metal, as were its spars and its furled sails too. Some hundred feet in length, its figurehead carved like a serpent's head, massive purple carbuncles for eyes, ivory teeth and a spitting tongue of razor-sharp metal.

It was supported on the ice by outriggers. Its deck arched gracefully to an elevated poop and prow. Its three masts were lateen-rigged, the sails tightly furled to the sloping yards. There was a large platform between fore and mainmast. A frame stood over the plinth: a heavy black canopy had once hung over the rails but the wind had blown it to shreds, and now only one or two threads of heavy material still clung to the metal.

Gangways, turned to slick chutes by the ice, ran down from the sides of the ships. Gingerly Golon pulled himself up using the icicle-covered guide ropes to either side.

To his untrained eye everything seemed in place. He looked to his right to Reh's ship, the *Windhover*, tied to the next wharf a hundred yards away. It too stood on the ice on outriggers. Beyond was the third wharf. The ship moored there had canted over to one side and was partially sunk into the ice. Perhaps its sinking had meant the unknown God had been left here in his mortuary pyramid.

A feeling of melancholy trickled slowly through his veins. It was evening. The pale grey sky was now streaked with rusty bands of red. The icy surface of the lake reflected the sky like a mirror. It was time to return to his inhuman lord and his new minions. With a heavy heart, Golon climbed back up to the mines and descended through the dark levels to the plague grave.

The chamber was thronged with the undead, in a vast semicircle. It was even colder here than it had been outside in the wind, as if the proximity of all the cold bodies had frozen the chamber even more. Golon put his cloak to his mouth and breathed through it once more. A futile gesture—the spores were most likely already inside him. If so, he must have the Chalice if he was to live. He forced himself between the undead, pushing away their groping fingers, his nostrils twitching at their rank smell. Faran sat on the metal throne on the dais, the Black Chalice still clutched in his hand.

For a moment Golon wondered whether his lord hadn't sunk into the second sleep, so still was he. An icicle had formed on the tip of his nose, and his hair was white with frost, but then the sorcerer saw his chest rise slightly. He still breathed, though he stared fixedly ahead, even when Golon had pushed his way into his field of vision.

Golon's eyes went to the Chalice. Faran's knuckles were white with the tightness of his grip. He was in some kind of trance communing with those who stood before him. Golon cleared his throat, and instantly Faran's eyes swivelled towards him. Golon's mind swooned once more and he was in his lord's thrall. He told Faran what he had seen, what the purple gem had told him: that the humans were still to the south and that it was dusk.

After he'd finished the Undead Lord stirred. "Good," he rasped. "Let us go to the upper levels. They will come this way. We'll be ready for them."

* * *

The day and now the night were a nightmare of fatigue and horror for Golon. He led Faran and the undead back to the surface where night had fallen and the stars shone crystal bright. Faran sent the dead miners off into the darkness, but Golon by now was beyond caring what they did. He sneaked away and in a side passage he succumbed to sleep not caring if one of the undead took his blood while he slept, so tired was he. But just before dawn he woke and found his master crouched over him and himself still alive. Faran told him what he must do: the Man of Bronze was coming with the humans. Only a demon could destroy him.

Again no protest came to Golon's lips but he rose as if in a trance, his mind wondering why his body obeyed even as he walked out in the predawn light and crossed the valley and climbed the opposite hill where there was a steep overhanging cliff overlooking the pass. He found that the undead had set ropes there overnight. He looked down. A five-hundred-foot drop, the road and the features of the landscape foreshortened, diminished. A new giddiness, this time vertigo, but he knew what he must do. For three days and two nights he lowered himself over the overhang of rock.

As he dangled high above the pass, he produced the obsidian knife once more and this time nicked his own wrist and with his quickly congealing blood painted a rune with his cold-numbed hands. Again and again he had to use the knife, until his wrists were scarred, but gradually his painting took shape. Like all runes of summonings it expanded from the centre like a flower. The blood would attract demons; the blood of summoners was the strongest, for that was what they craved most, to destroy those mortals with power over them. Had they not had enough of his family's, his six brothers? The demons would remember the sweet smell of their blood and rush to claim Golon's, and therein lay the trap. He would bring them and in their eagerness they would come faster than the eye could see and strike the cliff with the force of a meteorite. The mountain would be destroyed and the whole pass would be buried—with the Man of Bronze.

Each day he checked the pendulum. Each day it swung less and less. Dragonstooth was getting nearer.

And when one predawn it barely moved at all, he warned Faran to be ready that night and went out into the growing light. He took out his obsidian dagger and drew a pentagram in the snow in front of him: the spiky sigil of Akar, the demon of acute sight, of bright days, of clarity; whose medium was ice and lenses. Presently a pillar of blue light shaped concavely rose up in front of him. He approached it. The outside air was bitterly cold; the area in front of the shimmering lens was beyond cold. Nevertheless he leaned towards it, feeling the moisture on his eyeballs begin to freeze. And then it was as if he flew over the intervening terrain and was at the forest edge, staring in through the fringe of dark boughs of dripping trees, feeling that if he wished he could fly beyond even there, to Lorn itself.

He peered to right and left, each movement of his head causing a dizzying dislocation. There, he had it: the golden gleam of metal. He turned his head even further. The scene rushed past again and then Golon leaned back, astonished, the image dwindling rapidly, yet etched indelibly like an engraving on his mind.

The Man of Bronze, thirty feet high, occupied the whole of his vision. In his forty years he had taught himself to see the currents of magic not visible to normal sight. The air shimmered around the Man of Bronze with an aura smouldering with ancient magic.

He leaned closer to the lens and the scene flew towards him, past the Man of Bronze, into a snow-covered clearing. There he saw the humans. They were involved in some sort of meeting, Jayal Illgill standing at their centre, gesticulating in an agitated, distracted manner. Golon tried another of his arts, attempting to read his lips, but found the young knight's mouth was trembling too much: with the cold, fear or rage he couldn't determine. Presently he, Thalassa and the priest strode away to the Man of Bronze while the villagers busied themselves packing up their camp. They were coming: by nightfall they would be in the Duirin Hills.

It was time for the second summoning. He dismissed Akar back to the stars with a contemptuous click of his fingers. The lens elongated, then seemed to fold into space.

He pulled a glass phial from his side pocket and studied it, marvelling that it had not broken on its many adventures since leaving Thrull. The jar appeared to be empty but months before he had captured inside it the last breath of one of the Flame conspirators in the temple square in Thrull.

First, he as a summoner must take it into his being. He unscrewed the lid, took a deep breath and inhaled, feeling the man's unquiet spirit fighting with his own. He held his breath and rapidly began drawing a pentagram upon a large flat rock that he had cleared of snow in front of his vantage point. His face was puce red, his lungs bursting, as he finished the last of the elaborate sigils. Then, finally, he let out the breath, blowing it onto the chalk pattern on the rock.

Though it was a still day, he fancied he heard the merest susurration of wind, the dead man's spirit circling the surrounding rocks. But it could not escape, for it was bound to the area by the pentagram, its spirit the bait for the demon.

Golon began intoning the sacred text, staring at the eastern horizon where the snowfields met the sky. There he saw a shimmering, as if a portal had opened from this world to the next. The moaning of the circling spirit became more and more intense, and it circled ever faster, knowing its fate.

Ugly storm clouds were massing on the horizon far to the east. They began rolling towards him. Though they were yet far distant, a shiver went up his spine, for he knew what they contained: the snarling mouth and blazing eyes of the demon appearing and disappearing with each forward pulse of the clouds. He calculated their speed: they would reach him before dusk. Anything in their path would be flayed by their winds. There was no way the Lightbringer's party could avoid them. And when they reached the line of hills where the captured spirit waited, the demon would take its sacrifice and every other soul it could find.

CHAPTER FIFTEEN

To Scalprock and Maligar

The sleds had negotiated the last few stunted pines on the edge of the Forest of Lorn. Now they were out on the great snow plain beyond, the line of trees swiftly receding behind them. The dogs were driven on by the teamsters, their fear forgotten for the moment. There were no more hidden obstacles for the twenty miles to the Duirin Hills: no more of the ravines, roots and hummocks that had hampered their progress over the last months, just a flat sheet of virgin snow.

Urthred, riding in the lead sledge, suddenly felt very exposed, a familiar tingle playing up and down his spine. The sinister line of rolling black hills seemed to loom larger and larger by the second. Their enemies, the Worm, were ahead, but as long as the sun shone they were safe.

There were ten sleds in all, three to a sled. Urthred and Thalassa rode in the first with Garadas, the headman; Jayal came in the one behind with Samlack, Garadas's deputy. The ramshackle group of village warriors followed in the other eight, their excited cries mingling with those of the dogs. The sky was blue, as blue as any of them could remember. Despite the dogs' unease and the Man of Bronze's warning, there seemed little threat and they relaxed, joking with one another and joining in impromptu races with excited yells.

The Man of Bronze marched ponderously behind, each

step covering fifteen feet of ground, each impact sending a tremor through the earth that made the snow around him ripple as if it were liquid rather than crystal. But despite his giant strides, he was falling behind. Still Garadas let the dogs have their heads, and as the day progressed he became a smaller and smaller figure behind them.

The afternoon came: they had been travelling since morning, and the dogs were tired and needed feeding; it was time for a halt. The sun was still only halfway through its descent, but now as they slowed there came a chill, and the men's voices fell silent. It was as if the evening had already set in. The sky turned from blue to a livid orange and the snow all around them was shadowed and took on a shade of grey. Garadas muttered under his breath and thrust down the wooden rudder that acted as a brake. It bit into the snow. The sled described a half circle and came to a halt. The other team leaders did likewise, until the line of sleds formed a semicircle like a question mark with its back to the now invisible tree line of Lorn and the Man of Bronze.

All the riders descended, stamping the ground, their cloaks frosted with ice, trying to restart the circulation that had all but stopped during their inactivity of the last few hours. They broke out the sparse provisions that were left to them: the dog feed for the animals and hard tack and wind-dried meat, and a little apple brandy that warmed against the deadening chill for the men.

Behind, the Man of Bronze approached slowly, the dull orange sunlight of the afternoon blazing from his armour. The dogs began yelping excitedly, dancing in their harnesses, but as he neared and his shadow fell over them, they whined and hunkered low to the ground. He halted, apparently unconscious of the humans and animals far below him. His ruby eyes rested on the line of hills in front. Then after a few minutes of contemplation, he lifted the silver hammer in his right fist and pointed at the surrounding plains.

"I have not been here for five thousand years, but it is as if I left but yesterday. This is where I was buried. The final tournament: the sky was full of the roaring dragons of the gods as they prepared for the final tournament. There!" He pointed to a lonely buttress of rock standing up from the frozen plains. "That was where Reh's pavilion was set, and there," he said, pointing to the west, "in the darkness of the gathering night, there was Iss hidden. The tournament of the Duirin Hills. When the gods thought they could settle their mutual hatred with sport. Sport solves no hatred. But there I fought until the spider of the Worm laid me low and here I lay buried under the ground for many years until Marizian came and raised me from the earth." He sighed; his breath sounded once more as if it had been blown from iron bellows.

"Where is the pass through the hills?" Thalassa asked.

The Man of Bronze swivelled slightly. "There," he said, "that is the way Marizian came five thousand years ago." He pointed to a notch between two of the summits of the black hills. "The ancients called those two hills Scalprock and Maligar. Once a silver road ran through the pass, but when the fires of the final battle washed over the lands, it melted and became a river of molten metal. It washed back into the earth whence it came. Let this be a lesson for all the vanity of flesh: that what we bring from the earth will return to it, as do those who live on it.

"Humans once laboured in the mines beneath the hills, bringing metal to the surface; they built the topless towers and the great cities on Shandering Plain: Rolan Ber, Tian Garrec, Illintagel. But the land was hard, even then, in that age you humans call 'golden.' Dark misery and slavery: the only gold was that bought with men's blood. Thousands died. Either the God's magic could not save them, or the gods cared not to save them. I know not which, for though I served under them, I never saw their faces: Reh in his blazing pavilion; Iss, a thing of the earth and shadow that no human eye could see. But their hearts had as little compassion as this," he said, striking his cuirass where his heart would have been with a blow that seemed to echo back from the line of the distant hills.

"I remember that even as we came to the tournament the sky was thick with the black dust of the mines. Even from here I felt the misery of the human slaves that the gods had broken to their wills. Now their slaves lie buried in the very mines that they dug from the earth. And as with all things they abandoned they say a curse lies on all who pass this way."

The giant didn't turn his head to the hills. "I have lived ten thousand years. You may think you have seen evil things, that you have suffered. But though a metal heart only beats within me, and I shed tears of oil not salt, I have seen a thousand wrongs, have myself lain forgotten buried beneath the earth for five thousand years. What torture was that, when my brain lived, but my limbs had perished?"

He turned now and looked down upon the party, his bronze helm a hazy gleam, only the alien red light of his eyes visible.

Not one of them dared offer a reply. The villagers cowered, as terrified of this creature from the past as perhaps their ancestors had been of the pitiless gods themselves.

Urthred returned his stare: he felt the truth of his words. Once he had been a priest, but now, though he was still a priest in name, he wasn't sure whether he was in his heart. He'd seen the Books of *Worm* and *Light* reduced to dust in Marizian's tomb. The only record that humankind had of the gods. What were these creatures that man had worshipped? Who through their vanity had nearly destroyed the world in that battle ten thousand years ago?

Yet there had to be some core of truth in the holy scriptures: didn't they speak of the Lightbringer? And was she not divine, as they prophesied? Had not the Man of Bronze himself come to her aid? As with all things since the age of the gods passed and their miraculous works with them, only belief remained; there were no proofs.

So Urthred might not believe in the literal truth of the scriptures, or even that the sun was anything more than a source of light and heat, but he believed in Thalassa. She was part of the prophecy, part of the shifting patterns hidden in the stars that the gods had decreed would rule the fates of men. A pattern obscured now in the cryptic words of long-destroyed scriptures and the dust clouds of Shandering Plain.

But his father had warned him: a sacrifice was required if

the sun was to be restored and the world saved from darkness. She was that sacrifice.

He turned to her: now he thanked the stars that his emotions were concealed, albeit by a mask so cruel that even the gods would have approved its visage, for he was certain that his face at that moment would have revealed his sudden anguish at the thought of losing her.

"Let's go on," he muttered hoarsely. He hadn't eaten or taken water like the others; it would have choked him if he had. He was used to the day's asperities, he was a priest in name only, cursed by the God he had once worshipped.

It was the headman who broke the quiet that had settled, for even the dogs were cowed by the bass thunder in the Talos' voice. "Back to the sledges," he said in a tremulous voice. "Let's get over those hills before dark."

"Vanity," said the Man of Bronze. One word, but uttered with such menace that the men remounting their sleds stopped in midstride. The giant moved his head from left to right with a powerful grinding of gears and metal. "You have not listened. How many thousands have stood where you stand, over five thousand years? Do you think you will live when they did not? Dust: they have no graves, but fell here in the plains or in the forest. Their bones have long gone. For the sake of the Lightbringer who I have sworn to protect and for yourselves, turn back to Lorn. There is no safe way to Iskiard."

Thalassa squinted at the hills. Her voice was diamond bright, untroubled by the titan's words. "You know there is no turning back. We are near Iskiard."

"Aye," he replied slowly. "It is your destiny. But what kind of a destiny is certain death? Remember how Marizian fled from there after the gods destroyed themselves. I saw his face: his terror at what he had discovered in that place. Terror you had best take note of, because of all the humans I ever saw, he was the master of the greatest magic, of which yours is but a pale shadow."

"Our fate is settled now," Urthred said, shrugging off the chill on his spine. "Mount up!"

"Then go with the wind," the Man of Bronze said, pointing his hammer to the east. As one they turned. A line of clouds as dark as a raven's wing was hurrying over the horizon, filling the sky. "A storm is coming," he said, "and very fast."

"We have endured storms," Garadas said, but with no conviction as the clouds bubbled and fought one another, cumulus piled on cumulus, ever higher, filling the sky with purple and black thunderheads.

"Not a storm as this, for within it is a demon's heart, driving you on into Faran's trap."

Urthred turned back to the distant line of forest: already its edge was but a blur on the horizon, nearly lost in the darkness of afternoon and the shadow of the approaching clouds that now reared their heads high above them like dark giants. It was too late to return—now their only refuge was in the gloomy hills in front. They would never reach them before the storm broke. There came a moan of wind over the snow, which sent crystals spiralling up into the air.

"Hurry—you may still have time to pass the hills by nightfall," the Man of Bronze commanded. "I am slower than you. I will follow."

"Then Reh go with you, we will see you on the far side," Urthred called over the mounting roar of the wind, but with the growing force of the tempest he barely heard the words himself. This storm was no natural phenomenon.

"I will find you," the Talos answered. Already, twisting white snakes of a ground blizzard could be seen racing towards them from the cast. Now all was frantic activity as everyone leapt back onto the sleds and the dog masters whipped their teams into action. The dogs needed little encouragement, frightened by the sound of the wind. They strained against the harnesses and the heavily laden sleds started inching over the ground.

Soon they were racing north again, the preliminary gusts of the storm making the sledges dance sideways with their force. Urthred looked behind, but the Man of Bronze was already lost to sight in the curtains of snow. The other sleds appeared and disappeared intermittently with each squall. In the interlude between the blasts, the dim outline of the summits of the hills could be seen ahead.

To the west, the sun shone like a red haze through the snow. How many minutes were left before the shadows of the hills fell across the pass? The teamsters needed no encouragement, whipping the dogs into a fervour, the sledges flying through the blizzard, gaining a little on the storm. As they entered the lee of the hills the wind abated slightly and they saw ahead an icy, boulder-strewn glacis leading up to the pass between the two peaks.

The shadows fell long over the pass: they began to ascend, weaving between the boulders, the sleds bunching up, their momentum taking them forward for a little while, but then the dogs began struggling for purchase on the ice, their paws slipping back as often as they made a step forward. Garadas jumped down and everyone else followed suit, spears or bows at the ready. Jayal drew Dragonstooth and the darkness was cut through by its magical light: he held it in front of him, and a corridor of radiance raced up the boulder-strewn gully. He nodded at the priest—he and Urthred would go first.

Then the storm caught up with them again, snatching at them as if it were an animate being pushing them forward towards the pass. It flayed at their bodies, ice particles cut into their flesh through their several layers of clothes. Garadas shouted, his scream lost in the noise of the wind, and they closed up even further, hauling the sledges and their reluctant teams up the slope, the dogs worrying at their harnesses as they felt the hidden magic in the air.

Behind was the demon; in front the undead. They were caught in the jaws of a trap.

CHAPTER SIXTEEN

The Battle of the
Black Mines

The blizzard drove down into their faces from the pass, each gust of wind sending a snaking ice serpent hissing over the smooth ice slope. They had wrapped their cloaks around their heads for protection, leaving only their eyes exposed. As yet the epicentre of the storm had not caught them, but the ice stung every particle of exposed flesh and the winds threatened to tear them from their feet. The going was very rough with the sleds continuously jamming on hidden, snow-covered rocks.

"Leave the sleds," Garadas shouted, his voice slightly choked. "Take as much of the supplies as you can." The villagers glanced at one another. There was no way back without the sleds that had brought them all the way from Ravenspur. But Garadas gestured angrily. "We won't get through if we have to drag them with us," he shouted.

Reluctantly the villagers did as they were bidden, the sleds sliding back down the glassy slope up which they had so painstakingly dragged them.

They continued upwards, until their advance slowed and then stopped altogether as they peered vainly ahead through the curtain of snow. The wind howled bleakly, ululating around the fractured rock formations. Urthred risked a glance back into the teeth of the storm, the wind shrieking against the face of his mask. The sky was black with thunderheads, not a glimmer of light.

Another shrieking blast of wind came, driving some of the villagers sideways. The storm was mounting in strength. They would have to go on if they were to survive.

"Release the dogs," Garadas ordered, "we will need our hands to fight. Let them find their own way." He stopped and with a ruffle of its fur released his own. "Go!" he screamed. The dog hesitated for a second. It was an aggressive husky, albino in colour, its gums pulled back, yellow teeth exposed, its ears flat against its head. Its hackles had risen. It stalked forward, its growl audible over the wind.

Jayal turned to Urthred. "Are you ready?" he shouted. Urthred nodded, clenching his fists, feeling the fire burning in his veins. Fighting the wind, they led the Godans into the pass under Scalprock and Maligar.

They marched grimly upwards until the ground flattened out. They had reached the saddle of the pass.

Where were the vampires? Urthred stopped and quartered the gloom. Jayal stepped forward once more, his boots churning the virgin snow in front. Two of the villagers followed.

Suddenly the snow-covered ground in front gave way with a roar and Jayal and the two villagers fell into the darkness of the pit concealed beneath. Then it seemed that the entire flat area of the saddle around them began to cave in, to the left and right, before and behind. Several of those who had been standing on solid ground a moment before suddenly fell as if pulled downwards by strings; some of the dogs fell with them.

But miraculously Urthred still stood on solid ground. He caught hold of Thalassa as there was another roar of falling rock and the ground gave way right in front of them. A hand followed by a head, its lips pulled back in a snarl, appeared from the darkness and dirt—a vampire. The creature began to haul itself out of the freshly opened pit. Urthred lashed out with his boot and sent it crashing backwards into the hole. Another of the undead levered itself out of a pit to their left. He was too late to stop this one. The vampire dived forward, its fangs exposed. Urthred desperately pulled Thalassa from its path; it stumbled past and one of the villagers smashed it to the ground with an axe.

He saw movement on the slopes under Scalprock and an advancing tide of figures pouring from shafts hitherto concealed in the hillsides. For a moment he stood paralysed; not even in Thrull had he seen so many.

A scream from one of the pits, as a villager was pulled down. More vampires were climbing out of them. Jayal was still buried in the hole in front of him; for the moment the light of Dragonstooth was extinguished.

Flames flared from the tips of Urthred's gloves as he stretched them up to the dark heavens. Then he pointed abruptly down and to the left and a wall of rolling flame suddenly ignited in front of him with a dull thud. He swept his arm forward, sending it rolling into the close-pressed ranks of the vampires. The Wall of Fire. They saw it coming, but ran on towards it. The flame sizzled over the snow, rolling into the first rank, and the undead's desiccated bodies ignited, melting like wax.

Urthred watched, almost hypnotised by the strange beauty of the flames, as they turned from orange to purple, then back to gold. For a moment he had forgotten his own danger; then a claw raked down his back. He whirled round. His vision was suddenly filled with the face of a vampire. He smelt its putrid breath, then fangs splintered off his mask. He smashed it across the jaw with the flensing knife that once more sprang from his glove. The creature's head rolled away, still snapping, leaving its body teetering upright. Urthred toppled the body into one of the pits.

The surviving vampires had been blinded initially by the sudden light of Urthred's first spell, but now they stumbled on again fearlessly through the guttering flames. Melees had broken out over the small battlefield, villagers struggling with the undead, one or two of the dogs snapping at the creatures' legs. Some of the villagers who had fallen into the pits were scrambling out, but there were pitifully few left. Some were caught in a deadly tug-of-war as the undead tried to drag them back into the pits by their legs while their friends struggled to lift them out by their shoulders.

Now the line of vampires reached the outermost pits and fell on the villagers trying to help their friends. Screams and shouts intermingled with the frantic howling of the dogs, as the villagers attempted to bring their weapons into play. But their assailants were immune to pain, and though spears and axes made terrible wounds in the unarmed creatures, those in the front rank were borne down by the mass of bodies.

Urthred ran forward, more flames exploding from his gloves. A group of four vampires crouching over a prostrate body caught light, their bodies twisting and pirouetting as the flames consumed them. All this time the roar of the wind had got louder and louder—the epicentre of the storm was getting closer. The spinning column of a tornado connected heaven and earth. Out of the corner of his eye he saw some of the undead being whipped off their feet and carried into the sky.

Suddenly there was light. Jayal stood at the edge of the pit into which he had fallen, Dragonstooth blazing. He had cut down all the undead around him. He was surrounded by a circle of other pits that overlapped, forming a ditch that offered him some protection from another wave of vampires descending Scalprock. They threw themselves forward, but hesitated on its brink. Three of them tried to leap the intervening space and Jayal swung the sword in a wide arc. The coppery blade scythed through all of them as if they were grass, their upper torsos flying from their trunks. More flung themselves forward, and once more the sword flashed in a scintillating circle. One or two vaulted the drop and grasped Jayal's cloak, but the sword struck, and their bodies toppled away, the creatures' arms still gripping the cloak. Jayal shrugged free of the garment. Urthred and Thalassa ran to him, leaping across the gap, as another wave of their enemies came. Urthred was back to back with Jayal, both striking to left and right until no more vampires stood before them. They called to the surviving villagers to rally around them. Those who could broke off from their own melees and retreated to them.

A dozen of the twenty Godans was all that was left. Once

more the vampires surged forward towards them, once more they were completely surrounded, the ditch their only protection. At the edge of Dragonstooth's light they saw the funnel of the centre of the storm, now only a few yards to their south, sucking everything, fallen bodies, snow and rock, into its maw. Nothing could survive in its epicentre.

The vampires, seeing that they might be denied their prey by the tornado, pushed forward again. Jayal flung the blade forward and instantly there was a crack like thunder and a huge explosion in their midst.

The explosion: light, but no light. A blast of wind, even stronger than the icy tempest to the south. A scattering of pebbles and body parts flew past, two more of the villagers fell, a rock smashed into the side of Urthred's mask, sending him to his knees. He shook his head, trying to clear the stars dancing in front of his vision. Though a hole had been blown in the vampires' line by the explosion, the rest of the ring was still intact. Heedless of their terrible casualties they pushed forward again, the back ranks clambering over the bodies of their peers who had fallen into the pits, filling them almost to the brim with struggling life. In a few more seconds, the villagers would be overrun.

Urthred threw up his hands. No Wall of Fire this time; the lava flow fell limply a few feet in front. His energy was nearly spent, but the pools of smouldering magma spread over the ground, sending a steam of evaporated snow before them. Some of the undead spun round as the superheated steam overwhelmed them, others behind came to a halt, but those coming from the other side were now clambering over the bodies in the pits. Jayal swung Dragonstooth to left and right, scything them down as they advanced. One leapt forward, ducking the shimmering blade, and came running at Urthred. He swayed out of its path, using its momentum to push it to the ground where Jayal administered a coup de grace.

Once more they had cleared the small circle in which they were trapped—but they were still completely surrounded by the snarling host, rank upon rank of them, it seemed a hundred deep, their hands reaching out to them, nearly touching them across the pits, only the flashing weapons of the survivors keeping them at bay.

They drew back into an even tighter circle. Thalassa stood in the middle, her eyes closed, her brows furrowed, her body swaying backwards and forward as if in a trance, her arms raised to the sky.

Suddenly the noise of the storm ebbed away, the blizzard ceased on the instant, the sky turned white, a white that transformed the snow on the ground into a blazing glowing sheet. A star had appeared in the sky overhead, cutting through the storm clouds, burning with a phosphorescent light. It fell slowly towards the earth.

Thalassa, her white robe glowing like beaten silver, stood with her arms outstretched as if to gather the light. Around them the vampires fled like cockroaches caught in a sudden light, blinded by the star, some fighting with each other in their panic to get away.

Urthred looked to the south down the ravine up which they had struggled. The snow and tornado had disappeared. He saw in the harsh light a distant gleam of metal over the plains: the Talos, a mile away. The titan's arm was upstretched to the heavens and the falling star. He strode forward, sending geysers of snow before him.

Around them the undead had begun to slink away, emitting low, whimpering cries. The way to the north was suddenly clear again, but the star was falling by the moment, and its light would not last long.

Garadas and a few others were still alive. One or two more of the villagers crawled out of the pits; they were badly scratched, but otherwise unharmed.

"Quickly!" Urthred yelled, gesturing to the north.

He took hold of one of Thalassa's hands and they vaulted over the bodies ringing their position. A hand reached up and clutched his ankle but he kicked it free. They moved forward, as the light fell lower and lower until it was nearly behind the summits of the pass—the wind began to moan and then to howl as the light died.

CHAPTER SEVENTEEN

A Thousand Voices

.

Faran's mind was full of a thousand voices—the thousand voices of the undead. They were part of his mind, one organism. It had never been like this before, never had he fathered more than one or two in a monthly cycle, but now by his own hands he had reared all these and each spoke to him, their Dominant, and as never before he felt his mind was theirs; by thought alone he bade them come and go.

He turned to Golon. "It will soon be time for your spell, sorcerer," he said.

Golon stared at where he had placed the rune on the rock buttress under Maligar: they had to destroy the Man of Bronze.

"I will throw the mountain down upon the Talos's head and the coils of the Worm will drag him to the earth's core where Iss forever dwells."

"Let it be," Faran replied almost absently; he had other matters on his mind. Thalassa's party would be immediately below this vantage point by now. He must save her before his minions got to her. He exited the shaft leading out of the Black Mines, a hundred of the strongest vampires at his back, the others hidden in the subsidiary shafts below had run out when the humans had first tumbled into the hidden pits.

His brow furrowed in intense concentration as he stared

downwards calling out to his creatures. The clouds and snow driven by the storm obscured his view, but like a puppeteer—though one with a thousand marionettes—he pushed some forward and pulled others back until the circle was tight around Thalassa's party. The twisting centre of the storm was very near now, just to the south, sucking up all matter into its maw; the humans were exactly where he wanted them.

He descended the slope, nearing the battle. He screwed up his eyes against the lacerating wind. He could now see the melee, the tiny number of humans completely swamped by the undead. He sought for her and in a second found her. She stood next to the masked priest, her white cloak instantly recognisable.

The priest's gloves blossomed fire as he watched, sending it rolling into the undead that surrounded them. Faran's mind registered their death screams as the flame seared them, though he heard no sound over the howling wind. But the priest's magic would be exhausted soon. Sorcery had only a limited period.

Thalassa: even at that distance in the darkness, through the melee, he saw her face as clear as if it were day. Two hundred years he had looked on the faces of the Brethren and the Sisterhood of the Dead in Life. A month before he had seen the shadow of vampirism on her, but now it was gone. She was cured, but how? No magic he was aware of could reverse the effect of the vampire's bite. Yet she was free of the infection that had no cure.

And he rejoiced—there was a slight uplift in his heart's lethargic beat. She was not the blood slave of another of the undead. She might still be his: by mesmerism, by charm—or by the bite, whichever it had to be: she would be his.

Even if she was the one the scriptures called the Lightbringer, the enemy of his God, she would not die, but live to be with him.

He called to the thousand undead below, ordering them to spare her, not to touch her.

Instantly there came a feeling of dislocation as if his body had flown through unlimited space in a millisecond to where his soul was imprisoned in Iss' Palace of Grey. And there he saw it falling from its high place, falling and falling from where it had rested these last two hundred years amongst the other souls of the Dark God's elect. Now the God cast it down from its heights: Iss was angered. What he did was heresy: the Lightbringer must be destroyed. What would be his punishment? What would the God do to his mortal shell? Would his skin give birth to a million maggots, or the earth open and swallow him, suck him down to the gates of Hel?

He took another breath, his eyes going to the storm-streaked sky, the wild clouds driving from the east, but no punishment came. Still he lived this second life, this Life in Death. And again he called her name as the ring of vampires tightened on her, telling them, though she was the Light-bringer, to spare her.

He found he was running forward again, hurrying down the steep slope towards the battle, mindless of any fall, any injury to his nerveless body.

Then an explosion rent the darkness, and he tumbled over, the rocks ripping at his leather armour as he rolled down the slope. Over and over, blow after blow from stones and boulders. Then finally be came to rest.

His eyes remained tightly shut for through their heavy lids he saw the blinding light in the sky. On his retinas, a stamped image: Thalassa holding up her hands, summoning this blinding star. A light brighter than the sun. He began to crawl back towards the cave entrance, feeling blindly with his hands. Where was Golon?

The thousand voices of the undead that had filled his head with a kind of white noise were now one elongated scream. He felt them like a tide fleeing back to the mine shafts. Then, at last, Golon's voice. "I'm here, lord," he shouted above the sound of the wind and the howling of the vampires. The sorcerer's hand clasped his arm and pulled him to his feet. A vampire ran blindly into him. He staggered, pushing the creature to one side.

Golon led him back up the slope, his vision clearing

slowly. Now that they were back in the first chamber of the mines, the voices of the dead came back into his mind. They were scattered: he must rally them. He opened his eyes. He wasn't blind. Golon's pale face was beginning to emerge out of the darkness on his retinas.

"Where are they?" he growled, not daring to look out at the scene.

"They're over the pass, lord," Golon answered. "They're heading towards the wharf."

Faran cursed. Through the shadow over his eyes, he saw the Dead in Life cowered in the darkness of the mines, hiding from the light. He rose groggily and strode into their midst, striking out at them in a mad rage, until he'd driven them to their feet and into the warren of tunnels that led to the lakeshore. He turned to Golon.

"I'm going after them. Remember—the Man of Bronze must be destroyed," he growled.

The sorcerer nodded. Faran left him at the mine entrance and followed in the wake of the undead.

CHAPTER EIGHTEEN

The Windhover

In the falling light of the star, Thalassa and the others reached the gully leading down the northern flank of the Duirin Hills. Above them they saw a large cave mouth under Scalprock. As soon as the light died, they had no doubt more vampires would appear from its shadows.

Their feet slipped as they hurried down the steeply descending sheet of ice leading to the north. A thousand feet below they saw the vast ice lake, its smooth surface blazing like a pane of glass in the light of the falling star. Three pyramids stood on the shore below, surrounded by ruined walls. Wharves led out onto the lake where three ships were moored on the ice.

Suddenly there was another blast of wind: the storm was cresting the pass and coming after them. A volley of icy darts cracked into Urthred's mask. The light in the sky was falling lower and lower, and was almost hidden by the shoulder of Maligar.

Thalassa tugged at his sleeve and pointed at the frozen ships. He followed the direction of her hand, unsure of what she intended. She was already heading down the steep pathway towards the first of the covered causeways that led to the wharves. The rest of the party followed hard on her heels, stumbling over the boulders.

They reached the first of the walls: there was a breach in it where it had collapsed, revealing a covered passageway beyond, leading downwards. They climbed over the fallen stones into the sheltering darkness. They had no light: their torches had been lost on the sleds but Thalassa clenched shut her eyes, concentrating as she had done under Ravenspur; a strange nimbus of green light surrounded her as if growing from within her. Then she opened her eyes and snapped her fingers, and a green ball of light fizzled into being in front of her, hovering in the air. It showed broad steps leading towards the lake. They had made it to shelter just in time, for at that moment the pursuing storm struck the outside walls, the hail drumming against the stone like thunder.

They had time to get their breath. Somehow a dozen of the Godans had lived; each was pale, bearing scratches and cuts from the recent battle. Of all the sled teams, only Garadas's dog remained, its fur soaked and bedraggled, its legs trembling with the cold.

Through the breach in the wall they could see the light waning. They couldn't wait for the Man of Bronze: the vampires would be after them soon. They hurried down the sloping causeway, the steepness of the steps easing, until the floor levelled out altogether and they entered the domed chamber that Golon had discovered a few days before. A circular opening at its top admitted the light of the Talos' flare.

A vast marble slab, thirty foot long and twenty wide, lay at its centre, tilting towards the north. It would have held the Man of Bronze, maybe even a god, if this had been its function. A golden sun symbol was carved at its centre. Beyond, directly in front of the slab, through an entranceway they saw the ice-covered wharf some fifty feet wide and a hundred yards long stretching out into the lake. A ship, ghostly white in the light of the falling star, lay at its end.

Seeing it, one of the villagers ran forward into the entranceway. There was a sizzle of white light when he reached the threshold, his body was silhouetted for a millisecond, then he was gone, vaporised.

The others stopped, stunned at the setback.

"More magic," Urthred muttered. He looked about him quickly. He was sure the vampires would appear any second down the corridor. There must be a way out. The slab looked like a mortuary block. He inspected the single sun etched at its centre. Realisation dawned—this was where the dead gods would have been brought after Shandering Plain. This was where they would have been laid after the battle. The shafts leading to the barges of Reh and Iss had never been used; were still protected by the magical warding that the ancient priests had set there against intruders.

He heard distant footfalls echoing down the passageway from which they had come. The vampires. He hauled himself up onto the plinth and ran to the centre of the slab. He saw an upraised section of stone right at the centre of the delicate sun pattern. A button of sorts, activated when a body was placed upon it. He pressed down, feeling resistance. The gods had been titans, of greater mass than even the Man of Bronze. More force was required. He raised his right hand behind his head and smashed down with all the force of the glove. The impact jarred up his arm, but something had given way. The panel sank into the top of the slab.

Instantly the world seemed to slide away beneath his feet as the block started moving downhill towards the entrance, scattering the rest of the party. Faster and faster, under the doorway where the villager had died. There was a flash of energy as the warding dispelled and then he was out into the icy night. The block ran on grooves along the quay, before grinding slowly to rest directly in front of the ship.

The others had run out behind him, skidding to a halt in front of the ship. They saw in the dying light of the star that it was made not of wood but of metal, its spars and rigging were covered by dripping stalactites, its furled sails and its hull encased in a thick layer of ice. A gangplank led upwards to its companion rail. Urthred stared down and saw that the keel of the ship was not in fact frozen in the ice, but held up by runners on stanchions, much like those on the dog sleds.

He turned in the direction of the black cloud bearing down on them from Maligar. The wind howled past in streaming serpent tails of ice. The light in the sky finally fell behind the hill and was extinguished. The landscape went pitch-black save for the light of the glowing blade of Dragonstooth.

"Use your fire, free the rigging from the ice," Thalassa called. Before he could answer, she turned from him. The horizon above the hills was now totally black, save where, like a skeletal finger, the white line of the tornado pointed towards the earth. Then it struck the hillside: ice flew like arrow points past them. Men screamed as the shards found the unprotected flesh of their faces. All turned their backs except Urthred and Thalassa. He was protected by his mask, she by nothing. Instead of turning away, she spread her cloak wide. The finger of the twister rode over the roof of the mausoleum, touched down in a column of spinning snow and then raced down the quay straight towards her. She waited for the tornado, unflinching, as it reached her. Urthred could not take his eyes off her, even as icy arrow heads flew through the slits of his mask, and he felt blood pooling in them. He saw the back of Thalassa's cloak shredded by barbs of ice as the twister spun right onto her.

But then the twister was gone and she was left as if she were a statue, her wandlike figure standing where nothing could have stood a moment before. The villagers picked themselves up off the frozen quay where they had thrown themselves. The howling of the wind was gone, as if all the fearful tumult had been absorbed into Thalassa's body.

Then she staggered as if she had taken a blow to her chest, and sank to her knees, folding her cloak around her. Urthred stepped towards her, then stopped dead in horror: inside the folds of the cloak it was as if a fury struggled to get out. The white yak's wool bulged and heaved as if from murderous punches from within, her knuckles were tight on the folds of the cloak, her, face contorted in agony. He dragged her back towards the gangplank of the *Windhover*.

"Quickly," she gasped from between clenched lips, "free the ship!"

He looked from her back to the building behind them.

The rampway was choked by a hedge of bodies swathed in mouldering winding sheets. The vampires halted when the twister had struck, but now they swarmed forward. He could hear their hoarse yells in the sudden silence after the wind died.

He turned back to the ship and lifted his hands, seeking for the unfamiliar spell. His energy, drained by the battle under Scalprock, was returning: there was fire in his veins again. Now was the time for another spell. Spirits: the summoning from the air of mythical beings sacred to Reh, like the fire dragon he had summoned in the cave all those years before. But this was a lesser, more unfamiliar summoning, one that a pyromancer seldom sought.

He waved his hands as if coaxing a pot to rise on a wheel, and in the spaces between them a cloud of light appeared, within which, like a miniature aurora borealis, winged fiery spirits shimmered in the cloud of light. Then, at a small gesture from him, the creatures broke free of the cone of light and separated into a thousand glittering stars borne upwards by faery wings; they flew towards the ship, settling on every part of the masts and rigging and the outriggers on the keel, so it seemed it had been glazed with a molten, golden light.

The ice coating the ship vaporised in steam, meltwater fell like rain from the rigging. The hull of the ship creaked and groaned as the ancient glacial grip upon it was slowly eased. Rigging lines suddenly swung free; the sails shook and then fell from the spars, still perfectly preserved. A small gust of wind and they flapped and the ship moved sideways, sliding on the ice, bucking against its mooring lines, shaking more moisture from the thawed hawsers. The *Windhover* was free.

A warning shout came from a villager behind. The vampires were edging forward; cautiously, wary of the glowing light on the ship, inching towards the line that Jayal and Garadas and the other survivors had formed across the wharf.

Then with a strangled cry the vampires charged forward, falling upon them: figures lurched and swayed in the desperate struggle, the growls of the undead and the screams of the villagers intermingling.

Three more men were borne down. Without Jayal and Dragonstooth the others would have broken, but he stood firm at the centre of the line, thrusting and cutting like a demon. Eventually, though even he was forced back, Garadas and the others managed to rescue two of the wounded men: the other was lost in the scrum that followed.

Urthred threw himself into the melee, flailing at the snapping faces in front with his gloves. Then Garadas called out and they began to retreat slowly towards the gangway of the ship. Some of the undead were impaled on the villagers' spears, but still they struggled forward, wrenching the spearsmen from side to side with the embedded haft of the weapon. One villager who refused to let go of his weapon was pulled off his feet and over the side of the wharf, falling with a scream to the ice thirty feet below. Several vampires leapt down on him, careless of their bones breaking like so many rotten twigs as they struggled with each other, fighting to reach the dying man's neck and his blood.

Two of the villagers had retreated up the companionway and nocked arrows onto their bows. Now they fired and fired again: arrows struck into the vampires, like hammer blows on meat, and those in the front rank were quilled like porcupines, but they were undeterred, pushing the Godans back, grabbing at their thrusting spears, ripping some away, breaking others in half—the undefended villagers fell back, beating away the snapping teeth with their bare hands.

Urthred saw that when the line broke, that would be the end. He turned back to the ship: another gust blew it away from the wharf, the companionway releasing a shower of melted water.

They had now been pushed back to where he had left Thalassa. She struggled to her feet, her white cloak clutched tightly about her midriff, her face very pale as she struggled with the imprisoned energies in her cloak. Then she threw her arms out and there came an explosion of wind, the twister bursting it seemed from the centre of her body, arrowing down the quay, tearing over the heads of the villagers into the vampires, driving them back as if by a powerful hose of water: many were forced off the side of the quay, others rolled over and over backwards towards the pyramid, scrabbling for purchase.

Now Thalassa made a pulling gesture and the wind that had become a diminishing howl came screaming back upon their party. Urthred and the villagers ducked as the gale caught the rigging of the *Windhover*. The sails filled with a bang, the rigging tightened, the ship strained at her hawsers. The villagers retreated, blundering up the companionway, dragging their wounded friends with them. Jayal and Urthred were left guarding their rear, but for the moment, the vampires were only pulling themselves back to their feet.

"Cut the ropes!" Urthred yelled. Jayal nodded, running to the bow of the ship, leaving Urthred at the stern.

Urthred released his flensing knife from his glove and with one mighty blow slashed down at the iron-tight ropes: the first gave with a deafening explosion, strands of the fossilized hemp flying past his mask like shot from a sling. He hurried forward to the second: that too was cut with one blow. He turned and saw that Jayal had already cut the two lines at the bow and had flung himself into the ship's bowsprit rigging. Then there was a shriek as the runners freed themselves from the ice, and a dark gap began opening between the wharf and the ship: the *Windhover* was beginning to slide forward alarmingly quickly over the ice. The companionway slipped into the rapidly opening gap and smashed onto the surface of the frozen lake.

The vampires made a final despairing rush up the wharf. The first of them was nearly on Urthred; the gap between him and the ship was now already six feet, a dark thirty-foot chasm to the ice below. He turned, and his sandals struggling for purchase, took a running jump. He was airborne— something plucked the cloak from his back: one of the vampires had got a claw to him, then he fell into the mizzen mast chains, his gloves gouging great tears out of the rope and hull underneath as he slid down towards the ice. He clung on as the ship gained momentum, the razor-sharp outriggers and the ice just below his dangling feet. Now hands reached down and hauled him up the gunwales of the ship; he rolled over the deck, then pushed himself up.

Some of the vampires had also made despairing dives. Many of them had plunged to the ice and joined the ones who had already fallen: they crawled on the surface like broken insects.

But as Urthred looked, a vampire clambered aboard over the stern rail. Jayal was onto it in a flash, Dragonstooth sweeping around again, the decapitated creature joining its fellows on the ice.

The shoreline was receding fast, the hiss of the runners almost deafening, the wind thrumming in the rigging as the boat gathered speed, faster and faster over the ice. All that was visible behind was the black outlines of the pyramids on the shore and the hills silhouetted by the moon and the shining surface of the ice lake. There was no sign of the Man of Bronze.

Urthred looked at his companions: Thalassa, Jayal and nine villagers had survived, though two of the Godans were badly wounded.

"We have to stop, we can't leave the Man of Bronze," he shouted urgently at Thalassa.

She seemed to have been in a trance, from which his voice awoke her. She dropped her arms and on the instant the wind died away. The ship glided on briefly, its runners hissing over the ice, but then began to slow. Now there was total silence. Thalassa's face was screwed up in concentration as she looked back towards the pass: she was seeking the Talos, trying to hear his voice once more.

"He is coming . . ." she said. For a brief second they saw a distant gleam of metal as the Man of Bronze reached the top of the now distant pass. Then there was a violent flash of light right next to him and a second later a sky-splitting roar. The noise rolled on and on and over the ice. Thalassa groaned and staggered back, her hands held to her ears. Urthred had to reach out to stop her from falling to the deck.

"What is it?" he asked urgently, turning to the noise of the explosion.

She shook her head. "Rocks and earth, falling," she whispered.

He glanced back at the pass—something strange was happening, the hilltops seemed to shake. Then it was as if the top of Maligar peeled away, ripped away by an unseen hand. The sliding ruin of its slope fell into the narrow gorge where they had seen the Man of Bronze—there came a brief flash of flame, then nothing.

The shock wave from the landslide rolled on—there came a tremor through the ice, like a small wave that when it reached them made them all stagger slightly, and then a groan as the frozen water began to crack. Dark fissures sped out like flying hands from the shoreline: one ran unerringly towards them like a remorseless shadow, passing right under their stern. The ship lurched terrifyingly and the men cried out. The gap in the ice widened: soon the outriggers would fall through. Would the ship sink? Probably, or else it would capsize. Their fate would be the same in the icy waters.

"Quickly!" Urthred shouted to Thalassa.

She had been staring at the south, but once more she quickly raised her arms, her lips mouthing something quietly, and there came the whistle of wind again over the ice. The sails cracked and filled once more, and the ship began to pick up momentum. It seemed that it moved too slowly, for the crack in the ice was widening every second, the portside outriggers beginning to slide into it. But then the *Windhover* shuddered and began to pull away from the broken ice and accelerated. Now they had to cling on to the halyards as the ship slammed from side to side. Its runners hit small hummocks and mounds on the surface.

Urthred and Thalassa ran to the stern. The cracked ice was far behind them. Nothing was now visible of Maligar or the Man of Bronze.

"He's dead," she whispered.

"Maybe not," he answered. "He survived under the desert sands for five thousand years before Marizian came."

But inside his heart was empty. Even if the Talos had survived, he was rapidly being left far behind them. They had lost one of Marizian's artefacts, the Lightbringer's guardian. One, Dragonstooth, remained in their hands. The other, the Rod of the Shadows, had fallen to the Doppelgänger. Iskiard with all its dangers lay ahead, and Faran was not far behind.

The *Windhover* bore them north, flying ever onwards, over the ice.

CHAPTER NINETEEN

Spindel

Faran emerged from a mine shaft on the lower slopes of Scalprock—far in the distance he saw the first vampires flooding down towards the lake and the ship waiting by the first pyramid. He saw the humans emerge on the ice-covered wharf, and registered the sudden dying of the wind, and how the ship began to shift coltishly on its mooring, eager to be free of its hawsers. Then the mighty wind reached him on his lofty vantage point. His men fell back, and the ship began sliding away over the ice. Just as in Thrull, Urthred and Thalassa had escaped him again. With each foot the ship travelled over the ice the emptiness inside him grew.

Then over the shoulder of the pass high above him he heard the thunder of explosions and landslides. He had forgotten about the Man of Bronze. Some of the vampires ran down the slope in front of him, then he saw what they fled: the head of the monster rose like an apparition over the dark skyline. His mallet was raised. The slope and its running figures were suddenly crisscrossed by the twin red beams of his eyes. Then the mallet fell and a bolt of light hurtled into the undead. Fragments of stone and leathery parts showered Faran in his hiding place. The slope was wiped clean.

The ground shook as the titan came closer. Faran shrank

further back into the mine shaft. Why did Golon wait? He stared up at the constellations, at where Elgol, the demon's star, shone in the night sky like a red gem. Then the star's red centre seemed to explode and a comet shot from its surface; at first no more than a pinprick in the wider dimension of black space, it grew and grew to a mote, then a ball that suddenly filled the sky. There came a blinding flash on the slope of Maligar where Golon had fixed the rune. The earth began to shake, even harder than it had before. Faran was cast onto the floor of the shaft, dust raining down from its ceiling. Outside, it was as if the whole of Scalprock had turned from rock to jelly, its sides shaking, the slopes turned to liquid rivers of stone.

The titan turned his head towards the sound to his right as the whole of Maligar bulged out towards him. He raised his arms as the first boulders reached him like a giant wave, bearing him backwards. He toppled, engulfed by the avalanche of rocks. The rock slide continued for another few seconds, dust and snow boiling up into the air so that Faran's view was temporarily obscured. When it cleared, the hill opposite had disappeared, and the saddle filled with smoking rubble. There was no sign of the Man of Bronze.

Faran staggered out of the shaft and looked down to the lake: the Lightbringer's ship was a fast-disappearing dot. A horde of vampires had got down onto the ice surface and had set off in futile pursuit but the aftershock of the explosion had caught them a hundred yards out. Within seconds the lake had become a black and white mosaic of ice fragments and dark water. The vampires were sucked down, sinking like stones.

He heard a cry and looked upwards—there was Golon half running down the shifting scree slope, shaking his head like a madman, covered in dust. His arm was upraised as if still casting the spell.

As he stumbled past him, Faran seized the sorcerer's arm and wrenched it down. Only then did the man seem to recover his consciousness, though his eyes were still glazed. The spell was long exhausted but the landslides continued:

rivers of stone rushed past to left and right. More movement behind them and a large group of the undead emerged from the dust of the shaft.

A large boulder came crashing down the slope, narrowly missing them; it was time to move on. Faran looked out and saw that by a miracle, the other two ships were still moored by the other pyramids. He watched the boulder that had nearly struck them continue to bounce drunkenly down the slope and crash into the ice next to the furthest pyramid. The glassy surface splintered and the ship began to sink and then slipped below the surface of the lake. One ship only was left: Iss' own.

He ran, vaulting over the river of stones to his right, and started scrabbling transversely over the screes towards the second pyramid. Golon followed with the vampires but the undead were less dextrous than he and the sorcerer. Many of them were caught in the torrents of stone and swept down the hill.

Faran reached the walls and found an entrance. Here they were safe from the avalanches. He hurried through the ruined complex and into the domed chamber. The dock beyond was covered with the crawling figures of vampires injured in the struggle with Thalassa's party.

Golon grabbed Faran's sleeve and pointed at the doorway dedicated to Iss. Faran nodded and the sorcerer clapped his hands, dispelling the warding on the shaft leading to the *Dark Ship*. They hurried down it, and out onto the wharf, where the ship waited, still covered in a thick sheet of ice.

Out in the distance Faran could see the faintest glow far away on the lake's horizon. The *Windhover*'s white sails were still just visible. He inspected the surface of the lake around the *Dark Ship*. It held for the moment, but further out the ice was broken.

He whirled round and grabbed the collar of Golon's cloak, twisting the sorcerer towards him, fixing him with a stare. Golon's eyes glazed over once more as he succumbed to his mesmerism.

"Freeze the ice," he commanded Golon.

Golon turned and walked in a virtual trance to the lake-side, where he broke off an ice stalactite hanging from a rock. He pulled off his glove and rolled up his sleeve, exposing the under part of his forearm. It was then that Faran saw purple blotches amongst the blue veins so prominent on the sorcerer's pale skin—the first signs of the plague. Tonight or the night after he would be dead.

But for the moment Faran had him in his power and cared not whether he lived or died as long as he could get after Thalassa as soon as possible. "You know what you must do?" he asked.

Golon inclined his head. "Aye," he said in an expressionless drone, "I will bring Spindel, the soul of frost: he lives in the frozen star of Actiris, his blue eyes could freeze an ocean at a glance."

"Then bring him quickly!" Faran commanded.

Golon raised the icy dagger slightly, then stabbed, nicking his wrist; blood welled out. At the pain he seemed to snap out of Faran's mesmerism, but the Undead Lord crowded in on him again, fixing him with his glare, and a cloud once more passed over his eyes. He walked out onto the wharf, squeezing the wound, then raised his bleeding arm high to the stars. He muttered a prayer to Spindel, then allowed a single drop of blood to fall onto the gluey surface of the lake, throwing the ice shard in after it. As if a white brush had been applied to the cracks in the lake surface, the black areas of water vanished, the darkness in the depths suddenly marbled with ice, forcing its way up to the surface, One of the ship's outriggers that had begun to list into the ice was forced back upwards.

Immediately it was done, Faran and the five hundred undead who had survived poured across the gangplank onto the ship, pulling themselves onto its decks from the trailing halyards. "Brace the sails!" Faran commanded. The undead clumsily began to set about his orders, those slow to comprehend pushed and slapped into place. The black sails fell from the yards, which were swung around to the north. But still the wind was dead, the sails barely twitching.

Faran turned to Golon, who stared up at the rigging, slack-jawed, exhausted. Was he capable of another spell? The sorcerer, feeling his master's eyes, turned to him. No matter if he was at death's door, and this last effort might kill him: Faran needed his magic now. "Hurry! Bring the winds," he commanded. "Dawn will come in a few hours."

Golon didn't answer but walked to the prow of the ship. Though the storm had been strong enough to blow a man to his knees but half an hour before, now there was only the faintest of breezes. He stared out at the horizon but the white sail was gone, and with it Strag, the demon of winds. Thalassa had stolen his summoning. Her magic had grown since Thrull, since Alanda's death. He freed his mind, seeking not far away in the remoteness of the sky, for he knew he no longer had the power, but nearer, for a familiar whose body he could inhabit. No animal or bird had stirred since they had emerged from the Black Mines. But as if sent from Iss, immediately he sensed movement in the dark sky: a raven flying overhead. Golon released the shackles of his mind, and his spirit flew up, losing the chains that bound him to Faran, high into the freezing air to join the bird. There it was, beating a lonely path to the north. Now he swooped upon it and entered its body and flew with it towards the horizon where the *Windhover* had vanished. Onwards they flew, bird and man conjoined, until over the white vastness he saw the *Windhover*'s sails.

Now bird and man circled down, the ship looming up, and there was Thalassa on the poop, her hands upraised. Through his familiar's eyes he saw the glow of magic, of Strag, imprisoned between her hands. Down they flew, the deck hurtling towards them. At the last moment before impact, the raven swooped up, brushing Thalassa's cloak and tearing part of Strag's essence from her hands. As they bore it triumphantly upwards, Golon heard Thalassa's scream below, and the thundering of the *Windhover*'s sails suddenly in irons. Turning, the raven beat back to the land, where Golon's body stood motionless waiting for their return. As the bird alighted on the sorcerer's right shoulder, instantly he snapped back to consciousness.

The raven fell from him, stone dead. He pinched the thumb and forefinger of his right hand together and began moving them in the air, describing complex sigils there. And once more there came a faint unfocused whistling in the air, which grew and grew in strength. They saw the dust begin to rise up from the ruins of Maligar in a whirlwind and where all had been calm a split second before there was an explosion of wind, and driven snow and ice, and the sails of the *Dark Ship* began to twitch.

Golon felt the air currents, feeling their invisible eddies on his hands, caressing them as he might have caressed a woman's tresses, or the mane of a feisty stallion. The wind rose from the merest whisper to a raging storm, whose cloud steepled the heavens, whose wind robbed the air from his lungs.

He shouted to the undead to cast off the mooring lines, then unleashed the wind into the *Dark Ship*'s ten-times–reefed sails, sails that were as hard as iron yet visibly bulged when the tornado hit them. Instantly the ship bucked and then raced forward, its serpent figurehead eating up the ice and the night.

CHAPTER TWENTY

The Voyage of the Windhover

Most of them thought they were safe when the Duirin Hills had disappeared behind them. All the survivors save Thalassa and Urthred lay down and though the metal planks were covered with meltwater, as one, as if suffering some enchantment, they fell into a deep sleep.

But Thalassa could not rest: she controlled the winds that drove them forward to the north. She stood upon the ship's poop, her arms upstretched to the sky, her eyes closed. Her face calm, her arms a focus for the wind funnelling into the sails.

The ice rushed past the bows. Urthred stared at it, falling into a hypnotic state. He too longed for rest and he felt his eyes closing. He shook himself back awake. Were they safe even now? Nowhere was safe from Faran. Since that first night in Thrull he had been like a shadow, always following—even now.

They must be vigilant. Urthred stepped to the stern rail and stared hard to the south, looking out for pursuit. The wind blustered through the eye slits of his mask, keeping him wakeful. There was still nothing visible over the great sheet of ice save the two tracks of the runners pointing back towards the invisible hills where they had lost the Man of Bronze. Now he noticed an oar in a housing by the stern rail.

When lowered it would touch the ice, act as a rudder. But for the moment it seemed they needed no steerage. The twin tracks of the outriggers were arrow straight behind them. Thalassa directed them onwards as if she saw in her mind's eye exactly where over the horizon Iskiard lay.

Soon they would be there. Despite their loss, all might be well . . . Just then out of the driving wind from astern, like a flying black scythe, a bird swooped down from the sky, brushed against Thalassa's cloak before soaring upwards into the night. Surprised by the sudden touch, both of Thalassa's arms fell. The wind died. The ship juddered with sudden deceleration, slewing from side to side. She hastily raised her arms again. Another gust of wind, but much weaker now, and no longer under her command.

Urthred dropped the oar, which bit into the ice, sending up an eerie screeching, and pulled them back onto course with one hand, reaching out to her with his other. Her face was white and her body trembled, as if she had been touched by death itself.

"What is it?" he asked, staring skywards, past the rigging, wondering if the raven would return.

"Sorcery: Golon," she answered, her teeth clenched as she concentrated. "He has stolen some of the wind, taken it back to the south."

He stared over the stern rail, checking to see if they still were headed on the course of their wake, righting their direction, bringing the ship round into what little wind was left. For the moment they still sailed on, but at only half the speed before. Then a few minutes after the raven had come a dark thundercloud erupted upwards into the clear night over the southern horizon. Golon once more controlled the demon wind.

Something else was wrong. Despite their cries and the screeching of the oar on the ice not one of their companions had stirred from the deck: they lay like the dead. Urthred gave the rudder to Thalassa and climbed down into the waist.

Jayal leaned against the main mast, his eyes shut, mouth slightly agape, Dragonstooth still in his hand. No amount of shaking could wake him. Next he went to Garadas but he too could not be roused, and so it was with all the men. There was nothing to be done. A leaden feeling of exhaustion was beginning to overwhelm Urthred too. Ancient magic. The torpor of death.

He hurried back to Thalassa on the quarterdeck. She was leaning back against the rail, wrestling with the rudder in one hand while holding the other up to the fast dissipating wind. The cloud to the south towered higher and higher, apocalyptic, perhaps like the cloud that had covered the skies after the gods' final battle.

"I'm so tired," she murmured, swaying. He caught her as she began to fall and the wind fell to a whisper.

The ship was moving ever slower, the prow slewing round so that they now began to describe a wide semicircle. "Do not sleep," he whispered.

"No—with you I will wake, Urthred," she answered, forcing her eyes open. "Help me up, let me capture the wind." He took the rudder once more in one hand, supporting her frail body in his other. Another gust, then a steadier stream of air filled the flapping sails. He reached behind and seized the trailing rudder, altering its angle of deflection. The boat settled on its old course and skimmed on.

The feeling of fatigue was heavy on both of them, the smooth motion of the ship causing them to drowse. Each time Thalassa nodded off, the wind slackened.

Minutes and hours and days, even, might have passed and still the *Windhover* slid on over the endless ice. The night seemed prolonged, a thing beyond time.

Thalassa's head fell on Urthred's chest but he could tell she was still awake for the wind continued to blow. He breathed deeply the sandalwood scent of her hair, a fugitive fragrance that somehow survived the driving wind and the cold. How like a furnace was his heart, each beat of his heart like an anvil blow—his lethargy was forgotten.

He began speaking to her then, of the past, of Forgeholm, leaving nothing out, the things that had gone unsaid on the many almost silent nights they had spent together in Lorn.

And she replied, leaving nothing out of her history, the good and the bad.

The hours passed until they both sensed that the darkest time of the night had gone. There came an imperceptible lightening to the east, though the sky in that direction was now entirely obscured by towering cumuli. In front, against the greater darkness of departing night, a jagged line of mountains emerged from the gloom, and in its centre there was a notch in the ring of peaks. The entrance to a steep gorge. Urthred twisted the rudder, steering them towards it. These must be the Iron Gates that the Man of Bronze had told them about. The Iron Gates: a final name for a final place, at the end of the world.

He made another adjustment of the rudder. Beyond the Iron Gates was Iskiard. Not far now. He shivered, remembering his father's words: in that lost city the gods would demand their sacrifice: he would lose her.

"Thalassa . . ." he began, but the words choked in his mouth. How could that be? All this long night he had spoken to her, but now he had not a single word for her.

Her arms fell to her sides, and the wind died and they glided onwards in silence. She turned. How lovely she looked even in the dark. Her pale skin glowing, accentuated by the pure white of her cloak.

She regarded him with her grey eyes, the colour of an arctic sky. There were tears in them, and he realised he had never seen her cry, that she had never shown an ounce of self-pity, even when the fever of the vampire's bite had wracked her and she knew she was about to become one of them.

The ship was slowing, the wind slacker and slacker.

"Urthred, hold me once more."

Now he held her to his chest, and it seemed their hearts beat together. But where was the dawn? He prayed: Old Father, the Sun, Reh. Let your rays bring us joy, let them drive away the darkness. But the gloom of the Iron Gates was ever closer and still there wasn't the faintest glimmer of light in the east. Still Jayal and the villagers slept their enchanted sleep.

Thalassa pulled away slightly and looked up at him, a

challenge in her eyes. "Urthred, we are nearly at the Iron Gates. We don't know what dangers lie beyond them. Give me one last favour."

"Anything."

"Let me see your true face."

He looked away: the mask had protected him all these years from the world and the world from him. But now the time had come to cast it aside. They were nearly at their final objective. That day had come that Manichee had warned him of when he had come to him in Thrull. He must at last be free of his master's gift.

He reached up his gloves, releasing the steel tips, and unpicked the clasps that held the mask to his face.

It was as if his soul had risen to his throat, and like a bird fluttered there choking him. The moment had come. Now the last catch was undone and he held the mask free in his left hand. He turned to her and pulled it away, feeling the air on his face, on his scars. Her grey eyes never flinched.

Once before she had seen what lay beneath, in Lorn, in a room bathed by the sacred light of the Silver Chalice. But this was different. All things had appeared healed in that light. Now she would see him without its benefit. A strange defiance filled him as their eyes locked: he dared her to react, to scream, for her heart to give out as had Varash's back in Thrull when he'd revealed his face to the traitorous High Priest, but instead she reached up her right hand, slender fingers, so pale, the hazel wands of a sorcerer, and touched his ravaged cheek, and his lips, his devastated lips. But they were ravaged no longer; there was no line of ridged scar tissue: her fingers traced a smooth line over them, and upwards to his nose as if she modelled them from clay as she touched them. Now there was flesh where before there had been nothing but scar.

Now there were tears in *his* eyes and he blinked and realised he had lids that could blink, that could shut out the light. And she raised herself on her toes and closing her eyes, kissed him on those lips, those lips that had tasted nothing so sweet in all his life.

"You're healed," she breathed. She released him and took a step back.

He lifted the fingers of his right hand, but then remembered as the cold steel touched his skin: his gloves. Were his fingers healed too?

His head spun, he needed to breathe. He turned away to where the sun would rise. The ice lake was still slipping past rapidly below them despite the loss of wind. He held up the mask. Effigy of what he had been. Manichee once had instilled it with magic. But now its magic was gone as was his master. He saw it for what it was. Its lacquer was cracked and chipped, showing the wood beneath. The time of artifice, of hiding, was finished.

"I will not forget you," he whispered, and then, grasping the mask by its rim, threw it hard over the side. It spun away towards the horizon, like a disc, its edge flashing, further and further, like a bird. And perhaps it flew on forever, for swiftly it was swallowed in the darkness that hung on the far peripheries of sight and was no more.

He turned from the rail. Thalassa stood smiling at him and he smiled back. A smile? Had he ever smiled before? It didn't matter. He stripped off his gloves, and let them fall to the deck. Fingers, perfectly formed, were revealed. He went to her, and took her hands, and she sank her head on his chest again.

The hint of grey was more pronounced in the sky.

"Thalassa," he whispered and she seemed to stir from her trance, and looked up at him.

"Last night as we spoke, I was half dreaming, only half awake: I dreamed of the future as it will be after Iskiard, when the sun returns."

"The future . . ." she muttered dreamily as if it were an alien concept, as it was, for neither of them had ever discussed it before this moment.

The ship was now down to walking pace. The mountains reared higher and higher, until their heads craned back to see the summits. Frozen waterfalls like silver draperies latticed the black rock to either side. Behind, over the flat expanse of ice the grey thunderheads grew and grew, killing the light.

In the waist of the ship details started emerging where the sleeping villagers lay scattered on the deck. As the craft slowed, half of them stirred, raising themselves on their elbows. They looked around them blearily as if the magic that sealed their eyes had only worked while the ship moved. But the others remained ominously still.

Jayal too groaned and looked around, his eyes coming to rest on Urthred and Thalassa at the stern of the ship. But to him and the others it was as if a stranger and not the masked priest stood next to Thalassa. Only his cape remained the same: the mask and the gloves were gone. Jayal clambered to his feet, reaching for his sword. The two men eyed each other.

"Urthred?" he asked wonderingly.

"Aye, it is me," the priest replied.

Garadas too stood and stared. "Where is your mask?"

"It's gone—forever. I threw it overboard," he answered. "Now look to your men. Some have not stirred."

Garadas turned and saw the motionless bodies lying in the waist of the ship. He went hastily to the nearest and knelt by him. Urthred lashed the rudder to the stern rail and went forward to join him. Garadas had rolled the villager over. The man's cape fell away. His face was disfigured by blue-grey blotches. The plague. His mouth hung open. There was no doubt he was dead.

Garadas got to his feet and stepped back. He pulled the sleeves of his own cloak back, but his own arms were unblemished. But the look he gave Urthred said enough. In the confined space of the ship, it would be a miracle if any of them had escaped infection.

Thalassa had followed Urthred. "Not too close!" he warned her.

Urthred turned to the next man. Garadas had rolled him over, but now stood back. This man was still alive. It was Samlack, the headman's deputy. Under his sandy beard purple blotches discoloured his face—a white discharge issued from his nose and mouth. His breathing was hoarse and laboured. The other villagers, realising what was wrong with their friends, hung back, their cloaks held to their mouths.

"As I thought," Urthred muttered. The warmth of a few moments ago was gone, the dawn seemed suspended, a dawn that would never come. The plague: all over the earth it had decimated cities and countries, made nations weak, easy prey for the armies of the Worm.

Now it was on board the ship: it would kill within days. For the moment some of them were still apparently untouched; perhaps the gusting wind had protected them from the spores. But three men had died. Urthred peered closer, and saw scratches and cuts on the dead men's faces and arms where they had desperately fought off the undead. "We will have to throw them overboard, before everyone else is infected."

"It is not the way we would bury them in Goda," Garadas said bleakly. "There we would give their bones to Reh's sacred eagles."

"There are no eagles here," Urthred replied, looking up at the dark sky. "I have seen only a creature of Iss, a raven, and he was sent by sorcery. But the cold will preserve their bodies until the Second Dawn when they shall be resurrected. Come, let's wrap them in the sails."

The surviving men pulled some more sails out of their hampers and carefully wrapped the three corpses in them. When all was ready, they were lowered with ropes onto the ice. As the ship glided forward the bundles spun away behind them.

"May you find your way to the Hall of the White Rose," Urthred muttered as they were lost to view in the gloom of the storm.

From behind came a quiet "Amen" and he turned and saw Jayal standing there, a hand up on the shrouds watching the fast-disappearing bodies. The young knight's face was very pale. There was dry blood on a rent around the sleeve of his cloak.

"You're wounded," Urthred said.

Jayal looked back at him square in the eye. "It's only a scratch," he answered. "Attend to those who need it."

Thalassa was crouching near Samlack. She looked up as Urthred joined her. No words were needed: the deputy headman was breathing hoarsely and would soon be dead.

The ship still glided on slowly over the ice. They now saw in the grey light that the mountains were made of a rust-red sandstone, tortured strata of rock twisted and bent into strange shapes by some apocalypse of the world's past. The cliff faces loomed over them—the gorge appearing like a deep slit in the massive rock face.

"Take the helm," Urthred shouted back to Garadas, and with a nod the headman released the oar and steered them into the shadows of the great gorge. It was a mile across at its entrance, but still the little light there had been was instantly swallowed by deep shadows. A slight breeze still came from behind them. The ship now glided on down a ribbon of ice, the sky but a thin strip high above the lowering cliff faces. The canyon twisted away in front, the hiss of the runners on the ice amplified by the heights to either side.

Urthred turned back to Thalassa and looked deep into her tired grey eyes. "You need your strength—rest," he said.

"I must help those I can," she whispered. He remembered her in the square of Goda on the day they had set out for Lorn, healing the sick and the lame. But what could she do for the victims of the plague?

"Give me some water," she said. Urthred unclipped his water flask from his belt and unstoppered it, kneeling by her. She took it and heedless of the danger of the contact raised Samlack's head slightly, then began her prayer, praising Reh for the purity of the stream from which the water had come, the cleanness of the wind, the healing power of the sun and all natural things that had played upon its birth. Then she gently held the flask to Samlack's lips. "Let the water wash the poison from you," she prayed, tilting it so that liquid poured into the man's mouth. Samlack groaned, the water dribbling down his bearded chin, then he feebly opened his eyes and recognised her. "My lady . . ." he murmured.

She smiled. "Rest, sleep now. The evil has gone from you." She laid his head back on the deck, then rose so gracefully, her tall form unbending under the white cloak, that Urthred's breath caught in his throat.

She went around to the other men. Each of them was

given a draft of the water. When she rose from the last, she approached Jayal. He had retreated to the prow of the ship and was staring at the sides of the gorge drifting past.

Thalassa held the water bottle out to him. "Drink, cure yourself, you've been wounded."

He stared at the proffered object as if he would as soon consign it to Hel.

"I'm well," he said stiffly. "I need none of your water, or your cures."

"You could be infected."

"Not I," he said. A fleeting look of hatred passed across his face, like a flying shadow of the Doppelgänger, then it was gone. He was himself once more.

"Jayal . . ." she began.

But be shook his head, cutting her short. "Go," he said. "Do you think there is a cure for me? You forget I am Jayal. I am cursed. No physical affliction is anything to what I suffer in my mind. What value is this body, this body that is not mine, but stolen from an abomination; all that is opposite to me, but is me nevertheless. Death is preferable."

"There is still hope; Iskiard is near. You can defeat the Doppelgänger; why don't you drink?" she persisted.

For a moment his icy look softened and he appeared to be mollified. He reached forward and grabbed the flask, eyeing it for a moment. Then, in one swift movement, he hurled it over the side of the ship. It hit the surface and skittered away over the ice towards one of the sheer cliff faces.

"There," Jayal said, watching it disappear, "enough of your potions. It is done. Let it be death if that is my fate. I will perish and with me my line and my double too." He turned to the rest of the company, who stared at him as if he had finally gone mad. "Perhaps I *am* infected. Stay away from me if you would live!" Urthred made a step forward, a protest on his lips, but before he could say anything a cry came from behind, and he whirled round.

One of the villagers had been watching the flask receding on the ice behind them. Now he cried out and they all turned. Behind them, a mile or so distant, framed by the massive V of the entrance to the Iron Gates, they saw it: a black speck—a ship, like theirs, entering the gap between the massive buttresses. As they watched the edge of the thunderhead of dark cloud roiled up over the cliff faces, blanketing them from view. The ship flew on, growing larger by the minute.

"We need more wind." Urthred looked to the north. The Iron Gates ran straight and true. There was no way out, only forward. Whatever hint of dawn there had been was now gone.

Thalassa hurried back to the stern of the ship and raised her arms once more so the folds of the yak's wool cloak were extended like bird's wings. But only a faint gust of wind came in response. The sails flapped once, then twice as a desultory gust of cold air came from the south. The ship picked up a little bit of speed. They began to make way once more, but agonisingly slowly. Behind, the *Dark Ship* and its thunderhead cloud bore down on them swiftly.

In an hour or two Faran would catch them.

There had once been two hills, now there was but one; the other, Maligar, lay upon him, each rock, each fractured boulder, he felt as a man feels a pebble in his shoe, with an acute, specific pain. But he had been made by the gods, so that his brain encompassed each pain as equal, one as precisely delineated from the other as if they were a thousand different entities, as distinct as jewels.

He knew his right shoulder was separated from its socket, felt the pain of a thousand rocks that had buckled the cuirass on his chest, that one of his ankles lay twisted at a ninety-degree angle to the way it was intended.

But he still lived, and while he lived there was hope that just as when he had been buried five thousand years before Marizian came, he would once more see the sun. Yes, he would lie here until the next Marizian came, whether it be ten thousand or a hundred thousand years—the years were as nothing: he was nearly immortal—he could wait.

But then he remembered: the Lightbringer. Her time had

come: he must serve her, it was why Marizian had brought him back. He must free himself from his grave.

He raised his one good arm, feeling the rocks resisting him, tensed his musculature on that side, and thrust up.

A watcher from the shattered hills would have thought a geyser had just blown from the scree slope that covered the pass, for rocks and debris flew upwards a hundred feet. A mighty arm appeared, still clutching a silver hammer that burned in the grey predawn light. Then the great helm broke through, throwing the debris down the slopes in liquid screes, ever quicker the further the stones and boulders rolled until they crashed onto the refrozen surface of the lake, fracturing it once more.

Then the rest of his body thrust itself out of the rubble. Slowly, strange flashes of light buzzing and burning in the depths of the broken shoulder socket, the giant straightened himself, his head rotating left and right, its eyes opening slowly, their red beams cutting across the gloom of the pass.

He gazed over the ice. Nothing was visible there now: the *Windhover* and the *Dark Ship* had long gone, beyond the curve of the earth. But distance was no obstacle for the Man of Bronze; he intuited where the two barques were, over the dip of the earth. In their wake he saw the afterimages of the demons, like a faint trail of ether: Hdar, Strag and Spindel.

He looked at the lake. Slabs of ice bobbed on the surface of the ink-black waters. Time was short: the Lightbringer was in danger. He wrenched his ankle back into place and pushed as much as he could of the trailing metal back into his arm socket. He started down to the shore, paused for a moment, looked once more over the horizon in the direction of the invisible ships and then slowly began to wade into the lake, the ice cracking even further, pushing up into fractured slabs around his body as he forced his way through it. Further and further, sinking slowly into the frigid waters until his head disappeared beneath the surface.

CHAPTER TWENTY-ONE

The Iron Gates

The rust-red mountains reared up to either side of them, reaching up to the narrow band of grey sky that was all that was visible in that dark place. Dawn might have arrived on the cliff tops, but here at the bottom of the gorge it would take until well into the day to reach them. A lonely spot, perhaps the loneliest on the dying earth. Unvisited since Marizian had come in the opposite direction, fleeing from Iskiard five thousand years before.

The gorge had narrowed and had begun to twist like a snake. Garadas wrestled the rudder from side to side. The *Windhover* threaded the thin river of ice, the yards perilously close to the overhanging buttresses that rushed past them.

The wind had blown hard from the south for an hour, funnelled into the narrowness of the gorge, but however favourable conditions were for them, the *Dark Ship* was still catching them, driven by the dark thunderhead over its masts.

When they had first seen it it had been but a small blot glimpsed far away in the darkness of the twisting canyon and following storm, but gradually it had eaten up the space between and now the billowing black sails of the Undead Lord's ship seemed to fill the width of the gorge behind them, so close that the faces of the undead thronging the prow were clearly visible.

Ahead, the gorge twisted on, without a break. The Man of Bronze had spoken of a gateway through which they alone could pass with the magic of the sword. As yet there was no sign of it.

Garadas lined his surviving men up along the rear rail of the *Windhover* with their bows, waiting for the *Dark Ship* to get within range. After a few moments Samlack bent his weapon and let fly with a speculative shot, but the gale from the south held it up and it fell short, the black shadow of Faran's ship sweeping over it a second later, cutting down the intervening distance second by second. Half an hour and they would be on them.

A figure moved forward from the stern of the vampire ship. Tall, clad in black leather armour, his head bare. Faran Gaton. He brushed past the undead at the bow and stood on the bowsprit housing, clutching the jib sail halyard, staring forward at the stern of the *Windhover.*

The villagers, seeing him so exposed, sent a volley of arrows, but each of them again fell short. The headman issued a command to his men to save their ammunition. In half an hour they would need every arrow.

The distance was so short now that Faran's expression could be clearly seen. His eyes finally locked on Urthred's. Did he know who he was? wondered the priest. He had never seen him without the mask, and without it he was surely unrecognisable.

But nevertheless the Undead Lord's stare dwelt on him. Urthred's mind reeled, feeling the invisible coils of mesmerism reaching over the intervening space, twisting in his mind: he heard voices—whispers, insinuations. He felt his eyes begin to glaze over.

Jayal came hurrying back down the deck of the ship suddenly, snapping Urthred out of his near trance. Jayal's face was transformed, alive with excitement.

"The gateway, the way to Iskiard, is ahead!" he exclaimed, his voice strained.

They had all been staring at the pursuing ship but now, as one, they turned and followed the direction of his pointing hand, past the billowing sails of the *Windhover*. Far ahead there was a golden glow in the sky, different from the wan sunlight bathing the cliff tops.

"Faran won't catch us now," Jayal growled, unsheathing the sword. "Only Dragonstooth can open the gate to Iskiard; the Man of Bronze told us," he said, letting the grey light play on the naked blade. Once more the colour of the steel had changed. Now it glowed golden, just like that strange light in the sky. "See? The sword responds; it's alive. It knows it's nearly home."

Urthred peered forward once more. The ship swerved around another curve of the twisting canyon and suddenly he could make out a shape in the brilliance ahead. A golden bridge arched over the gorge, from which fell traceries of light, spilling like golden and silver veils to the bottom of the ravine. Beyond the shimmering screen nothing was visible.

"The moment is coming." Jayal turned to Thalassa. A look of yearning sadness such as had not been present since he returned to Thrull was painted on his young-old face.

"What is it?" Thalassa asked.

"It is farewell, Thalassa."

"Why? The sword will take all of us to Iskiard."

Jayal shook his head. "No. As I watched the bridge a voice came into my mind. Marizian's voice. It told me this: the sword will take me to the city, to where Marizian found it, deep in the underworld, but not you. So, farewell. Maybe I will see you again in the next world, if Reh grants me rest in the Hall of the White Rose. My life is borrowed, forfeit to the Rod of the Shadows. I give it back most willingly, for it was nothing better than a curse these last seven years."

"But through it you lived when you would have died on Thrull field."

Again he shook his head. "When I woke resurrected in my father's tent, I knew. Magic cannot make you a man or bring the dead back to life." He turned to Urthred. "Remember the favour I asked of you."

"I remember," Urthred answered. "If I find the Rod, I will bury it where no man will ever find it again."

Jayal nodded earnestly. "That's it! Let no man ever again become what I have become. I came back to Thrull and the memories came back too—the ones I had suppressed. And instead of hope, I was given despair—the knowledge that only a ghost of me lived on, that the rest of my life was forfeit to *him*, my shadow. How well he has used me, how he has played with me! And all because of the magic of the Rod."

"But you can still use the Rod against your shadow, send him back to Shades."

Jayal shook his head. "The Doppelgänger has it: he will not be separated from it until he takes this shape and I assume once more that broken body that I left on Thrull field. Will I be able to withstand the pain of those wounds that he has lived with these last seven years? Probably not, for he is my opposite. It is the battle against pain that has kept him strong. And what of this vessel? This body of his that I carry? Should I not cut my wrists or fling myself from the ship so every bone in this borrowed body breaks? Then he would die, for only while his old body lives does he live.

"But, friends, I am a coward. My father saw it, back in Thrull, saw that without the darkness of my twin I was not a real man."

"But you fought at the battle, passed through many dangers to get the sword, have travelled with us to the top of the world. Who would call you coward?" Urthred asked.

"My conscience, priest: for when I could act, I didn't. But now fate has decided for me. See what the Doppelgänger will inherit!" he spat, a strange gleam in his eye. He pulled up the sleeve of his tunic and showed them his arm. It was covered in large blotches of green-brown discoloration, like a bruise except that at its heart was a suppurating wound, oozing liquid. All those at the stern rail recoiled from the sight.

"The plague," Jayal said with grim satisfaction. "That will be my gift."

"Oh, Jayal, why didn't you drink, why didn't you take the cure?" Thalassa asked.

He shook his head. "It is over, my lady. The curse, everything."

"I have more magic; you may still be saved. Live," Thalassa pleaded.

Jayal managed a wan smile. "Live? I told you; there is no life. Good-bye."

He began to back away, to the prow of the *Windhover*; Thalassa took a hesitant step after him, but as she did so the wind dropped again and the *Dark Ship* behind surged forward. She stopped, looking from it to the retreating figure of Jayal. As they had spoken the luminance of the golden veils had become stronger and stronger so when he reached the bow he was but a silhouette against it, then the light became a blaze and it seemed he had been consumed by the golden effulgence.

They were only moments away from the light. Urthred twisted round. The sky was lightening away to the east, down the length of the Iron Gates. Already there were purple and golden highlights in the towering clouds overhead. The serpent figurehead of Faran's ship was now only fifty yards behind. Golon stood next to the Undead Lord, and as Urthred watched Golon's hands began to weave in the air in front of him: a spell.

Garadas had steered the ship around the curve in the gorge but suddenly he cried out in alarm as the rudder began to twitch in his hands. He wrestled with it, but it seemed to have a mind of its own, twisting out of his grip as if possessed. The *Windhover* began to slew alarmingly from side to side.

"Magic!" he cried. "Fire your volley, lads, hit the sorcerer."

The villagers hastily nocked arrows onto their bows and let fly at the prow of the *Dark Ship*, where the vampires were crowded together shielding their eyes against the golden glow in front as if it were the brightest sun. This time they were within range. One arrow thudded into the wooden serpent head of Faran's ship, another flew straight at the Undead Lord himself, but with a swift movement he batted it away with his gauntleted hand.

The *Windhover* still weaved from side to side. Golon was shaping another spell: now he released it with a final gesture. A storm of magic broke over the *Windhover*'s decks. The coiled ropes lying on the deck and the loose rigging lines began twisting and whipping through the air like snakes, striking the archers, snatching their bows from their hands, flinging one man bodily overboard. A second later one of the flying outriggers of Faran's ship ran over him.

Urthred looked round: the golden veil filled the horizon. Jayal was there somewhere at the prow, lost in the brilliance. Five hundred feet above their heads was the golden span from which the veils of light fell. Now he could see a massive keystone hanging from its centre towards the bottom of the gorge. They were nearly under it.

The ship was slowing, the sails losing wind, shuddering, nearly in irons. Now the gap between them and Faran was only some fifty feet. More arrows flew back at the Undead Lord standing so proudly at the bowsprit, but the arrows seemed to slow in the air as they neared him, bending away, deflected by some magical warding. Garadas screamed and finally relinquished his tenuous grip on the tiller. Black scorpions scuttled over his face and arms. The barge began veering towards the right-hand cliff.

Faran's gaze swept over the few men left standing. Urthred felt light-headed, swooning under the influence of the mesmerism. He tried to shout a warning, but already one of the villagers had thrown down his bow and drawn an axe from his belt. He brought it crashing down on the neck of his neighbour, who fell like a slaughtered steer. The possessed man turned, striking to left and right. His eyes were staring, blind, hypnotised. He fought with the strength of two men, as his fellows grappled with him.

Urthred tried to barge past him and grab the tiller, for the side of the gorge loomed in front. But the possessed man lashed out, sending him spinning back. Then the glare of the bridge was gone as if they had entered another zone of light. He caught a glimpse of the prow of the ship: in startling clarity he saw Jayal for the final time. The knight lifted Dragonstooth aloft, towards the keystone.

Then one of the ropes twisting on the deck flew round, smashing Urthred in the side of the head. The *Windhover*'s starboard outriggers crashed into the cliff face, and were torn away with a screech of wood and iron. The ship rolled over, its mainmast snapping off. A tangle of spars and ropes crashed overboard, dragging the ship further into the side of the gorge, everyone slipping towards the starboard rail as the deck canted over forty-five degrees.

Urthred held Thalassa as they slid into a pile of sails and rigging. He threw the wreckage off him desperately. Somehow they were still creeping forward, the rigging trailing over the side acting as a giant brake. But the bowsprit of Faran's ship was overlapping the stern of their own, the area crowded with vampires ready to leap across. A shadow passed over them—the shadow of the bridge. Then the world exploded in golden light.

The vampires leaping forward into the *Windhover* were vaporised. Then the *Dark Ship* and the gorge were gone. The horizons seemed to explode outwards, fleeing beyond sight. All was blinding white.

Urthred's eyesight gradually ebbed back. The *Windhover* rushed on, still on its side, trailing wooden fragments and cordage.

Then gradually the ship began to slow until it slewed around in a semicircle and halted. They had stopped in a vast ice-bound emptiness, whipped here and there into lonely mini tornadoes of whirling snow by a little wind. There was no sign of Jayal. Where he had stood at the prow was marked by a single scorch mark. All was silent except the howling of the wind. Its sound came not from north, south, east or west, but seemingly from all those directions at once, converging on the wreck as if dead spirits came, eager to inspect these intruders into their world.

Urthred pulled himself out of the tangle of rigging, the icy fingers of the wind plucking at his tattered robes. The cold was mind-numbing. Already the wreckage-strewn deck and the dead villagers were covered with a grey patina of hoarfrost. Only one or two of them stirred. Garadas was one of them. He looked wonderingly at where the scorpions had swarmed over his face and hands—they were gone. Only two other Godans, Samlack and a man called Ostman, had survived.

Urthred helped Thalassa to her feet as Samlack climbed through the shattered cordage and timbers to the prow and peered ahead. Now he shouted and pointed. "Towers. It looks like a city."

Urthred strained his eyes. It might have been nearly dawn in the Iron Gates, but here, there was still only a faint grey in the sky. They had come even further north, many leagues further in latitude from the gorge. There on the dark rim of the ice plains stood black silhouettes. A hundred or more. Behind them a blazing star that he had never seen before rose up into the sky more rapidly than he had seen any star rise.

"It is a city, but what is the star?" Thalassa asked. "I've never seen its like before."

They both turned to the headman, since he was more familiar with the constellations of these northern reaches of the world. But he too merely shrugged. "Nor I—see how swiftly it moves, like a comet. Perhaps it is a sign sent from Reh." As they watched it assumed a position right over the towers in the mid part of the horizon.

Urthred glanced at Thalassa and she returned his look, her grey eyes not wavering. "Yes, perhaps it is a sign," he said. "Reh has sent his star to welcome the Lightbringer to Iskiard." He shivered, remembering his father's prophecy and to disguise the shaking of his limbs said briskly, "It's cold. Let's salvage what we can from the wreck and get moving."

They scrambled back up onto the deck, avoiding the bodies of their dead comrades, scrounging what they could from backpacks and picking up fallen weapons, even scavenging canvas from the sails as extra cloaks. Finally they were ready. They set off through the cutting wind to the north guided by the star. They had nearly reached the Lost City.

CHAPTER TWENTY-TWO

A Gallery of Ghosts

In the blink of an eye, Jayal had flown through space, just as he had flown with the others, transported by the magic of Dragonstooth, from Thrull to Goda. But this time when he awoke from the darkness of unconsciousness he found he was alone, in an alcove.

It was very cold—the walls surrounding him were covered in ice. The sword was still clutched in both his hands. It glowed with light. Once more as it had in the Iron Gates a voice came into his mind, seemingly coming from the sword itself. The voice of its onetime owner: Marizian. It told him he was in Iskiard, in the underworld, where Marizian's great journey had begun five thousand years ago. Where his journey would end. The Doppelgänger couldn't be far away. Marizian's voice died and now like whispers he heard an undercurrent of other ghostly voices, a multitude of them, welling up in his mind.

There was a grey light seeping through the darkness before him, as if filtered through an immense thickness of ice. He lifted Dragonstooth and the blade flared with light. Now he saw a long nave running to left and right in front of where he stood. The nave was some hundred feet across, its walls were made of grey stone. The ribbed vault of the roof was high above, almost lost in the steely gloom. In the wall opposite him he could see an unending line of alcoves and plinths similar to the one he stood in. Each of them was occupied.

He must have stood motionless for some time; he found that icicles hung from his hair and his eyebrows. His hands, he saw in the light of the sword, were very pale, blue with cold, but in one place it was now mottled black. The plague was spreading quickly. He must hurry, find the Doppelgänger, end the curse that the Rod had brought into the world seven years before. Otherwise dishonour would stain the Illgill name forever.

Honour? Where was it? Not in feats of arms, for he had fought as best he could yet evil still had won.

No, if honour lived, it lived only in the individual, in action taken without hope, without hope of redemption, or reward, even as the iron jaws of fate closed. Honour was in giving up the self and all the hopes of self; all positive things. Honour was in stretching out one's arms to the emptiness, to blackness, and embracing it.

The buboes throbbed on his back, his groin, his armpits. Hdar was inside him; the demon was unforgiving. A dull ache, which grew and grew implacably hour by hour. Was this what the Doppelgänger knew in his crippled body, this never-ending pain? How long before he died? Or maybe it was the curse that he could not die, even as the Doppelgänger could not die on Thrull field? What kind of monster would he become before it was over, an abomination to his own sight? A mass of black, sloughing flesh, of putrescence, his face liquid with sores, his eyes gone, but still living, breathing.

There would be no revenge if be was reduced to that before he could find the Doppelgänger. He must find him soon. Perhaps it would be the Doppelgänger himself who would lead him. He waited now, waited for the Doppelgänger's voice to return and command him, as it had for these last weeks—telling him to come, come to the Rod, and surrender his body. But strangely, for the first time in days, the voice now chose silence and only the ghosts whispered.

The hilt of the sword was burning his palm. Its colour

changed before his eyes from the gold of the Iron Gates to the coppery glow it had showed in the underworld under Thrull, and as it had when Erewon, the God of the Moon, had blessed it at his tomb in Lorn. The sword, his companion so long, for all those years since he had seized it from the wizard's tower in far-off Ormorica: all that time he had barely understood its powers, only the heat of its blade that could cut stone, but now it was as if Marizian's intelligence passed from its hilt into his being, as if it were speaking to him, guiding him. Its light shone in a nimbus around him and as his eyes adjusted to the gloom and his thoughts cleared, he saw swimming in the light a new vision. He clearly saw the actuality of the cold grey nave in front of him, yet superimposed on the sheen of light, like the grey lines of a faint map, he saw the plan and elevation of the city, the levels of its underworld, spiralling down and down towards the centre of the earth like the inner funnel of a whirlpool, and near the centre of the whirlpool he felt an answering pulse of energy. The Rod of the Shadows. Glimmering far below. Far but not too far now. The route he must take was clearly visible, and it began here, in this hall.

He felt a numbing chill in his feet: he tried lifting them, and they came away with a crack of ice; they had been frozen to the floor of the alcove.

He walked out into the cold light of the nave; now he could see that yet more of the same alcoves stretched up his side of the great hall. In each stood a silent frozen figure. He understood: these were his brethren, warriors like him. Perhaps he wasn't alone after all.

Some impulse drew him across the nave to the alcove directly opposite his. He lifted Dragonstooth so the light flared on the face of the statue. A pale face varnished with ice, its eyes open, staring. His heart stopped: a face he recognised. Furisel, his sergeant from the legions: the man who had abandoned him that night those months ago in Thrull: that night when he had searched for Thalassa, the night he had lost and found Dragonstooth. Furisel, whose corpse he had later found in the house on the Silver Way. Furisel stood upright, his hands resting on the pommel of a two-handed sword. Why was his body here? The blade in Furisel's hands began to glow. Jayal stepped back, his heart thudding. He saw that up and down the nave, all the warriors' swords had begun to glow faintly, answering the blaze of Dragonstooth.

Then it was as if the shadows cast by the swords began to detach themselves from the statues in each niche. Was it a trick of the harsh shifting light? The shadows drifted towards him. He backed away even more, into the centre of the nave.

The other faces now materialised from the grey spirit bodies. His long-dead companions of Thrull field: Vortumin, Jadshasi, Edric and Poluso. Surely of all the dead these warriors deserved to be in Reh's warm paradise in the sun? Instead, they were here, imprisoned in this cold annex of Shades. This was not the Hall of the White Rose. They were accursed: their bones lay scattered upon the earth.

The grey drifting ghosts closed, surrounding him. As one they raised their swords and pointed them directly at him.

A cold chill ran down his neck. Beyond the surrounding ring of spirits from the very end of the nave, he saw a single figure drifting towards him. It came on silently. Though the other figures were grey, this ghost still had the vestiges of colour about him as if time and death had not as yet faded some vital spirit in him as it had the others. Through the thronging ranks he came, dividing them so they drifted to each side, their spirits roiling like clouds, then re-forming behind him.

Jayal had seen enough. He knew who came.

The ghost's face was altered, almost unrecognisable under the burns and hoary beard. But the faded black and red armour was what he had worn on Thrull field, and the glowing eyes were unforgettable.

It was his father's ghost that came. To lead him to the place where he had died, where the Doppelgänger waited for *him*, Jayal Illgill.

CHAPTER TWENTY-THREE

The Last Summoning

Gone . . . The Iron Gates stretched on ahead of the *Dark Ship*. There was no sign of the *Windhover*. The demon-driven wind had also gone. Faran's ship rested motionless on its outriggers. Behind them, at the end of the gorge, the sky was streaked with red. Dawn was coming. There was nowhere on the ship or on the gorge where they could hide.

It had taken a few minutes after the blinding light for Faran to recover his sight, even then dark spots swam in his vision. He sat heavily on a thwart at the prow of the *Dark Ship*, amongst the villagers' arrows that porcupined the bulwarks and masts.

Golon stood in front of him, staring at the Iron Gates: his face was deathly pale.

Faran pulled himself to his feet. "Where have they gone?" he asked the sorcerer.

Golon pulled the little purple gem from his cloak and held it out in front of him, frowning with concentration. The gem swung north, up the length of the Iron Gates.

"Iskiard," he murmured, turning to Faran. "Just before the explosion I saw a comet arc through the skies. Dragonstooth has taken them, just as it took them from Thrull. The ship, the people—everything."

"How far is the city? A league, a hundred?"

Golon shook his head. He looked about him at the dark cliffs bending over their heads. "Only the gods were meant to travel through this place. To us, it's a prison. We could sail down it forever and never reach Iskiard."

"There is a route to every place," Faran retorted. "There must be another way out."

"Only back into the rising sun, or upwards," Golon replied, pointing at the narrow strip of sky far above them.

"Upwards?" Faran too looked up at the overhanging cliffs. Already their tops were bathed in the golden light of morning. "If the sky was going to be dark forever, we would have time to scale those cliffs. But the light comes, and there is no shade, nowhere to hide."

"Then there's only one solution."

"What's that?"

The sorcerer stared back at his lord. The plague was spreading rapidly, through his veins, outwards to his skin. He had tried to deny the evidence of the growths he felt there, alien presences, numb to the touch but full of corrupt matter, but the fire in his veins was undeniable. Where did such as he go after death? Would Prince Iss admit him into his purple halls? Or would he spend eternity as a wailing ghost in the abyss?

The practice of his magic had kept his mind occupied up till now. He had harnessed the demon in the wind and driven them here, concentrating like a fury, to the exclusion of all else. But now that they were stationary, and the thrill of the chase was over, all he was left with was that one certainty: a mortal chill—soon it would be over for him too.

All the time the sky was lightening and the sunbeams inching further down the face of the cliff. A few more minutes and the light would be at the bottom of the gorge. Then Faran and the undead horde would be reduced to mist. Faran's eyes fixed on him and he felt once more his soul being sucked from his brain, into those hooded eyes.

"Golon: we need a spell, quickly." Even through the mesmerism, Golon registered the urgency in his master's voice.

He dragged his eyes away from Faran, and stared at the ground, noticing his faded and torn purple slippers as if they belonged to another man, not him. He had been wearing them that last day of Thrull, the day he had searched the streets for the masked priest.

There remained only one more summoning that could save his master. Not a single demon, but a host of them: the very creatures that dragged the edge of the night over the land, conquering Reh's Light. As sacred to Iss as Harken's dragons were to Reh. They would leave this gorge and the whole world for that matter in the darkness forever.

But he, who had summoned Nekron and Acharon, Hdar and Strag, feared even to speak the name of the creatures out loud, least of all invoke it; for of all the pantheon, their summoning was a right that belonged solely to Lord Iss, and not to servants such as Golon.

"Well?" Faran prompted, snapping him back to the present. He realised that he had drifted, broken the bonds of the vampire's mesmerism. It had never happened before. Was this the power of death? "What answer do you have?" the Undead Lord said impatiently.

"There is no answer, lord, lest . . ." His voice trailed off.

"Lest what?"

Now Golon looked up and met Faran's stare again. Yes, either it was the power of death, or the fact that Faran had been partly blinded by the flash of light when the *Windhover* had disappeared: the vampire's eyes were occluded, the effect of his mesmerism muted. "Lord, I should not even speak of it—" Golon hesitated.

"Speak of what? Spit it out, man."

Golon swallowed. "I have done your bidding, trespassed even in the purple halls and in the stars."

"We have trespassed alike, you and I," Faran interrupted again, "for the glory of the Worm and the defeat of the Flame. That was the pact we made in Tiré Gand when the Elders bade me march on Thrull: that Iss would be triumphant, whatever the cost. I have kept our oath since. I have taken even Acharon's curse—we are equally damned and cannot be damned further. Speak, whatever the sacrifice, whatever the toll, we must pay it. The Lightbringer must not escape."

Golon closed his eyes. "Very well. Listen, my lord, and you will understand my fear. The demons of which I speak will bring the eternal darkness, the Midnight at the End of Time.

"All who read the *Book of Worm* know their names, yet also that they will be cursed for uttering them aloud, for the names of these creatures are for Lord Iss alone to speak." Once more Golon looked up at the skies. "But I will quote the passage from the scriptures: *'In the golden age of the world, there were no cycles, no night succeeded by day, and day by night; but kingdoms where the gods' influence was ever present. Where Reh dwelt, there it was always sunshine; and in Reh's brother's kingdom, Erewon's, it was always midnight with a full moon shining; and in Iss' land there was only pitch-darkness with no sun or moon. But then came the wars of the gods and each strove to have hegemony over the other, so Reh sent forth his fire dragons to carry the chariot of the sun into the land of Iss, and Iss sent his creatures forth dragging the canopy of night into Reh's kingdom.'*

"So say the books of law. Now Reh's dragons have not the power they had of old: they had not been seen or heard of until we disturbed their nest under the Palisades. But every day we see the power of Iss' creatures: they fly round the world ever faster so that daylight becomes infinitesimally shorter. In a thousand years from now, or in a thousand thousand they will catch their tails. Then black night will stretch from one horizon to the next, so all is dark and the sun never rises and time will end."

"But can you summon these creatures?" Faran asked.

"It is in my power. But before I do, consider this: when the demons are called, the words of the prophecies will be overturned—the warp and weft of the fates will be unravelled, time accelerated, Lord Iss' will precipitated. What would have been inevitable, given aeons of time and the maturation of fate—the coming of the eternal darkness—will be brought forward. It will come when the Lightbringer, Iss' enemy, still lives; and when those who follow Reh still have hope. But when she is dead there will be no hope, nothing to stop the coming of the kingdom of Iss."

"You're saying we should wait? But how can we wait when daylight comes? Soon we will be destroyed, the Lightbringer will escape, and Iss' coming will be forever jeopardised," Faran said, gesturing at the creeping light.

Golon stared back, his own impending death freeing his tongue, giving him the courage he had lacked these last few years to answer back to his lord. "Perhaps extinction is preferable to the curse this summoning will bring. For this, all other curses upon our heads will be superseded. *My* soul will never enter the Place of Grey. But what of yours, that already rests there? Think of it: Iss himself will come and pluck it from its lofty pinnacle and cast it out and it will wander Shades until the ashes of the earth's fires have cooled and there is no world, no man or god. Now tell me, lord, whether extinction is not better?"

Golon paused, and studied his master. The fight seemed momentarily to have gone out of the Undead Lord; his pale face was beyond weariness, the mask of a two-hundred-year-old corpse, drained of life, of hope.

"A man can only suffer for one eternity," Faran whispered. He inched a step closer. "Bring these demons. In return, I will give you the Black Chalice. You are dying, you have the plague, do you not?"

Golon flinched from him. "You think I didn't know?" Faran sneered and sniffed the air. "Aye, I smell it. If you were like me, you would smell it all. The hundred thousand scents of the day, some beguiling and some repellent, that those who live exude." Golon hung his head. "What have you got to lose?" Faran continued. "Help me and instead of death you will live forever, like me."

"It is heresy to even name the demons . . ."

"Just speaking their names troubles you? Then let me speak them for you: I fear no curse. Even though the God be angered, he will not cast me from the Palace of Grey, for I am his elect, whose actions will bring his glory back to earth."

He took a deep breath and stared at the heavens as if daring them to send punishment. "On the very edge of that curtain of night," he declaimed, "fly a thousand thousand of Iss' steeds, trailing in their horned feet the darkness behind. These creatures are called the Athanor."

Golon's heart froze in his chest at the naming of them and his eyes flicked up to the sky to see what retribution might be cast down from the heavens for his master's foolhardiness. But none came, save the slowly advancing light of sunrise.

There was now a triumphant gleam in Faran's misted eyes. "See? I have named them and we both live. Now we need your powers. The sun is nearly on us. We cannot wait: they must be brought."

"But, master, it is Iss' prerogative alone . . ."

Faran cut him short. "Man must seek to master the world's destiny; the great man's will overrides all other scruples, all other powers, even a god's. How otherwise has humankind progressed, but by the inspiration of those who were nearly gods themselves?"

Golon didn't answer him, though a chill had gone up his spine at his master's heretical words.

"We will precipitate the darkness that is inevitable—that is all," Faran continued. "Then all the creatures that fear the sun, the Brethren, the hobgoblins and trolls who live underground in dark eaves, the damned spirits of the cursed glades, the rock giants frozen by the sun, the ghosts and wights who only inhabit the darkness—all these will praise us, and join to our cause. And Iss too, when he comes in dark glory in his chariot, will he not thank us for shortening his exile in the stars? Will he not lift up our souls and place them near the top of that pyramid in the Palace of Grey, there to look down upon his other servants? And will he not curse those others, Marizian chiefly, who wrote the prophecies and consigned him to that darkness which I, Faran, have liberated him from? Yes, Iss himself will thank us, Golon."

Golon didn't answer, but hung his head. For he knew Faran's words were those of a madman, unable to see the inevitability of the curse that must follow this summoning. What did Iss care for even one of the elect like Faran? He was no more than an insect in the God's eyes, a tiny whirring nuisance that would be stamped out the moment Iss' will was done on earth.

Yet Faran still had that one thing Golon must have: the Black Chalice. And though this scheme of his lord's was insane, and no doubt they would be cursed, was it not better to be cursed and alive than blessed and dead?

"So, still you are silent," Faran growled. "Still you are too afraid to summon them?" He pointed to the east. "I have named them, but what good is a name? My tongue will not bring them, only yours. Each minute the sun creeps towards us until that moment when its cursed face will shine upon us and we will be no more. The Athanor have passed over the Astardian Sea and over the edge of the world. If you know the words of the ritual, bring them back and cover us with darkness."

Strangely, Golon, who had never been seen to laugh in all the years since Faran had summoned him to his palace in Tiré Gand, now chose to let out a dry mirthless chuckle. "Why, lord, every priest of Iss is taught the words of that summoning, for each day and night we wait for the Prince's coming, his eternal darkness. The words are those that we will greet him with that dread night."

"I'm not interested in prayers, Golon, for then I could have brought every preacher from the Mother Temple in Tiré Gand with me. Instead I brought you because you have the power to change prayers into action, scripture to magic."

The smile passed from Golon's face. "The power?" he repeated. "Aye, I have the power, and with it comes knowledge, knowledge you would best be afraid of." He clenched his fist, so the knuckles showed white in the darkness. "I have studied long, poring over the codices where the demons are named. Studied them so long that their voices called to me, from the vellum in front of my eyes, called to me all the way from their homes in the stars. They tempted me, those voices, calling me to summon them unbound by any wardings to earth. Their voices were plaintive, persuasive. I felt my resolve weakening, yet I knew what would happen if I did so: had I not seen my six brothers ripped to a thousand pieces?

"And, when the demons' laughter and mockery became too much, I would flee my tower, my hands over my ears, trying to keep the voices out, and I would wander upon the high moors above Tiré Gand, sometimes all day until the dusk fell. And as the darkness crept over the land, there came a voice a thousand times stronger than the other demons' voices, like the chattering of bats. And I looked up and saw them, right upon the edge of night, the Athanor. A thousand times mightier than the others, for only Iss has the right to shackle them and bind them to his will: a thousand times more dangerous than those that killed my brothers."

"They won't harm us—they will see we do Iss' will."

"No, I tell you, our souls will be forfeit," Golon replied vehemently.

Faran took a step nearer him. "The sun grows old, eternal night comes. You are dry: in your soul, in your thinking. You have lived too long in musty libraries, splitting the hairs of a theological point, deciphering the head of a book worm for a full stop. Our lord does not live in the shadows of the library, on the dusty pages of a book. He is in the stars. And because be is there and we here, he needs us to act, to interpret his will. Show you are a true servant, not one who has merely swallowed the dusty lessons of the tomes and choked on them."

Golon did not flinch away from him but stared levelly back, eye to eye in a way he had never done before. "Perhaps you are right. But what good are words?" He pulled up the sleeve of his cloak and showed Faran his plague-mottled arm. "See? I will die as surely as you will when the light reaches you."

"So, not even your own magic can save you," Faran said with a thin smile, "but only this." From his dark cape he withdrew the Black Chalice. Its black surface gave off not a glint in the gloom of the ravine. "Do what I ask of you, and you will have it."

Golon stared at the Chalice. His heart's desire. But then he remembered the scenes in the tomb in the Black Mines, and he wondered. Was this what he really wanted?

Faran noticed his hesitation. "We only bring what is inevitable. Hurry! We will live in darkness forever and Iss will bless us!" He held the Chalice out, his eyes never leaving Golon's. "Yours is the only living blood left in our company, fill it and drink."

A small gleam of triumph flickered on Golon's face as he took the Chalice, but inside him there was terror as well. Was this how all men felt when confronted by the irreversibility of the Death in Life? He swallowed hard, pulling the obsidian knife from his belt. Then he knelt on the deck, placing the Chalice in front of him. "Let my blood give me eternal life," he whispered.

He cut down on his wrist, releasing a purple-red flow into the cup, and the knife fell from his fingers with a clatter. He grasped the Chalice with both bands, gazing into its depths, as if he stared into a whirlpool sucking him down.

"Hurry," Faran ordered. "The light is near. Your part of the bargain is required." Golon looked up at the sky. The sun was coming, the symbol of his enemy, Reh. Yet, in truth, when he had come from many a dark hour of study in his lonely tower or from the crypt beneath the temple of Tiré Gand, had the sight of the sun not cheered him? No, this was heresy: darkness only would he love. He closed his eyes and brought the vessel to his lips in one swift movement and tipped it back.

He waited. What would happen? The sip of bitter gall that was his blood coursed through him like a line of fire that ran into his heart: there was a sudden stillness there—the world was spinning. The Chalice fell from his hands and tumbled to the deck, joining the knife.

Faran was by his side, helping him to his feet. "Courage, man: see, it works," he said. "Now hurry, dawn is coming."

Golon's heart had almost stopped beating, his breath was frozen in his chest—yet he was conscious. He felt the blood drying in his veins. He shook his head, trying to clear it. His eyes narrowed against the sudden brightness of the light on the cliff face. Dawn. A grey gleam at the eastern end of the Iron Gates. The sun was coming and he would be reduced to a mist.

His tongue was strangely thick in his mouth, as if he had been drugged; his skin was cold, dead cold. Inside was an emptiness: only one appetite was left, the taste for blood. All other needs and desires were forgotten. His soul had gone, been given to the Prince of Darkness; now it rested in the Palace of Grey. He was one of the Dead in Life.

He leaned down and picked up the dagger and the Chalice, then he began walking forward, Faran steadying him. They reached the bowsprit. Faran pointed to the west.

"There—the Athanor are far away, on the other side of the world. Bring them now,"

Golon nodded. He stripped off his cloak. No longer did he feel the bitter cold, it was as if his skin had become numb. He stared once more into the Chalice. A small amount of his blood had survived the fall to the deck. He knelt and poured it on the deck in the area between bowsprit and foremast. The blood sizzled on the wooden planking, scoring a hole. Around it, Golon began carving an intricate sigil with the tip of his knife, of involved and cross-latticed patterns.

Minutes passed as the light continued to grow. The pattern expanded and expanded, like a spiderweb, but even more intricate, some shoots running right across the deck to the rail and bowsprit and back to the foremast. It was a work of art—it should have been his lifetime's work but it was dashed off in moments. The pattern had a strange life of its own, leading the eye into hypnotic ellipses and curls.

Then it was ready. He lifted his gaze and saw that he had but a few moments left; the sunlight was only a little way above them. How he now hated that golden light; how he longed for sable night to return. He would bring it back. He looked at Faran: strange, those eyes that had held such mastery over him but a few hours before now had none.

Now Golon was as great as his lord. Sadness and emptiness. How Faran had misused the gift that now he, Golon, possessed! Faran, in thrall to a mortal woman, Thalassa. Brought down by mortal desires, when only the satisfaction of blood mattered. How his weakness had imperilled them all: for Golon guessed that even if Faran had caught her, he would have kept her alive. Kept the Lightbringer, the enemy of Iss, alive!

But he was not like Faran. He would be immortalised. When the world was dark in centuries to come, it was his name, Golon's, they would remember, not Faran's.

"Begin the ritual," Faran commanded.

The two men eyed each other for a beat. "I need blood for the ritual," Golon said finally.

"What's wrong with the blood in the Chalice?" Faran asked.

"It's mine," the sorcerer answered.

"You want another's blood?" Faran answered with a thin smile. "But yours in the Chalice is the last living blood on the *Dark Ship*."

Golon looked at the copper drinking cup lying on the deck. His blood still stained the rim, though its depths as always were hidden. He felt a chill. *His* blood? He felt events were accelerating, getting out of control. A summoner never used his own blood if he could help it. Always another's: a slave or sacrifice. But once already he'd broken the rule, summoning Spindel when he'd sprinkled his own blood on the lake surface. But Spindel was a minor demon: the Athanor were a thousand times mightier.

He needed blood. The sunbeams would soon be upon them, there would be no hiding from them. Even if they climbed down and hid under the ship, the beams would be reflected up from the lee. There was no escaping what he must do: he was one of them, the undead, now: his fate was theirs.

Of the seven brothers he had been the most cautious and methodical: he alone had survived; but now he knew he was taking a risk greater than those that had killed them.

"Very well," he answered, then turned and raised his arms to the departing night in the west, and began to chant in a quavering voice that any who heard would have known was the voice of a dead man.

"Come, Athanor, dread steeds, who haul the dark chariot; Galadrian's thread is lost; Reh wanders the depths of night: come, Darkness, end of the light forever."

Silence on the ship save the eerie whistling of the wind over the ice, yet strange stippled shadows seemed to winnow across the dawn sky like cirrus cloud. Then a strange rumbling was heard. Loose rocks began to topple from the heights above them, smashing into the surface of the ice, filling the air with spinning stone fragments. The sun had just reached the edge of the cliff above them, but they saw a dark aura around it as it hauled itself up, as if its shining disc had been eclipsed and only the light around it still shone. The violet of the sky began to deepen.

There came a shrieking in the air. Dark forms, like migratory birds in the autumn, passed over them, then turned, circling down towards the ship. Down and down. The vampires watched, hypnotised. Golon still stood with the Chalice in his hand. It became colder and colder as the creatures closed.

The forty years of caution had been as nothing, for in his moment of triumph, when he had achieved his life wish, he had made the fatal mistake. *His* blood had been the lure. Now the Athanor had come for him. He was the sacrifice.

The dark flying shapes hovered, casting the whole ravine into an inky blackness; a stunning chill came with the shadow, black ice covered the deck in seconds, the sound of the wind stopped. Then the Athanor swooped. They made no noise as they fell on Golon. The only sound was the sorcerer's single agonised scream.

CHAPTER TWENTY-FOUR

No Dawn in Tiré Gand

In Tiré Gand the blaring of cow horns announced that it was the hour before dawn; the undead thronged the streets, hastening to their daytime resting places.

On the highest of the city's seven hills, the religious leaders of the city, the Elders, repaired to the ivy-hung sepulchres set in the cliffs beneath the great stepped pyramid of Iss. The temple guards and the priests went to the mouldy catacombs that honey-combed the hill, the burying place of Tiré Gand since the city's foundation.

Elsewhere—the other ranks of society made their own arrangements for surviving the daylight hours. The lowest of the laity took themselves to the cellars of their houses, while the merchants pulled down the dark blinds of their shops and retired to the storage vaults where many a glass flask gleamed ruby with the blood that was the life of the city. But the nobility did not deign to dwell in the slums and shambles of the lower town. When the bone trumpets were sounded, they were carried in litters to shuttered mansions on the other side of the Furx, the great river that guarded the city on one side. The snaking lines of palanquins proceeded without benefit of lantern or torch, across the three bridges with their seven great spanned arches: the Bridge of Sighs,

the Way of the Hollow Crown and the Bridge of the Risen
Dead.

On the boggy ground on the opposite bank the latter-day
lay rulers of the city had laid out palaces with many a Gothic
spire and steeply pitched roof. These palaces had but one
gateway and one door and no windows. Their gardens were
filled with weeping willows and poison ivy and creeper-
hung walls and many an umbrageous plant and shrub that
cast a twilight over the dewy lawns even at high midday.

Only one of the buildings stood out from the rest. Several
of the litters passed a sizable mansion that stood at the end
of the Bridge of Sighs, directly overlooking the river. This
building, unlike the others, had windows, now boarded over,
suggesting that once one of the living had resided here, perhaps as recently as two hundred years ago. There the ivy
hung thick on the gargoyles guarding the gates, and the
weeds in the formal gardens behind were knee high.

The nobility of Tiré Gand had never had reason to like
this neighbour of theirs. The man who had owned this place
had been an upstart, a mortal; doomed to die a natural death,
unlike these nobles who had lived the Life in Death for a
thousand years and more. Only the damp river air ended
their second existence as their bodies rotted at the joints,
their heads and their limbs loosened and finally fell, quite
literally, apart from their bodies. Then their families would
take their constituent parts to the darkest area of their vaults
and leave them, all jabbering skulls and twitching limbs,
until the second sleep took them forever.

But this man had once lived and would have died, under
the assassins' knives bought by a noble who envied him his
influence with the Elders. But even in death, his status had
been enhanced, for the Elders had brought him back to the
Life in Death through the Black Chalice.

The rotting walls and towers of this house, the mildewed
pier stabbing out into the sluggish grey water of the Furx,
the formal gardens fringed by weeping willows, all had once
belonged to the city's general, Faran Gaton Nekron, victor
of Thrull. He who having been granted a draft of it to bring

him back to life had been entrusted with the city's greatest treasure, the Black Chalice. Perhaps one or two of those who passed wondered what had become of him in the lands to the west.

There had been no news from Thrull for a long time. The Elders had despatched scouts from their armies in Surrenland. They had returned a month before: Thrull was a ruin, empty of life. Of Faran Gaton there was no sign. Had its master gone to the second death? It was difficult to believe: his had been a haughty confidence mixed with military competence that far outshone the capabilities of the other enfeebled denizens of the city. He of all their number had been the ideal candidate to subjugate the western lands. But few mourned his disappearance, for if he had lived, he would surely have returned one day and challenged even the power of the Elders. In five centuries or so perhaps, his mansion would sink quietly into the marshes, and then these self-same lords would pass down the causeway without being troubled by memories of its erstwhile owner.

Now the nobles' palanquins were brought through the gates of their mansions, into gloomy halls down marble steps to damp crypts where they spent the daytime hours, cursing the moisture that seeped through the stones, that rotted their bodies, that would one day reduce them to mere simulacra of those who lived.

An hour passed. All now was quiet in the city and on the causeways. Tiré Gand was on a more easterly longitude than the Iron Gates. Dawn arrived an hour earlier. The sky became grey and presently, over the eastern moors, came the sun. Yet the light of the rising purple orb barely penetrated the mist that drifted down from the high moors and over the River Furx. The grey streets were filled with dripping condensation.

At this daylight hour, the places open to the sky were empty save for the men the city's Elders, the elite of the priesthood, called disparagingly the day priests of the god Iss. These were the living servants of Iss who came from elsewhere in Ossia hoping eventually to be granted the

Death in Life. Generation after generation had come, aged and died, and very few had been granted the final viaticum of the Life in Death.

In the streets living slaves passed about their business, their heads hung low in abject despair, knowing that their lives might be ended at any time by the blood lust of their masters.

The vast edifice of the Mother Temple of the Worm dominated the city. The lower courses of the temple were set as a pyramid, serving as a pendentive for the drum of the dome. Between the four arches holding the dome were four apses in which hung a thousand copper bells.

Beneath the high corbelled ceiling, the cloaks of the day priests' purple and brown robes were barely distinguishable in the gloom as they moved about their tasks, the sound of their shuffling sandals echoing about the vast space like sighs.

Strangely, there was still some pride even in these lowly castes though so few were called to the Death in Life: for in the books of prophecies they were singled out for a signal blessing: as the only living acolytes manning the temple during the dawn hours, they would be the first to see the beginning of Iss' eternal night, when first would come Reh's burning chariot and then the eternal darkness that would forever snuff it out.

Through the generations, each day a priest had been assigned to watch for this event. This morning it was a young acolyte. He stood on a rickety platform suspended under the glass-lined lantern above the temple dome. Below him was a vertiginous drop of two hundred feet to the great mosaic of the Worm devouring its own tail set into the temple floor. In front of him, suspended from a metal beam, hung the great bronze bell of the temple, twenty feet in radius. It would never be rung until the great day when the sun was extinguished.

His was the highest vantage point in the whole city, sitting only just below the bleak grey moors behind, where the sorcerers' towers were silhouetted like broken teeth on the horizon.

The land of Ossia stretched below him: the falling tangle of the mist-filled streets of Tiré Gand stretched over its seven hills, the brown fields, the dun-coloured river, more drear, treeless moors rising beyond. The horizon was lost in the grey mist, but nevertheless, as the sun rose, the sky lightened imperceptibly, bringing new details out of the shadow from that tenebrous landscape.

But as he watched he fancied he heard a faint rumbling and the lantern tower seemed to rock back and forth, the movement exacerbated by the great height at which he was situated. He found his teeth had started chattering in his head. The glass dome around him began to crack.

He turned in the direction of the newly risen sun. It was as if the sky to the east of the purple orb, which should have shown the violet of the day, was now black once more. Around the sun stood an aureole of darkness, as if it was in eclipse. Stipples of darkness carried on westwards past it, swallowing the little light that still remained in the sky. The darkness rushed over the moors and swooped down upon Tiré Gand like a great wave, pitching the observatory into shadow.

The air suddenly felt oppressive, his eyelids leaden. He felt so tired, as if it were indeed deep midnight once more . . . He shook his head, trying to keep himself awake.

What was happening? Was this the last day? Had Iss finally triumphed? He must act. Rouse the Elders from their tombs.

Without thinking, the acolyte grasped the clapper of the great bell that hung before him and yanked it furiously. The noise rang through him, shaking the unstable scaffolding platform; the weakened glass of the dome shattered with a dry crack, shards of crystal fell slowly like snowflakes two hundred feet to the mosaic floor of the nave.

The sound waves pushed out, reaching the thousand lesser bronze bells situated in every niche and upon every flying buttress, and they in turn began to ring, filling the vast space and the streets outside with a cacophony of sound.

Below, in the darkness of the catacombs, a thousand smaller bells situated over the sarcophagi of the Elders picked up the reverberation and began to tinkle urgently. The eyes of one and then another sprang open in the darkness, knowing what the bells portended: the Endless Night had come. With unaccustomed speed, they levered themselves up onto their emaciated elbows and dropped to the marble floors of their tombs.

The guards thrust open the bronze gates of the tombs and the Elders shuffled out in their mildewed robes and stared up at the sky. Not even a faint nimbus of light now surrounded the sun. It was total eclipse. All was dark. As one they sank to their knees and raised their hands, giving thanks to Lord Iss: he had restored the world to the primordial darkness from which it had come, a world that they would now inherit, in which they need no longer flee the burning rays of the sun.

Around the dark streets of Tiré Gand bone cow horns moaned, and drums were beaten, a mournful sound, yet triumphant, a bass refrain to the continuing clangour of the bells.

CHAPTER TWENTY-FIVE

Iskiard

Once more, Thalassa brought forth a light, a gentle green light that glowed over them. Then she, Urthred and the three surviving villagers, Garadas, Samlack and Ostman, left the wreck of the *Windhover* and set off over the tundra, the distant towers and the single star blazing over the ruins acting as their waymarks.

It was still dark and now they were even more conscious of how far the sword had brought them. In the Iron Gates the sun had risen, but in this more northerly latitude there was still no hint of dawn in the sky. Perhaps light only came for an hour or two a day. Instead there was a black sky, no stars, save the one that guided them, a bitter cold eating their bones and every inch of bare skin. The canvas sails they had wrapped around themselves for extra warmth were little use. The ice and snow beneath their feet had been smoothed flat by the centuries of scything wind that now drove into their faces, sending up a dismal howl. Gradually the towers and the star disappeared from sight as the wind mounted to a frenzy, and ice devils spun towards them. They stumbled on blindly, following the guttering light of Thalassa's magical orb.

The ice devils circled nearer and nearer: before spinning away once more like tops. But the further they marched, the nearer the ice devils got, their sound higher and higher until it was as if they were surrounded by a wall of whirling white tornadoes, spraying ice particles into their faces whichever way they looked, the sound deafening. Thalassa and the others halted, afraid to move on.

"Lead on," Garadas entreated, "before we all go mad!"

Thalassa took Urthred's arm and pressed forward, her hand outstretched, palm outwards: the circling ice devils spun away at her sign, forming an avenue, which folded away on either side of their path, like a parting of waves.

Without the mask Urthred's face was unfamiliarly numb from the cold, frost hung on the newly grown eyelashes and brows. It seemed to him he glimpsed faces in the whirling columns of snow: ghosts, *his* dead—Randel, sacrificed in the dark inner sanctuary; Seresh dead in the underworld; the screams of the thousands burned in the temple after the undead had risen; Furtal perished out on the marshes. Alanda, their faithful guide; his father, unexpectedly found and as suddenly lost; the population of Lorn; the dead Godans who had followed them trustingly across half the world, only to die.

On and on, the faces leaning in towards him. He heard their voices: incoherent, warning, bewailing, accusing, cursing . . .

His head reeled. Why had *he* lived, the voices seemed to say, when they had perished. Guilt ate his soul, he had a hunger to die, to give up and join these others, wandering the plains of Iskiard—those who had been more worthy than him. Anything to shut out the maddening noise . . .

Then silence, the ghosts had vanished in a second. The light of the star once more filled the northern night sky, blazing, giving hope, and under it, suddenly looming across the entire horizon, the towers and minarets of Iskiard.

Then a hundred gouts of flame tore apart the night, and there was a roar like the sky being ripped asunder: the roar of dragons, the same they had heard on the Plain of Ghosts and over Ravenspur. The dark horizons turned to gold. Everything was revealed in the stark light.

A massive granite wall punctuated every few yards by steepling round towers stretched away to left and right. The wall was covered to half its height in banked snow. The sky was starkly lit by dazzling gouts of flame that came from a hundred high points: the towers and the tops of huge buildings including a number of pyramids that stood within the walls. For one more second Urthred saw as clear as day, then all was dark again.

The villagers fell to their knees, terrified, their mouths slack, gaping. Urthred stood unmoved: he had heard the call a second before the shock wave of noise and explosion of light had actually reached them. A call that sang in his blood, blew away the clinging webs of despair, rekindled his inner fires. Reh's dragons. Once in Forgeholm and once again on the edge of Lorn he had become as they. For he was their brother. Was not his blood as fiery as theirs, was there not kinship between them?

The dragons from Harken's Lair. As he had always known they would be, waiting for them in Iskiard—and for whatever followed them. He felt each one's expectant heartbeat, rapid with excitement. They could see what he couldn't see: their enemies were coming, the battle would be soon. Then Urthred would lead them as once Harken had led them. Brothers of fire . . .

But first they must get into the city. Urthred squinted at the wall. It was broken directly in front by a massive stone gateway, its bottom half lost in a snowdrift, a smooth glacis of ice leading steeply up to where there was a gap in between the half-open double gates, broken by a glassy portcullis of stalactites hanging from its coping. Black sky showed through behind.

The villagers had by now slightly recovered from the shock of the dragon fire. "Follow me," Urthred commanded and set off up the slope. Thalassa followed.

Centuries of snow had been windblown to a glassy, icy slipperiness and he had to dig out foot- and handholds with his feet and gloves as he climbed. He reached the point where the slope gave way to the top of the open gate and the dark night beyond. There was a narrow treacherous ice ridge here. He helped Thalassa up and then inspected the top of the gateway.

The huge stalactites hung down, twenty feet in length, blocking progress. He reached forward and caught the spear of ice immediately in front of him in the pincers of his gloves. It broke with a sound like the snapping of a limb. The dragons remained silent, though he felt their silent heartbeats within him, knew that the creatures waited, to see whether they would enter.

In the narrow gap he had opened he saw a steep ice chute leading downwards on the other side: the northern star shone down on a massive snow-covered square. On each of its sides, he saw distant boundary walls beyond immense buildings and colonnades.

Thalassa stood just behind him on the ice ledge. "I'll bring more light," she whispered, and opened her arms to the star. Suddenly the light that had accompanied them all night and now hovered slightly behind his head increased in intensity, throwing Urthred's shadow across the square.

How far the shadow ran! Over the unmarked snow of the massive square, a mile across. Beyond the colonnades rose the looming bulk of the pyramid and the hundred towers that had led them here over the icy waste. He saw on top of each of them, reflected back by the light, the stirring forms and flaring metallic wings of the dragons. Two hundred red eyes fixed upon them from their several vantage points. Once more he felt their heartbeat accelerate, acknowledging the Lightbringer had come. Another air-splitting roar, then silence as if the dragons watched what they would do now.

Urthred looked around the city. Where should they go? What were they looking for? He had no foreknowledge of this place; Manichee's books had referred to it with no great certainty, small wonder since Marizian was the last man to have been here, and that five thousand years before. But Marizian had left a trail of clues—had given them the prophecies of the Lightbringer.

To the left, a mile or more distant and occupying almost

half the side of the square, was the largest of all the pyramids, five times the size of the temple pyramids in Thrull, a thousand feet high. On its eastern side, fronting the square, was a peristyle building. Perhaps a sanctuary, a place of purification for pilgrims.

"There," he said, pointing.

Thalassa gestured, sending the magical ball of light flying far across the square and upwards to the pyramid summit where it hovered, so now it seemed there were twin stars beaming down upon them from the velvet black sky. In the augmented light of star and magical sphere, wreaths of smoke could be seen coming from the distant summit, just like the smoke that had billowed from Reh's temple in Thrull. But this was no smoke; the light showed it forming into distinct shapes. These were the ghostly forms of the dead pouring into the Mundane World from Shades. They eddied about in the bright light, then fled up into the sky.

Urthred turned, shielding his eyes from the glare of the twin stars. Already he sensed a lightening of the sky, the blackness giving way to a steely blue, and the very topmost of the cloud-touching towers suddenly glowed with a roseate hue. From high above he heard the roar of one of the dragons, greeting his master Reh.

At a gesture from Urthred, Garadas produced a length of rope salvaged from the *Windhover*'s wreck. The headman tied it tightly round the pommel of a dagger that he hammered into the ice shelf as a piton. When it was anchored, Urthred seized it with one gloved hand, and offered Thalassa the other. She stepped in close to him and he lowered himself and her down the steep reverse slope behind the gate until they reached the level of the snow-covered square fifty feet below.

As their feet touched the ground, there came from each vantage point more roars and gouts of flame, and the beat of armoured wings as if each dragon was about to take flight— the sound echoed off the ice-clad walls of Iskiard.

Urthred felt the fire in his veins respond. His limbs and heart ached with yearning to be with them: he remembered how it had been, when he had flown over Lorn: that had been freedom.

The snow at ground level was shin high, its flat virgin expanse unbroken to the foot of the pyramid. The buildings flanking it now seemed even more imposing than they had done from the heights above. The stepped pyramid itself looked as high as a mountain from ground level.

"Come," Thalassa said, "though it is nearly dawn, something evil stirs. Iss is close." Urthred looked up at the eyries of the now-silent dragons: a hundred of them. Surely there were enough to defeat whatever was coming to Iskiard? But still he felt a sick unease: whatever stirred against them was dark and very powerful.

Thalassa set off across the square at an oblique angle, heading towards the westwards pyramid, the starlight still blazing over the distant summit, her footsteps leaving a lonely trail in the virgin snow.

It was only a mile but it took half an hour to get there through the deep snow. More and more of the tower tops now glowed with light. But despite this favourable sight, Urthred's heart was still oppressed with a gloomy dread. At last, the massive steps were in front of them, leading up to the peristyle building they'd seen from the gateway. Its steps were strangely free of the snowdrifts. There was a gap in the colonnades directly above them. Now Thalassa called the burning orb down from the summit of the pyramid, so it hovered brightly over her head.

She began to climb, her sandalled feet silent on the stone. Urthred and the three others followed close behind: until they stood on the top. Thalassa's orb burned in front and they saw that beyond the colonnade was a granite wall. Right in front of them was an entrance and a long corridor, plunging into the darkness.

They stepped closer, the light flowing before them. The corridor walls were lined with glass mirrors, covered with a thin sheen of ice. They gave back a hundred reflections of their ragged selves and the light now blazing behind them. In the mirrors the four men, reflected a thousand times, their clothes dripping with snow and meltwater, seemed a pauper's army, led by a single goddess clad in a glowing white robe.

For though the men were reflected countless times from the panels, Thalassa's image gave back only one, from the panel right at the corridor's end. Her white cloak glowed like a star in the mirror. Only her reflection, and not Urthred's and the villagers', showed in that one glass. Looking at it, it was as if she, and she alone, stood there in the corridor, and that she alone was destined to pass through that doorway into the unknown. The Godans shrank back when they saw this, and whispered fearfully amongst themselves. Urthred too felt a shiver of fear at this magic, but Thalassa was already moving away from them, down the corridor towards the mirror.

She approached the panel, the light glowing brighter and brighter in the reflection so it seemed no longer a mere reflection but a coming apotheosis brighter than any star, as bright as the sun. The men held their hands in front of their faces, shielding them. She reached the panel and flung up her arms. With one more flash of light, the panelled mirror shot up into a hidden notch in the ceiling.

Now that the glaring reflection was gone, they saw that another corridor stood behind, lost in darkness. But right at the threshold was what they at first took to be a bundle of cloth and bones. Urthred hurried to Thalassa's side. A leathery mummified face stared up from the bundle, the skin stretched tight on the framework of bone, the corpse's mouth agape. Apart from the shrinkage, the face had been perfectly preserved in the cold. The robes were velvet, faded with age, embroidered with elaborate decorations: priestly vestments. Urthred knelt, his breath misting so thick in the bitter cold that he could barely see in front of him.

Some colour, though faded, still clung to the man's robes: orange and red. The colours of a priest of Reh. One hand was outstretched, still covered by leathery brown skin. A yellowed scroll was clutched in it, as if the dead man was offering it to whoever next came through the doorway. A quill and an ink pot lay on the floor next to him. Urthred gently prised the scroll away from the skeletal hand. He pulled it open and it unfurled with a dry rustle.

He recognised the words on the paper, the language of the Flame.

"I, Cronus, will now die, my soul forfeit forever to Shades, unless a fellow priest comes and sends my ashes to heaven. You who come beware, if you are a friend. Beyond lies the temple: there the Marishader lurk. Everywhere the ghosts that Marizian released fly through the air. All they speak to, they send mad. There is no hope in Iskiard."

He stood slowly, looking further down the corridor to where it seemed to break into a mazelike hall bisected by columns: there lay the temple and the underworld. And their fate.

He looked back down the reflecting corridor. There was grey in the tiny area of sky visible. Dawn at last. The prospect of seeing it tugged him back, towards the square.

A distant roar, magnified by the confines of the corridor, as the dragons greeted their lord again. Iss was powerless after dawn. Reh had not forgotten his handmaiden, the Lightbringer.

But then a strange thing happened: the light had feebly grown from grey to a subdued white even in the few seconds Urthred had been watching, but now it was as if dawn had been replaced by dusk, or as if reaching its ebb, the darkness like the tide came flooding back, filling the world.

He could feel a slight vibration in the air, through the floors and walls of the corridor. It grew and grew. His teeth began to chatter. Brittle cracks sounded from the mirrors, then, one by one, they exploded and a shower of glass rained down on them. The villagers clung to each other in terror. The light at the end of the corridor was fading fast.

"Priest, what is it?" Garadas asked, his face pale under his beard.

Urthred was silent. The mounting dread that had been with him these last few hours had suddenly peaked and he was speechless. It was Thalassa who answered. "It is the darkness of the eternal night."

The men let out a moan of terror. "The spirits of the dead protect us!" Garadas whispered despairingly. "What's that noise?"

Again it was Thalassa who answered. "The Athanor: it is the beating of their wings."

"What are they?"

"The demons that drag the edge of night from dusk till dawn, but now they have circled the world and there is no sun. Now only Reh and our faith can save us."

Now Urthred spoke. "Reh and our faith, and the dragons. I must lead them," he said quietly, staring towards the end of the corridor.

"Lead them? How can a man lead dragons?" Garadas asked.

"Remember Lorn, when Fenris Wolf had us pinned in the tower?"

"Aye, you summoned the dragon."

"Then I summoned, but now I will become one. I will lead the dragons against these Athanor. Go on, into the underworld: I'll join you when the darkness is defeated."

CHAPTER TWENTY-SIX

The Battle of the Skies

After Golon's scream, the darkness was full of the rustling of wings and a strange masticating sound, half sucking, half chewing. Then the darkness passed, and the intense cold and a fraction of light returned. Once more Faran could see the area between the bowsprit and the foremast. It was empty save for a charring around the summoning circle and a dark smear of blood. Golon was gone.

Faran had never known fear, not since his first death, that night of the assassins' knives when he had woken by his mistress's side, drowning in his own blood: not since then (for what terror was there beyond extinction?) had any experience or sight caused his inner soul to tremble: not even as he lay beneath Nekron's thundering feet, nor when Acharon had taken him upon his barge. But now, as he stared at what he and Golon had brought, he felt ice in his veins, ice that would freeze even the thick viscous tar that served as his blood.

In the sky over the prow of the *Dark Ship* and the steepling sides of the gorge, it looked as if a shelf of darkness flew westwards. He saw the confused mass of beating wings at its edge, silhouetted against the light of what would have been dawn, but which was now being overrun by the darkness: the Athanor.

The undead gibbered all around him in the demons'

shadow, foam at their mouths. Only the whites of their eyes showing. Now the Athanor swooped once more towards the ship: the denizens of Hel, bat-winged, their bodies armoured a dark scaly brown, cruel-fanged, their heads peak-shaped, ending in tufted ears, their eyes blazing red malevolence. Perhaps Golon had not been enough: now they came to take Faran to where the sorcerer had been borne, down to the abyss.

Instead they landed without a sound upon the spars of the ship, grappling them with their dark claws. Now there came a faint tremor, and the ship bumped and shifted from the icy bed of the ravine with a clatter of ratlines and halyards.

Then there was a sudden lurch and the ship lifted up as if it weighed no more than paper, and Faran saw the walls of the gorge dropping away, faster and faster so the rust-red cliffs sinking past either side became but a blur.

Above, and to either side, he saw the Athanor like shadows, their claws gouging the hull and spars so the black metal of the ship buckled and turned white. Their wings barely beat the air beneath them, their tails swept away in the slipstream as far as the eye could see.

He fought the sudden absence of gravity and struggled to the rail. He thrust his head over the side, and the wind rushed past. On either side the Iron Gates fell away. The ship flew higher and higher. The golden archway spanning the ravine that had seemed so impossibly high a moment before shot past and fell away below like a plummeting stone. Beneath them the dark line of the ravine was no more than a diminishing scar running through the jumbled red wilderness of mountains five thousand feet below. And then the ship settled just under the layer of darkness above and he saw a thousand and a thousand more of the creatures, so intermingled that their shapes *were* the darkness.

Now the upwards movement was replaced by a lateral one, and the air rushed into his face from the bow. How fast they were carried forward, swifter than the swiftest horse. Did they still point towards Iskiard? He fought the howling wind and ran forward to the foremast stays. He clambered up into the webbing trying to get a view of what lay in front.

The wind thrashed at his face, the blackness ahead still impenetrable to his eyes. Nothing, utter nullity.

He reached out as if to touch the dark cloud that trailed from the black edge far in front of him: his right hand plunged into its depths; it was as if it had been cut by a million freezing razors, and he pulled it back quickly. A handful of what looked like black soot came away in it, but it was not powder, but rather the essence of darkness, impacted, made solid. The blackness of the last day. He felt its darkness pass through his leathery skin, its cold seeking out his heart. Even *his* dead heart. Dark life, squirming in his hands—he threw it down. On the deck he saw what looked like inky black worms wriggling where he had flung them.

Yet some of the darkness remained stuck to his leather glove. He stared at it with a strange and dread fascination. The darkness spoke to him, perhaps in the same voice that the demons had once spoken to Golon, tempting him, cajoling him to join them.

Though he knew destruction lay there, he pressed the darkness, not understanding why he did it, to his mouth, and it was as if the dark soot entered his spirit. Darkness entered his veins, a sustaining darkness that drove away everything from his mind, even his blood lust; for it was more satisfying than any blood he had ever tasted.

Voices echoed in his head, the demons' voices. And then as if a veil had fallen from his eyes, his sight came back and he saw the world below as perhaps Iss saw it from his starry home. He saw the curvature of the earth, the horizon no impediment, as if his eyes flew around them. And he saw how the darkness raced on over the blue of the sea and the green of the land until it encircled the world, so not a ray of sun fell upon it.

And upwards, where the light of the stars had been snuffed, there, like a shadow upon the darkness, he saw a dark mass, a black star, getting closer and closer . . . The God himself, coming from the stars to take his inheritance.

On they drove, the force of the wind ripping out Faran's cloak, plucking at his limbs, threatening to snatch him from

his precarious hold on the foremast stays. He peered ahead.
Below, he now saw that the mountains had given way and
that an ice field stretched all the way to the north. The
shadow of the great cloud fell on the ice plain as it snuffed
the light of the dawn that blossomed, then died. They pursued and began to outrun the sun struggling through the
morning sky to its zenith.

Then, as the shadow swept on, he saw the distant towers
and pyramids of Iskiard in front. The Athanor carrying them
saw it too, for they began to drop down from the belly of the
cloud. The forward motion became even more violent. Like
a plummeting hawk upon its prey the ship tilted steeply
down, and on either side the Athanor came crowding in to
escort it to its target. From this height, the black granite curtain walls, the pyramids, temple roofs and towers were as
clearly etched as a map before his eyes.

Urthred ran back down the corridor towards the square. He
stepped out under the colonnades and peered out. To the
east, in the direction of the rising sun, there was a line of
inky black. The risen sun was eclipsed, the barest rim of
light showing at its edge. This was it: the endless night, Iss'
demons covering the world with their darkness—unless the
dragons could overcome them.

The dragons roared, and gouts of flame exploded from a
hundred different vantage points. He felt the intensified
hammering of their hearts, and his own stepped up its beat
in sympathy. He felt the weightless, anchorless joy that was
an anticipatory thrill of flight.

Yet elation was mixed with fear—the snow on the square
barely glimmered, its colour turned from white to black as
the shadow passed over it. Urthred felt the cold hand of Iss
on his spine.

Faran and he. This morning, a morning that had begun in
light and ended in darkness, they would fight and one or the
other would live.

His head swam. It had been at Forgeholm, in the sanctuary, when he had first brought the Fire Dragon. Years had

passed before the second occasion, on the edge of Lorn, when he had become the dragon and fought Fenris. His soul ached for flight, his veins burned with a molten fire as if in addiction for the sky. He fought his spirit like one who fights a kite that wants to break free of the string that holds it to the earth and soar up and up into the blue sky.

He strained his eyes, imagining himself upon the tops of the towers. Then the earth fell away, perspectives blurring, the edge of vision grey. And he *was* at the top of one of the towers, and he was inside one of the creatures, standing upon taloned claws, metallic wings flaring out to either side.

Now he was high up he saw that the edge of the cloud seemed to boil with a furious life; was not darkness all but comprised of a million batlike demons, drawing the darkness behind them. Where their leathery wings overlapped one another and touched, wisps of darkness broke off like waves, and tumbled downwards in shadowy curtains, showers of darkness that seethed and roiled where they fell upon the snow-covered tundra like acid.

Something was moving under the canopy, nearly lost in the darkness, but Urthred's eyes were sharp as an eagle's. The *Dark Ship,* beneath and slightly behind the line of whirling claws and gaping fanged mouths and beating leathery wings. Black creatures held the ship's masts and spars in their taloned feet, dragging it under them as their peers dragged the edge of the night.

A shadow passed over his soul—he felt fear. He shut his eyes against the sudden dizziness, then snapped them open again. Once more he was in the great square and no longer high in the dragon's eyrie. He had failed. He felt his human frailty, imprisoned in this human body, cowering on the steps of the temple annex, his friends gone on and he alone, powerless. Now the thunder of the approaching darkness was as loud as the sound of galloping hooves, and he could see the pillars on either side of him begin to shake. Snow and ice fell from the cornice above him.

A burst of brilliant flames and then, as one, the dragons thrust off their towers. They fell into space like stones, but then with a single beat of their mighty wings, they soared up once more. A hundred or more of them—all that had escaped Harken's Lair. As they beat upwards into the inky sky each spewed long traceries of golden fire that underlit the advancing shelf of darkness overhead. They circled the towers and the rooftops, in a long serpent's tail, the stragglers joining the end of the tail, beating their mighty wings to catch up with the others.

At their head, the brightest scales, the rainbow spectrum plumage, were those of Vercotrix, chief of all of them, Harken's own mount, leading the spiral of dragons higher and higher and in ever-widening circles towards the Athanor.

Urthred followed them with his eyes, hypnotised by the spiral pattern, his neck craning higher and higher. Against the darkness of the cloud they appeared a hundred miniature suns. That was the only life, that life of flight, the world left far behind, the elemental battle, light and dark, in front.

Before conscious thought could hinder him, the cord that tied Urthred to these creatures fastened around his soul and tugged him upwards. His soul soared, then once more he was one with them. This time he was Vercotrix, the dark sky roiling with his fiery breath, its moisture turned to mist; he saw with his diamond-bright eyes. He was part of the dragon's past and future, bound by the fire that ran in their veins, and as his heart lifted to Vercotrix, so the chief of the dragons climbed, higher and higher, the rest following in his trail, his throat spitting molten flame as he called the other dragons. The noise of two hundred wings was like the thunder of a waterfall; so closely did they come together, they obliterated the sound of approaching thunder from the dark cloud.

The edge of the cloud had been ten miles away, but the distance narrowed quickly as the two approached each other at breakneck speed.

In the cloud now Urthred saw through Vercotrix's eyes the turmoil of creatures, some human limbed, yet fanged, a span or more wide even at this distance, drawing after them a swirling dark canopy, darker than the sky of a moonless night: darker and deeper than soot.

The dragons flew right upwards towards the dark maelstrom, one thousand feet, two thousand feet, five—until the city was but a tiny blot far behind. They were level with the cloud. Ahead was the *Dark Ship*.

Urthred and Vercotrix: their will was one, fused. Let them destroy the ship, and Faran: then maybe the Athanor would be destroyed as well. His tail twitched so that he hurtled straight towards the ship. But now the leading edge of the dark cloud peeled away and dropped towards the ascending dragons, and Vercotrix and his followers, one whole, one spirit, thundered into the bubbling darkness in a train of fire.

Then the darkness was all around, seeping through the armoured scales, dousing their internal fires. Some of those who followed fell, down and down, their wings spinning like falling sycamore seeds, their metal armour breaking away from their bodies. And even he, Vercotrix, the strongest of all of them, felt his fire begin to dampen. Now he was lost, his eyes failing to penetrate the dark, the flames of his breath no more than brief pulses of orange. He spun, his tail lashing from side to side, trying to keep himself on an even trim. A sweeping talon of mist scythed towards him—Vercotrix banked steeply. Up and down were indistinguishable; did he rise or fall?

The darkness would destroy even him. Nullity, entropy, the destruction of all that was positive. It was as if his spirit were slowly sucked away, Now he knew he was falling once more; he reeled, struggling to keep consciousness. Then he heard Thalassa's voice, like an echo from far away, calling him back. Telling him to leave the dragons, return his spirit to the ground, find her in the underworld.

His eyes blinked open once more: again he stood on the temple steps. Far away were orange explosions in the midnight sky, burning debris plummeting downwards falling from the dark edge of the cloud. As he watched, dozens more fell, spinning to the ground, and each exploded in a geyser of dark smoke and roaring orange flame as their acid and fire commingled, lighting the underside of the cloud five thousand feet above.

Thalassa's voice came again. "Urthred, there is nothing you can do. Come to me." He looked around. The corridor into the underworld was empty save for the corpse of the long-dead priest and the shattered glass of the mirrors. Where was the voice coming from? But like an echo in his soul, it came again, calling him.

Her voice tore him one way, the cry of the dragons the other. He looked back at the advancing cloud. Flashes of muted orange like burnt sienna deep from within its heart showed that the battle still raged there. And he heard Vercotrix call to him, as clearly as Thalassa had done.

He could not turn away from his brothers: he was still one with them, even as he stood beneath the colonnades.

Once more it was as if his soul were sucked back into the air: through the darkness. Back to Vercotrix and to death. The dragon still flew, but only just. He felt a terrible wound at its right wing base, and acid ichor flowing away in the currents of air beaten from behind its hurtling body. Vercotrix's talons and gouts of flame rent the sooty darkness to shreds: though the dragons died, so did the Athanor. He heard them wail, and ahead, through a tear in their ranks caused by another lance of flame, he glimpsed the target he sought, deep in the darkness, the place whence the magic came that controlled these demons; the *Dark Ship*, its masts appearing through the darkness for anything like a ship breaking through a fog-bound sea. It sailed serenely through the air, undisturbed by the apocalyptic battle all around it. He tucked his right wing under his body, banking once more. As he hurtled down he saw the throngs of the undead, white faces turned towards him, then black clouds blanked out the view once more.

One beat, then two. Would he make it? The dragon fire in his heart was failing, the wound in his side leaking more life blood. More and more of the dragons behind fell spinning out of the air, only he the strongest, and one or two others, struggled on towards the *Dark Ship*. Another gout of flame, the cloud parted once more, and then he saw his enemy. Faran at the very prow of the ship.

Then the dragon banked, aiming at the Undead Lord, and

the world in front ignited in orange flame as it breathed a stream of magma. But he hadn't allowed for the deflection caused by the airspeed of the ship and his own swiftness. The long tongue of flame narrowly avoided Faran, bending past him to strike the mainmast and the poop. There it exploded, pouring across the packed decks and shooting up the rigging of the main and mizzen masts. The sails ignited and burned to a white ash that flew away in the air.

The dragon thundered over the ship, perilously close to its blazing mainmast, but even as he passed he saw some of the undead caught in the rolling flame, toppling over the side, falling like meteorites to the invisible ground. The flame had reached some of the Athanor carrying the ship by its spars: they shredded like crepe paper, while the ship lurched forward and fell, toppling even more of the undead who had survived the flame over the side. They tumbled after their burning brothers.

Vercotrix thundered on, the other dragons behind, carving a whirlpool in the dark cloud. A sudden confusion in the edge of the cloud, and the face of the sun suddenly appeared. A few stray sunbeams struggled through, stabbing part of the flaming wreck of the *Dark Ship*. More of the undead began to dissolve into a thick, tarry mist and the ship started to plummet ever faster towards the earth.

But then Vercotrix had overflown the vessel, was deep in the cloud once more, the ship left far behind. The demons were thick all around. Dark talons scoured at his eyes and he veered away. He turned in a tight arc, trying to beat his way back.

More thunder far below as more of the fallen dragons struck the ground, the orange explosions like erupting volcanoes seen through the cloud. The few left followed on his tail, his brethren—dark shapes whirling over the face of the dark cloud, but he felt their wings beat slower and slower as the darkness snuffed out their fires, as starved of oxygen, their fading breaths lit the underside of the cloud. They would not survive much longer.

He called, a deep roar, to the six who remained. Up they soared, Urthred going with them, to where the air was thin and the sun still shone. Then he broke free, into the violet blue of the sky, higher than he had ever been. Below him were two layers of cloud: the cloud dragged by the Athanor, boiling in angry confusion where the dragons had broken through it, and another layer, a veil that hung above it, a strange pearly grey-white, the colour of glue. The ghosts of Iskiard—the veil over the sun.

Here, the sun was stronger than he had ever known it, free of that veil that had obscured it all the years he had looked upon it from the earth. Radiant orange, white, at its core, where, at its heart, in the Hall of the White Rose lived Reh's elect. He felt the dragons respond to its light. Its beams ignited the dying coals of their hearts. Up a little while longer, towards their father the sun, the God who had fashioned them ten thousand years before. The dragons called to one another, their dying song, the last few beats of blessed flight, the last ever . . .

Then, when they had reached the apex of their climb, as one, they folded their wings close to their bodies and plummeted down, faster and faster until they were beyond speed, were a blur only, where sight and sound had ceased to exist and only intent was left.

The first cloud layer flew past, then the darkness parted, as dark water parts before the diving kingfisher, shredding before its speed. There as if at the end of a long tunnel was the *Dark Ship*, its decks still ablaze with the dragon fire, grappled by the claws of the Athanor who laboured to stop its fall. Vercotrix aimed himself straight at its burning mainmast.

And Urthred went with him. But in that last instant before the collision, he heard Thalassa's cry and woke just as Vercotrix and the others reached an impossible speed and exploded in orange light in the air around the deck of the ship.

Chaos and death had come to the *Dark Ship*. Faran barely kept his perch on the wildly bucking deck. The sky was split with the roar of the dragons, the sound of their passage only reaching him after their bodies had hurtled past and disappeared once more, so swiftly they flew. Now they returned once more: this time he heard them before he saw them, a keening whine that rose to an ululating shriek. The world was suddenly not black but orange as, like mini-suns, geysers of flame exploded all around him. Fire raked the ship, marching up the rigging like lit touchpaper, the sails exploding. The flame swept the massed undead from the stern, shredded the wings of the Athanor. His heart was left in his mouth as the ship dropped like a stone, smoke and smouldering tatters of sail left a contrail behind them.

But still the shadowy forms of the Athanor came after them, and where the darkness pooled on the ship, the fires died out, their dark talons gripped and their breakneck fall was slowed. He looked down. They had dropped a long way: they were much nearer Iskiard, two thousand feet up at most.

But once more he heard that banshee shriek cutting the air, and the dragons came again. A few seconds later the darkness below was lit up with volcanic explosions, their orange-red flames showing like magma, ripple upon ripple of fire expanding outwards.

The clouds parted and there were the walls of the city just in front. But now there came a whistling in the air, and Faran looked up, directly above the mainmast, and saw seven meteorites plunging towards the deck with such speed that sparks and flame flickered about their bodies. The last of the dragons. The noise of their approach rose to a deafening whine. He took one last breath into his leathery lungs.

Seven stunning explosions, milliseconds apart, like claps of thunder. Iron and magma swept the decks, cutting the undead to shreds, the mainmast was caught by what looked like a broken wing that cut through it like a scythe, rigging toppled overboard, and the ship exploded from stem to stern, fire blazing all around.

The *Dark Ship* fell like a stone, broken spars and bodies, all dropping at the same pace towards the distant earth.

Once more Urthred stood on the temple steps, dizzy from the explosions and the shared speed of the dragons' descent.

His skin was cold and he found he was shivering. He looked to the south. The dark cloud was almost overhead, a thousand feet high. Orange light blossomed at its heart followed by an earth-shattering roar; fire rent the sky, gouts of flame shot out like firecrackers from the cloud, and plummeted to the earth like burning resin dropping from a torch, while behind them fell the tumbling bodies of the dragons, mangled and ablaze. In their midst was the hull of the *Dark Ship*, ripped from the grip of the Athanor. Now the darkness would be defeated, Faran would die, his sorcery dead with him, and the cloud would die too. And yet, even as the ship fell, the cloud of darkness swept on through the fiery rain, flowing over the walls, covering Iskiard, running down the sun.

An absolute darkness. He heard Thalassa's voice again, barely audible over the roaring of the flames, but he understood her well enough. She was calling for help. She was in danger. He must join her.

But he must see what happened to the ship first. The last scintilla of light was sucked from the air: it was like a total eclipse, only the afterimage of his surroundings and the burning plummeting bodies illuminated the scene. The *Dark Ship* was lost from sight. Would the Athanor hold it up, or would it fall like the dragons? He heard distinctly each black leathery wing, a fluttery thunder, as they flew over the granite curtain wall and began to settle on the towers. Their summits were lost in the pall. Raining debris smashed into the ground, exploding with earth-shuddering concussions.

He couldn't wait. Her voice was now a scream in his mind. She was nearly lost. He turned. His feet carried him unconsciously. It was as if he glided, his mind disengaged, now hearing only that siren voice, Thalassa's, calling him forward into the darkness of the ruins.

CHAPTER TWENTY-SEVEN

The Last Dawn
in Imblewick

The White Tower. Just as it was getting dark Creaggan gently rapped on the door of Fazad's room. The soothsayer did not return the boy's greeting after he entered but placed his fingers to his lips, cautioning him to silence. He closed the shutter, then shut his eyes and cocked his head, concentrating on the sound of the court preparing for the night.

Apparently satisfied with what he heard, he opened his eyes. He gave Fazad a strange look, alert like an eagle's as if he had learned something from the everyday noises echoing through the corridors and stairwells. "It's all quiet for the moment."

"What are you listening for?" Fazad asked.

"Why, don't you of all people sense it? Our enemies are stirring."

"The Worm?"

"Aye—you have seen them with your own eyes. Don't deny it," Creaggan answered, with a little smile. "The night of the wolves' howling: I followed you, and saw what you and Gurn saw, though it was only what I had seen a dozen times before: on the nights of the full moon when the dead's blood rises like sap in a long-dormant root. The Worm have been in Imblewick for many months. Treachery surrounds us; the forces of Iss are marshalling. I wanted you to see for yourself, see what was stirring in this city of ours.

"But now," he continued, "time runs out. All last night and today, the queen and I have been casting the runes and making horoscopes. Tomorrow will be the day."

"What day?"

"The queen will explain by and by. I have come to bring you to her chambers. Tonight you will dine with her. But first"—he pointed at the cupboard—"fetch the cloak, boy."

Fazad looked down at the floor. "You know the queen has forbidden me to wear it."

"Perhaps you no longer want it? You're afraid of it?" Creaggan asked. He craned forward like an overzealous schoolmaster, his eyebrows raised. The boy didn't answer. Creaggan took this as assent. "It is good; you are weaned of its wild influence, you are fit for human company: yet wildness has its uses. Tomorrow you will need your old skills—go fetch the cloak and your dagger while I fetch Gurn."

Fazad went to the closet and opened it, taking down the cloak once more: his fingers trembled as he gazed into the dead wolf eyes on the cloak—they seemed alive. Creaggan returned with Gurn, who frowned when he saw Fazad holding the cloak. The boy merely shrugged. Creaggan led them through the White Tower. The two had been expecting a dinner with the soothsayers and widows who made up Zalia's inner court. But the meal with the queen was unlike any they had taken before.

They were the sole guests. The queen's steward, a lank-faced man wearing a black ankle-length cloak and a yellowed but once-white neck ruff, ushered the three of them into an empty antechamber. The queen stood on the top step leading to the hall. She dismissed the steward with a curt nod and led them into the hall. There were no other servants present within. The last of the evening light slanted down onto the massive walnut dining table that had once seated a hundred guests. But now there were only four places set, all at the far end. They sat, the queen at the head facing the vast unoccupied space stretching away from them.

Silence for several minutes. The queen sat, impervious, it would seem, to Gurn's and Fazad's curious stares. A golden goblet and a golden dish were the only ornaments on the varnished table. They expected servants to come bearing trays of food as they had done every night they had dined with the queen. But the double oak doors of the chamber never opened. The queen appeared abstracted, staring down the table to where, at the far end, they guessed, her husband must once have sat.

After a few moments' silence she lifted one of her hands. The sorcerer bent down and produced a large pouch that Fazad and Gurn had not previously noticed from under the table. Inside was a selection of withered, dried fruit. Blackened apples, peaches, apricots and pears. He placed them in the golden dish. Next he produced a wrinkled wineskin. From it he squirted a line of brown liquid into the goblet. It smelt sharp and vinegary.

When he was done he turned and arched a white eyebrow at the queen.

She nodded and then turned to Fazad and Gurn, who had watched Creaggan's actions with curiosity and bewilderment. "Forgive me, my friends, this mystery. Everything has its reason which I will now explain. The world is full of prophets, those who see what the future brings. I have had many brothers and sisters in the art, brothers and sisters I whispered to in my dreams, and they to me. But now the darkness has come and their voices are cut off. Only Creaggan and I remain of all the hundreds there used to be."

She looked at Fazad. "Once the greatest of them lived in Thrull. She was called Alanda. She was Illgill's prophetess."

"I remember her name."

"She saw that Illgill would be defeated and the city destroyed. But she saw brighter things ahead; how one called the Lightbringer would come from the city and save the world. So, though the city was under Faran and she could have escaped, she remained, waiting for this woman to be revealed."

"And was she?"

"A month or so ago, I had a dream. A vision came of Alanda in the far north, where all our kind, the Witch Queens, came from. She was there with Illgill's son, and a masked priest of Reh and a young woman, clad in a white cloak: there was an aura about that woman. Just looking upon her I knew she was the hope of the world: the Lightbringer. But then the vision faded. Alanda I know is dead. But the Lightbringer still lives—I feel it in my bones."

She paused once more, looking intently at Fazad, her head slightly cocked, as if judging him. "Creaggan and I have cast the runes. Tomorrow will be a dark day, but always remember to have faith in the *Book of Light*: for in it we are promised that the Lightbringer will come. When the darkness comes, look to the north; there you will see a new star. As long as it shines, remember my words: the Lightbringer lives.

"There are revelations at every turn of the diviner's art. In the fall of the rune stones, or the divining sticks, in the opaque mysteries of the crystal ball, in the gyres of the astrolabe. But now I have seen dread things that I hoped never to see. The treachery of my people revealed when it is too late to act, for tomorrow the terrible day comes, the Day of Iss.

"Tomorrow you will see terror, boy: the day of no light that is written of in the book of Flame. Tomorrow the dawn will die even as we watch. This is the last night. I have seen it in the runes, in the *Book of Light*, in the gyres of the astrolabe, in every medium, the crooked flight of the ravens at dusk, the cloud plumes of the summits of the mountains. All the signs are complete. The only light after tomorrow will be that star of which I have spoken. That night will last not for a night, but forever, unless the Lightbringer prevails."

"You have seen all this?"

"That and more—you have seen the undead in the old graveyard?"

Gurn and Fazad nodded heavily. "They are preparing to strike," Zalia continued. "I have not enough loyal followers left to stop the plot. You and Creaggan and only a few others are the only ones I can really trust. Tomorrow an hour before dawn, the twelve men of the council will come here. I have summoned them so they are here rather than elsewhere when the darkness comes. There will be a guard outside. They are all picked men. They will come in and arrest the ringleader and his accomplices when they make their move."

"Who is the ringleader?" Fazad asked.

The queen smiled. "I think you know that already, boy."

Fazad was silent. Yes, he could guess. Rutha Hunish. But how could a hero of the war against the Worm be a traitor?

The queen didn't let him dwell on his thoughts but hurried on. "We must prepare. The last dawn is coming. You wonder at these?" She gestured at the fruit and the evil-smelling wine. "It is written in the *Book of Light* that this is what shall be served at the last supper. The fruit is rotten, the wine is sour, just as the land is barren and the sun is dying. Now we need Reh's redeeming light to bring back to life that which seemed dead. For it is written that this will happen even to the Lightbringer, that she will fall into the jaws of death only to spring free again." They all stared at the golden dish and goblet.

"Creaggan, restore the offerings," she commanded the soothsayer. He rose stiffly and grasped his staff of office. He held one hand palm downwards over the plate and goblet while passing the staff slowly over the top of it. Suddenly there came a golden glow from the vessels and before the eyes of the boy and the seneschal the blackness began to disappear from the skin of the fruit and the red and green and orange flesh was restored, moulding itself once more to its original shape. Fazad and Gurn looked on amazed as the light from the plate and goblet slowly dwindled to a barely visible nimbus, then disappeared.

"It is done," the queen said, rising from the table. "Let this be a symbol of the resurrection of the sun. The Lightbringer will show herself, and once you have seen her sign, be sure to have faith. The sun will return."

The four now leaned over the table and each took one of

the fruits and ate it. Then they passed the goblet, finding that the wine that a moment before had smelt sour now gave off the hint of damsons and violets on the nose. And as each tasted it, it was as if purple nectar passed their lips. Though it was late, the tiredness of the day lifted off them. It seemed as the liquid passed over their tongues as if they would be able to speak the language of the gods all night long, and as the liquid sank into their bellies it felt that they were lifted up towards the heavens on a cloud.

When the fruit and wine were gone the queen held up a hand. "I will not sleep tonight. Yet, tomorrow I will sleep forever."

The three men made as if to protest, but once more she stilled them with a gesture. "Peace. I have that knowledge that all soothsayers have—the knowledge of their own deaths." She turned to Fazad. "The kingdom has no heir. My husband and son drowned in the Inland Sea, as my brother and his children died on Thrull marshes. Our loyalty to the baron has cost my line dearly. I am old. Who will possess this land after my death? If the dark prevails over the light, one of the traitors I spoke of. And if the light? A stranger probably, for no one lives here now who is royally born, and of those noble-born Galastrians, none deserves the crown, for were they not the ones who lingered here while my husband went over the seas? They are cowards who dared not fight our enemies.

"So, wolf child," she said, facing Fazad, "I have decided that tomorrow, in front of the council, I will name you my heir, and as you are but thirteen, Gurn and Creaggan your guardians." Fazad's mouth must have opened in surprise and he struggled to speak. But the queen silenced him once more. "You are a nobleman's son. Let the last of the Falarns rule in this isle."

"Amen to that," Gurn and Creaggan answered, buoyed by the wine and the queen's words.

Still Fazad wished to speak, but the queen touched her fingers to her lips. "Silence, always silence," she whispered, "tonight we will watch. I have summoned the council to this room an hour before dawn. Until then, dream—dream of what you have learned here in the White Tower, and what you were when you first came here, half boy, half wolf."

Fazad looked away, but she stretched out a hand and rested it on his shoulder. "You have tamed the wildness, but you will need it again soon: when the darkness comes, you, too, must be dark and fell, as the cloak taught you to be. Before the council enters, put the cloak on. Now sleep." The weight on Fazad's shoulder suddenly seemed very heavy, his eyelids felt like lead. How? When he had felt so euphoric but a moment before? He shook his head, trying to clear it, but the queen's voice came again, droning inside his head like the sound of bees. "Sleep, for after tomorrow there will be so little." He was slipping away. Sliding down into that first sleep, full of dreams and wild visions.

The queen looked down at the sleeping boy. "Are you armed?" she asked the two men.

The seneschal and Creaggan nodded, pulling back their cloaks. At their belts both men carried poniards, a foot long, with pronged sword catchers at the front of their hilts.

"The boy has one too," Gurn said.

"Good. Tomorrow we will know who, apart from Rutha Hunish, are traitors. It may be all twelve, or only one. But where there is one, there are usually two, three or more."

"You don't suspect who the others are?" Gurn asked.

The queen smiled thinly. "When you have ruled a long time, suspicion comes as naturally as a second breath. It is too easy, for madness lies beyond the first doubt. Over the years I have accepted: nothing is ever truly known. Of course, Rutha Hunish is a traitor. But can I arrest him now when he heads my army, who believe him a hero and their saviour?"

"Who is he, really?" Gurn asked. "Where did he come from?"

The queen turned away. "Seven years ago, after the death of my husband, as my army marched on Thrull, on the plains beyond Darvish Forest where your city Perricod stands, this man Rutha Hunish came at the head of a small group of rough-looking highlanders, claiming he was from that far-away land, the Land of the White Clouds, far up the west coast, where the mountains and the clouds merge as one with the sea. The men he led all had strange accents and looked ill disciplined. But the armies of the Worm marching on Thrull were known to be formidable and my general needed every man he could muster. So he greeted them and invited them into their ranks. They marched on together.

"Trust only came slowly. Perhaps only on the battlefield. Before our general fell and several others who took command after him, Rutha Hunish had already been at the head of every charge, at the heart of every defence, and every soldier called him a hero. Then when all was lost, he led the survivors back from the battlefield, back over the sea to Galastra. Here the men hailed him as their saviour and their leader.

"But he has deceived us—I fear he comes not from the Land of the White Clouds, but from the land of the Worm, Ossia. And his masters are not the cloud spirits of his ancestors that are said to rule that near-forgotten country, but the Elders of Tiré Gand." Her face was haggard and drawn in the lamplight. "So. My friends, the last I may have in Galastra, let your daggers be ready, and your hearts be hard for what you must do when the traitors are revealed."

Then she motioned for them to sit around the table, and so they remained, the wine still buoying them up, through the remaining hours of the night in an unsleeping vigil, in a kind of enchantment, staring at the plate and goblet. The boy slept on, his head resting on his arms on the table.

And as the hours passed strange visions came to them, of past times and times to come, perhaps as potent as those that Zalia had seen in her astrolabe. Just before dawn, when the candles had burned low, Fazad groaned and lifted his head, groggily coming back to consciousness, trying to remember what he was doing there. The queen hushed him, quietly telling him to put on the cloak. He looked to where he had left it, draped over a high-backed chair. Zalia inclined her head. He threaded his hands through its sleeves and pulled it on, then sat again, rigidly immobile, as if fearful of what the garment might do to him.

A few more minutes passed: the first suggestion of grey came through the great oriel window at the end of the chamber. Then, without any visible sign from the queen, Creaggan rose and went to the door of the chamber. There was flickering torchlight beyond. The twelve members of the council waited outside, having assembled as silently as ghosts. Creaggan led them in, through the great dining chamber into the oval audience chamber beyond, where the throne and the council seats sat. The twelve and the queen's party took their seats as silently as they had entered.

Rutha Hunish was the last of the twelve, being the youngest. He waited patiently as the elder men arthritically seated themselves, then he moved across the room with the stealth of a panther.

Queen Zalia sat on her high throne with her astrolabe in front of her, her face wrinkled and almost transparent, each blue vein showing, her shock-white hair glimmering in the slowly maturing grey light of dawn that came through the great window at the end of the chamber. Her advisors stood ranged in a semicircle in front of her throne on high-backed seats, Creaggan at their centre, the *Book of Light* open on a lectern in front of him. To his right sat the proud captain of the guard, Rutha Hunish, his dark face aloof and saturnine. To Creaggan's left were Gurn and Fazad.

Fazad sat uncomfortably. The smell of the wolf pelt was pungent, almost overpowering. He was far too warm in it: the room was stuffy from the blazing fire and the galaxy of lamps hanging from the raftered ceiling. Contrary emotions coursed through him: tameness and wildness, and a growing unease.

The instant he had felt the familiar garment on his back again it was as if he had woken from the dead, or at least from a deep enchanted sleep in which all his senses had been numbed. His heart beat faster, his senses of hearing, sight and smell were a hundred times enhanced.

Now as he waited before the queen it was as if the castle had come alive with sound, movement, smell. He felt it like an organism all around him. A door opening far away in the predawn dark. The smell of bread baking in the distant kitchens. Even a spider slowly weaving its web in the rafters. And outside he heard the distant cry of his brethren hidden in the streets of the city and the surrounding mountains.

And inside this room? An unmistakable smell: sharp and acrid, emitted by nearly every person present, the smell of human fear, an acid sweat that prickled in his nose. Only the queen was calm, her pale face expressionless. She, like them, could only wait.

Fazad was conscious of Rutha Hunish's malevolent stare. It was as if Rutha knew what he knew: that he was the traitor.

Now for the first time in the hour, the queen moved: she leaned forward and spun the astrolabe, its gyres and arms forming a hypnotic pattern as it turned on its axis. There was not a flicker on her face as she watched it. What visions of the once and future world did she see? All was silent in the room save the faint whirring of the orb: not a cock crow to herald the dawn, nor the cry of the wolf pack that suddenly fell silent, no early drovers passed in the streets below

Fazad looked about the room and caught Gurn's eye. The older man nodded imperceptibly: he was ready. Fazad felt the reassuring weight of the dagger concealed under his wolf fur.

The minutes passed inexorably. Then abruptly the queen turned to her right. "Are the soldiers in the barracks?" she asked Rutha Hunish.

For the first time since they'd entered the chamber, Rutha Hunish broke off his dark stare at the wolf child. "Aye: it is as you ordered—in their barracks, the shutters drawn."

"Everyone?"

"All that could be spared from watching the ice for our enemies."

"I told you: everyone should be confined to quarters, no exceptions."

"And I, madam, cannot allow our enemies free entrance to our city," Rutha Hunish replied, curtly.

Fazad expected the queen to rebuke him but she seemed to have achieved what she wanted from this exchange and turned her attention to the man directly to Rutha Hunish's right. The mayor of the town, dressed in the charcoal-grey cloak of a burgher: the man had a shifty, weasel face.

"Ogil: what of the townspeople?"

"The crier went through the streets last night announcing the curfew. No one will stir from their homes until they hear him again."

Next she turned to the High Priest of Reh, an old man, with a beaked nose that almost reached his chin and melancholy drooping eyes. His orange and red robes of office were faded with age.

"Matach, are your acolytes ready with the temple bells?"

"Yes, they are ready, but what they wait for they do not know," the High Priest answered.

"But you know, Matach?" the queen asked.

The priest inclined his head. "Aye, I know the *Book of Light*. With heaviness in my heart I have seen the signs, just as you have, my queen."

"What signs are these?" Ogil asked, breaking in.

"Those that betoken the death of the sun," Matach answered, his features curled slightly in contempt at the layman's ignorance. "Prepare yourself. Iss' eternal night comes."

Ogil appeared flustered and shot a glance to his left to Rutha Hunish. So, thought Fazad, those two are in collusion. Rutha Hunish didn't return the mayor's look, but continued to affect an air of nonchalance now that his exchange with the queen was over.

The High Priest had turned back to Zalia. "Even in the darkness the bells will ring out, announcing the rebirth of the sun. Let Reh preserve us."

"And let the Flame burn forever. Let them be rung as

long as the priests have strength to ring them," the queen answered.

Fazad expected her to move on to the next member of the council. Instead she surprised them all by turning to him and gesturing for him to rise. The boy did so. The queen indicated that he should approach her throne. He crossed the room and knelt on the deep piled rug in front of her. Outside, the first grey light of dawn silhouetted the delicate floral traceries of the oriel window.

"The hour has come, child. Darkness will cover the morning sun, Reh's barque is lost in the labyrinth of the night, yet he will find Galadrian's thread once more, the thread that is lit with human prayer and hope. You are the youngest in the room. Remember in the future, when all those assembled here are dust, that when you pray in the darkness, Reh will always listen to you. Pray for our souls and the Lightbringer."

"Amen," Matach muttered. The other council members murmured the same response, but it seemed with none of the old man's ardour.

The grey light through the window had increased as the queen spoke, and now the first bare branches of the oak that grew in the courtyard outside the White Tower could be seen. The queen continued, "Our enemies will rejoice when they see the darkness. Thrulland and Surrenland have fallen; Galastra alone remains. Beyond is only the ocean. Here is mankind's last hope. But I am old, have no heir. Now I will name one."

There came a stir from the assembled worthies. Only Creaggan remained impassive, though his knuckles were white on the staff of office.

The queen continued, "Fazad Falarn, noble born of Thrull, you will be king of Galastra. Let every man heed my words."

A gasp of shock went round the listening men, and Rutha Hunish half rose from his seat, the calm of a moment before gone, a look of thunder on his brow. The queen rose too, like a woman a third of her age, and confronted him.

"You name a foreigner as the prince?" he hissed.

"Don't forget: you are a foreigner too," the queen retorted. "One who commands the Galastrian army. But that also will change. Know that from this moment, Gurnseneschal of the Iremage family, will be general of my army."

The previous announcement had sent up a buzz of animated conversation, but now complete silence fell on the meeting hall. Rutha Hunish's face was very pale under his dark brows. "Now, madam, I believe you insult me. I have proved my loyalty to the state a thousand times, but these men are unknown, could be spies . . ."

"No," the queen interrupted, pointing at him. "Here is the spy. Before the council, I declare your treachery. You are an agent of Tiré Gand, joined to my country's cause by lies. A ruthless man who has put to the sword and to the stake a hundred of his brother worshippers. You have spread evil throughout this island. Worse, you have brought an Ossian legion and hidden them within the walls of the city."

The council looked in amazement at the queen and then back at the general. Rutha Hunish made a noise like an enraged, cornered animal, and threw back his cloak, revealing a dagger at his belt. He drew it in one fluid motion and flung himself at the queen.

For the rest of his life, Fazad would wonder whether when the queen had beckoned him to stand before her throne, she had expected him to have anticipated what happened next: had she not asked him to put on the cloak, checked he was armed? Told him and Gurn that they and Creaggan were the only ones to be trusted? Surely he and Gurn had been her last hope?

But he was still kneeling on the carpet between them as Rutha Hunish lunged. It happened in a split second, the man leaping past him. He had no time to get to his feet: instead he launched himself from a squatting position just as Rutha Hunish fell on the queen. The two collided. A split second later Fazad was on his back, grappling with the general, feeling his dagger slice through his cloak. A sharp pain and then wetness, spreading down his arm; he was wounded.

Shouts of consternation from the watchers as they saw the blood. It was an unequal struggle: Fazad was but a boy, Rutha Hunish a full-grown man. Fazad was flung to one side and tumbled down the steps from the dais. He rolled and saw the queen leaning to one side, her hand clasping a red stain growing on the front of her white dress. Where were the guards Zalia had said would be waiting outside the door?

Now, suddenly the grey light suffusing the room began to die, as if someone was drawing a black drape over it, throwing the chamber into a deep gloom, as if the process of dawn had reversed itself. The light leached away and the darkness grew yet more dense. All the candles snuffed on the instant, as if starved of oxygen. The pale features of the queen slumped in her throne and the councilmen frozen halfway between sitting and rising were the last things Fazad saw before the light totally faded away.

He heard muttered prayers in the darkness, a groan, and bodies moving about. He waited, his heartbeat and the throbbing of his wound the only measure of how long had passed.

Rutha Hunish was near, seeking him out. He crawled away from where he had come to rest, then struggled to his feet, giddy from blood loss, drawing his dagger.

He stared into the blackness, seeing nothing. The room grew colder and colder. A shouted challenge, then the sound of a scuffle. More curses, weapons being drawn, a clash of metal, a scream.

Then the desperate scratching of flint on tinder; a spark thrown onto a pitch torch. The light exploded but it was as if it were the opposite of light, a black blossom instead of one of light. Rutha Hunish stood over him, holding the nacreous flame, his eyes deep pools of shade, his teeth black stones as he opened his lips to speak, his stubbled beard shining with ghostly translucence. Ogil stood next to him, a tinder box in one hand, a sword in the other. All around were struggling figures: those loyal to the queen fighting with any weapon that came to hand.

Rutha lunged forward, but Fazad threw himself to one

side and the general's dagger ripped through his cloak. He struck back, but Rutha Hunish jerked away, and was lost in the melee and the darkness. All was strange in the striated light. Another shadow lunged at him, but Fazad again dodged the blow by a whisker. Where was Gurn? And those guards that the queen had spoken of?

He thrust out with his own weapon, and a jar ran up his arm. In amazement he saw his adversary topple like a rag doll. He stared at the dagger, not believing he had killed a man. Nothing seemed as it should be in the negative light.

Then he saw Rutha Hunish again. The general had climbed the three steps to the throne, where the queen sat, lolling to one side, her hands clasping the wound in her chest. Then Rutha Hunish's dagger fell again and again, and the queen tumbled off the throne, rolling down the steps.

At that moment Gurn appeared on the dais, his bloodied dagger in his hand black in the sorcerous light. Rutha Hunish slowly straightened and the two confronted each other. It was as if Fazad were in a kind of vacuum, in which he heard the sounds of the battle only vaguely, but every syllable uttered by Gurn and Rutha Hunish was clearly audible.

"Now, for an even match," the seneschal growled. But what match was he, a one-armed man, against Rutha Hunish. Yet there was something so fierce in the grizzled veteran's demeanour that Rutha Hunish took a step back: he had seen the stone eyes of a killer. "Ogil," he said from the corner of his mouth, to the mayor cowering at the base of the dais ten feet away, "throw me the sword!"

For a moment Ogil stood paralysed, but then he reversed his sword, and tossed it two-handed across the intervening space. Rutha Hunish had to take his eyes off Gurn for a split second as the sword seemed to hang motionless in the air. A flash of movement. Gurn's dagger shot out, the sword catcher deflecting the blade, sending it spinning in a drunken, flashing circle. Its blade rather than its hilt struck the general's hand and he screamed as the blade lopped off one of his forefingers.

The general stared at the bloody stump. Gurn reversed

the direction of the dagger and slashed back at Rutha's head—the general pulled aside just in time, but the blade scythed open his cheek. He desperately tried to parry but Gurn stepped around his blade, sending his own weapon thudding to its hilt into Rutha Hunish's sternum.

Rutha fell to his knees, bubbles of blood frothing between his lips. His mouth opened into an O, and both hands clutched at Gurn's protruding dagger. But even near death he wasn't finished: a strangled curse came from him, and he lunged forward weakly with his weapon. His feeble blow missed Gurn. Then the traitorous general overbalanced and fell down the steps to the feet of Ogil, who stared on in wide-eyed horror. Rutha Hunish lay unmoving, dead, next to the queen's body.

"So die all traitors," Gurn pronounced fiercely. The rest of the fighting had stopped. One or two of Rutha Hunish's conspirators cowered in the dark corners, others lay dead around their former master.

In the sudden silence, they heard cries of despair coming from all over the palace. Rutha Hunish's picked men were seizing the gates and the towers, securing the barracks. Then, the bells of the Temple of Reh began to peal, startling them all, first one, then another, until each of the hundred bronze bells rang out and it seemed the room was full of their sound. But if that was not enough, now came another layer of sound, high pitched, weaving in and out of the minute silences left between the clangour of the bells. The howling of wolves.

All was chaos within the room as the survivors wrested themselves from their apathy and started moving. It was not quite dark: Rutha Hunish's torch had long ago been extinguished but one or two of the lamps had been rekindled and now flickered in their wall brackets. And, as if only made visible by the surrounding darkness, they could now see how Creaggan's staff of office and the queen's astrolabe glowed with magical light.

Creaggan knelt by the queen. Gurn wiped the blood from his blade. "How is she?" he asked.

Creaggan was holding his cloak to the queen's chest as a compress. Already it was stained a dark red. He looked up. "Fading fast. Bring the boy."

Gurn gestured at Fazad and he hurried forward, clutching his wounded arm. Suddenly he was afraid. He may have killed a man in the heat of the battle, but the prospect of seeing his friend dying made him shiver with terror. He forced himself to kneel by her, taking Creaggan's bloodied cloak and holding it to Zalia's wound. "I am here," he whispered.

Her eyes opened a glint, seeing the bloodied rent in his cloak. "You took a wound for me," she murmured.

"It was nothing," he replied.

"No," she answered. "You are as brave as your father was. Though you were once a slave, now you are a Falarn again. Remember: you are my heir, as those councilmen who are loyal will testify. Reh has decreed that a young man will lead my armies once more." She paused, struggling for breath against the pain. "Go with Gurn, carry the banners of the Galastrians across the Astardian Sea. There is still time before Iss comes from his dark star to the world. March on Tiré Gand, destroy the city. Let the centre of the Worm on earth be destroyed and the Lightbringer come.

"Encourage my soldiers—though they are good men, it will be dark midnight throughout the march, and their spirits will be low. Look to the skies. Remember: even in the darkness one star will burn, the last star at dawn. It is a symbol of the Lightbringer. She will be with you. And one day, let it not be long, the sun will return."

"I will do all this," Fazad breathed.

The queen nodded feebly. "I know you will. Raze Tiré Gand. And afterwards travel on, up into the high steppes, to Valeda: find out what happened to the Emperor."

Fazad seized her hand. "I will do so, but only promise me you will live," the boy said passionately. But the queen's eyes had closed and Fazad saw that her chest no longer moved. She too was gone.

He got to his feet unsteadily. His whole body shook, from fear of the darkness, the deathly cold that had settled on the room, the shock of his wound, his loss. He found there were tears in his eyes.

He looked up to the oriel window. It faced north. It should have been an hour into the morning by now, yet it was sable night again outside; not a star shone except one. As the queen had promised, right at the middle of the window there now burned a single star, a star he had never noticed in the constellations. It blazed with an incandescent light that seemed to sparkle, like a miniature sun. His eyes were drawn into its fiery heart. A vision came to him, as if it were a trick of the light through the tears: a beautiful woman clad in a white cloak: the Lightbringer, just as the queen had promised.

His heart rose, and he blinked his misting eyes. Though it was Iss' dark midnight, there was hope.

CHAPTER TWENTY-EIGHT

The Battle for Galastra

Fazad wrenched his eyes away from the Lightbringer's star as a series of bangs echoed up from below. More enemies were trying to break down the gate at the base of the tower. It sounded like they were using their hand weapons. He turned and faced the other survivors.

Only four of the council stood with Gurn, four bent old men staring at their murdered queen. But then Creaggan braced himself and took back his bloody cloak, which Fazad still held in his hand. He laid it gently over Zalia's face.

Gurn had found Ogil the mayor, cowering behind one of the thick curtain drapes. He dragged him out unceremoniously with his one arm. "So, one of the rats still lives," he spat, throwing him to the floor in front of Fazad.

Suddenly the boy was uncertain; what should he do with the mayor? Remembering the queen's confidence in him, he fixed Ogil with a stare.

"Tell me—what was Rutha Hunish's plan?" he asked as harshly as he could.

Ogil didn't meet his eyes, but looked away shiftily. "The soldiers loyal to Rutha Hunish never went to the barracks. Instead they joined the Ossian legion hidden in the catacombs. Together they have taken the streets, the walls of the citadel, the harbour, the temple: the Flame is lost. Save yourselves and surrender."

"Surrender to the Worm?" Fazad snorted. "I have been one of their slaves; I know how it goes with the followers of Reh. I would rather be dead. Tell me, how many are there of them?"

"Six thousand men, or more."

"It is enough to take the city," Gurn said grimly.

"How long before they break into the tower?" Fazad asked.

"The door will hold for a little while," Creaggan replied. "It is solid oak, a hand thick. They will need a battering ram, not maces, to break it down."

They were all looking at Fazad, waiting for orders. The queen's words had made him her heir but how was he to change from a mere boy to a king in a moment? "We had better see for ourselves," Fazad said, feeling responsibility like a weight bowing him down.

"What of him?" Gurn asked, pointing at the prostrate mayor.

"Tie him up. When we return we'll deal with him. And if we don't return"—he paused—"let his new friends, the Dead in Life, do what they like with him."

Ogil was swiftly bound, then they hurried to the doors of the chamber and flung them open. Outside they found the guards who had ushered in the councilmen slumped dead on the ground, black bile running from their mouths. To a man they had been poisoned.

Creaggan knelt by them, sniffing the air. "Hemlock—slow acting—I didn't see this in my auguries."

"Rutha Hunish had his sorceries too," Matach the High Priest said. "How else could he have shielded the darkness of his heart for so many years? So he hid this act, knowing that you would search the future. Don't blame yourself, old friend."

They hurried down the stairs. On each level the sight that met them was the same: dead servants, and guards, the white-haired widows and the other soothsayers dead in their studies: all the staff of the White Tower. The entirety of last night's supper must have been poisoned. Only the strange fruit that they had dined on had saved Zalia, Creaggan, Gurn and Fazad.

Finally they reached the first floor. The sound of maces, their flanged blades biting into wood and then being wrenched out again with a squeal, was very loud. But if the door was as thick as Creaggan said, it would take many hours before it was broken down.

Here they found some twenty soldiers commanded by Gurn's friend Valence, holding the stairs that led to the door. They looked up sharply when they heard Fazad and the others coming down the steps. There was a heap of bodies on the floor. Gurn looked at Valence.

"We posted our own men to shadow Rutha's," Creaggan explained.

"Aye." Valence nodded his head. "We ignored the curfew as you asked. Followed them from the barracks and when they tried to seize the gates we dealt with them." The sergeant grunted, toeing one of the corpses.

"Then it was well done," Gurn said, "for otherwise we'd all be dead."

The sound of the maces had stopped a few seconds before. Now they heard a scuffling in the passageway below. It sounded like a body of men carrying a heavy object. Then, a few seconds later, the tower shook as something very solid and very heavy was crashed into the door.

"Battering ram," muttered Gurn. The boom came again, echoing up and down the tower like the peal of doom.

The grizzled sergeant gestured for them to come with him. He led them to the murder hole that Fazad had noticed when they had first been brought here—through it they could see down into the murky passageway below. Underneath was a heaving mass of bodies, clad in purple and brown leather armour, their faces hidden by skull masks. Between them they held the battering ram, a fifteen-foot length of oak in leather slings, which they swung forward once more. Another boom. Fazad and Gurn recognised the uniforms from Perricod: the undead legion, the Drinkers of the Viaticum, the same that had followed them all the way through Darvish Forest.

"Have you any oil?" the soothsayer asked Valence.

"It is coming," the sergeant replied. There was a banging of a metal pot on stone, and two soldiers hove into view down the steps from the kitchens. They carried slung between them a wooden pole looped through the metal hoops of a glowing red metal crucible. Some of the liquid spilt over the lip and landed on the flagstones. Instantly there came steam and a crackling sound, as the red-hot liquid cracked the cold stone on which it fell.

"This will drive them off for the moment," Valence said, gesturing at the murder hole. The two men staggered to the opening and tilted the pot up. Burning liquid fell down it. The effect on the men beneath could only be imagined since immediately steam rushed back up the hole obscuring their sight. But there followed inhuman screams and the scent of burning flesh, then the heavy thud of the battering ram being dropped.

A couple of minutes passed and the steam dissipated. They peered down the hole. The corridor below was filled with oily smoke and blackened corpses, burning oil still licking around their bodies.

"The way is clear, let's get out," Fazad said.

"Caution first. The tower may be the only refuge left," Creaggan replied. "There is a balcony on the floor above, let's see what's happening." He motioned for Valence to remain where he was. While he, Matach, Fazad and Gurn hurried back to the second floor, where they found the balcony looking east over the city and the port.

It was deadly cold outside, a thick hoarfrost forming on the stone railing of the balustrade: their breath instantly condensed into a mist in front of them. None of them had witnessed such a dark night, yet by the hour it should have been day. The bells of the Temple of Reh had died one by one since the dawn's light had been obliterated. Now as they stood on the balcony one bell alone rang out defiantly.

In the sudden near silence they heard cries of despair coming from the dark town and the faraway clash of arms, like knives being passed rapidly over whetstones. Orange fires raged fiercely in one or two quarters, their light and the northern star the only illumination. The citadel itself was deadly quiet—it seemed the Drinkers of the Viaticum already had possession of all of it apart from the White Tower.

"One bell only tolls. One acolyte is left alive. The temple has nearly fallen," Matach lamented.

Now from within the citadel itself there came the sound of clashing arms, much louder than that which could be heard in the lower town. Someone loyal to the queen must have rallied the surviving guard in the outer buildings and fallen on the Drinkers of the Viaticum.

Across from their vantage point they could see the keep of the citadel. Flames suddenly burst from the windows, partially illuminating the scene. The courtyard was packed with heaving bodies. Small melees like eddies in a deep-running stream appeared in the packed throng.

Further away, over the curtain walls, they could just see the drill ground in front of the barracks. That too was lit by fires that had begun in one of the neighbouring houses. They revealed a chilling sight: rank upon rank of the skull-masked undead legion, standing stock-still in front of the locked barracks. A stout oak bar had been thrown across the barracks gates. Even from here the small group could hear the cries of alarm from the soldiers trapped within.

Fazad and the others could see what the undead were waiting for. Some of their living collaborators had gone to fetch fire from the burning houses, and were now returning with flaming brands and ladders. They climbed onto the barracks roof, negotiating the steeply pitched slate. Reaching the chimneys, they threw the brands down them, then blocked the openings with cloaks. Smoke was already billowing out of the small gaps in the sealed doors and windows of the ground floor. The cries of the garrison increased in volume.

"They're going to burn them to death. What can be done?" Creaggan asked.

Fazad was silent, surveying the darkness, as if waiting. Now he had the wolf cloak again, his hearing was acute. On the surface was a bedlam of contradictory noises. But he listened for another sound beyond those of destruction and death. One that had ceased when the light had died. But he knew they would be coming soon. They were his brethren.

The howl caught all of them but Fazad by surprise. It seemed to come from all around them: from the battlements, the courtyard, the drill ground, the roof of every house, much nearer and louder than it had been when the dawn light had first been snuffed out.

In the light of the burning houses next to the drill square, he saw the confusion in the Drinkers of the Viaticum.

Fazad turned to Gurn and Valence. "Though we have but twenty men left and out there are thousands, we will win a victory, I promise you. We will do as the queen wished." A strange look had come over the boy's face with the howling of the wolves. Unbridled ferocity shone from his eyes, and the gums were pulled back over his teeth in what might have been a snarl.

In the citadel square, the struggling figures of the guard made some headway, though their mortal weapons could not slay their adversaries. Beyond, the serried ranks of the undead were suddenly broken as the wolves leapt from the shadows and fell on them.

Fazad hurried down the stairs once more, trailed by the others. "Get the men ready: we're going to break out of the tower," he shouted to Valence.

He led the whole party to the very bottom of the tower, to the entrance level. Gurn thrust a sword into Fazad's hand, then threw down the bar on the door. Steam and black smoke eddied down the corridor, the charred bodies still smouldering. They threw their cloaks round their faces and ran out through the poisoned air.

Then they were out of the passage and could breathe

freely again. But in front was a line of skull-masked Drinkers of the Viaticum.

Creaggan was just behind Fazad. As he emerged from the entrance tunnel, the wizard saw the undead and pulled up short, striking his staff hard against the pavement of the courtyard. The tip of the staff burst into incandescent light, the Drinkers twisted their heads away from the brilliance, and Valence, Fazad, Gurn and their twenty fellows raced forward.

In that moment only one emotion burned in Fazad's heart: the blood lust of the wolf. His blood sang, his sword arced back. He smelled the scent of rot and decay, accentuated by his heightened senses: his mouth was full of angry bile. He swung the sword—it bit into flesh and bone.

But they still had to force their way past the line of undead to the gates of the barracks square. A mace swung past his head. He struck back. The first blow fell on the neck armour of one opponent, biting down through cartilage and breastbone, the force felling the creature. He hauled the sword free, seeing how his blow would have killed a man, but how the creature immediately tried to push itself back to its feet. Now he attempted a cramped stroke up at his left-hand opponent, just as his mace swung towards him. Steel met steel. For a moment, they matched each other's strength, the creature's jaws snapping behind the skull mask. But Fazad was only a boy, was being pushed backwards . . .

A blur of steel whistled past his cheek, and the creature's head fell like a scythed bushel of corn from its neck as Gurn's axe struck home. Yet still its torso grappled with him. Fazad stepped to one side and it overbalanced and fell twitching to the ground.

His ankle was grasped, and he looked down: the one he had thought he had felled with his first stroke was trying to pull him down. He swung the sword again, severing its wrist.

He turned. Gurn was now engaging another of the creatures. One more hay-making stroke, and this time an arm and most of the chest were cut through by the razor-sharp blade, yet still the creature stood.

"We must get to the gates," Fazad screamed. Gurn turned. His eyes blazed in the light of the burning citadel, then he seemed to regain his senses, gesturing with his axe for Creaggan to come up with his light. The old man hobbled forward, the rallying undead flinching back from the light as he approached. Fazad looked round. Several of the men had fallen, but there were still some fifteen of them left. Enough.

Gurn led the way, his axe a blur of motion. His handicap had made his single arm very strong, but now he needed every ounce of strength. Fazad followed in his wake, even his own madness dimmed by Gurn's unfettered ferocity. Six thousand vampires, that was what Ogil had said. Now every one of them seemed to block the way, choking the stable yard in front of the White Tower, clawing, snapping, clutching. More of Valence's guard fell, grappled to the ground or struck by blows. Surely there were too many of the undead for their tiny party? They needed a miracle.

But then he saw that a miracle had occurred. They had struggled halfway across the courtyard. In front of them the gates were ajar, left so no doubt by the insurgents who had betrayed the citadel.

Fazad and his remaining men pushed towards them. The square beyond was a confusion of struggling Ossians and leaping wolves. Those Drinkers of the Viaticum caught alone or in small groups had been overwhelmed, their still-writhing bodies being torn apart by the maddened wolves. But others had formed into a small square, keeping the animals at bay with their pikes. The area around them was piled with slain animals. Gurn halted, swinging the axe in a wide are, felling three more of the vampires that had rushed at him. Fazad pushed ahead, struck out at another Drinker, going low so the blow caught him on the thigh. He heard the crack of bones and the creature toppled to the ground.

He raced on through the gate, followed by Valence, Gurn and Creaggan with his blazing light. Some of the wolves broke off from worrying the fallen vampires and ran towards Fazad, surrounding him with a protective cordon.

Arrows whistled through the darkness from the packed group of legionaries: Fazad heard each one, though he couldn't see them. He twisted, letting one pass harmlessly by his ear and away into the night. The roof of the timber barracks building was now blazing, flames and sparks flying up into the sky, lighting the undersides of the clouds. The men hurried across the cobblestones towards the gates, their rear and flanks now covered by the wolves. A new sound: a thousand cries came from within the barracks as smoke leaked from under the lintel and from the shuttered windows.

Fazad shouted out more orders—his voice high with excitement. The few survivors hurried to the gates of the barracks. Valence and Gurn were at his side; the one-armed seneschal dropped his weapon as did Fazad, for the arm wounded by Rutha Hunish was stiffening. The three of them reached up and raised the oak bar, letting it fall to one side. Immediately, the double doors sprang open, nearly knocking them to the ground. A wall of smoke came rolling out, and in it, choking men, staggering like drunks. Some sank to their knees, but others were armed for the fight. Those still standing saw Creaggan and called to their fellows, so that within seconds some two or three hundred Galastrians had rallied around the soothsayer, ready to do battle.

"Speak to them," Fazad told Creaggan, picking up his sword again, "they don't know me, won't obey me."

Creaggan raised the blazing staff, and ordered them to fetch fire from the burning roof. The spearsmen raked down the glowing thatch with their weapons; the bowsmen pulled oil-soaked rags from their packs, wrapped them round their arrow tips and set light to them. Then they advanced until they stood in a line just behind the snarling, worrying wolf pack, not fifty feet distant from the trapped vampires. Some of the creatures weren't going to wait for their fate and broke rank, stumbling forward snarling. The wolves surrounded them and the vampires were borne to the ground, fragments of bones and desiccated skin flying up into the air.

At a signal from Valence, a deadly hail of burning arrows and spears ripped through the remaining Ossian ranks. Half of the square was struck, the vampires' parched skin erupting like papyrus, and as the fire spread to their fellows, the packed mass began melting before their eyes, too closely grouped for one vampire to avoid his neighbour.

Then the Galastrians fell on them. A clash of metal, but no screams from the falling vampires, the broken square fragmenting still further, until men fought in tiny gaggles. The fight lasted several minutes until most of the vampires were too battered to fight on. The Galastrians torched their bodies or let the wolves rip them into even smaller pieces.

Then silence, save for the moaning of the human wounded and the dragging of bodies across the cobbles, vampires still struggling to haul themselves away, or wolves carrying off their prey.

They knew this had only been one part of the Ossian legion—there were many more in the lower town. Below, the single bell in the Temple of Reh still tolled out, slower and slower, as whoever rang it tired or lost hope of rescue. No words were spoken in Fazad's party, but as one they seemed to know that if that solitary ringer should cease, the city would be lost, Galastra and the world too.

Creaggan turned to the men. "Listen to me—the city is betrayed, the queen is dead. But she chose an heir before she died. Matach, the High Priest, will be my witness."

Matach stepped forward. "It is true. This is your ruler, chosen by the queen before she died." He seized Fazad's free arm and lifted it, as one who adjudicates a boxing match signals the winner. A buzz of conversation ran round the ranks of the assembled soldiers, then stilled, and they all stared at the small group in their midst before one man cheered, and then another, until they had all joined in.

"Go, boy," Creaggan whispered to Fazad. "Step forward, let them see you." Fazad did as he was told. Creaggan swept the burning staff over his head, lighting him, and the cheering increased in volume.

Fazad lifted his sword and pointed down the sloping rampway to the open gates into the town. Immediately the wolves left off their savaging of the mutilated bodies in the square and as one black tide began swarming downhill towards the gates.

A murmur of wonder came from the ranks, but Fazad had already stepped forward, with Creaggan, Matach, Valence and Gurn behind him. The seneschal had unfurled the Iremage banner and fixed it to a spear shaft. Now he held it high as a rallying point. The soldiers all took torches from the blazing barracks and surrounded Fazad. "To the Temple of Reh!" he cried.

"To Reh! To Reh!" came the answering cry from a thousand throats.

They marched into the lower town towards the temple, the wolves running in front of them. There was no immediate resistance: the only signs of their adversaries were small knots of wolves, worrying at one or two bundles of rags in the roadway that had once been vampires. But as they got lower the streets began to fill with Ossians: small skirmishes broke out, arrows whistled out of the darkness, striking men down—invisible death.

They struggled on, down and down until the pyramid loomed up into the sky and they stood before the beaten bronze gates. The design of the relief shone back from their torches: Reh mounted, his chariot of the sun circumnavigating the earth. The gates stood slightly ajar. The temple had fallen.

They approached cautiously. Inside they saw a carpet of bodies. The scene of the slaughter within had even the most grizzled veteran choking. Red and orange robes, in stark contrast to the dead-white faces of the corpses, lay in a multicoloured swathe right up to the temple steps. Each man still held a bronze bell.

It was the bell in the tower that still rang. They entered the pyramid, with its corbelled roof, reaching in steps up to the aperture open to the sky. The hearth fire had been extinguished, doused with the acolyte's blood. Here they found a few sated vampires, lolling like drunks, their skull masks cast to one side, their pale faces smeared with the blood of the dead priests and acolytes. These they put to the torch.

They passed on to the entrance of the bell tower. Here they dispersed a gaggle of vampires with fire-tipped arrows and found, barricaded behind a thick door that had been splintered and scraped down to an inch thickness by the desperate claws of the vampires, the last acolyte, his face white, half dead from fright but still ringing the bell. They had to physically drag him from the bell rope before he would stop. One of the soldiers took hold of the rope before its chimes had faded and began tugging at it frantically lest those listening in other parts of the town lost hope at its stopping.

Fazad and his advisors returned to the sanctuary of the temple where the hearth fire had once burned. As they stood among the corpses, it felt as if the cold damp heart of the Worm had replaced its heat forever. But when they looked up, the solitary star stood right over the apex of the pyramid, shining down through the chimney vent, giving light to that lightless place.

The soldiers crowded into the temple interior, eyeing the scene of slaughter and their new king uneasily.

Fazad issued orders—he couldn't remember what—and Gurn, Creaggan and Matach passed among the men, dispensing words of comfort, of courage, rallying them once more. First they scoured the lower levels of the Temple of Reh, killing all the enemy they could find, burning the undead with magic. Down and down, into the very sewers of the city, the wolves running before them in the darkness, scenting out the decay of the undead, sparing not a single one.

Fazad left the scene of destruction and with his advisors climbed slowly back to the barracks square, where the corpse pyres were burning fiercely. He saw that Ogil the mayor had been fixed on a stake on top of one, and that it had just been lit. The mayor was pleading for mercy, but the members of the guard betrayed by Rutha Hunish were not likely to show clemency. Fazad watched him burn without a flicker of emotion.

Below, the clamour of fighting continued for many hours over the sound of the single bell, until the day would have turned to night. Gradually the vampires were defeated by the fire and the wolves. But those who watched from the battlements saw that Hel had come to this city, a Hel where there would be no light again save the orange light of the corpse pyres and the burning buildings, where the air was filled with smoke and sparks and cinders, where the wounded groaned, pleading for release from their suffering.

Fazad, the Wolf King, a child who had grown beyond pity, stood with the guardians of the throne, Gurn and Creaggan: he looked not at the scene of human misery below, but always upwards, to the solitary star, the Last Star at Dawn, the Lightbringer's star. There, only, was hope.

CHAPTER TWENTY-NINE

The Golden Hall

U rthred ran down the mirror corridor, past the corpse of the priest and into the pillared hallway beyond. He slithered to a halt before the entrance, his worn sandals seeking purchase. This far into the complex it should have been pitch-dark, but instead there was a faint grey glow, like the phosphorescence of a ship's wake, snaking away between the columns. The trail of Thalassa's magic light, left to guide him onwards.

But he was still virtually blind. He hastily pulled out the torch he had salvaged from the *Windhover*, and extending the claws on his gloves, raked them down the stone walls of the corridor. A torrent of sparks caught the oil-soaked cloth at the end of the torch, and it burst into flame.

He followed the snaking grey ribbon of light. Where was Thalassa? Her voice had called him back from the combat in the skies. But now it seemed she was far away: he heard it no longer.

He peered down the avenues of pillars as he went forward: columns and diagonals, shifting perspectives and shadows lent a feeling of unreality. Then, at the end of one of the avenues, he saw a dark basalt statue of the hooded Iss, his head sculpted like a python's, the basilisk eyes staring red, the tongue ready to spit the serum that would transform a man forever. A figure knelt before it, shrouded in a white cape.

His light had not disturbed the kneeling figure. He advanced. Now he saw that the cloak was not a cloak at all but a thin silky web cocooning the person inside. He lifted the torch. Samlack, the deputy leader of the village, his face cocked to one side, his mouth open in a frozen look of surprise, his eyes fixed and staring.

Urthred recoiled, thrusting the torch left and right, seeking the danger. Movement in the shadows, white shrouded figures like Samlack, advancing slowly. The Marishader. There were four of them, coming slowly towards him, utterly silently, as if their feet too were made of the spun cotton of the cocoon.

One suddenly pulsed forward. He swung the torch at it, the flame flaring across the creature's chest, burning a wide gouge of the white substance. The Marishader recoiled. A strange wail of horror came, not from it, but from a point behind Urthred. He turned: nothing but the pillars and the darkness. He whirled back: another of the creatures was nearly on him, its mouth gaping open, issuing a stream of white mist which fell on his cloak, instantly starching it white, the filaments racing like cracks on a frozen pond over his clothes. Another wail came from just behind his head. The hairs prickled on the back of his neck. He nearly turned but fought the temptation. This was the creatures' way of hunting their prey, projecting their voices. He let his eyes not his ears concentrate. Sweeping the torch in a semicircle, driving the creatures back. He looked beyond the statue of Iss, and saw a corridor running away into the darkness. The grey trail of light led the way.

More white shapes were appearing in the hall by the moment. He had to retreat. He began backing away down the corridor, the Marishader crowding in, their voices echoing from behind him. He steeled himself to step blindly back towards them: he dared not turn. In front, the creatures crept ever closer. He felt his chest and arm stiffening where the breath of the second one had touched him. He thrust the torch forward again, driving them back, then knelt rapidly.

The filaments spread by the creature's breath were covering his body just as they had Samlack's. Already his gloved fingers were shrouded and stiff. He forced open the claws of his glove and scratched clumsily on the floor. He drew the symbol of Reh, the same he had inked on the foreheads of his companions in Marizian's tomb. Then he stood and stumbled back a step and touched the torch to the rune. A white phosphorescent light. Shadows raced away into the hall to where the Marishader had stood, the air was punctuated by a thin wail, then the hall was empty. He looked down: the white filament was slowly dissolving in a mist from his body: he could move his hands freely again.

But the darkness and the Athanor still came; he felt them like a snake slithering through the corridors, seeking him out.

He hurried down the dusty corridor, following the grey glow. It ran for a hundred yards or so. Alcoves to either side held large gold jars. He held up the torch: the reflection of his unfamiliar face loomed back distorted by the curving of the metal. The torch was nearly burned down to his glove: he felt the heat through the leather and metal harness. But suddenly it snuffed out as if pinched between giant fingers: darkness, a sudden absence of air, a bitter chill. The darkness had reached him.

He threw down the torch and ran, cloak flying out behind him, sandals flapping noisily on the flagstones. The line of grey light still hovered in midair, guiding him. In its light he saw that he had come into a new hall, similar to the first one. In the gloom ahead he saw a green halo of light a hundred yards away through the serried ranks of pillars. The grey spore led straight towards it. He hurried in the same direction, like a moth towards a faraway candle, and as he neared, details grew more distinct: the corniced ceiling of the hallway, the strange hieroglyphics that covered the length of each of the pillars and, at the avenue's end, vast squatting granite statues, Thalassa's magic light glinting off their polished bodies.

And there she was, her white yak's wool cloak glowing in the light of a torch. She was with Garadas and Ostman, inspecting the base of one of the statues. It was another statue of Iss, but different from the first. This one showed the God seated on a throne: in one sculpted hand he was shown holding the mirror in which he revealed to humanity its mortality, in the other he held the sceptre of judgement.

Now the echo of Urthred's sandalled feet hurrying towards them must have reached their ears, for as one the three of them swivelled round, the villagers thrusting their torches in his direction.

"It's me," he cried breathlessly, for it seemed that all the oxygen was being drawn from his lungs by the pursuing darkness. He struggled forward through it as if it were a black, viscous liquid. Thalassa's light was still far in front. Why wasn't he getting any closer to them? He turned, and saw the dark shadow sweeping through the hallway behind: not so much a shadow as a complete absence of light that obliterated everything, the pillars and their pictograms, the high ceiling.

Time seemed to distend, his movements became slow. He struggled on, fighting the pull of the darkness. Suddenly it was as if he broke through an invisible barrier. He was right in front of his friends as if he had been catapulted forward. He nearly fell straight into Thalassa's arms.

"Urthred . . ." she began, but at that moment the edge of the darkness caught them: the villagers' torches guttered as if they had been doused in water, darkness flowed around them, filling every nook and cranny. Only Thalassa's light still burned.

"The Athanor," shouted Urthred. He swung his arm, which was suddenly free, sending it in an arc: a scythe of flame spewed out, cutting through the darkness. The snarling faces of the demons were lit up in the magical fire, the shadows retreated back down the corridor.

"That'll hold them for the moment," he said hoarsely, still struggling for breath.

"Are you all right?" Thalassa asked.

"Better for seeing you," he answered. "But the darkness will return." He looked around, seeking the way onwards.

"Here," Thalassa said, pulling him towards the statue. He inspected it. There stood Iss, his hand held out palm forward, showing the mirror of mortality to all who approached. As they neared he saw his and Thalassa's faces reflected in it—two grinning skulls. The two villagers' skulls showed behind.

He turned to Thalassa. "What must we do?" he asked.

She took a step forward and plucked the mirror from the statue's hand. "The only way forward is through Iss. We must do as his servants would do."

"What is that?"

She brandished the mirror, the reflection of their skulls swaying wildly. "Iss shows us our mortality—he asks us to reject it, to live forever." She threw the mirror down on the floor, where it shattered into a hundred fragments of glass.

A faint hum issued from the statue as if it were coming alive. A chill went up his spine: she had invoked Iss. But now she spun round and seized the staff in the statue's other hand and lifted it up. The humming sound increased in volume. Between the squatting statue's knees was a small area of blank wall: but as she lifted the staff the stone swivelled open, revealing a dark shaft leading downwards.

She led them forward down the steeply sloping corridor, the green light in front, which once more left a trail of grey wafting mist behind it. After five minutes, they saw a dull blue gleam ahead and a striated light that washed down the corridor towards them like ripples in water.

They entered a high stone-flagged chamber, two hundred feet square, shaped like the interior of a pyramid, with a corbelled roof supported in each corner by four vaulted arches. There was another corridor opposite the one they had entered by under an archway in front. Set into the pavement were several pools of glittering water, each one lit from beneath by a single beam of light. The ceiling was awash with shifting patterns of golden light. And at the very centre, as a sea that is set alight by the setting sun, a million flecks of gold burned off a large central pool.

Again the strange conflicting symbolism: light, symbol of hope, after the threatening statue of Iss, as if whoever had designed this place, perhaps the gods themselves, believed one must be counterbalanced by the other. They had passed from death to this symbol of rebirth: water. The four of them walked further into the chamber, marvelling at the glowing pool.

"Drink if you are thirsty," Urthred said, "we are safe from the shadows for the moment. This is a place dedicated to Reh."

Ostman looked questioningly at Garadas. The headman moved forward, and setting his spear by the side of the pool, knelt and cupped his hands and raised the water to his lips. He closed his eyes. "It is good," he whispered, splashing some more on his face, so the grime of travel was washed away. He took yet another cupped handful and pressed it to his lips. Now Ostman joined him and he, too, drank thirstily.

Urthred turned to Thalassa. "What happened to Samlack?" he asked her.

"We split up, trying to find the way. I found him covered in that white web—dead; then the creatures came out of the darkness and we ran." She looked at him, steadily. "I called to you."

"I heard you; it saved me," he replied. He told her of the edge of darkness that had killed the light of the sun, the battle of the skies, the falling dragons. He looked behind him, down the shaft. "The darkness still comes. Let's drink and be on our way." They too knelt by the water and drank and splashed their faces, some of the fatigue washing away from them.

"Let's see what lies in the next room," Thalassa said, rising and going through the archway on the opposite wall.

Urthred and the villagers followed. The next room was walled with undecorated rendered stone: it had only one feature, a plinth that stood at its exact centre, upon which sat a golden quill and a small golden pot. Urthred approached cautiously, and stared at the two objects, wondering at their purpose, but not daring to touch them.

In the light from the chamber behind he could see another square entranceway ahead. A rising sun, symbol of Reh's rebirth, was etched into the stone lintel of the entranceway. He left the quill and the ink pot behind and passed into the next chamber followed by the others.

Rather than being corbelled, this chamber had straight walls rising to great heights lost in the gloom. He craned his neck back. Stone steps led up the walls immediately to his left and right to a gallery that ringed the room, and above that there were more staircases leading to three more galleries above it.

On the walls behind the galleries were row upon row of lively frescoes, hundreds of figures, wearing an ancient style of dress—silk gowns, wide pantaloons and broad-brimmed hats—each in a different hue: gold and orange-yellow and red: the colours of the sun, and cerulean blue, and the emerald of grass just after rain. Each of the figures was painted in mid action: conversing, or walking or playing with complex-looking mathematical tools: dividers, protractors, rules, globes. Above the last gallery the ceiling was so high that it might have been the sky—it was painted as the night firmament in which the constellations not seen since the sun began to die blazed in their original majesty.

Who were these people—warriors, statesmen, noblemen and noblewomen, scribes, priests and priestesses—crammed so tightly into that space? He peered closer. Strangely each painting was incomplete; the central section of the figures was missing, like a girdle about their middles that showed only empty space, as if the work had been left off hurriedly. He puzzled over it for a few moments: then he understood. He turned and went back into the antechamber with the pot and the quill. Thalassa came behind.

He picked up the quill and dipped it into the mouth of the

pot, then withdrew it. On its tip was golden ink. He turned and found Thalassa looking at him curiously.

"This place is a riddle," he said. "You have already solved one with the Iss statue. Now here is another, these figures: so real, so lifelike. As if they waited for something."

"You mean they have a purpose, like the statue?"

He nodded. "More magic, of a kind long passed from us, but which our ancestors commanded. We already know from the Man of Bronze that the ancients of Iskiard stayed here, waiting to receive the bodies of the dead after Shandering Plain. But after the battle none came. The humans dragging the bodies of the gods were lost in the snow and ash that covered the earth and the sun. What had once been an oasis became an arctic wasteland. The people of the city longed to leave. But they were imprisoned here. Generations passed and even the little magic that the gods had left slowly died.

"Then came Marizian. He was the last great magician, so great that Iss himself singled him out and tempted him to go to the lower depths, to find the Rod of the Shadows. He did so, opening the way to Shades, thinking his people might find the road to freedom through that cursed zone. Instead the unnumbered ghosts of history poured out, driving him back, forcing him to flee the city, covering the sun. And the ghosts slew all they found above the surface. Yet some of the people of Iskiard survived."

"How?" Thalassa asked.

"The answer lies in those wall paintings." He stepped, through into the next chamber. There, just to the left of the door, before the mounting steps, was a painting of a kingly figure clad in a gold hauberk, a halberd in one hand. Golden rays of energy had been painted emanating from him in thin lines, radiating like a blaze of dawn light to each and every other figure in the crowded tiers above.

Urthred applied the quill to the blank section: as the nib touched the wall, it was as if life blossomed from the quill. Immediately the middle zone of the fresco was completed, colour bloomed, golden light shot out in the radial pattern to the other figures in the fresco. A thousand invisible fingers seemed to paint the missing detail of the warrior's armour in a blur of speed, each ring of armour, each shade minutely picked out.

There came a faint rumble and the chamber began to shake, then the plaster around the painting cracked asunder. Urthred stepped back, the quill still in his hand. The whole surface area of the walls was alive with movement. The two villagers sank to their knees in terror.

Then dust exploded from the wall where Urthred had begun drawing and a figure burst abruptly out of an alcove in which it had been concealed. It was right in front of him, holding the halberd towards his chest in golden gloves, its face hidden by a golden visor. Urthred flinched back from the apparition.

Though its armour was coated from head to toe in plaster dust, Urthred could see it was the living form of the painted warrior. Plaster rained down from the galleries above and they saw that other figures had burst out of their imprisoning alcoves and now stared down at them with pale faces.

Urthred and the warrior eyed each other for a few moments, then the latter spoke.

"Who are you?" he asked.

Urthred bowed his head. "Urthred, a priest of Reh. I have released you."

The warrior considered his words for a few seconds, then dropped the halberd point from Urthred's chest, and slowly raised the visor of his helmet. Underneath, his face, too, was caked in white dust. "My name is King Unam, last of the rulers of Iskiard, the final city of the north that man lived in after the gods departed the earth. My subjects are the Drusilites, the People of the Mist. But when I woke I expected the hall to be full of my servants."

"Five thousand years have passed since you were locked in these walls." Urthred pointed at the figures staring down from the galleries. "These are all the servants that are left."

The king nodded slowly, the dark eyes in the chalk-white face looking far beyond, as if no walls bounded his vision and he could see clear to the outside, to the city beyond the sanctuary. "Generation after generation had been imprisoned in this city: how we longed to be free of this place! How we snatched at the chance to be gone when Marizian offered it to us. He said he would open a way through Shades with the Rod of the Shadows. He would lead us away from this arctic hell to warm climes; we would live forever, not realising he had been deceived by Iss. Now most of my people are dead and the final darkness comes, as Iss promised when he made his boasts before Shandering Plain. Five thousand years have passed, you say? Patience and deception: those are Iss' attributes."

"There is still hope," Urthred answered. "In the south, Marizian wrote books of prophecy—telling how one human would come and redeem the world; a person called the Lightbringer." He turned and pointed to Thalassa. "She is that person."

Unam took a step towards her, dust spilling from his armour, and inspected her keenly. "You are the Lightbringer?"

Thalassa's face was pale and her lips trembled. "So it is written," she answered faintly. "Somewhere in the depths lies the gate that Marizian opened—only I can close it again."

"That road into the underworld is very long," Unam said, "and very dangerous. You will need a guide." He turned in the direction from which they'd come, as if once more he gazed directly onto the Great Plaza outside. "You will also need more time." He turned once more to Thalassa. "Even now Lord Iss comes from the stars to enfold us in eternal night, so he has dominion of this world forever. Hurry, Lightbringer: the Drusilites will win you time. I will lead my army once more out under the dark sky, and there the People of the Mist will fight their final battle. I will leave you a guide who will take you to the place you desire."

"Who will be the guide?" Urthred asked.

"A spirit who has lingered in this place as long as I. He hides from me now, ashamed that he betrayed me five thousand years ago. But I command him, as my last act, to lead you," Unam replied, raising his voice slightly as if addressing someone hidden in the shadows at the back of the room. Urthred and the others turned but there was no one there. "Go carefully, for the Shadow Ones are abroad, not far from here." Then the king raised the halberd high in the air. "Now we will issue forth for the last time, into the Great Plaza, and do battle with our enemy, the night."

There came a rustle of dust-choked clothing and the Drusilites began swarming down from the galleries: the ranks of the servants, grim-faced warriors, beautiful courtesans, ascetic monks, the elite citizenry of long-forgotten Iskiard, gliding over the marble.

They passed through the antechamber into the room with the glowing pool. One by one they stooped and took water into their hands and sprinkled it to their lips and over their clothes, washing the plaster dust away, the golden light making their dusty clothes seem bright once more.

Unam watched them, until all had washed. Then he, too, passed through to the pool room, and knelt and threw water over his own face. When he had finished, they saw his features properly for the first time: his high intelligent brow, the handsome face, the generous mouth, yet tinged by sadness. He smiled faintly and held up a golden glove in a farewell. Then he gestured, and his people began to file out towards the Great Plaza.

The southerners turned: back in the painted room a silent figure had emerged from the same shadows that Unam had addressed but a moment before: the guide that the king had promised them. He was clad in a dark cloak, spangled with stars and miniature suns, white-haired, his head bowed, a cowl covering his eyes, but, below, his mouth was set and grave.

Thalassa approached him. He looked up then and stared at her solemnly with piercing blue eyes.

Thalassa stopped dead. "I know you," she whispered.

"Aye, my lady; we have met before, in my tomb—I am Marizian, here at my lord's command. I have come one last time to guide you to the depths, to the Hidden City."

All the colour drained from Thalassa's face. "You wonder what I do here, I who saw you five thousand years before your birth?" the spirit continued. I am a shadow of Marizian; just as all our shadows live in Shades, so I, this shadow, this simulacrum, have dwelt in these walls, while my other half wandered the earth—wandered until he died."

"Then why haven't you died too? A shadow cannot live without its substance."

"It is true. Now that my soul is released from its bondage, this image will soon fade and I will once more be part of that skeleton you saw in my tomb in Thrull."

"We saw a ghost in the tomb."

"Aye, that too was part of me. My unquiet spirit has drifted over the world these last millennia seeking she who will redeem the world: the Lightbringer. Have you any understanding of the care with which I sought you? The doubts that tormented me: that though I wrote of you, you would not come? In the book of prophecies I left signs that you should follow, not knowing that you would ever read them. In lonely places I raised shrines to you, so later generations would remember you and one day you would visit them. Now you are here: the dream is flesh."

Thalassa hung her head. "I am but a woman: others have called me Lightbringer. But I know I am only human: weak, mortal."

"No one who has travelled to Iskiard is weak. I salute you, Lightbringer, and this man, the Herald: he too I wrote of five thousand years ago. But who are these?" he asked, pointing at Garadas and Ostman.

Thalassa looked at them. "Noble men who followed us from the Palisades, from a place called Goda."

"Goda?" Marizian responded. "I remember it. It was the first place I stopped at as I came with the Man of Bronze over the mountains to Thrull. There was peace in those mountains and in that valley I sat in a grove of the sacred trees, resting. And there I set the first shrine for you, Lightbringer, so you, too, might rest on the journey to the north. Goda—a place of refuge."

He drifted towards Garadas. The small, wiry man looked at him, his nut-brown face drained of colour, just as Thalassa's had. "Headman, your journey in the north is over. I will send you back to Goda, for there I received a welcome in my lonely travels when all others shunned me—in return, you at least will live, though so many of your men have perished."

Garadas's brows darkened in a frown. "How will you do this?"

Marizian gestured around him. "A man can go anywhere he cares to from this room, as long as he can find that place he seeks."

"Your words are dark, sorcerer," Garadas replied. "But I will not leave the Lightbringer."

Thalassa reached out a hand to Garadas and touched the sleeve of the headman's tattered furs. "You have done enough. Think of your daughter. Will you make her an orphan? I asked you to bring me here, to Iskiard. It is done. Go now, with this magic, before you, too, pay the price."

"I will pay it rather than leave you," Garadas said stubbornly.

"No, Garadas, I command you," Thalassa interjected. "Go with my blessing, back to Goda. Give them hope in this sunless time, and if I succeed and the dawn comes once more, remember me, in that shrine where you first found me."

Garadas looked at her and then at his one surviving man, then relented—perhaps after all the others who had been lost, he owed it to Ostman to get him home safely. "Very well. We will not forget you."

He turned to Marizian. "What do you want us to do?"

Marizian pointed at a section of the wall in the shadows. No figures had been painted on it, but instead a mountainous landscape was shown: high snowcapped peaks, the greys and blues of alpine ridges, and below, a green valley with a rushing river. "Do you recognise that place?" he asked.

Garadas squinted at it. "Why, it is Segron Height and

Goda, and there," he said, narrowing his eyes even further, "I see the old city and the sacred grove before the shrine!"

Marizian smiled faintly. "Yes. It is all those things. Now, headman, go towards that place with your friend, walk to the mountains, be free. And may Reh be with you."

Garadas and Ostman looked at each other uncertainly, then, bowing to Marizian and Thalassa, they turned and advanced on the wall. As they neared it, it was as if the line between the floor and the wall opened, and all became a plain perspective field, stretching away, and then Garadas and the other man walked on into it until it was as if a mist passed over the painting. Suddenly they were gone, and the painted wall swam back into view.

Marizian nodded in satisfaction. "They will be safe as long as Reh triumphs. And their wives and children will see them again and have some comfort, even if the darkness succeeds." He turned to Thalassa and Urthred. "You two alone remain of all those who set out from Thrull and Goda. So I wrote it, five thousand years ago, in the prophecies. Your faith has kept you together, and what I wrote in weak words has become strong in the flesh and the spirit. Time is short: let us go to the Hidden City."

"Before we go on," Urthred said, "there is one of our companions who might still be here: Jayal Illgill."

"Illgill?" Marizian closed his eyes and concentrated. "I see each of my artefacts in the darkness: the three magical items that I left behind me at my death. Jayal Illgill has one of them: my sword Dragonstooth. It brought him through space and time to Iskiard, and took him deep into the underworld. But I see my other artefacts too."

"What of them?" asked Thalassa breathlessly.

"The Man of Bronze: he follows, he is somewhere south of the Iron Gates. And I see the Rod of the Shadows. It is where we go to, near where I first found it at Iss' prompting. It is with Jayal's shadow, the Doppelgänger."

"Then Jayal's dream was true," Urthred whispered.

"Your friend is near it now," Marizian said.

"Then let's hurry."

Marizian nodded. He gestured for them to follow him, beckoning them towards another opening at the far side of the Painted Chamber. "To the great pyramid," he cried. His feet and cloak made no noise as he glided forward.

CHAPTER THIRTY

King Unam's End

The *Dark Ship* fell with such speed that Faran knew the Athanor that carried them were dead or gone, but as they fell, the fires that had spewed all around him began burning out, starved of oxygen by the speed of their descent. Through the dying flames, Faran saw the snow-covered square of the city hurtling up towards him. He prepared for the bone-shattering impact, but then a miracle occurred—the ship began to slow. He looked up: perhaps one or two of the demons still clung to its shattered rigging. The ship was levelling out, approaching the ground on almost a flat plane.

And then they were there. The ground suddenly reared up at him as the ship tipped forward one last time and they landed in a geyser of snow, ripping planks and trailing rigging as the ship wobbled perilously on its outriggers. Then one of them collapsed and the ship slewed round, smashing to a halt in the side of a massive drift that had half buried a building. The foremast snapped at its base and came crashing down. Faran was entangled in ropes and still smouldering sails that threatened to ignite his cloak. He kicked the burning material off and stood shakily.

Burning figures lay in a jumbled heap on the canted deck. But somehow there were still some vampires that had survived; they, too, struggled to their feet. The flames were already turning the remains of the *Dark Ship* into a pyre. Faran vaulted down from its side into the deep snow, the vampires that could still move followed.

Now he took stock. The square was full of oily smoke, plunged into the deep gloom of the demon-brought night. But Faran could still see. The ship had come to rest on the eastern side of the square. He saw a large fire-charred crater where one of the dragons had crashed in the square's far northern corner. Yet though the flames leapt a hundred feet from the hole in the ground, somehow the dragon still lived, its wings arcing upwards in agony as its metal plumage was reduced to molten ore. Even from here, a quarter of a mile away, he could feel the intense heat.

In all quarters fires raged where more of the dragons had fallen. As he watched he saw one of the towers lean slowly over and fall with a dull crash that sent dust and snow steepling into the air.

The vampires were now ranged about him, waiting for his orders. He guessed there were some two hundred left. He studied the ground around him. Apart from where the ship had landed, leaving a great gouge in the snow, the snow was still virgin. But out in the centre of the square he could make out footprints leading from the south towards the great pyramid on its western side.

Faran pointed at the footsteps. "That is the way." The other vampires crowded around, scenting the air. They like him could just detect the faint scent of blood even over the smell of smoke: a lingering, musky scent preserved by the arctic chill.

He led the vampires across the square, hard on the scent. *Her* scent, he realised. Thalassa was just ahead. Soon she would be in his power. The thought made him increase his stride; he cut through the deep snow, his eyes fixed on the dark entrance he could now see under the colonnades in front of the temple.

He was nearly at the steps but then through the colonnades came a golden glow, the light beaming over the square. He slowed. Suddenly, ahead of him, rank upon rank of figures appeared, their golden raiments glowing in the darkness, their faces aglow. They spread across the top of the steps, waiting.

Faran halted, confused. Who were they?

He drew his weapon from his belt, the mace that had belonged to the last of the Reapers of Sorrow, and held it up, its metal flanges cruelly sharp where the blueing gave way.

Faran gestured and the undead surged towards the temple. One of the golden warriors took a step forward to meet them and there was a whirl of contrasting hues, the gold of the Drusilites mixed with the dismal sacking and winding sheets of the vampires. Weapons clashed, the fiery swords of the Drusilites against the iron bars that the vampires had salvaged from the Black Mines.

The line eddied back and forth. Their opponents were creatures of light, quicker than the vampires, but there were fewer of them. Soon the undead had driven a wedge through their middle.

Faran followed his men, avoiding the melee. He had a scroll case in his hand, an item salvaged from Golon's abandoned backpack. The thing gave off a strange oily mist where the demons had touched it. He pulled open its top, revealing the document within, which he unfurled and read. One of the Drusilites broke free of the melee and threw himself at the Ossians, his sword upraised, but Faran held up the scroll and the descending sword seemed to hit an invisible object surrounding them, spinning off into the darkness. Golon still lived on in his works: the spell, a warding, had worked. The Drusilite hesitated, surprised by the magic. A second later the creature's head was staved in by Faran's mace.

Faran reached the top of the steps, the scroll of warding keeping his enemies at a distance. He saw a mirrored corridor that ran beyond, into the interior of the complex, and thrust himself forward, the mace raised. The vampire in front was touched by one of the golden blades and fell to the ground. Faran stepped into his place. He found himself confronted by one of the strange warriors, its eyes golden, dazzling him, so all he saw were shadows of its form and not the form itself. He slashed down with the mace, crushing the glowing creature's skull. It was as if it evaporated before his eyes, into a drifting mist that he now realised was filling the corridor as more and more of the golden warriors fell.

He had fought his way nearly to the chamber. Then he saw what he had been looking for: the leader of these strange warriors, the king, in the very last group blocking their way, guarding the entrance into the temple. Strangely the visor of his helmet was up, revealing his face. He swung a golden halberd in a wide arc to left and right, the blade cutting down two of the undead who had confronted him. The blade flashed back again, humming with energy. More vampires fell; the others dropped back, cowed by the magical blaze.

Faran threw himself forward into the gap left by one of the fallen vampires, the mace upraised in his right hand. The king must have felt his presence for his eyes swivelled to confront him, fearless but recognising death as the flanges of the mace swung in towards his head. The blow glanced off the open visor of the king's helmet and caught him on the cheek, smashing the bone back into the skull, and he toppled backwards into the throng of his men. But unlike the others, his figure didn't dissolve into a mist. Faran swayed past another sword thrust and threw his weight into a blow that smashed into the top of the very point of the king's helmet. The helmet's rivets burst asunder, its metal bottom edges driving deep into the warrior's neck, and blood exploded over the man's chest, a curious blood, red and gold commingled.

The air warped and shifted, as if seen through a curved mirror, then the vision of the king disappeared.

All around the golden warriors began to fade as mist fades with the coming of the sun, their golden souls rising up and up until they struck the top of the corridor and flowed back towards the interior of the temple like a river of golden ore.

Now Faran had time to draw a breath into his lungs. The air percolated slowly down his parched larynx into his desiccated chest. His heartbeat calmed to the rhythm of the Dead in Life: four a minute, all that was needed to keep his torpid blood circulating. He found himself looking at one of the mirrored panels in the corridor. Two hundred years had passed, yet still he expected his reflected face to loom back at him. Once more it came as a shock. No reflection there: nor from any of the undead who surrounded him. Only those with souls cast a reflection in a mirror.

He looked down and noticed that a large wound had opened on his thigh, the skin hanging there like a thick layer of yellowed papyrus.

A mockery of life—no more. But he would find the essence of life—make it his once more. Thalassa—she was the key.

He strode forward into the darkness of the pillared hall. He sniffed again. Her scent hung in the air, jasmine and musk; the sweet smell of her blood. He was close. He hurried on, the flap of flesh at his thigh forgotten. Ahead, like an omen, he could see a statue of Iss at the end of one of the avenues of pillars.

CHAPTER THIRTY-ONE

To the Valley of Fair Light

Imblewick

The sky was black as coal, the streets and houses filled with the dead and the cries of the dying. The garrison pursued the undead through the streets and cata-combs, flaring torches in their hands. More fires were inadvertently set. The conflagration spread with the gusting wind.

Fazad, Gurn and Creaggan watched from the battlements of the citadel as below half the city burned, and the undersides of the driving clouds were lit by the flames. Matach the High Priest had ordered that the bodies of the slaughtered priests be carried from the Temple of Reh and placed on corpse pyres in the square outside the citadel. Now these were set alight, adding to the hellish glare of the sky. The inhabitants who had survived the vampires' rampage hid from the terrible lights and sounds in their houses.

A day and another evening would have passed had there been light. When the fires had subsided and it would have been midnight again if the world had still had time, Creag-gan rode through the smoking ruins with the crier calling the people to come out, go up to the citadel. At first, there was no response, and he wondered if there were any left alive. But slowly one or two shutters were drawn back, and nervous pale-faced men and women looked out from their windows. Doors opened and a crowd gathered as the procession continued round the city.

Yet some of the streets were still ominously quiet. None of the soldiers wished to enter the houses in these places, even if they had once lived in them themselves; they knew what they would find: lifeless corpses or worse, their loved ones returned as slavering revenants.

Gradually the procession swelled, the townsmen lit torches, and they started the climb up to the parade ground in front of the barracks.

Fazad had Cloud brought from the stable by the White Tower to the barracks square. Here he mounted. From his vantage point he could see over the whole city and a swathe of the Astardian Sea. The torches of the population were like a serpent trail of light winding its way up towards the citadel through the darkness. He looked from it to the strange star on the northern horizon.

Behind him the garrison stood at parade, each man with a torch alight in his hand. Supply wagons and dray horses had been taken from the stables next to the smouldering barracks. The shadows around the square were full of the yellow eyes of the wolves.

Creaggan rode to one of the open-topped supply wagons and swung himself stiffly onto it. He had been in the saddle many hours. Slowly the following townsfolk filled the square. When they were assembled, Creaggan held up his staff of office and the people, seeing it, fell silent.

"Brothers, the hour of the Worm has come," Creaggan called to them. "Black Night sits upon the skies, and Reh is lost in the Dark Labyrinth. Yet look, see on the horizon over the Astardian Sea!" He pointed to the north. "There glows a star even though the others are dead. Did that star shine last night, or the night before? No, it is a sign, sent by Reh, that though he lies imprisoned deep beneath the world where no mortal eye can see him, he has not forgotten us. He has sent his redeemer, the Lightbringer. Hope is at hand."

As he spoke all eyes had turned to where the star glimmered.

"Come," continued Creaggan, "though the queen is dead, in front of the council before the l.ght was extinguished, she has elected an heir. Foreign born, yet a nobleman." He gestured at Fazad on Cloud. The boy whispered and the horse trotted forward into the light of the torches.

He returned the inquisitive stares of the townsfolk boldly, unintimidated. There came a whispering murmur from the crowd, in which some raised voices could be heard. To the boy's ears they sounded hardly less hostile than those in the council chamber that dawn when the queen had announced her decision. Only a few of the townsfolk had seen the half-wild boy, that frozen day months before when he had been led up to the citadel. Since then there had been nothing but rumours about him, how a lycanthrope now inhabited the tower and how he had brought the wolf pack across the Astardian Sea, the same that howled at night from the Dragon Mountains and the abandoned wharves. The sight of the wolves, silently ringing the square, their mouths carmined by the blood of their enemies, their odour drifting on the freezing air, scarcely reassured them.

Fazad stared back at them, then drew the sword that he had wielded during the battle. As he did so, the wolves sent up a baying from around the square, a howl that seemed to echo back from the distant mountains. The assembled throng looked about them wildly, wondering if they, like the Drinkers of the Viaticum, were about to be ripped to shreds.

Then Fazad held up his hand again, and suddenly there was a deathly hush. When he spoke, it might have been a boy's high timbre, but it bore the authority of one who had travelled far, seen much, particularly death. "You do not know me. Only this good old man and the High Priest can vouch for me," he said, indicating Creaggan and Matach. "The rest of the council are dead. Yet the queen put her faith in me—you in time will have faith in me too. First, let my actions speak for me. Let not the wolves sway you against me nor the dead queen's words make you love me. But let the soldiers who have seen me in the battle speak. Have I not shared your dangers?"

There came a rumble of "ayes" from the ranks of the soldiers, many of whom had been saved from the burning barracks by him.

"The battle was close run," Fazad continued. "And if we had lost, the city would have been destroyed. I have seen the end of Thrull, Bardun and Perricod. Galastra is now the only land free of the Worm. But we cannot wait, praying that the light will return. We must act: gather our arms and take the fight to the enemy. Let us go, brothers, across the frozen sea. Let us be as the wolves, for our enemies are crueller than these," he said, pointing to his brethren, "who merely follow their natural instincts."

Another murmur of approval from the soldiers, now joined by at least some of the townspeople.

Fazad sheathed his sword and dismounted from Cloud. Gurn waited for him.

"Did they hear me?" he asked the seneschal.

Gurn looked at the dispersing crowd. "Many did. And the rest? They will hear too sooner or later. Tonight they will sleep, sleep away the weariness of the battle, here in this square, or in their homes if they dare. But tomorrow when they wake and see that no dawn comes, they will understand that the only hope is to fight. Then we will gather them and march on Tiré Gand."

"Amen," said the boy, looking at the thinning crowd, wondering how many would return.

He and Gurn climbed to the White Tower. Behind them the soldiers lay down in their cloaks and slept on the cold cobbles of the square, for their barracks were destroyed and they had nowhere else to go. The burning corpse pyres gave them warmth in that freezing night. Death warmed them.

When the morning should have come, but didn't, those who had gone away returned, as Gurn had predicted, and even more of the townspeople joined them. Gurn and Valence set about marshalling the men, distributing arms and armour to those who didn't have them. Orders were issued;

some of the men were redirected back into the town, with blazing torches, there to root out the surviving vampires in the underworld with their fire. The rest were readied to march.

Fazad led Cloud from the stables, followed by Gurn, Creaggan and Matach. There in the barracks square stood a legion. Ten thousand men in all. Five thousand army regulars, the rest volunteers. The Wolf King rode past them, eyeing them. They stared back stony-faced, determined, and as he rode out of the square, the huge serpentine column with its supply train followed behind, down from the citadel into the lower town.

Ten thousand. Ten thousand against the armies of Ossia? Once the army of Tiré Gand had been over a hundred legions strong: a hundred thousand men.

How many legions had the Ossians now? Unlike the living, their numbers grew day by day.

Many of the Galastrians who marched through the dead streets of the town dared not think at all of what lay ahead. Others, fewer still, believed that despite the odds, a miracle would occur, that the prophecies of the *Book of Light* would come to pass; the Lightbringer's star was a promise of their victory.

At the front of the column the white banner of the Iremages and the yellow and gold banner of the dead queen were mounted side by side on a gonfalon carried by a squire. Before the two flags Fazad rode erect, without a saddle on Cloud's back. Gurn, mounted beside him, was the army's only general since every Galastrian general had perished at Thrull or been part of Rutha Hunish's plot. Otherwise the men were led by warrant officers, like Valence. Creaggan rode behind Gurn on his mule; Matach, his arthritic bones too frail to ride, was carried in a litter.

Through the gates and onto the quays; the masts of the frozen fleet were like a forest of leafless trees against the light of the star. They passed through the broken hulks and out onto the iron-coloured sea, the soldiers in their mailed overshoes fighting for purchase on the slippery surface.

To either side ran the wolf packs, like dark squalls on the edge of the darkness.

Fazad clutched a map he had taken from the queen's study: it showed the coast and Surrenland and the roads leading to Tiré Gand. He whispered to Cloud and the horse started off on a slight tangent to the southeast.

How lonely and desolate the frozen sea, like a desert of small grey dunes stretching away, each briny wave captured in mid pulse as it had pounded towards that invisible shore!

One or two watch fires burned on the heights behind them, but they were soon swallowed up as the army passed further and further out over the frozen sea. Fazad halted Cloud and inspected the men as they shuffled past, sullen-faced, bleary-eyed, unshaven, some muttering prayers as their home finally disappeared from view in the darkness behind them.

It was nearly windless in that endless dark, and no blizzards came to hide their path over the corrugated wilderness of frozen waves. On they marched, for several hours. Creaggan had proclaimed that they must act as if the sun still shone, and for that purpose had brought an hourglass that he carried with him on his mule and assiduously turned, counting the passage of morning, afternoon and night. So after they had marched for eight turnings of the glass, Creaggan deemed that darkness would have come, if there had been day and night, and called the first halt. Immediately the men began making their bivouac on the ice.

Fazad and Gurn had their tent erected at the centre of the camp, but such was the superstition surrounding the Wolf King that none, not even Creaggan and Matach, dared pitch their tent within a hundred yard radius of it. The wolves halted on the perimeter, waiting for the camp to settle. Then they came through the gaps between the fires and laid themselves down around the solitary tent. Fazad and Gurn slept that night ringed by the pack, the air full of the acrid odour of their fur and their breathy sighs. Outside a thousand yellow eyes surveyed the frozen grey sea and the fires of the Galastrians.

When it should have been morning, Creaggan awoke and called to the trumpeter to sound reveille. The men stirred and saw the darkness and with heavy hearts formed their line of march. They went southeast, avoiding a landfall on the as yet invisible shore of Surren for as long as possible. Days passed, broken only by Creaggan announcing the night's stops and by the morning trumpeter.

The army went to sleep in darkness and woke to darkness. And each time he woke Fazad expected the men to be gone, back to Imblewick. Yet at each awakening they were miraculously still there, their tents glowing in the light of the single star, the embers of their fires burning down into the ice of the frozen sea.

Their tenth stop. A message came to Creaggan's tent: the king requested him to attend him for an augury. Creaggan set off across the ice to Fazad's tent a hundred yards away. His hazelwood staff glowed, showing him the way as he stepped carefully over the wolves who lay closely packed, the air thick with their scent. They stirred as his feet brushed close to them, but did not move, only their eyes following him.

A single light burned in the king's tent, and no guard stood at its entrance. Creaggan pushed aside the flap and entered. The young king sat on a rug studying the map; Gurn stood in the shadows behind. Fazad rose when he saw Creaggan.

The old man looked wistfully at a scroll-armed stool to one side of the tent. He was weary from the day's ride.

"Sit, I beg you," Fazad said quickly, as if remembering his manners. Creaggan did so with a sigh of relief.

"How goes it with the army?" Fazad asked, with the look of haunted wildness that was always there.

"Matach and I do what we can to keep up their morale," Creaggan answered. "But in this darkness, when all the time they look up at the sky and expect to see Iss' serpent ship blocking out the horizons, they despair. If we could engage the enemy, they might feel less impotent."

"Tiré Gand is a month's march away. We must be patient." Fazad held up the map. "We have marched far to the south; each night, when you sleep, I send the wolves to the shore, to spy on what lies there."

Creaggan expressed no surprise at this intelligence. "What do they find?"

"The shores and hinterland are empty, razed of life: the creatures are uneasy. We have to turn in to the mainland soon, but when?"

Creaggan nodded slowly. "So that is why you called me tonight?"

Fazad nodded. "Let the runes decide."

"Very well," Creaggan answered, and produced from his cloak the velvet bag that he had brought with him. He emptied its contents onto the fur rug covering the ice: ivory bricks scattered over it. He gathered the bricks once more, and threw them up in the air so they landed in a random pattern.

He frowned, studying the pattern, watched by Fazad and Gurn, who had now stepped forward from the shadows.

"What is it?" the boy asked eventually.

Creaggan looked up, his blue eyes slightly distant. "It tells us that the most direct road to Tiré Gand is due east."

Fazad turned to Gurn. "Do you know of any road that leads through Darvish this far south?"

The seneschal shook his head. "Perhaps there are roads made in the springtime of the world, when the people of light populated this land. But such a road would now be lost."

"The bricks never lie," Creaggan said.

"I believe you," Fazad replied earnestly. "If this is what the augury suggests we do, we should do it."

But there was clearly something else bothering the soothsayer. "It is the most direct route, but the runes show there is great danger too." He pointed at the centre of the pattern. Each of the small ivory bricks was delicately painted with symbols: the sea, the ice, the sun, the Worm, the star, the wolf, the trees of the forest, and many others. "See here the ocean, and ice, and here the sun." But then he pointed at the black tiles with the serpent symbol of Iss painted on them. The pattern of those tiles was a semicircular fan that half surrounded the sun and star symbols. "Iss is waiting on the shore."

"But the wolves have seen nothing; neither on the sea, nor inland."

"We have our sorcery, and they theirs. Perhaps our enemy is invisible, even to the wolves," Creaggan answered.

"Nothing escapes the wolves of Bardun," Fazad answered, the savage glint back in his eyes. "I will send them further ahead. They will find the undead: we will have warning."

Creaggan returned to his tent with a heavy heart. He slept long into the next day, well past the time of reveille, but when he woke he found the camp still dead, the men as exhausted as he, wearied by the unvarying monotony of darkness and ice. It was as if they had all fallen under an enchantment, the trumpeter still snoring by the entrance of the tent. He woke the man with a curse, and presently the trumpet's brassy call stirred the men.

When they broke camp, Fazad turned Cloud's head in towards the coast. Behind him he heard a murmur of approval from the ranks of the army. At last there was to be some relief from the unrelenting ice and darkness.

After two more turns of Creaggan's hourglass, the coast of Surrenland appeared in front, like a dark iron bar lying on the horizon. Enemy territory. Fazad sent the wolf packs forward. Once again he saw what they saw: the empty beaches by the frozen sea, the deserted headlands, the grass and the trees dying under the sunless sky. Nothing stirred as if they alone still lived in this midnight world.

He ordered the army to advance. They reached the shore where the wolves waited for them and marched south, flanking the southern extremes of the Darvish Forest that here extended a finger into the Gorvost peninsula. They sought the eastern road through the forest promised by Creaggan, but the forest lay in an unbroken line to their left: no roads led into its interior.

More days passed. The fringe of Darvish Forest still appeared through the darkness as an impenetrable, trackless barrier. At each turning of Creaggan's glass, the star shone ever more weakly, its dying an omen, filling the men once more with despair. Tiré Gand was yet four hundred leagues away, up the coast of the Inland Sea and northwards through the barren moors of Ossia. As the star died, the only real light left was that of their torches, endlessly renewed from the saplings at the forest's edge.

After a week of seeking the eastern road, they reached a frozen estuary. Creaggan's glass told them it would be dusk in a world with light. The road bent southwest, now heading slightly inland. At the head of the estuary they came to a place where the armies of Ossia had passed recently. It was not marked on Fazad's map. The cliff road dipped into a hollow where a walled town had once nestled by the water. It had been razed. From their vantage point on the cliffs they could see blackened shells of houses, still smoking. The harbour ice had melted in the intense heat of the conflagration and a thin scum of ice was only now reforming on its surface. Whatever had happened here had occurred recently.

They rode down. A pyramid of skulls stood by the gateway into the place, the flesh rendered from the bone, the bone white in the darkness. A warning. Only Fazad had seen the like before: on the battlefield on the marsh outside Thrull. He studied the grim memorial as he rode past on Cloud, each skull grinning as if sharing a joke at his expense. The soldiers averted their eyes as they followed, some cursing, the others silent.

Their enemies were near. But where? A week's march, yet not a single person alive or dead had been seen, and the wolves had ranged many leagues forward and into the fringes of the forests too. The enemy had left the town, but the smoke and the absence of ice in the harbour suggested that the Ossians were now only a day or two away at most.

He urged Cloud forward. Suddenly the horse reared, and he had to cling to his mane to keep his seat. Gurn spurred his own animal up to him, uttering soothing words to Fazad's skittish mount. "What is it?" he shouted over the clatter of hooves and shouts of alarm from the column behind.

The boy had by now calmed Cloud. He cocked his head. "Listen," he said. The seneschal heard. The far-off howling of the wolves—a warning.

Gurn looked through the gate at the dark streets ahead. At least here they would have the protection of the town walls for the duration of their halt.

He sent men into the houses with torches and into the cellars and the sewers seeking the vampires. But there was nothing, not a soul alive, dead or Dead in Life. They prepared uneasily for the night. But none could settle to sleep, as if some enchantment had been placed over this place: those who drifted off snapped back awake, their minds full of dark images, of Iss' dark chariot being borne slowly to earth through space, of a vampire's mouth outstretched above their throats. The night was full of the stifled cries of those men who had drifted off, only to be woken by nightmares.

Most gave up the uneven struggle for sleep. And many—after they had lain exhausted and unsleeping staring at the starless skies, thinking of home, of Imblewick, imagining another undead legion sent to attack the city, their loved ones slain, the houses smoking ruins—rose from their sleeping mats and stole off through the ruins to the gate and back to the road to the north.

When it should have been dawn according to Creaggan's glass, the trumpeter bestirred himself and blew a few mournful notes, waking the few who still slept in the camp.

A cry went up as the empty sleeping blankets were discovered, and then another from the watchmen on the walls. A line of men had appeared on top of the bluffs above the town. They wore the uniforms of Galastra. Five hundred or so stared down at their onetime comrades, but instead of rejoining them, they remained on the bluffs, their white, haunted faces taking in the scene below. Their friends called out, shouting for them to return to town. But their voices died when they saw how still they were.

"What has happened to them?" Fazad asked.

Gurn turned to him. "They have crossed over; they are the undead."

Fazad looked back at the line of men, a twentieth of their entire army, taken in one night. "What now?" he asked in a quiet voice.

"Fire," Gurn answered and called for torches to be thrown over the walls. There had been no rain for days and the icy brush in the moat smouldered, then caught, throwing up flames. The haggard whiteness of the undead was now plain for all to see. The light of the flames seemed to trouble them—they held up their hands, trying to shield their eyes, letting out low cries. Then they stumbled back out of the circle of light and over the lip of the ridge.

There were vampires behind them, and in front. Perhaps the darkness hid them, even from the wolves who had run for leagues all around and seen nothing. Fazad looked about him. "Where are they?" he asked, turning a circle.

"They wait, wait for one greater still to triumph over us," Creaggan answered.

"Who is this other enemy?" Fazad asked.

Creaggan turned his wise eyes upon the boy. "Even the wolf feels it, boy. Its name is despair. Those on the cliffs have given themselves to it. It is the single mightiest foe any of us will fight. For is this not the purpose of Iss' dark night, to cow mortals to his will, make them give up hope, so as one they bend their knees to him when he comes to earth and makes them his slaves?"

He drew a heavy breath. "But it is written in the *Book of Light* that while there is hope in some men's hearts, and while the Lightbringer's star still burns, Iss cannot come into his kingdom. Only when all light is extinguished, and every single man and woman has abandoned hope, can he come to earth."

Fazad nodded, understanding. He looked up at the bluffs, but the tops of the cliffs were now empty.

"So while we believe, they cannot defeat us."

"Only while we believe," Creaggan agreed.

Fazad gathered the members of the council. "The wolves see nothing, but I sense it. Our enemies are all around us. Should we turn back, try to save Imblewick at least?"

Matach rose slowly. "You have heard the soothsayer. That would be to admit despair, and Iss grows stronger at every despairing soul who has abandoned Reh. What would we save the city from? Those who have deserted were thinking of their loved ones, thinking they could help them. What good are they now? Instead of helping them they have become their enemies, desiring their blood. But we who remain know that the only way to preserve those we love is to go on. We must reach Tiré Gand, fight one last battle against the Worm."

"But we have only covered a hundred leagues of the journey, if that," Fazad said glumly.

"Aye, a hundred leagues of five hundred. Again despair. But do you think that Reh would forget us? That is our business, my king; the business of miracles. We will find one, you will see." He turned to Creaggan, who nodded at his words and intoned a solemn "amen" that was echoed by the other members of the council: Fazad, Matach, Gurn and Valence.

"Come, let's march," Fazad exclaimed. "We lose time: a day should have dawned and we're not yet on the road." He motioned and the trumpeter sounded again. The remaining soldiers formed into their columns and they marched from that accursed city. Later Fazad realised he had never even learned its name.

Further and further they went to the south, towards the vast, barren land on the southwest of Surren where sand dunes blown by the prevailing winds stretched ten leagues in from the Inland Sea. According to Fazad's map a road had once led to a city now sunk under the waves of the sea. Some of its course could still be discerned between the fifty-foot-high dunes that had drifted over it, and they zigzagged over them trying to find it, but it had been buried centuries before. Somewhere to the east was the ghost port of Gor-

vost; beyond the salt marshes, southern Surrenland and beyond that Ossia.

Fazad marched in a trance: half of him with his army, half
with the ranging wolves. Far ahead he saw the skull-masked
battalions falling upon the towns and fishing villages where
the people had resisted the Dark God's priests.

The landscape changed from the giant dunes to a bleak
waste of marram grass and pines; the fringe of Darvish Forest became ever more distant in the darkness on their left.
Now they neared the devastated villages: the wolves waited
for them, crouched by the roadside, their ears pressed low
on their heads. They heard the call of the distant sound of the
bone horns. The noose was tightening around them. Fazad
and the council sought out tracks to bypass the battalions of
the Worm in front.

They camped, without fires, their provisions low, the
quiet more sinister after the noise of the march. The wolves
lay down like dogs on the perimeters, seemingly as spent as
the men, the men not caring anymore how close the animals
were to them: suddenly the wolves seemed their only allies
in the dark land.

Gurn ordered a roll call: another thousand men had
melted away. The legion was down to eight and a half thousand.

Fazad called an urgent council of his advisors.

"Friends," he whispered, keeping his voice low, for their
perimeter had been pushed right in, the men clinging to one
another in mutual sympathy against the invisible dangers
that menaced them. "The time has come for action. Our enemies are all around. The men despair."

He unfurled the queen's map and knelt on the ground, as
did the others. Creaggan held a flickering torch so they
could see the old document better. To an onlooker in the
camp it must have looked as if they knelt in prayer.

There was the island of Galastra and the craggy shoreline
of Surrenland, leading to the southeast. Fazad traced their
route to where the estuary of the River Gant narrowed just
ahead of them. The name of a city, Morigar, was marked

upon it, once an important port after Gorvost harbour had silted. A spur of the road they needed would lead them rapidly towards Ossia from there.

Fazad looked up and stared at his companions. "That is the route we must take. But our way is blocked. The wolves have reached the heights above the port, and I have seen what they have seen. An army is in front: the brown and purple of the Worm occupies Morigar."

"How many?" Gurn asked.

"The wolves don't count," Fazad said with a rueful smile. "Anyway, more than we muster."

"There are no routes around Morigar: only the forest and the sea."

"Then we are lost. The road through Darvish that my augury promised has not appeared," Creaggan said, the torch shaking in his hand. Gurn and Fazad had never seen him so downcast in all the months since they had first met him in the hall of Imblewick Keep. But now it seemed that his hope too had gone. Iss was one step nearer the earth.

Gurn laid his hand upon the soothsayer's shoulder. "Have faith, old man. The star that you so believe in still shines."

"The star grows dimmer. We have been too slow. The men have lost hope."

As the two older men had been talking Fazad had risen suddenly and stood in silent communion with the star to the north. In its dim refulgence, the dead wolf's eyes in the hood of his cape gleamed eerily. "Then I will show them the light."

Gurn and Creaggan looked up at his unexpected words. He turned suddenly, the cape swirling behind him, and stared at the two men, his eyes alive with the wildness that both had come to recognise so well. "You gave me the answer, seneschal, when we first passed through Darvish Forest. That night we camped in the woodcutter's hut." The seneschal looked at him blankly. "Don't you remember: the spirits of the light that only shine in the darkness?"

"Ah, boy," Gurn said, shaking his head with a small,

hopeless smile, "that was but a fairy tale. You have seen the forest—it's as Creaggan says: there is no way through it."

"No!" Fazad exclaimed, taking a step towards them, his feet stamping on the frozen ground. The soldiers within earshot left off what they had been doing and stared in their direction. "As I slept, the shadow of one of my wolves came into my mind. Not the wolves that even now wait above Morigar, but their leader, the most fearless, the boldest, the fastest. Catscar is his name. I sent him into Darvish when we first began to lose men, hoping he could find a way through, as was promised by the runes." He leaned in even closer, his eyes alive with excitement. "He found a faint trail, running to the east just as the augury predicted." He pointed to the dark line of trees to their left. "I was with him, running on roads that humans will never know about: the highways of scent, of hearing, of sight. Invisible roads down which he flew as swift as the wind."

His gaze had become abstracted and he breathed heavily. "There, my friends, is true freedom, the freedom of the senses . . ." And indeed it seemed that his eyes were those of the running wolf's: they were flecked with yellow, alive with animal ferocity. He closed them and once more his face lost that quality of fierceness, its tension; a vestige of humanity returned. His fists were so tightly clenched they showed white at the knuckles.

"Yes, my friends," he continued, "when I saw there was no hope out here, that our enemies were all around us, I followed the wolf deep into the forest, looking for these people of light that the seneschal told me of. We ran very far, until hope almost gave out. But then I saw a curious thing. . . ." He opened his eyes again. "I beheld in the darkness ahead a glowing valley full of light, each tree still in leaf though winter has gripped the land for months. Yet there in that valley it seemed it was mild, and each tree had an emerald spirit captured in the covering of its leaves, softly glowing. I drew close into my wolf spirit, suspicious, scenting the air: but all I smelt was myrrh and incense and honey.

"And there below, in a clearing, I saw them, moving in a

stately dance, more intricate than those I have heard were danced once in the courts of this land: a valley filled by golden people of light. They were creatures of Reh, the spirit of the sunlit glade and the moonbeam. Golden warriors and maidens, forgotten long ago, only visible now the world is dark. You were right, seneschal, they exist!"

Gurn shook his head. "You are moonstruck, boy. You dreamed them. These people fled the earth with the gods."

Now Fazad knelt once more, so his eyes were level with the seneschal's. "You must believe, like you made me believe, when I came in out of the wastes of Bardun. You helped me, as Queen Zalia did. You made me human once more." He seized the older man's cloak by its single sleeve. "Tell me that you believe."

Creaggan had remained silent during the interchange, but now he spoke. "We must listen to the boy, Gurn. Not because he is our king, but because hope is all that we have left. I have heard of these people, but like you had thought them lost with the gods.

"I too wandered the earth in my youth and passed through Darvish. I have heard their name from the foresters' lips a hundred times: the elves—Reh's messengers who flew as swift as sunbeams over the earth in the ancient time. They will surely help us."

"You too?" Gurn answered. "Then I would accuse both of you of staring at the moon, if there were a moon, or even the stars. But there is only that one star."

He sighed. "You're right, though. We need to believe in something, otherwise another thousand of our men will be gone after this stop, and a thousand more the next. Let us seek these people of light."

Just then one of the watchmen who had been posted to the north of their camp came running up. "Sire," he said, kneeling in front of Fazad. "There are Ossians advancing to the north of us."

It was as if the men had been stung. They stiffened, and swivelled to the north.

"How many?" Fazad asked.

"Twice our number at least . . ." The man hesitated. "They rose up out of the dunes, digging themselves out like moles."

Fazad swallowed hard. So that was it. Now he remembered the stories of how the undead had burst from the marsh at the battle of Thrull. The colour had drained from Gurn's face: the boy saw that he remembered too. The vampires had buried themselves so deep even the wolves couldn't scent them.

They were trapped in a narrow funnel between the forest and the sea. Their only clear escape route was the frozen ocean. If they retreated that way, their march on Tiré Gand would be over. There was only one way: the forest and the sanctuary of light that Catscar had glimpsed at its centre.

"We have no option," Fazad said. "We'll go into Darvish."

"How will we find our way? There are no tracks," Creaggan said.

"Catscar will guide us as—he waits for us on the forest's edge."

At this moment there came through the endless darkness the mournful sound of a bone cow horn, very near this time. The note of death, of the legions of Tiré Gand. A shout rang out from the outposts, followed by a noise like a roll of thunder, the sound of maces thudding into leather shields as the legions advanced. Fazad ran towards the noise, Gurn, Matach and Creaggan hard by his side.

Valence held the advance post with a company. His men had hammered sharpened stakes cut from the scrub into the ground as a rudimentary perimeter. Even in the darkness, they could see a solid line of infantry preceded by the trumpeters heading through the rolling dunes.

The High Priest shaped a spell while Valence called a group of his archers forward. Suddenly blue-yellow flames ignited from Matach's fingertips, underlighting his face. He applied the magical fire to the arrows stretched out to him, and their metal points glowed with a sudden light. The archers lined up again at the line of stakes, each man drawing a bead, and at Valence's command let loose a volley that sizzled through the bitter air. Immediately it was as if a fiery scythe hurtled through the undead's front rank; it halted in confusion as those following fell over the bodies in their way, the blaze spreading from the desiccated corpses to the leather armour and clothes of those behind.

Matach smiled in grim satisfaction, turning his hands palm upwards. "A spell I have not used since Thrull field, but I never forget a good one." But even as he spoke more of the undead flowed round their fallen comrades and came on remorselessly.

"Quick, another spell!" Fazad called, but Matach shook his head and looked sadly at his hands.

"I am old. That was all the power I commanded, more than I had even to give on Thrull field. The days of the great pyromancers are gone. Manichee was the last."

Fazad glanced behind, to the forest that showed as a darker line against the dark of the sky. "We'll never reach Darvish before they fall on us—we're lost."

"No," Gurn said, "we have time. We just need a contingent to hold our rear."

Valence looked at his old friend and then to Fazad. "Let me lead the rear guard. We can hold them and die fighting as we should have at Thrull. Instead we lived and saw our honour and our strength leached away these last seven years. We can buy you enough time to reach the forest."

Gurn looked from Valence to Fazad, then nodded his agreement. What was left of the army must reach Tiré Gand. "No sacrifices, friend: just hold them for a little while, then fall back. We'll wait for you," the seneschal said, but there was a hollow tone in his voice, as if he didn't really expect to see his friend or his men again.

"I will hope to see you in Darvish," Valence answered. "But if I don't, take the Wolf King to Tiré Gand; that is where the true battle will be, not here."

The undead were nearly upon them; they reached the line of stakes with a cry of triumph, the ranks behind pushing some of those in front onto the tips, impaling them.

"Go now," the sergeant called, and ran forward with his men, their weapons smashing down onto the undead vainly struggling to pull themselves off the sharpened poles.

Gurn, Fazad, Matach and Creaggan hurried back to the camp. There they found chaos: men running to and fro, their possessions and weapons scattered all about them in the tangle of canvas and guy ropes of the half-struck tents. Many had already fled in panic.

Gurn rallied those he could and led them eastwards, the sound of screams and the clash of arms ringing clearly in their ears as they crossed the two miles to the forest's edge. A lone wolf waited before the tree line: Catscar.

The animal disappeared into the dark trees but when the men got there the edge of the forest seemed to present an impenetrable barrier of interlocking branches, the ground between the boles broken up by fallen, moss-covered trunks. Another blast from the bone horns, now from the south. A lookout on the flanks called a warning: an even greater army approached, the undead legion from Morigar. They had already crossed their tracks and were behind the rear guard.

Valence was lost, caught in a pincer movement, and they would be too if they didn't move. "Break up!" Gurn screamed at the men. "Follow the star. We'll meet at the valley of shining light."

The men all too eagerly broke their ranks. Fazad, Gurn, Creaggan and Matach watched them stream past and plunge into the depths of the forest.

The four briefly linked hands, then followed the remainder of their army into the trackless and pitch-dark waste of Darvish.

CHAPTER THIRTY-TWO

Marizian the Guide

Marizian glided in front of them: silently he passed through more of the huge chambers, each decorated with burnished gold leaf and frescoes glimmering with rainbow hues. The golden hue of his skin glowed as these brightly lit rooms gave way to darker ones, where no magical lights shone. The gloom increased the further they passed into the dust-choked interior of the ancient temple.

Then the succession of chambers ended. Looking back down the mirrored avenue of doorways behind, they could see the faintest of glimmers far away from the Pool Room, a tiny pinprick of light. They had already come a long way—it was absolutely quiet.

In the last chamber the far wall was broken by the entrance to a long corridor—it disappeared into the distance down a perspective of diminishing arches.

Marizian halted here. "This is the way. It leads to the great pyramid."

"We saw it from the square—what is it?"

"In my lifetime, no one in Iskiard was allowed to enter it; not the king, nor his chief sorcerer. It was said that the God's secrets were buried below it, in the Hidden City."

"Is it far to the Hidden City?" Thalassa asked.

"Yes, very far. Into the depths of the earth, into the darkness." It seemed he shivered, even though he was a ghost, as he remembered his descent. "It is strange," he said finally, "I never came this way in life, for it was a forbidden place. Yet I remember it now from my dead self's journey, like an afterimage on my mind."

"What lies ahead?" Urthred asked.

Marizian's brows creased in concentration. "A name comes to me. Ancient guardians of this place." He looked up. "The Marishader," he whispered, his face paling even further.

"We've already met them," Urthred said grimly.

"They're deadly to those who have souls, but not to me, for I had left my soul behind in the Painted Chamber before I came this way. They were kept imprisoned in the blue room, behind a magical barrier, but I set them free."

"Set them free? Why?"

"You have heard from the king of my treachery. Lord Iss spoke to me in my dreams. Like a spider travelling the web of the moonbeams, he came and lighted by my pillow, and whispered poison in my ears, tempting me to steal a god's power all to myself. I betrayed my city for the promise of that power. I released the Marishader, for some of my fellow sorcerers did not trust me, and would not go into the Painted Chamber. They followed me and would have stopped what I was doing, so I set the Marishader on them."

"We found one of them, by the entrance to the temple. His name was Cronus."

"Cronus?" answered Marizian sadly. "Aye, a powerful magician, almost as powerful as I, but the Marishader would only obey me. One touch, and a man's soul and memories are theirs. Below in the underworld lie a hundred like Cronus. But they were just the beginning, for when I opened the gates of Shades thousands more died in this city. And since? Who can count the millions?"

Urthred didn't reply. Ancient betrayals sat as heavily here as the gloom, as if these events of five thousand years ago had just happened, rather than transpiring so long ago that countries and kingdoms had risen and fallen in the intervening space and the sun meanwhile had guttered like a candle.

So deep was he in thought that he didn't notice a shadow settle over the ghost's face. "They are coming," Marizian said.

They turned. At first they saw nothing. But in the silence they heard a faint wailing noise, seemingly emanating from the corridor in front, and then they saw a throng of grey forms, the size and shape of men swathed like mummies in a cocoon of spun cobwebs that covered their limbs and heads and bodies. All that was visible in the grey floss of their faces was a dark cavity, and within it total blackness like the entrance to a pothole. The creatures glided forward rapidly, in a wave, a dozen or more of them, keening loudly, their swaddled arms outstretched towards the three intruders.

Thalassa and Urthred flinched back, but Marizian held his ground, the palms of his ghostly hands turned to them. The creatures came to a stop like an undulating grey cloud a few paces from him. Their wailing died out.

"Do you know me?" Marizian asked.

"Aye." As one the dozen voices came back, high and singsong. "Marizian, you who set us free from captivity, you who set us to destroy the ones following you."

"And did others come?" Marizian said sadly.

"Aye, when you went to find the Hidden City. Priests of the god Reh followed. We took their souls."

"Alas. Their deaths are upon my shadow. What then?"

"A period of waiting. Weeks, maybe months. Perhaps you reached the Hidden City. Then you returned, fleeing, it seemed, in terror. And behind we saw the ghosts spill from Shades and fly up to the sun, and veil it. No others ever came. We wandered here without sustenance for years and years, as the grey twilight covered the sun, until these last days."

"What then?"

"Men came. Led by one who carried that selfsame device

that you brought back from the Hidden City: the Rod of the Shadows."

"Baron Illgill," Urthred whispered.

"What happened to this man?" Marizian asked.

"We could not touch him, because of the Rod. He and his companions went into the underworld. But one or two became separated from him, and lost their souls, became one with us."

"And after?" Thalassa asked. "Did others come?"

"Aye, another came, and he too bore one of Marizian's artefacts. The sword, Dragonstooth. The same with which he sealed the Iron Gates. And he too descended to the depths."

"Are these men who came still alive?" Thalassa asked.

Silence. Then a solitary figure glided forward from the mass. Its voice was a falsetto like the others. "I stole the memories of one of them."

"Then let that man's voice speak once more," Marizian commanded.

The Marishader's voice changed to a deeper timbre. "I am Otin, one of the last of Illgill's legion."

"Speak, Otin. Where is the baron?" Urthred asked.

"I last saw him by my grave, in a tunnel far below here."

"Is he still there?"

"I still hear faintly, though my former body is but a husk from which my senses slowly recede."

The creature was silent for a while, the black hole of his mouth fighting for words. "I hear a voice, it is muffled . . ."

"Can you hear what it's saying?"

"It is the ghost who came after the baron—he has slain him and stolen the Rod."

"Then the baron is dead, just as Jayal dreamed it," Thalassa said.

The creature had fallen silent again; then, as if dimly heard through a sounding box, a faint reverberation sounded in his throat, and a high-pitched nasal whine came from the dark O of his mouth: the Doppelgänger's voice.

He spoke in a slightly distracted way as if he was preoccupied doing something. They heard a faint dragging. "There—all done. A present for you, cousin Jayal. See what I have done to our father. To make sure your rage is bright enough to follow me into the dark depths."

There came a faint laughter, then the voice got dimmer and died away completely.

"The baron is dead then," Thalassa said in a whisper. She looked down the long avenue of arches, remembering. "In Thrull they said he would return from the north one day and conquer the Worm—now that will never be."

"You are the hope now, Lightbringer," Marizian said. "It is you who will come from the north and shine upon those who are covered in night."

"Aye, the hope," she said wistfully. She held her hands palm upwards in front of her face as if inspecting them for the first time. "See, these hands are flesh; their touch is human, as is my soul. You expect too much of me."

"Those hands have healed dozens while I have watched," Urthred said fervently. "I have seen the light shine from you, light that was sent from the heavens."

"Perhaps," she answered. She turned and their eyes met. They were the last of all those who had set out from the south: the Lightbringer and the Herald. "Tell me, Marizian," she said in a stronger voice after a moment of silent communion with Urthred, "for I will need to know when we have it, what you did with the Rod."

The magician was silent for a while. "It is a long history. In the God's time, it was kept far from mortal eyes in the Hall of the Mirrors. The gods agreed that none of them might touch it, for whoever had possession of it would be too powerful. And so it remained, buried here in Iskiard even when the gods fought on Shandering Plain, where many were destroyed and Iss and Reh were gravely wounded. Both of them went to the stars: Iss to the Palace of Grey and Reh to the Hall of the White Rose.

"After the battle the clouds of ash subsided and the sun shone once more and Reh who had gone to his palace in the sun held sway, and men were content with his light and feared the night, when Iss spied upon them from his dark stars. That was the time that we know as the Golden Age. But Iss could not forget this earth of ours; he remembered the Rod of the Shadows here in Iskiard, protected by the wardings of the gods. A magician would be needed to circumvent them. I was supposedly the greatest mage this world had seen since Shandering Plain. And so night by night he came into my dreams.

"He showed me what we are, we humans: no matter how good or evil we think ourselves, we are but halves of one whole. We are half light, half dark. He told me of the magic by which the two are separated, one half to live here on this mortal plane, the other in Shades.

"On the one hand I was content with my life. But on the other hand, there was darkness, envy, an acid burning my soul: a desire to be like the gods. Divided between the light and the dark: Iss' voice was forever in my ears.

"Yet here is another lesson, priest. For however balanced between light and dark a man's soul begins, once the dark voice is given a hearing, resistance breaks down, and evil cannot then be denied however virtuous the heart before. The light is overwhelmed. Evil will always prevail.

"I tricked my king. I told him I would lead the people from Iskiard to freedom through Shades. I went alone into the pyramid. I found the Rod and when I had it in my hands I saw what no naked eye ever sees. Do you not feel it too, priest? Look around you: you are blessed with magic. Can't you hear the ghosts that swarm about this place, the unnumbered dead of the whole history of the world?"

Urthred nodded. "Aye, I have heard them; seen them too, flying up to the sun."

"Know that this earth and mankind is old, older than the gods: they were but the last arrivals," Marizian continued. "Man has lived a million years, and his ghosts up to now have been penned into Shades. But the Rod changed that. I travelled to the Hidden City and released it from its magical bonds. There I found a portal that led across the desert to a dark pyramid. A shimmering gateway stood there and I thrust the Rod into it. It opened and I saw within a roiling white mass of what I took to be clouds towering to the heavens of the Mirror World. Yet they were not clouds, but the spirits of the damned and the cloud exploded in front of me into this world and I fled. Perhaps the spirits in the cloud spared me, for they sensed the evil in me, I know not, but everyone else abroad in the city was slain, by them or by the Marishader."

"Then we must go to the pyramid and shut that gateway again. Lead us there, master," Thalassa asked.

"Don't call me master," Marizian answered.

"But you created me," she said. "You wrote of me in the books of scripture."

"You would have existed without me, and without a thousand other scribes and prophets. You are that thing that never dies, Thalassa. You are hope."

Now she was silent once more, her look abstracted as she pondered his words.

It was Urthred who said softly, "Lead on, Marizian: time is short."

Marizian nodded. "The route stands in my memory like a ghostly trail, through the many dangers. Five thousand years have passed since I last travelled that path: perhaps some of the corridors will be blocked and stairways fallen, but we will find a way."

He stepped forward into the long corridor, and the Marishader parted in front of him, letting them through, though their cobweb fingers brushed the humans' garments, and where they touched there sprang a pattern of white filaments, and a cold chill touched their souls.

CHAPTER THIRTY-THREE

Father and Son

"Father . . ." Jayal began, but then the words died. Illgill's ghost wavered in the air before him. It was so cold in the long nave, it was as if his blood had frozen. The baron held up his hand: though it bore the mark of a terrible burn, it shimmered, transparent, as if it were made of the air itself. "See, I am but a ghost. My spirit will soon go where it has longed to go these last seven years. To Shades, where all the unaneled must go, those whose bones lie neglected in the field, like the twenty thousand that lie scattered at Thrull. I am with my legion again."

"I will find your body, carry it to the sacred eagles . . ." Jayal cried, but again the baron raised his hand, silencing him.

"Aye, you will find it right enough." He fixed his son with such a piercing stare it was as if it irradiated the innermost core of his brain and he would go mad. "But to find it you must live. The journey is long, to the depths of the world beneath this city." Once more he was silent; his eyes, though but belonging to a wraith, seemed to his son to glow with the fervour they had in life. "I am proud of you. You have followed destiny. I have seen how hard it has been: I have seen the curse, the shadow that follows you, the same shadow that slew me, and is now in your mind. Yet you brought the sword, have found your way to Iskiard. After the harsh words of your youth, too late the words of love: a ghost cannot give much comfort . . ."

Jayal felt tears in his eyes. "All is lost: now we will never know one another . . ."

But again the baron silenced him. "Son, we both left our regrets behind in the ruins of Thrull. We have no time for them. The Illgills must fall, and our line disintegrate, until it is dust. Then you will have peace like me, though your lodging be only the Plains of Grey where the winds with supernatural force howl all through that endless twilight. But before we are reunited in that place there to sigh together until the sun rises once more, remember: the curse must be taken off. Manichee was right. Find once more that evil that I brought into the world. Destroy your twin."

Jayal braced his shoulders, meeting the ghost's eyes once more. It was as if the zeal of his father's words entered his ears like a fiery balm, thawing his ice-cold limbs: his heart beat again, with newfound purpose, a new identity. "Tell me where to go," he said in a strong voice.

"You must hurry. He is near his mark, the gateway of the Hidden City. He has the Rod of the Shadows."

"Cursed that I ever lived by it, cursed when I first saw my twin as I was borne onto that bridge that arcs between the Mortal World and Shades: where the two of us came together and I was transformed."

"You must recover the Rod. And when the gateway to Shades is shut, and the Doppelgänger destroyed, throw it into the abyss, where no man may ever find it again."

"I swear, by this borrowed life: he and it will not survive."

The baron's ghost smiled. "I will lead you, but only for a little while. Our time is short—Shades beckons. Many dangers are before you, but you must succeed."

"Only show me the way—I'm ready."

The elder Illgill gestured and they passed down the long grey nave, the other ghosts falling in behind them like a white bridal train gliding over the stone floor. At the far end of the hall, just before an arched doorway, they came across a rectangular pool set into the stone floor. Its surface was covered with a layer of undulating mist. Something struck Jayal as familiar about it. He stared at it. Suddenly a secondary vision came. The Doppelgänger. He had come this way, through the pool. But even as he moved on, the baron's apparition began to fade: his soul was nearly at the Plains of Grey.

"Do not go, Father; ghosts can live for a little time in this world: I need you," Jayal pleaded.

A dry laugh came from the baron's blistered lips. "The world is a sad place for a ghost. This is what your twin discovered all those years ago, after the exorcism. Many times I saw his shade around the Palace on the Silver Way. I saw him, yet I pretended not to—for only by human acknowledgement is the ghost's hold on the living strengthened. I denied his existence: ignored, he slowly faded away; powerless to find a way back to our world. Powerless, that was, until I used the Rod and I myself brought him back.

"And now I know what he suffered. Seeing the world but never being part of it. I look on you, my living flesh, and it is a fiercer pain than even the pain of death knowing that I can no longer touch you. For my soul has gone, and without it I am but a phantasm, gifted with speech but nothing else. Soon even my voice will die." His pale eyes stared deep into Jayal's. "Will you remember me when you no longer hear my voice, when the vapours of which I am made are sucked into the underworld?"

Jayal was about to protest that he would, but the baron silenced him, once more. "I was a cruel father, yet I tempered you in steel, for how else could you have gone to the south and brought back Dragonstooth? How would you have crossed the Palisades, followed me through Lorn into this place?"

"But, Father, I took seven years, I came too late . . ."

"If you had spent but a week on your quest, you would still have found me dead, for we were never meant to meet each other alive again. Such are the dictates of fate. Nothing can change what is written. You are here now, that is all that matters." He paused, and though a ghost addressed him, Jayal felt for the first time in many lonely months the warmth of a kindred spirit, a warmth he had never felt with his companions, Thalassa, Urthred and Alanda, on his haunted journey to the north. Yes, bitterness was futile. The past was gone, spent; nothing mattered but the future, however long or short fate had determined it would be for him.

"Lead on," he said. "I am an Illgill yet."

A smile glimmered on his father's pale face, and he glided onwards. Beyond was a circular chamber with a hundred-foot-wide shaft at its centre. Several passageways branched off the chamber and Jayal wondered where these led. Back to the outside world? To the air, the light of the sun? Those things that the living enjoyed? They were not for him: he was as good as a dead man—the plague boiled in his veins.

His father guided him to the edge of the shaft. Jayal peered down. Immediately vertigo pulled him forward into the drop. Down and down it plunged, seemingly to the centre of the world. He pulled back and inspected the rim of the shaft. A series of empty groove sockets descended in a spiral into the gloomy depths. All that remained of the original staircase were one or two rotten steps right under the rim. A rope hung down over the side fastened to an iron strut.

"That is the way we descended," the baron said, pointing at the rope. "The Doppelgänger too. It is the only way down to the lower depths." Jayal stepped forward and seized the end of the rope and gave it an exploratory twitch. A pulse ran down its length; the rope bowed outwards, flicking the far side of the shaft, sending a shower of dust into the darkness. The rope seemed sound enough, though slightly frayed around the metal stanchion at the top.

First he must leave a sign for the others, Urthred and Thalassa. If this was the only route to the underworld, as his father had said, then they too must come this way.

He knelt at the lip of the shaft, pulling from his belt a short poniard, a weapon it seemed that had been at his side forever, had been given him by his long-dead mother. He glanced up—the ghost of his father looked down: he too remembered. He scraped the point into the stone on the lip of the shaft. The message had to be short. It was slow work making any impression on the rock, which seemed as hard as adamantine. So he merely scratched his name and an arrow pointing into the depths.

Then he sheathed the dagger, and slinging Dragonstooth on his back, seized the grey rope in his gauntleted hands. He looked at his father's ghost.

"I can come no further, my journey is ended," the baron said. Already his face seemed transparent. Jayal could see the brickwork of the wall behind. "The Doppelgänger is near the Hidden City and the way to Shades. Hurry, son, hurry as if on Reh's chariot." As he spoke he had faded to nothing, and the other ghosts also dissolved in the air, drifting away, like coils of smoke.

Jayal reached out a hand, but only caught the solitary wreath of vapour that hung where the baron had stood. He whirled round: Vortumin and Jadshasi, Edric and Poluso; gone like his father.

Now he was utterly alone, without even the company of ghosts, the transitory warmth gone so quickly—like life. Isolation returned—loneliness like a metal vise upon his throat and his chest, as when he had stood in the Ormorican desert that bitter day when he had thought of suicide. He felt wetness on his cheeks and realised he was crying. He had never cried when he had been a child, his father's harsh regime had forbidden it: disappointment or injury had to be met with a Spartan indifference. But now he cried those lost tears of childhood, the tears feeling like an emollient for his soul. Where had the years gone? Gone to this curse, the curse that had withered everything.

Anger replaced the tears. He swung out over the darkness, planting his feet on the walls of the shaft. He began to walk himself down, peering into the gloom below, now only dimly lit by the glow of Dragonstooth hanging from the sling on his back. But the magical light of the sword was faint: as if it realised that the lights of the gods that had sustained it—Reh and his brother moon, Erewon—were conquered by Iss. All that remained was a dim halo. He looked up at the top of the shaft; he was already fifty feet below the lip.

Down and down. The rope was knotted where the first length had run out and another had been attached. The lower he got, the more splices he found: every scrap that the baron had been able to lay his hands on had been tied together.

Eventually his heel touched something in the darkness below. A piece of wood clattered away in the stillness. He felt down with his foot. A pile of crumbling wood, the wood of the broken staircase now fallen into a heap at the bottom of the shaft. He stepped onto it as gently as possible, still grasping the rope firmly. Though it had been partially preserved by the intense cold and dryness, it still gave way with a series of cracks as his weight settled on it. Planks slithered and crashed to the invisible floor. Abandoning any pretence at stealth, he lowered himself the last few feet off the mound of wreckage onto the floor.

Instantly be drew Dragonstooth and its reduced light filled the chamber in which he stood. The shaft soared up overhead, as dizzying looking up as it had been looking down, the swaying rope like a tapeworm swallowed by its black maw.

He stood in another circular area, similar to the one at the top of the shaft. It was frescoed with blistered wall paintings, gold and blue and white. Tunnels led away like the spokes of a wheel. The Doppelgänger had come this way. Which tunnel to take?

He tried to guess, tried to bring an afterimage of the Doppelgänger to his mind. Nothing. He closed his eyes, trying to pick up a trace, a scent of his twin.

And then suddenly there it was: a simulacrum of the Doppelgänger as if made of a winnowing mist, just on the borders of the blackness in his mind, superimposed on a vision of the tunnels and the shaft. It disappeared into the tunnel immediately in front of him. He followed it down a gently sloping shaft. It was very dark, the only guide the simulacrum of himself gliding away in front, like one of those ignis fatui on Thrull marsh that lured so many to their doom.

He blundered forward, as blind as a mole, scraping his knees and elbows on the side walls, following the image. The gloom was like a caul around his head. He breathed deeply. The air was bitter with ancient dust and grime.

At the end of the shaft he entered another circular chamber. On the side by which he had entered was a semicircular ring of high pews. A ramp led down a sloping staircase between the tiers to a wide funnel-like shaft some hundred feet across, which was set into the exact center of the room. It was as if the seats had been arranged to view something that was due to come from the shaft. In the pews were the mummified remains of long-dead ancients, clad in gossamer-thin robes, the nearest garments waving in the slight air disturbance he had caused by his entry, the material spinning away like broken spiderwebs on the faint gust of air. He accidentally brushed one of the forms near him and it seemed to fold in on itself, as the fragile remains of its bones crumbled in the disturbance and fell in a gentle susurration of dust onto the floor beneath the pew.

The afterimage of the Doppelgänger drifted downwards to the shaft. Beyond lay another ramp leading up to an iron grille, hanging open on its hinges. A single rope was attached round the grille over the abyss and to one of the wooden pews behind him; the line sagged downwards in the middle. A bridge must have connected the two sides at one stage in history. Its stanchions were still visible on both sides, but the structure itself must have fallen into the chasm a long time before.

The ghostly image drifted over the top of the shaft and disappeared through the grille on the far side. The only way across the hundred-foot abyss was by the rope. He reached up and tugged at it. It seemed sound enough.

He slung Dragonstooth and reached up and clamped his hands on the rope, swinging his legs up so he gripped it between his ankles. Hanging upside down, he began to claw his way across, one hand over the other, the rope bucking and sagging, creaking ominously where it was attached to the pew. Inch by inch, until he hung over the shaft, the dead ancients in serried rings looking down at him from their high seats, the grille invisible behind him. And now from the depths far beneath his feet, he heard a sudden explosion of noise. He froze. There was a displacement of air, and he felt himself being sucked downwards into the shaft. Now he heard another noise, a slow scraping as something hauled itself up towards his exposed back. He was helpless, like a worm wriggling on a line, the pike rising from the depths.

He snapped to: the noise was nearer now, he must act. He anchored his feet as best he could, slowly released one hand and painstakingly reached behind his back towards Dragonstooth. He found its hilt and began to haul it out of the sling.

The noise had almost reached him when the sword came free and its blade shot light down into the depths.

Then he saw it, a scuttling shape like a giant tarantula, scampering up the side of the shaft. The vibrations of the rope must have woken it. It opened its maw. He swung and there was a burst of light. The creature screamed, blinded, and toppled back, throwing up a gluey tendril of web that flew past Jayal's nose and anchored itself to the crumbling ceiling high above his head. The creature fell, then rebounded back, stayed by the elasticity of the web. It started to scuttle up again. It would be back on him in seconds. He extended his arm, stretching to reach the gluey tendril that it had shot out, the rope swinging wildly so he could barely hold on to it. Then the tip of the sword touched it, its natural heat doing the rest. The shroud parted with a hiss and fell towards the creature, which seemed to remain motionless for a moment before it too fell out of the circle of Dragonstooth's light into the depths below.

Jayal brought Dragonstooth back, clumsily threading it through the sling. Only then could he afford the luxury of taking hold of the rope with both hands again. He rested then: a minute, two minutes, while his breathing calmed. He had nearly dropped the sword. If he had lost it, he would have been defenseless. His palms were clammy with sweat.

Yet his heart beat strongly; his blood pounded, circulating the plague fever through his veins. He felt its fingers reaching out towards his heart. The sands were running out.

He began to drag himself along the rope again. He had survived the first step, but there would be many more.

CHAPTER THIRTY-FOUR

The Fair People

The noise of fighting two miles distant followed them into the choking depths of the forest: the clash of arms and screams was crystal clear as Valence's rear guard fought its final, doomed battle against the Ossian legions. A single errant flaming arrow arced high into the heavens above the trees and fell earthwards like a comet, then suddenly the only sounds were breaking branches and men's curses as they fought further into the creeper-choked stands of ancient oak and beech, dense thickets of underbrush and thorn, limbs and roots tangled and tangled again, a thousand years of interbranching boughs and leaves. Trailers and burrs snagged every part of their bodies, each step forward was a struggle.

Soon the survivors were scattered into tiny groups, and then even these were broken up, so difficult was the way. But Fazad still held together his group of Creaggan, Matach, Gurn and a dozen soldiers. Here in the depths of the forest his wolf sense was most acute. He sniffed the air and immediately detected the musky odour of other animals. He followed the scent and presently they came to a game trail so wide it was almost a path, with enough room even for Cloud between the trees.

He called out, trying to rally the men to him, but the

sounds of a few moments before had died away. He looked at the horn hanging at Gurn's belt: the seneschal had carried it with him all the way from Perricod. A call might be heard, but it might be heard by the Ossians too. His voice would have to suffice: he shouted again but his words were swallowed by the ghostly green depths of the ancient forest. It seemed they were completely alone.

They moved on down the game trail. The scent of the animals, deer he guessed, was very strong in his nostrils. But there was something else, an invisible charge in the air. As they went on, the scent of the deer died out, as if they had not dared to go deeper into the forest. He felt the wolves close by: their unease, their fear. The hairs on his neck were standing up.

He turned, seeking the light of their star but it was lost, hidden by the tangled undergrowth, not even a glimmer making its way through the interlatticed branches. Invisibly the wolves passed like a shadow, following their leader, Catscar, to the north.

They struggled on for many hours. Now Fazad reasoned they must be far enough from the Ossians. He halted, and Gurn brought out the ivory horn, blowing upon it so tentatively at first that only a dry whistle was emitted. But finally he got his courage, and this time the horn produced a note that carried through the still air. One or two answering cries came, and some men fought their way through the tangle to their side, their faces showing relief to have found some friends in this benighted place. There were now some thirty men in Fazad's group.

"Light your torches," Fazad ordered. "I will lead you to the golden vale." They scratched at their tinder boxes and presently the darkness was shot through by flickering light. With it their situation seemed less desperate.

Matach's palanquin had been abandoned at the forest's edge. He leaned against a tree, gasping for breath, his face haggard, almost beyond hope. But as more and more torches were lit, he straightened slowly, staring at what lay ahead in the gloom.

"Look," he said, pointing. A few yards to the north the game trail expired. The surrounding dense tangle of undergrowth gave way to a widely spaced plantation of trees. What was more, they saw that on the further trees there were still leaves on the branches. They had broken through some kind of barrier, from winter into summer, almost from darkness to light, for once more the Lightbringer's star was visible shining through the trees to the north. They pushed forward into the plantation. Suddenly the air seemed warmer and they were in a grove of leafy beech trees, each standing clear of its neighbour, grass in between their trunks.

Behind, they saw other Galastrians emerging from the dark line of trees, brought to the spot by the horn call. They looked around them, bewildered. Gurn now produced the gonfalon holding the Iremage and the queen's standards, and unfurling the flags, he held them aloft as a rallying point. The survivors congregated around them. They were only a tiny few of the legion that had departed from Imblewick. Many asked after Valence's detachment, but it soon became clear that none expected to see the little sergeant or his men again.

White and yellow flowers grew on the grass in front of where they had gathered, glowing in the darkness like stardust scattered over the earth. Matach knelt and fingered the leaves of the plant, which were narrow and thick and pulpy, a deep vernal green with a white streak down their middle. Stalks rose from the leaves, striped on the backs with lines of green; their insides were milky white.

"It is a good sign. This plant is called the Lightbringer's flower," the old priest whispered. "The flowers open just before the dawn in anticipation of the rising of the sun."

"There will be no sun here," Gurn said, looking at the inky sky.

"No, seneschal. But it is a sign: it shows if the very flowers of Reh's creation have hope of another dawn, so must we."

"Amen to that," the old soldier said gruffly.

They pressed on. Scattered among the plantation of

beeches they now saw silver birches whose trunks glowed like metal in the darkness.

The wolves waited ahead of them, looking to Fazad and then back towards the north, waiting for his prompting to run ahead again. He nodded and they leapt forward, scouting through the lush meadows.

Ahead, they sensed a faint glow coming through the trees—in its light the silver birches seemed to shine even brighter. "When the sun shone, no one knew where this land was: it is only revealed in the darkness of the end of time," Creaggan said.

Fazad turned to Gurn. "You spoke of a people, a faery folk, who lived here, seneschal. But where are they?"

Gurn shook his head. "I didn't believe my stories in the first place: how there might be people here, who have lived hidden from man through the millennia, is beyond me."

They went forward again, the wolves preceding them. Both humans and wolves were utterly silent, awed by the strangely glowing flowers of the meadows and glistening silver bark of the trees. They ascended a slight rise. In front the sky seemed to glow as if the now-invisible moon was about to rise. A solitary wolf waited for them, silhouetted against the light on the skyline sitting on its haunches. Catscar. He turned and looked at Fazad and let out a low growl. Fazad went forward and petted him on the head, like a dog.

The others followed him to the ridge, where the ground gave way beneath them, revealing a valley stretching as far as the eye could see to left and right. It, too, was dotted with the glowing trees and flowers, but this was not what initially caught the eye.

From left, right and in front came the golden glow of what seemed a thousand lamps hidden in the groves and hedgerows of that place. The wind blew gently and it was warm, the cutting arctic wind that had been with them all the time during the march was now completely absent.

A path led through the trees to a river meandering across the valley, and beyond that was a grassy meadow The noise of the river running over its bed of stones carried up to them, a merry tinkling.

The path continued over a wooden bridge that arched over the stream, then led on to a ring of standing stones in a wide rolling meadow glowing with the white flowers. Beyond were more beech trees and low wooden buildings hung with the golden lanterns.

The Lightbringer's star burned exactly over the northernmost stone of the circle.

Creaggan, Gurn and Matach stood silently. Fazad turned from the enchanted valley.

"What do you think?" he asked them.

"It is them: the fair people, the elves," Creaggan answered. "We've found them."

"I see no one, neither do the wolves. Where are they?" Fazad asked.

Creaggan shrugged. "They and they alone elect to reveal themselves to humans. They're watching us, waiting to see what we do. Shall we go down?"

Fazad nodded and started to descend the slope, Catscar beside him, the wolf hunkered low, cowed by the brightness of the lights. But before either man or beast had gone more than a couple of steps, there came a thrumming noise in the air and a golden arrow embedded itself with a dull thud into the ground in front of him.

He whirled, wondering where the shot had come from. Another fiery dart flew across his face and thwacked into the ground, crisscrossing the first and thus forming a miniature barrier. Still there was no one visible. He turned again.

No more arrows came. Creaggan's eyes went to the crossed shafts on the ground and then narrowed as if he was focusing on something barely glimpsed. "Now I see," he said, and held his staff of office high. At a word of power from the soothsayer, magical light blazed forth from it.

It was as if the doors of Fazad's perception were instantly wiped clean and he saw for the first time.

The trees melted away, like a tide running out, the mile back to the forest thicket. As the wave passed over them their forms dissolved and in each of their places stood a creature: upright, six feet tall, dressed in silver armour, some bearing a blazing bow in one hand, others golden bowls, their faces silver, their cloaks golden, and on their feet winged sandals.

A gasp of dismay came from the men behind. Some of them dropped their weapons from nerveless hands, others sank to their knees. The wolves began to slink away, but then seeing they were completely surrounded, hunkered down, snarling. The creatures began advancing, pulsing forward in shivers of silver light, until they circled the soldiers.

"Steady, men," Gurn growled, although there was a tremor in his voice and he too took a few steps back toward the path leading to the stone circle and the bridge.

The men followed suit and began retreating down the slope into the valley. The creatures of light came behind, herding them down towards the meadow and the stone circle.

Presently they came to the bridge and crossed over it. The stone circle was full of more of the glowing creatures, each of wandlike beauty. These were not soldiers, for the man who stood in the middle of the grouping wore a glowing wreath of leaves and berries and was clearly the king of this fair people; next to him stood a lady, also with a wreath, but this of corn and roses intertwined. It was he who spoke first. The tone of words was light and lilting, but their import was not.

"Mortals, with mortal breath, have come into this immortal place. Speak, before your corrupt exhalations blast this clearing, turn the fair rose brown and the green leaf sere. For we have the power of the land and of ancient alchemy with us—we can take a living soul and turn it into any of the fair forms of nature. Speak before I transform you into trees or rocks or part of the babbling brook."

"Lord," Fazad began, recovering his wits. He pointed north, overhead, to where the Lightbringer's star shone directly onto the heads of the glowing folk. "We have passed through Darvish, following that star. The star is the only light that now burns in our world. The night of Iss has fallen. We come not to trespass but merely to follow it to where we must go."

"And where is that?" the Elf King asked.

"Tiré Gand in Ossia."

"That is the home of the Worm."

"It is the Worm that has brought this dark night upon us. We are children of the light."

The Elf King nodded his head solemnly. "Aye, the Worm is at the core of all the fair fruit of this world, burrowing away until it withers and blackens. The stars have been snuffed from the sky, and the sun too. How else have we become visible, we who have hidden in these fair trees for ten thousand years, who revealed ourselves to mortals only when we cared to? If this night continues, the golden grove will die and rot back into the ground and my people will be no more."

"Then are we not allies?" Fazad asked. "We both wish for Iss' defeat and the sun's return."

The Elf King was silent for a beat. A silvery hand came up to ruminatively stroke his beard. "This star you follow— what is it?" he asked.

"It is the symbol of the Lightbringer: the last hope of the world; she who will restore the light of the sun."

"Ah, we too believe in this person, this Lightbringer," the king answered.

He turned to his queen, as if passing to her a decision on what to do with these humans. Now she spoke for the first time: her breath was like a golden exhalation in which flowers fell to the ground, starring the green meadow white. "You are welcome, seekers of light."

Fazad bowed low. He saw where her breath had landed, columbine twining and rising up towards her white dress from the grass, twisting into the fabric of her glowing garment. "Thank you, my lady," he replied. "But I fear many of us who sought the light are now lost."

"What is your name?" she asked.

"Fazad Falarn, king of Galastra."

"Trust me: those men you speak of will find their way here," the queen said. "All paths in the forest, however faint, lead to this sacred grove. You will see. But as you wait, come, King, feast with us."

She pirouetted, sweeping the hem of her golden dress in a wide arc about the clearing, and instantly a table appeared before them covered with golden plates laden with fruit and bread and flagons of wine. "Come," she said, "eat this food and your spirit will become light, will travel more quickly over this dull earth with its mortal weight."

Fazad, Creaggan, Gurn and Matach looked at one another: suspicion mixed with hunger in roughly equal parts. An unspoken agreement was reached and they bowed and reached forward and touched the food. As they did so it melted at their fingertips and their skin too was suffused with a golden glow. At once, their weariness flew away, their limbs felt light, as if they were made of an airy substance.

"Tell your men to come forward," the queen said. "Let them all eat of this food, for they have far to travel tonight and a great battle on the morrow."

"A battle tomorrow?" Gurn asked. "You misunderstand, my lady. Tiré Gand is far away—another month's march at least."

She smiled. "We'll see," she said enigmatically, then nodded at her husband, who had stood silent all this time. Now he opened the palm of his right hand and a glowing sword suddenly materialised there. He lowered his glowing eyes on the four men.

"Aye, though you are made of clay, eat the food and you will have the celerity of light, and the hand of magic that can transform pelf to gold, that can reduce the undead to ashes, for your weapons will become enchanted. You will be of the essence of fire and light, and travel as quickly as those twin elements of our father Reh. I and my army will come with you and battle Iss' minions: we will find the Lightbringer and she will return the sun, the moon and the stars to the sky.

Then we will be able to live invisibly in Darvish once more, far removed from the sight of man."

Fazad turned and saw that more and more of his army were coming down the slopes, drawn from the depths of the forest by the light. It was difficult to guess in the darkness, but it seemed to him that nearly half of those who had entered Darvish had found their way here.

He stepped to the front of the glowing circle so they could see him, and raised his hand, gesturing for them to approach. He ordered them to form a line, until a long column snaked back over the bridge and up the slopes. Then one by one he bade them come forward. They slowly filed into the stone circle, touching the magical table, and their weapons gleamed with an ultraplanar light.

Creaggan touched his staff to it and there came a noise like thunder, and the soothsayer held it up and they saw how it glowed like frozen lightning.

Fazad called Cloud and the horse whinnied and stepped into the golden circle and gently took a small sheath of corn and he, too, was transformed.

When all had passed through the circle Fazad turned to the king. The golden eyes seemed to bore through him. "You are strange," the king said. "Half human; half animal—commanding both."

"Aye, for only those with the nature of both can hope to survive in this savage world."

"The Mortal World was always savage—only here in the greenwood has there ever been peace and light. Now we must leave: we will find this star of yours, grow it into a sun so the world is restored."

"Which way will we go through the forest?" Fazad asked.

The king shook his head. "We won't go through the forest."

Fazad looked around, confused. "How then?"

"You will see. Tell your men to prepare themselves," the king commanded.

"And what of them?" Fazad pointed up the slope. The

last of his men had filed through the stone circle. But the wolves ringed the high bluffs around them, Catscar in their midst. His mind was full of their yearning, of regret, sadness.

The king shook his head. "They are not creatures of the light, they cannot pass through the portal. Release them— send them back into the wild, for creatures like them should never be subject to human will. You must empty yourself of the wolf if you are to fight on the side of the light." As he said these words the wolves set up a dismal howling, and Catscar took one or two steps down the slope towards Fazad, their eyes making contact with each other's over the hundred yards of space. Fazad felt himself torn two ways; both back into the heart of wildness, and forward into the paths of light, forever away from the wolves. Zalia's words echoed in his mind: he must abandon the wildness in his heart, find the humanity within him.

Slowly he reached behind and stripped the wolf cloak from his shoulders. He held it up so Catscar and the other wolves could see it, then let it fall to the ground. Instantly their howling ceased and there was silence. They watched him, unmoving.

"Go," he called. "No more will we run together in the wild forest, on the scent of the deer; no more will your blood sing in my veins. Without you earth will be a dimmer ace, the dead confines of rooms will hold me, no longer the majesty of the forest and the plains and the wheeling skies. All will be cramped and limiting." He drew his breath, staring at the army. "I must be with my people, but my people fear you, and when I am with you, they fear me. A monarch cannot win the hearts of men with fear. So farewell."

But still the wolves sat unmoving and silent on the bluffs above the meadow. Fazad turned to the king. "It is over. Show me the way you spoke of that leads out of the forest."

The king pointed his sword: the table and banquet had disappeared. The circle of stone was now filled with light. In its centre was what looked like a glowing staircase reaching up to the heavens. "There," the king said. "Follow me."

"Where are we going?"

"Why, to Tiré Gand. Isn't that where you were heading?" Fazad looked from the king to the glowing staircase, but before he could ask another question, the elf continued. "I will go through first with my army. Follow with your men."

He gestured and from the meadow all the elves came flowing forward towards the staircase in lines of silver fire and began to climb up it. As they did so, their light began to dim and the tops of their bodies melted away followed by their legs, until they had completely disappeared. And as more and more passed into the circle, the light of the lanterns in the trees began to die one by one and the clearing became darker and darker, creeping ever closer to the circle of light that also began dying, until the Stygian gloom of Darvish had almost returned once more.

Only the king and queen were left. He held out his hand to his wife and she took it and stepped forward to the staircase. "Wait!" Fazad called, suddenly unsure. "Where will I see you again?"

The king turned then and stared at him with his alien silver eyes. "I told you—at the gates of Tiré Gand. We will be waiting." Then he was gone, and the light had disappeared from the clearing apart from a faint glow around the stones and a rapidly fading image of the magical staircase that glimmered in the air.

"Quickly before it vanishes," Fazad pried, but Gurn seized his arm.

"No, master," he hissed, "they might be devils come to tempt us to destruction. What if it leads to Shades?"

"Then we will only have found it a little earlier than others," Fazad answered. "For all men must go there sooner or later." He raised his hand and gestured for the column behind him to enter the circle of stones once more. Now there was confusion in the ranks, the men looking from one to another, too scared to be the first. Fazad turned on his old friend in frustration. "I must be the last to go." He pointed up at the bluffs. "See, the wolves are still waiting. Now I no longer have the cloak, I cannot control them. But they won't attack if I remain. You must lead the men," he hissed. "Quickly, take Cloud before the portal fades away and we are stranded here."

The seneschal's face worked with contrary emotions, his hand gripping the pommel of his sheathed axe. "Very well, then," he said. "I will go—even if it be to Hel's gate."

Gurn gestured and stepped forward, palm out to Cloud, who whinnied nervously, eyeing the seneschal and then Fazad. The boy leaned forward and petted his mane. "Go with Gurn," he whispered. "I won't be far behind."

The horse neighed, then turned, and tentatively placed a hoof on the first of the glowing steps. Immediately he did so, the hoof and fetlock seemed to dissolve from view. He took another step and another: hocks, quarters, back and then head vanished. Gurn, Creaggan and Matach followed. The soldiers, seeing the council men disappearing, hurried forward, sensing that the portal was fading fast. And as each stepped up to the stone they vanished as if swallowed by the thin air.

Fazad stayed, watching the light fade, anxiety eating his heart. Would they all get through before it went out forever? Would he and those who remained be left stranded here, lost in the centre of Darvish? He shut his eyes, trying to blank out his fear. He heard the gentle footfall of boots on grass. Half an hour, an hour passed. Surely the light would be gone now?

He opened his eyes. Now the last men were shuffling past. The faintest grey outline of the staircase lay faintly etched on the night sky above the stone circle. The clearing was very dark. He felt the thousand eyes of the wolves on him, like magnets. They were waiting to see if he would go. He still heard their voices, calling him to return, dragging him back into their world . . .

But he must go into the light . . .

Suddenly he snapped to and he realised that the last soldier had been gone several minutes. The glow had disappeared from the stones, and no image of the staircase was left . . . He was alone. He stared and saw that there was still a faint luminance coming from the northernmost of the standing stones.

He heard a footfall behind him, and whirled round. In the light of the single star he saw the old woman of Bardun, her face haggard and ghastly, her eyes dark pools. She was walking slowly towards him over the meadow. When she passed the glowing white flowers, their light went out like snuffed candles. He felt a chill on his spine. He could not resist her, he knew. If she asked him to pick up the cloak again, he would. At his back he sensed that the light of the last stone was fading; he was lost forever in Darvish.

Now she was right in front of him, and their eyes met. He saw the cunning in hers, the cruelty. She stooped where he had dropped the cloak and picked up the garment. She looked at it and then at him, and he remembered the cave that day when she had told him first to put it on in the early morning light. But she said nothing, merely held it up before her and with her free hand made a small sign, almost of benediction, or perhaps farewell, then turned and hobbled off into the darkness.

Suddenly he no longer heard the wolves in his mind. Their voices were silent for the first time in these last several months. As he looked he saw them melting backwards, through the sacred grove towards the forest's edge, back into the heart of Darvish, their home, whence they had come all those months before. The wolf woman of Bardun had let him go, had freed him. He could finally be human once more.

He whirled round. Though the staircase had disappeared, there was still the faintest of glows from the northernmost megalith. Perhaps it was not too late. He ran and then flung himself forward, expecting his hands to encounter only hard unforgiving stone.

CHAPTER THIRTY-FIVE

The Battle of Tiré Gand

One second he was diving towards the standing stone; the next it was as if the hard stone had become flesh, but not soft flesh. Muscle overlaid by scale armor. Fazad crashed hard into a man, his momentum bearing them both to the ground. He rolled away, winded and disorientated. It was pitch dark. The other man cursed. Fazad recognised the voice.

"Gurn?" he called out.

"Aye," the seneschal grunted. "I waited for you, but now I wish I hadn't." He sounded winded. Fazad must have struck him in the midriff.

"Are you all right?" Fazad asked as he clambered to his feet.

"Only a bruise or two, and short of wind," the seneschal answered, trying to push himself up on his single arm. Fazad saw him in the gloom and helped him up. Then he looked around.

What he saw took his breath away.

The forest and the standing circle were gone. Gone too was the warmth of the valley. The blustery wind was bitterly cold, as if snow was threatening. Thick banks of low-lying cloud rolled towards him from the darkness in front. He was facing north. Above the layer of cloud, the solitary star shone, higher in the sky than it had seemed to have been a moment before in the stone circle.

Through the mist, to left and right stood the shining spirits, like lines of fire reaching as far as his eyes could see, their golden light forming a huge crescent that stretched ahead into the darkness, winking dimmer and then brighter as the thick cloud rolled over it.

Now, as his eyes adjusted to the tenebrous gloom, he saw that he stood on a low bluff. He began to make out more details: the ranks of his own men on top of the low ridge to either side, still glowing faintly from that strange inner light bequeathed to them by the elven banquet. In front stretched a marshland, pale reeds waving and rustling like bones in the breeze. The Galastrians for the most part gawked about them, slack-jawed, as dazed as he was at the sudden change in location. Creaggan and Matach stood a little way down the slope, peering forward into the gloom.

He went forward and joined them. "Where are we?" he asked the two wise men.

"The heart of the Worm: Tiré Gand is right in front of us," Matach said, a faint tremor in his voice: excitement or fear, or both?

Fazad stared into the rolling clouds. As yet nothing of the city was visible, but he didn't doubt the priest's words. Tiré Gand. The king had brought them through the ether, right to its gates.

"And the Elf King?"

"He has gone on. He wouldn't wait. He's gone forward to the walls of the city."

Fazad strained his eyes again. There was a road that became a causeway running down into the marsh to the right of his position. Beyond, where the furthest horns of the golden spirits were ranged through the marshland, he saw a river. Its waters looked grey even in that light, the colour of cement, and barely a ripple disturbed its sluggish flow. And now he picked out a series of gloomy mansions, covered by a rust-coloured ivy standing on either side of the causeway, rising up from the sinister reed beds, their towers and machicolations appearing and disappearing in the drifting fog. The city must lie directly in front.

Gurn led Cloud forward and Fazad mounted. He drew his sword, then raised his free hand, and there came a rustle of armour and weapons from right and left. It was frighteningly loud to his ears, but as the ripple passed down the lines through the fog the sound was dampened. Perhaps those in the city had not seen the ring of flaming spirits nor heard the sound of their armour. He sensed no alarm.

"Are you ready?" he asked his three advisors. Each man nodded. Creaggan held aloft his staff of office, and Gurn the gonfalon with its two standards. Then Fazad rode down the slope onto the causeway, the horse's hooves ringing off the stone, a flat echo from the ivy-hung walls of the mansions to either side, but nothing stirred from behind their walls. Perhaps their owners had already fled and were warning those in the city of their arrival?

He urged Cloud forward and there came a pulse of acceleration from the lines to either side though the men were struggling through boggy ground. How like Thrull, these ringing marshes. But just as the marshes had not protected Thrull, neither would these now protect the Worm. He was more and more convinced that their arrival had caught their enemies by complete surprise. What had been visited on Thrull would be visited on Tiré Gand.

Then the mist blew away and he saw what lay ahead.

On the opposite bank of the river stood walls so high that they showed like the sides of grey mountains, reaching up to the jet-black sky. Over the walls, seven hills rose up to a mist-shrouded moor that seemed as high as the sky. There was a confused jumble of towers and hanging buildings on the flanks of the hills, but all seemed to pay homage to the monstrous stepped pyramid mounted on the central and highest of them.

In front, the level of the river was high, though the flow was sluggish, dead reeds and lily fronds lazily spinning down its length and crowding under the spans of the corbelled arches. An odour of decay hung in the air.

The city was dark save for one or two guttering lights flickering from the walls and towers. In front were three bridges. Fazad was facing the middle one; the two horns of the elven army had reached the ones to left and right. Each of the bridge ends met with a narrow, triangular gateway, more of a slash than an entranceway, set into the high walls in front.

Still no sign of any movement in the city at their approach. Where were the watchmen? He saw the Elf King ahead, surrounded by a company of his men. They fell in beside Cloud as Fazad rode forward. They were nearly at the bridgehead: Cloud's hooves were louder and louder on the walls in front. On the two bridge posts facing him were statues of winged gargoyles, their gigantic red eyes made of huge rubies reflecting back the lines of the elven folk coming towards them. Then it seemed as if a shadow passed over them, and their wings moved, and then he saw that far from a shadow, they *had* moved, the creatures were alive. These were the guardians of the city.

A screech like the ripping of cloth, echo upon echo about the seven hills, the same noise repeated from the bridges to the left and right. He spurred Cloud onto the bridge, his men running with him, and slashed at the right-hand creature. Cloud reared, a talon whistled past Fazad's ear, then acid burned his face, the creature's spit. Through the mist of pain he saw the gargoyle fall, nearly decapitated, into the turgid waters below.

He whirled round, but its companion too had gone, toppled by the soldiers. He wiped the acid from his face. His men were already swarming forward past him following a company of elven archers led by their king. To left and right the elves flowed forward onto the flanking bridges. So closely packed were their ranks they seemed like walls of golden light.

Now he heard a tattoo sound on kettledrums from far away in the city, drums he recognised from long ago, beating men to arms . . . Where? Thrull once more. Lost in the mists of time, the imperfect recollection of infancy, but be had not forgotten though he had been but five. The last day of the city as it had been, that dawn as the sleepless night had finally ended, and the day of the battle had come. Each successive rank of Faran Gaton's army revealed as the darkness fled; each line marked by the standard pole of its cohort, each surmounted by a grinning skull.

He remembered the flicker of fear that crossed his father's face as he stared down from Thrull's ramparts at the size of the army arrayed against them. How was it he remembered it all?

Suddenly fire overarched the river, delicate traceries of flame that fell about the gloomy city like stars: the elves on the banks behind had let loose their arrows. What were they firing at? The arrows soared under the overhanging machicolations of the city walls. But some of their shots found marks, for even as he neared the end of the bridge, Fazad saw one and then another winged creature toppling from the heights and falling into the river with leaden splashes, geysers of water flying upwards, sprinkling him and Cloud as he cantered under the gate arch.

There in the gloom he saw that the gates were shut. They were huge, fifty feet high and thirty wide at their bases, massive bronze casts, more metal on one of them than he had seen in his entire life. How would they ever be breached?

Elves and Galastrians milled about him. The drum on the opposite side of the gates began to beat more urgently. A humming sound was in the air. Missiles rained down from the turrets onto them. Dead men fell like puppets whose strings had been cut; others cursed and groaned at their wounds.

Creaggan advanced through the ranks, holding aloft the staff enchanted in Darvish. Still it appeared as if he held a lightning fork in his hand, its light blinding. More arrows flew through the darkness but they bent and warped away from him in the air. A magical warding, like a bell jar surrounding his body. Fazad followed, as the sorcerer flung forward his staff of office. A shaft of light flew from it and struck the gates dead centre. Then a scintillating explosion lit up the entire city, the sky and the mist-shrouded moors. There was a groan of metal, and the gates swayed inwards. One of them toppled away from the other and landed with a deafening clang; the earth shuddered and shattered cobbles flew through the air; distant bells rang from the temple as the aftershock reached it.

His men streamed past, screaming with excitement. Tiré Gand lay open. Revenge for all their defeats and injuries, booty: all the rewards of a soldier were in their grasp.

But Fazad remained still, braving the rain of missiles that continued to fall from the walls above. On the bridges to left and right the line of elves and humans had come to a grinding halt in front of the other gates. They were paying a heavy toll; bodies toppled over the parapets into the water. There was no one with them with Creaggan's magic. He could quickly lose two-thirds of his army. He would have to divide his own force, open the gates from the inside.

He urged Cloud forward through the throng of soldiers. The narrow streets rose steeply behind the walls. They were full of Galastrians struggling with troops wearing the bronze armour and skull masks of Tiré Gand: weapon struck on weapon; the lines ebbed back and forth as if the two sides were involved in a deadly tug-of-war. But though they fought the undead, the Galastrians' enchanted weapons opened smoking wounds in the enemy, who fell, burning, to the ground.

Creaggan brought his staff down in a wide arc, lightning forked and cracked, sizzling over the heads of a company of the undead advancing from a side alley. They stood frozen for a second before their smoking corpses fell to the ground. Then Gurn and his men crashed into the disorganised ranks, Gurn hacking to left and right. They beat the Ossians further and further back until they were retreating uphill towards the Mother Temple.

Fazad circled the square on Cloud, his sword held high, the men rallying to him. He looked up at the temple pyramid atop the highest of the hills. The Mother Temple of the Worm—if that fell, surely the city's resistance would be broken!

But already the bridge behind them and now the square were littered with the dead. Their comrades on the other bridges were being cut down. He called to two of his ablest lieutenants. They listened as he gave orders: they must go and open the other two gates of the city from the inside. The lieutenants shouted out to their buglers, who sounded over the din of clashing arms and screams. Presently some order had been brought to their detachments' ranks and they set off to either side, following the line of the massive walls to the gates.

Fazad's remaining men numbered only some thousand with a hundred or more elven archers, their king still at their head. As he watched, the creatures ran off lightly uphill, their bows held up, high in their hands.

He urged Cloud uphill after them. Gurn was by his side holding the gonfalon, Creaggan and Matach were close behind. But as they began their ascent, it was as if the Ossians melted away into the darkness. Why? Fazad and his men were so few compared to the garrison of the city. There must be more Ossian soldiers than those they had already fought.

Then, as they climbed, the resistance began again. He heard screams from the rear of their column. Archers fired from the dark buildings, their arrows unseen in the blackness. Now, from doorways on either side of the narrow street came vampires dressed in ancient armour, blood-crazed by the humans' scent. They staggered out and flung themselves on the nearest soldiers. Minor skirmishes, a whirl only in the ranks, but the enchantment of their weapons had, as the Elf King promised, turned their steel into magical swords, and the vampires ignited, then evaporated into a tarry puddle.

They reached the first inner wall. Fazad looked down to see that the city was divided as Thrull had been: a lower town full of dwellings, and an upper town containing the principal temples and barracks. A battle now raged throughout the lower town, the squares surrounding the two gatehouses the scene of desperate melees, as his men tried to open the other gates.

He urged Cloud on again: even the horse's indefatigable energy seemed to flag, as if he now carried more than just his master's weight. A narrow gateway in front led through another defensive wall. Surely the Ossians who had fallen back in the face of their advance would fight them here? The elves ran forward fearlessly into the darkness, holding their glowing bows up like torches, illuminating the thick cloud of cobwebs hanging from the ceiling of the tunnel. There was no one at its end.

Fazad crouched under the low arch and rode through, dusty mould and mildew showering his head. Then he was out in the open and the Mother Temple stood before him. Tier upon tier rose into the cloud that tumbled down from the bleak moors of Ossia.

The area in front of him was a hundred yards square. It was unpaved: circular stone headstones and dark yew trees crowded closely together on packed earth.

A cemetery.

"Why would the undead need graves?" he said aloud, keeping a wary eye on the entrance to the temple.

It was Matach who replied. "Iss' element is earth. Perhaps this is where they bury those vampires who have been visited with the second death and can never return."

"Then if they have died the second death, they can't harm us," Fazad replied, urging Cloud on towards the headstones and the trees. The horse was skittish, stepping sideways, not forward.

The elven archers ran ahead of him with their king, fanning out into a long skirmish line. Still Cloud would not obey him. He kicked his heels into the horse's flanks for the first time since they had been together. But once again Cloud balked, rearing up. Fazad could only watch as the elves reached the shadows of the branches of the yew trees, then they were gone, in the blink of an eye vanished, as if the shadows had eaten them.

Pandemonium followed. The Galastrians stopped dead, some stunned silent, others screaming in terror. Fazad gave up his struggle with Cloud and dismounted quickly, and the horse galloped off to a far corner of the square.

Fazad joined Creaggan and together they advanced to the edge of the cemetery.

"Where have they gone?" Fazad shouted.

"Banished, interred into the lightless prison where Iss keeps his damned," the soothsayer answered. Just then there came a sinister rattle of chains, and a portcullis dropped down abruptly in the passageway behind them. Now there was no escape from the square. It was a trap.

There was only one way to go: forward, over the cemetery towards the entrance to the temple.

"Follow me," Fazad cried, holding up his sword. The soldiers rallied behind him and with a rattle of arms pushed through the yew trees towards the gates of the temple.

He ran. Past the first gravestones, to the point where the elves had disappeared. Still nothing. Then screams came from behind. Before he had a chance to turn to look, Fazad slipped on something slimy and unyielding underfoot. He grabbed a tree trunk to steady himself and came eye to eye with a viper, its tongue darting towards his face. He leapt back. Snakes were all around, slithering and hissing in the trees, covering nearly every inch of the ground.

More screams as the serpents fell from the trees. Men panicked, blundering through the dark grove, the magical light of the weapons almost gone. The ground opened and some plunged into the graves below, where they were clasped by the bony fingers of mouldering skeletons. Fazad shoved himself away from the tree and its hissing denizens and ran on. Finally he was out of the graveyard.

The great temple wall loomed in front of him into the sky. The great twin bronze gates of the temple decorated with beaten reliefs of the end of the world stood before him. Pagoda-topped towers stood to either side of the gates. The gates looked solid, verdigrised copper, almost as imposing as the ones on the first wall.

Now that the light from the enchanted weapons slowly ebbed away, where was the Lightbringer's star? Hidden by the temple? Or had it vanished? Fazad shouted out for more torches to be lit, but only one or two of his terrified men had the wits to obey, and try to strike sparks from their tinder boxes, and even these failed, for the sparks would not catch on the resin heads of the torches: it was as if the whole atmosphere of the temple precluded light or flame.

Fazad drew a deep breath. Creaggan had made it across the square with about a hundred soldiers. Behind them in the graveyard one or two men struggled in the graves and amongst the writhing serpents. The rest were dead.

"Can you open the gates?" Fazad asked the soothsayer.

The old man looked spent, exhausted, his eyes half-closed. "Maybe there is still magic in the staff. I'll try."

He hurried forward, the staff extended before him, but it no longer glowed with anything but the faintest light. The wood shook in his hands, glowed briefly, then died. Whatever magic he had once commanded, it was all used up.

Then Fazad saw movement in the watchtowers above them.

He was about to yell out a warning, but it was too late: what looked like a hail of black soot fell from above, hissing like rainwater on drought-dry earth as it fell on the soldiers below. They screamed in pain, whirling as if a million hornets bit their flesh. Somehow Fazad escaped but he saw the faces of those touched by the deadly hail as they beat frantically at their bodies. Their features turned from pink flesh to black and withered skin that resembled rotten apples: flesh to dust in a second.

Matach's orange and red vestments seemed to empty of his body, leaving only a mummified skull poised in midair. Then he silently toppled into a pile of rag and constituent bones.

Gurn was unharmed, and so, too, Creaggan, though those to either side of him had fallen. But Fazad saw the soothsayer stagger: he had thrown his cloak back the better to fight and one of the dark hailstones had grazed a wrist, and now corruption ran up and down his arm.

He went forward to help him, but Creaggan waved him off angrily. He swayed from side to side, then took a few steps forward and hurled the staff at the gates. His last drop of life energy must have been sacrificed in the spell, for though the staff had lacked magic a few seconds before, now there came a blast like forked lightning as it struck the metal. Creaggan's body fell towards the gates just as there came a blinding flash. His body was silhouetted for a split second before it was blown to a hundred pieces by the blast.

Fazad flinched back, half blinded, but heard a mighty crack as the gates gave way where they were joined.

When the smoke had partially cleared, Fazad saw through the light spots clouding his eyes the gates leaning inwards. He shouted at the few remaining men and rushed forward to the gap.

Figures materialised between the shattered gates, soldiers in an armour be had never seen before. Black steel, great helms, maces glowing with purple fire, a strange vortex of spinning darkness where their shields should have been. Fazad felt his eyes being drawn into the centre of the pattern—his head began to spin. He looked away, warning the men to do the same, but some of them were already staring blankly at the shields, mesmerised.

Gurn swore. "It is their elite guard, the Legion of Purple Lamentation. Steady, boys," he shouted, but before the stunned survivors had a chance to ready their weapons, the Ossians were on them.

Fazad struck out with his sword at the nearest enemy. The legionary's shield came up to block him. As the metal touched the whirling pattern of mist, a numbing cold sprang up his sword arm, down his veins, a freezing fist feeling for his heart. The sword fell from his nerveless hands. The Ossian swung his mace, but suddenly Gurn's axe appeared, parrying it before it smashed Fazad's skull. The boy stumbled back, groping for his fallen weapon. He brought it up, parrying another blow.

They were driven back from the gates, back across the cemetery. More and more of the Galastrians fell. Fazad looked to the north. There, finally, above the square he glimpsed the star. It still shone, but for how much longer on him and his men?

CHAPTER THIRTY-SIX

Talos

The rust-red cliffs of the Iron Gates gave way to the Man of Bronze; he raised the silver mallet high over his head as he remembered his master Reh had done when he had entered the city ten thousand years before. In a mighty flash the magic barriers parted like cobwebs and fled away, until there was no gorge left, but only the empty tundra spreading on and on for miles to either side. The giant strode on over the plains. He was nearing Iskiard.

His ruby eyes stared fixedly ahead. There the sky was dark, as dark as it could be. The dark of Iss' time: the Athanor had come. Those who pulled the night over the sky, covered the sun. His ancient enemies.

All around he sensed the dead dragons, smouldering on the ground. A hundred destroyed. Truly the Athanor were strong.

A lance of red light beamed from his eyes and curved to the horizon, catching the top of one of the distant towers of Iskiard.

Now he heard a thousand wings beating as the Athanor swooped to do battle with him. He raised the silver mallet in his right hand, and immediately the blackness of the dark night roiled up into a purple thunderhead. Then he smashed the hammer down to the earth, and a crack of lightning ran from the ground to the sky, the sound of the thunder deafening. Far in the distance he saw two of the towers slowly lean and topple. Yet no flash of lightning this, for like a writhing tornado of white energy, it twisted above the city, bringing light, hurling the demons from its midst.

Now there was confusion in the sky, as the two contending forces struggled for dominion, twisting, wrestling. Shafts of light from the westering sun broke through the cloud showing the ruined city and the demons circling over it, the darkness in their claws.

Then the light of evening grew and the creatures that held the blanket of the night fled momentarily, gibbering and chattering, to the horizon, where they circled, regrouping. They would return soon. For the moment the evening sunlight bathed the ruined city.

His heart was metal, yet he had lived long amongst humans: he felt joy when he saw the light. How long would it last? As long as it took him to get to Iskiard. He strode on. He heard a humming in the air and the ground shook: the demons were returning. Flight upon flight of them fell towards him. He raised the mallet once more and bolts of energy exploded from it, forking and crackling amongst them. They spun to earth in a confusion of wings and mist.

He strode forward, the ground between him and the surviving towers eaten up by each monstrous step.

As he advanced, he called to the Lightbringer, as he had called to her in Lorn, in a voice above human pitch, that only she could hear. Her voice answered him. She was already deep into Iskiard, near the Hidden City, where the portal opened to Shades.

He reached the walls, but didn't break his stride; instead with one blow he smashed a thirty-foot-wide gap in the granite, the rock flying far and wide over the snow-covered plaza beyond. Burning dragons were scattered over the square. Some vampires too, crawling about the shattered wreck of a ship. And by the great temple complex he saw more corpses wearing the golden armour of Reh, but that sight didn't stay him either.

He reached the temple. Some of the demons still lurked in its shadow; they flew forward like bats, their claws reaching up, grabbing at his bronze harness, trying to drag him to the ground.

He threw the mallet in a semicircular motion around his body and there was another blaze of lightning and an explosion and the demons were gone. The air reverberated with the sound of the explosion: more of the towers fell. In front of him the temple complex had begun to collapse in on itself. He waded forward through the dust and rubble, oblivious of the falling pillars that fell across his back, not bothering to fend them away. More of the walls tumbled, until he could see, a little way in front of him, the great pyramid reaching up to the heavens.

CHAPTER THIRTY-SEVEN

Into the Underworld

Faran and the remaining hundred vampires from the Black Mines passed through the empty halls, past the Chamber of Life and into the Painted Chamber with its thousand alcoves and the floor thick with plaster dust. Faran followed the scent of blood. That slight muskiness, like a desert flower: Thalassa. He followed it down a long avenue that passed through a succession of arches, the scent getting stronger all the time.

The avenue opened up into a snow-covered courtyard. The great pyramid stood some fifty feet away. Two sets of footprints led from the entranceway around the angle of its base: Urthred and Thalassa. Alone now, no allies left. just the two of them.

Yet he hesitated before moving on, some sixth sense staying him. Some of the undead passed him, drawn by the scent of blood. But still Faran held back. Why? He stared hard at the snow in front as if seeking a sign, then suddenly its surface shook like water shivered by a fierce concussion. The footprints were wiped clear, obliterated. A dark rumble came from over the walls and buildings like the roar of a raging fire. He heard the building behind groan on its foundations and then the shock of the explosion reached him: a mighty tremor that nearly threw him to the ground. He clutched a pillar. It swayed from side to side, like a ship's mast in a storm.

Now he guessed what was coming: the Man of Bronze. Not even a mountain could bury him for long.

A stab of whiteness suddenly bathed the snow-covered square. Light was beginning to come through a rent in the absolute darkness to the west. He flinched back from the entrance. One of the undead who had passed him was caught in a beam that suddenly appeared over the snow-encrusted battlements. Its skin began to smoke and its mouth opened in a silent scream as it saw its flesh begin to dissolve into mist.

Now more stabbing beams of light broke through the cloud and raced across the face of the pyramid, lighting up its towering peak. Another tremor and now he heard towers falling behind him with dull roars. He turned and saw the temple walls shift and waver from one side to the other, as if they were made of paper. They were on the point of collapse.

More of the vampires stumbled past in panic only to be caught by the low beams of the sun. In an instant, their cloaks fell smoking to the ground and the mist that once had been their bodies blew away like spindrift.

If he stayed here he would be buried. He would have to risk the light. The entrance of the pyramid must be around its massive stepped corner, where the footprints had led. Perhaps fifty yards away, perhaps more. Fifty yards of light. It was evening: the sun cast a deep shadow to the east. All he had to do was venture across the brief intervening distance to the side of the pyramid. He threw the cape of his cloak over his head. His hands were already covered with his gauntlets. Not an inch of skin was exposed.

He ran blindly out into the snow, feeling even the weak beams of the sun like a furnace heat, scalding his back. He screamed as he felt his dried flesh begin to strip away, despite the covering, but ran on, the heat increasing, each step taking, it seemed, an hour, knowing his goal couldn't be far away. He collided with the base of the pyramid, his cape nearly falling off, but he snatched it back over his face, groping his way around the base until he felt the coldness of the shadow in front. He flung himself into it, tossing back the cape: steam was leaking from his cloak and from his gauntlets, but he was now surrounded by shadow. He was safe.

He heard over the thunder of the titan's approach a thin keening in the air, then a figure stumbled round the corner of the pyramid: a vampire, his exposed hands melting away, so white bone showed through. Faran reached forward and yanked him by his collar. He fell into the snow by his side. Now others came, their rags thrown over their limbs, having taken their cue from Faran. Some sixty were left. Several were badly injured, but he and they would be enough to subdue the dangers ahead and the only two remaining humans: Thalassa and Urthred.

The noise was getting louder. The buildings behind him imploded with a roar. He started off along the eastern edge of the wall followed by the surviving undead. Now he saw a shaft set into the side of the pyramid ahead. The entrance. He ran forward and into its welcome embrace. Behind him the thunder of the footsteps continued to grow.

The shaft angled down into the base of the pyramid. The first few yards were covered by thick blue ice, slightly glazed as if feet had already passed over it. Again, Faran detected the faint, alluring scent of Thalassa's blood. He went on, his feet slipping on the ice, but quickly gained a flatter section of corridor. A series of square arches led away to a distant vanishing point. The slabs of stone above weighed down upon them, showing dangerous cracks where the ice had forced open fractures in the massive blocks. The corridor walls, though much corroded by the moisture that had seeped in through the shaft entrance, had once been painted with gold leaf that now covered its floor like an umber carpet. Figures could still be seen faintly etched on the surface. As in the Temple of Iss in Thrull the frescoes showed the progress of the dead into the underworld.

Behind them the vestige of twilight was snuffed out: they

looked back and saw a mighty arm and shoulder groping through the entrance, all the Man of Bronze could fit into it. There came a bellow of rage that sent blocks crashing down from the ceiling. But he wouldn't be able to follow unless he pulled the pyramid apart brick by brick.

Then the pyramid shook again and there came the sound of shattering stone as the giant began to claw away at the fabric of the edifice. But Faran and the other vampires would be safe for an hour or two.

He went on with the survivors. The corridor ahead broadened out into an oval chamber. At the centre of it stood a vertical shaft leading down. In the darkness he saw a faint grey mist rising from the depths, fleeing upwards ever faster as it was caught by the breeze running down the corridor at their backs. As the mist flew up he heard a faint moaning, on the very periphery of sound. Ghosts, the ghosts of the damned escaping.

He strode to the side of the chimney. Ropes spiralled downwards. A name was scratched into the stone. Jayal. He puzzled over this. Jayal was still alive and a threat, but it was clear that the humans had become separated. He had more than enough vampires to deal with all of them.

He gave orders and the undead hauled up one of the ropes and fashioned a sling at its end in which they lowered him to the bottom of the shaft. He cast off the sling and stood on the pile of wood. He sniffed the air: more scents had joined those of Urthred and Thalassa. They all led in one direction, down one of the shafts that issued from the chamber.

The vampires came climbing down, one or two slipping and falling with the brittle crack of atrophied bone on the stone surface. Faran left these crawling like broken insects on the floor and led the remainder down the shaft. They went on for half an hour, over another pit and down more shafts past clustered heaps of yellowed bones, victims no doubt of the millennia-old disaster that had overtaken the city. Still the stream of vapour emitting its high whining sound streamed past: all the ghosts of the world before his eyes.

Faran heard a mighty roar and the fabric of the under-world shook: the Man of Bronze descending the first shaft.

They had time, but not much. He sniffed the air again. Humans and something neutral smelling as well, like the dead scent of metal or stone. Ghosts, the scent of ghosts. The twin trails led downwards and he followed.

CHAPTER THIRTY-EIGHT

The Hidden City

Thalassa, Urthred and Marizian's ghost had reached the bottom of the underworld. The journey had taken many days; they had lost count of how many exactly. It had brought them through numberless chambers, some packed with skeletons, others crowded with iron machinery, derricks and winches perched like birds of prey over huge rusted platforms. On the fate of the dead and the use of the machinery, Marizian's ghost was silent, reflecting perhaps on the destruction he had unleashed five thousand years before. Urthred and Thalassa didn't ask him, because between their fitful stops for rest, they hurried: to catch up with Jayal and to flee the enemies they knew would be following.

But on perhaps the tenth day they found the baron's body. It had been left in a place where it would be easy to find.

Surkut and Endil lay in front; they had been disembowelled and beheaded, their heads placed in niches to either side of the baron. Illgill himself had been propped in an alcove. His throat had been cut and his tongue pulled through it, so it seemed he had two mouths. He too had been disembowelled: his intestines garlanded about the cramped space, his arms and legs stretched out in a crucifixion pose.

No doubt the horror had been meant for Jayal, but the effect was strong enough on them. Thalassa had turned away and retched. Urthred could only stare at the carnage, appalled. The ghost hovered silently.

For many hours more they had continued, at first too shaken to speak, down more shafts, their circular stairs intact, along stone-clad corridors and now, as the gradients eased, through rock fissures. They were now at the very heart of the earth, the air getting warmer. A mile deep at least.

Then the long succession of stairs and rooms ran out and they entered the last chamber. A huge rectangular vault some fifty yards square. Their footsteps echoed back from the distant walls. There appeared at first to be no other exits. A square jade sarcophagus stood in the centre of the room, glowing in the light of Thalassa's orb.

The skeletons of a great number of large animals, cattle as it seemed, lay thick about the sarcophagus. Withered stalks of wheat lay on top of it, somehow having survived the centuries. The chamber's roof was supported by row upon row of palm-tree-shaped columns.

The walls of the cloister were covered with frescoes, as bright today as they had been when they had been painted millennia before. They showed the buried king in triumphant war scenes. The armor of the warriors was strangely styled, with extravagant wing tips on the cuirasses and wide-brimmed helmets now passed from human fashion and memory.

In the mural, a rival lay dead at the king's feet; the king stood over the body, proud and merciless with a scimitar in one hand, the head of his vanquished enemy in the other.

Other reliefs showed different scenes right up to the ruler's own death. Then the funerary service: drove after drove of cattle being herded to the tomb, so the king would have sustenance on his journey through the underworld. Another panel showed the king's slaves bringing the harvest in from the fields, so that he would have bread, and still others depicted the king hunting and fishing.

Finally, two more reliefs. Where the rest had been flat,

without depth, these pictures had perspectives and vanishing points as if painted by a completely different hand.

The first scene was a desert that must once have stretched away from the tomb when it stood above the earth. The king and his courtiers were all arrayed in splendid cloaks and head dresses; they stood looking out over the dunes. The sun was behind them—the artist had taken care to show their shadows on the ground. Yet the king's shadow was longer than his courtiers', stretching forward miles and miles over the dunes to a far horizon.

The second picture showed the skeletons of the courtiers still arrayed in their gorgeous costumes, lying on the ground. The sun had swung round, so that now its rising disc starkly silhouetted the desert horizon and a figure, casting a monstrous shadow, was seen returning towards their point of view. The shadow of the king returning from whatever place he had been to.

"What does it mean?" Thalassa asked Marizian. The ghost's form as they had descended lower and lower had begun to fade. Now it was almost transparent. Urthred saw his lips move in reply, but only the barest whisper floated to them in the stillness.

"I see with my other's eyes, my ghost now in Shades. I remember, and with remembrance comes my end. Now that memory and substance join, I must leave you.

"The desert lies before you: beyond is the Hidden City. There is the gate to Shades. Lightbringer, find the Rod of the Shadows—use it to lock the gate. And let the sun shine, let there be a true balance between Reh and Iss, day and night, and the world have peace once more." So saying, his form faded completely from view and all that was left of the great magician were a few wisps hanging in the air, like the threads of the thinnest gossamer.

"I will do so," Thalassa said to the rapidly dispersing mist, the sibilance of her voice echoing back faintly, as quiet as Marizian's last words.

Urthred turned and stared at the walls of the chamber and its frescoes. What had Marizian meant when he said that "the desert lies before you"? These were only pictures. He stepped closer to the first one, the picture of the king and the courtiers staring out over the desert. He sensed a breeze playing against his face, felt the dry heat of a desert. Then, as if by a trick of perspective, the planes and shading of what lay ahead changed abruptly, and a vista opened up before his eyes. He turned in panic. The tomb was gone, Thalassa too. The setting sun shone into his eyes, blinding him. He turned, saw his shadow race away, just as the king's had. Dunes stretched in gentle rolls far away, the sand glittering in the light.

He looked at the ground in front of him. There were two tracks in the sand, both of them bare human footprints. They were identical: Jayal's and his twin's. He remembered that day in Lorn: Jayal placing his boot print on that of the Doppelgänger's on the frosty forest floor.

Now he heard Thalassa's voice calling from the direction of the fast setting sun, but when he looked behind him he still saw no one. He called back and presently Thalassa's slim body seemed to unfold from a gap in the sky and she stood in front of him.

"You touched the painting and vanished," she said.

"Is there a way back to the chamber?"

"We'll find one," she said. There was a tremor in her voice, as if she thought it unlikely they would return.

"Let's follow the footprints," Urthred said quickly.

Behind them the sun set abruptly and the sky became pitch dark: no moon, nor star. But now the sand shone with a silver light. They followed the footprints over the palely glittering powder.

After an indeterminate time, a greater darkness loomed up from the horizon ahead. A large building of some sort. They stopped and peered forward. Its outline gradually revealed itself as the top of a pyramid. Its bottom was obscured by one of the pale dunes. Behind it, the sky seemed to be lightening: dusk had not seemed so long ago but here another day hastened hard on its heels, as if time were accelerated, were flying past.

A shiver went up Urthred's back. The final pyramid, more ancient than any structure on earth. Each successive one—those in every city in the world that had survived the departure of the gods—Iskiard, Thrull, Tiré Gand—had taken its form from this original.

The footsteps in the sand continued over the summit of the dune and disappeared in the direction of the pyramid. The mystery of what had happened to Jayal and the Doppelgänger would be waiting for them on the other side.

Urthred took one of Thalassa's hands. She smiled at him, her teeth pearl white in the strange light. Together they walked up the final dune, he with a leaden certainty in his heart that this was the last time he would ever walk with her, though he had crossed half the world with her at his side. Their sandaled feet barely disturbed the silvery powder.

Then they were on the summit of the dune and the whole of the pyramid was revealed. How high was it? The light distorted everything, robbing it of perspective. Each tier reached up in giant steps, ever diminishing to where its summit seemed to touch the dark sky, yet the sky seemed no higher than the dune on which they stood. The horizon swam with black and red stripes, like a last sunrise.

But their eyes were not looking at the horizon; rather at the base of the pyramid, where the footsteps in the sand ended and there was a blaze of magical light. A figure stood there, holding a glowing staff in his hands. Though Urthred and Thalassa had never seen its light before, they had heard Garadas tell of it many times, and they knew that the light could come from only one object: the Rod of the Shadows. Again it was difficult to tell how far the figure was from them, but in that unearthly light they saw his face clearly: it was not the ravaged visage of the Doppelgänger, but Jayal's. Dragonstooth lay in the sand at his feet.

Instantly the weight lifted from both of them. Jayal had lived; the Doppelgänger was gone. Thalassa called out his name and Jayal, looking up to the summit of the dune, saw them, and waved the Rod, so it cast a semicircular blaze of white light over his head. Urthred and Thalassa looked at each other and smiled, and hand in hand ran down the slope of the dune. Urthred stumbled slightly and Thalassa slipped from his grasp; she laughed and ran on alone as he regained his balance. But when he got back to his feet, his own laughter died as his eyes fell on the footprints in the sand. Two tracks, and now Thalassa's.

A tingle of unease shot down his back. Two tracks. Where was the Doppelgänger? He pushed himself upright, shouting a warning, but his cry came at the same second as her scream as she slid to a halt in front of Jayal. He reached out a hand and grabbed her by the hair and yanked her back into the arc of light. The features that a moment before had been indubitably Jayal's twisted into a sneer.

Not Jayal, but the Doppelgänger. Once more in his old body. Urthred cried out and threw himself forward, but the sand gave way beneath him and he fell once more, over and over, down the dune, coming to a halt only a few yards from the others. He scrambled to his feet as the Doppelgänger struggled with Thalassa, clicking a stud on his glove: a knife sprang out with an almost-silent click. He took a step closer, peering into the blazing light of the Rod in which the Doppelgänger and Thalassa were only barely distinguishable.

"Priest," came that wheedling voice just as it had in the Temple of Sutis in Thrull, and under Astragal. Both times the Doppelgänger had had Thalassa in his power, but never before had he had such magic to defend himself with. Now he swung the Rod through the air and a blinding scimitar of white light hurtled just over Urthred's head. "Come on, priest, if you would go with your beloved into Shades."

Urthred halted. He looked at Dragonstooth lying on the ground. "Where is Jayal?" he asked.

The Doppelgänger laughed. "Him? He is gone—I don't know where. He fought well at the last. I took a wound in the chest from Dragonstooth but with one stroke I was through his guard and I smote him." The Doppelgänger paused, his head thrown back, his gauntlet ever tighter on Thalassa's neck. "What a sight it was. As I struck him we were both carried through the ether to where the bridge stands that spans this world and Shades, and there our bodies fused in a flash of light. And then he was gone, and here I stood, alone, in my old body. He has gone to his fate; I to mine." He yanked Thalassa back by the hair. "Come, priest, come to your whore. Will you risk damnation forever for her sake?"

And Urthred did step forward, the knife pointed at where the Doppelgänger's face was half hidden by Thalassa's. Now that he was in the halo of light surrounding the Rod, more details began to emerge. There was something different about that face that had once been Jayal's but now was the Doppelgänger's. There was a shadow on it, and just at the collar a purple mark—the same marks that the doomed villagers aboard the *Windhover* had borne: the plague.

The Doppelgänger saw that he knew, and his face creased into an evil mask once more. "Yes, Jayal cheated me, at the last. He got his old wounds and I got this—the plague. Now we will both die. But at least I will take your precious whore with me.

"Now," he continued, "I'm going to take her where you can't follow. Into Shades." Urthred started forward and the Doppelgänger gave ground, sending another flare of light at him, but though Urthred felt his face burn, he didn't flinch back. Through the glare he could see that he was nearly where Dragonstooth lay on the sand.

The Doppelgänger, seeing the threat, thrust out the Rod again. "Don't forget, one touch of this and you will follow us. And for you, unlike me, there will be no return." As he spoke, he took a step back, and Urthred saw a shimmering portal behind him, like the portal he had seen on the Isle of Winds in Lorn: the doorway into Shades. Dragonstooth was only a yard in front. But the Doppelgänger was still backing away rapidly, nearly at the portal. "Farewell, priest," he called.

"No!" Urthred cried, lunging forward, sweeping up Dragonstooth and swinging at where the Rod was outstretched in the Doppelgänger's hand. The two met with an explosion of light and sound. Urthred flew backwards as if struck by a giant's hand. He landed on his back, winded and blinded by sand and the white light. His whole body hummed with a buzzing energy transmitted through the sword.

The sand and light spots cleared from Urthred's eyes; he saw the Rod lying in a small crater in front of the shimmering portal. Of the Doppelgänger and Thalassa there was no sign.

Thalassa had gone into Shades. The light of the world was extinguished forever.

CHAPTER THIRTY-NINE

The Last of the Illgills

Jayal lay on his back. He felt hard stones pressing into him. His fingers reached out, exploring. Not hard stones but skulls.

Now he knew where he was: where it had all begun. Thrull. This was the pyramid of skulls that Faran Gaton had erected on the marshes after the battle.

His chest was on fire. He craned his neck forward. He wore an unfamiliar makeshift tunic, the same one that the Doppelgänger had been wearing when they had fought. This, then, was the Doppelgänger's body, and the Doppelgänger's wound. The area under his sternum was a deep red. The red-hot fire of Dragonstooth's wound, and warm blood welling up. He had struck well. A mortal wound, delivered by himself. The gods must be laughing. Such were the jokes played on man since they had given him magic.

Here as in the north, the sky was dark: the darkness of the end of time. The single star shone in the velvet black of the sky.

He was back in this place again, where he had begun the quest seven years before. Even in the dark he heard the croaking of the birds of death circling overhead, as he had heard them the day of the battle when he had lain dying in his father's tent. Nothing had changed; as if no time had passed, as if the seven years had never existed.

He struggled to his elbows, fighting the pain of his chest wound. Through the glimmering of Thalassa's star he could see over the endless reed fields to Thrull. But the familiar skyline had changed. The cliffs were only half their original height, as if an explosion had blown away the tops. Not a house or temple remained on the heights to show that man had once lived here, though a faint rim of ruined walls still ringed their lowest extremities.

Above the new wound he felt the pain of those older wounds he had carried for so short a time that day seven years before. He saw with one eye only, and his head ached as if that mace that the Reaper had struck him with had only just been withdrawn. He tried to stand, but the pain in his chest was too great, and he fell back.

The end would be soon. Either he would die of these wounds, or the Doppelgänger of the plague: then both would cease to exist.

He lay back, praying to the single star: the Lightbringer's star.

He fixed his eyes on it. It glimmered for a second and then his eyelids grew heavy. He felt himself being carried out on a dark tide: everything was slipping away, just as it had as he lay dying on Thrull field so long before.

But this time he knew the journey was forever. Out and out, the ebb tide, when all was swept back to the sea, the sea of death. The darkness came, the star became dim: Thalassa's star . . .

Then like a candle cast into the sea the starlight guttered, and the end did come, as it should have done seven years before.

And as oblivion came, the light of the star, the last light in the sky, his hope and mankind's, was extinguished.

And the world was covered in darkness.

Tiré Gand. Only some fifty or so of the Galastrians survived. The Legion of Purple Lamentation was in a solid phalanx, pushing them back into an ever-tighter circle towards one of the minor buildings of the pyramid temple. Now that the enchantment had gone from their weapons, the Galastrians' blows smashed ineffectually into the undead's armour.

Another push threatened to overwhelm the few who still stood. A shouted order from Gurn and they fell back, leaving the dead and the dying behind them. They retreated into the building at their rear, throwing a heavy oak door shut behind them. Some of the men leaned against it, others looked about the room looking for material for a barricade. They found themselves in a domed chamber, its walls lined with hooks from which hung the mauve and brown vestments of the priests of the Worm. Heavy oak pews were stacked against the walls; these they dragged to the door, blocking it.

Strangely there was no assault on the door, as if their opponents paused, waiting for something. Now the Galastrians had a brief respite in which to draw their breath.

Cloud had followed them into the vesting chamber, his grey flanks scored with wounds. He came and nuzzled the boy king, and Fazad in return soothed the horse, murmuring in his ear. Then, slowly, Cloud sank to his knees, and then onto his side. His master knelt by him. Froth bubbled at the horse's muzzle. Fazad looked up in despair. Gurn hurried over and reached out and felt the horse's neck.

"His wounds are grave," he said sadly.

"Yes," Fazad answered. "He speaks to me, as he has always spoken; ever since that night that Jayal Illgill brought him to Skerrib's Inn and charged me with his care. I remember when the vampires came and I hid in the stables, under the straw in his stall knowing that I must die. Then his voice came into my mind and he bade me, in words as clear as yours, to mount up and ride away on him."

Gurn looked from the boy to the door where he expected the Ossians to renew their assault at any moment. There was still no sound, just an ominous silence.

"And what does he say now?" he asked.

"His masters, the Illgills, are dead. He was old, even when the baron first mounted him: he has served generation after generation. Now the ties that bind him to this earth are cut. He will follow his masters to the Hall of the White Rose."

"The Illgills are dead?" Gurn shook his head. "Why didn't we all die on Thrull field? Then we wouldn't have had to suffer this vain hope, this belief that one day we would be avenged." He clenched his fist so the knuckles showed white.

Fazad reached out a hand and touched the seneschal's sleeve. "Courage, my friend. For Cloud has one last message: the Lightbringer still lives—we must have hope."

The horse whinnied once more and spasmed, kicking out his hooves. Then he was still.

There was a sudden loud crash and the door to the chamber and the barricade were knocked flat. Dust fell from the ceiling. Some of the Purple Knights stood outside, a battering ram held between them. They threw it down as if it weighed nothing, and stood motionless, thronging the doorway, their dark armour lit by the one or two flickering torches still left alight in the chamber.

The silence was broken only by the laboured breathing of the Galastrians. The heavier sighing of the wind through the knights' jaw guards was clearly audible though they were a good forty feet from the centre of the circular floor where the Galastrians stood.

"Good-bye, boy," Gurn muttered. "It was a brave thing we did. Let no one forget it when the earth is dark forever more."

Fazad looked up: the ceiling was a domed one, with a glass observatory right at its top. The Lightbringer's star shone directly down from above, gleaming on the marble floor separating them from their assailants. The last attack would not be long. He wished someone had told him how to pray to her, for now he needed her help more than ever. But Creaggan and Matach were dead. Zalia too. And so would he be soon. He was not afraid to die: the fearlessness of the wolf still lived in him though the cloak of Bardun was gone.

"Let Reh preserve you, seneschal. You were like a father to me," he said.

Gurn would have replied, but at that moment the light of the star above them died abruptly. There was a sudden and utter blackness as there had been in the queen's tower in Imblewick that last dawn.

The vampire knights screeched in triumph; their call was taken up by others, it seemed thousands strong, thronging the cemetery outside; all who had gathered to see the humans die. Soon the whole of Tiré Gand echoed to their baying.

Only the dead saw anymore. Fazad was blind. His courage was spent. He reached out and clutched the seneschal's hand. The end had come.

The Man of Bronze had struggled for many hours at the entrance to the pyramid, the smouldering bodies of the fallen dragons illuminating the lightless sky all around with Hel fire.

Painstakingly, stone by stone, he cast the blocks aside until he had burrowed to the heart of the pyramid and saw the great shaft descending into the depths. Ropes snaked downwards and he sniffed the air, telling from their scent signature every person who had climbed down. The baron and his men, Jayal, Urthred and Thalassa. All were here, all were in front, a mile down. There was something else too, a neutral odor, an absence of soul. The Doppelgänger and the undead.

He was late, he must hurry. Iss was coming from the skies. He, the Man of Bronze, would fly down the shaft. Flying as the God had taught him when he had flown with the dragons and fallen upon his enemies five thousand feet below, out of the glowing disc of the sun.

He stretched out his arms and stepped forward and fell. Down and down he plummeted, the depths looming up at him, the fractured remains of the steps a spiraling blur to either side. Then he closed his eyes and stilled the dizzy speed of his descent and when he opened them again he was floating, even he who weighed so many tons floated those last few feet and landed on the fractured rotten wood at the bottom of the well of the shaft as if he was no more than a feather.

He drew a breath into his metal lungs, and once more there came a hollow ring from them as the plates buckled under his titanic cuirass. Again he detected the faintest scent on the air, of the humans who had stood here. The ruby beams of his gaze lit up the dark interior of that dark place.

He set off, following the spore of the humans and vampires in front, the beams of his eyes catching movement to either side. He heard the thousand voices of the Marishader, who waited in ambush, the voices of all the memories they had stolen. He shredded each and every one of them with the red beams of his eyes, their cobwebby bodies burning away like gossamer.

Many miles yet he travelled. He hurried, his feet ringing down those echoing tunnels built by slaves in the time of the gods.

He arrived at the emerald tomb chamber and saw in front the portal to the other plane, hidden in the fresco. A star shone in the picture, showing that this was where she had gone.

The last pyramid was near. He raised a foot to begin the journey.

But the step was never taken. Just then the Lightbringer's star in the wall painting disappeared and with its death his burning heart became instantly cold, his limbs seized and he stood frozen, like a giant statue left as a memorial in that forgotten tomb.

CHAPTER FORTY

Into Shades

They came over the final dune like a dark tide, Faran in the middle, the forty remaining vampires from the Black Mines curved like dark horns on either side. One person only stood before the pyramid below them. It was the priest. Faran held up his hand and the line of vampires halted, on the crest of the slope. Four sets of footsteps led down to where Urthred stood, but only he was visible. There was no clue as to what had happened to the other three; no sign of Thalassa.

Urthred held Dragonstooth in his right hand, but his head hung low and his shoulders were slumped. A glowing staff lay on the sand in front of him. Even from this distance Faran recognised it: the Rod of the Shadows. He had seen its light once before, blazing through the dark night on the battlefield of Thrull. But in that darkness it had been lost, Baron Illgill too.

The quest for it had drawn him from Thrull and under the Palisades, through the Nations of the Night and Lorn, through the Iron Gates and into the great underworld of Iskiard. Marizian's greatest artefact; the key to Shades. Here it was, guarded only by the priest.

Faran had once imagined that to recover it he would have to lead the armies of the Worm into a final battle against Illgill, an even greater host than had met on Thrull field. But here was the final reckoning: he with his forty vampires and only the priest to oppose him.

Once he had desired a final apocalyptic battle. But now the desire for all things, including combat, had gone. Perhaps from the priest too, for still he didn't stir, though a minute or two had passed since Faran and his men had appeared.

There was a certainty in Faran's heart. Now he would have the Rod, and the world would be made safe for the return of Lord Iss. The Lightbringer was gone: the northern star had died and so had the hope of the Flame.

And with the death of light, of the sun, the moon and the stars—in short, anything that reflected Reh's glory—died the appetites of the undead. The monthly cycles of blood lust and satiation had ended. They would never hunger again, for now no light would ever shine, and in the *Book of Worm* it was promised that when that time had come, Iss' children would thirst no more.

Faran licked his lips. The scriptures were right. The blood thirst had gone. He was free, but empty as well. No days, or nights, no cycle of thirst and satiety, no battle to stay alive, just Iss' endless midnight. Now inside he felt dead indeed, as his outer body had been these last two hundred years. What was life without desire and need?

He should rejoice, rejoice that it would remain forever thus: darkness, uninterrupted, immutable, the bone horns eternally moaning in tribute to their lord. Yet the prospect seemed as bleak as the sunless earth.

It was as if the spirit went out of him on that instant of recognition; if he could have, he would have melted into the dusty sand beneath his feet and become part of it, let the million grains of his consciousness merge with the endless dunes. Desire, the reason for his existence, was gone.

He stared down. He still held the mace he had taken from the last of the Reapers of Sorrow. It seemed a lifetime ago. Its cruel flanges were as sharp as knives. Perhaps there was one more task that would bring him release. He would kill the priest. He gestured for his men to advance and they started down the steep reverse slope of the dune, the silver sand running before their feet in mini avalanches.

The priest must have heard them coming, but he did not turn; only continued staring forward. The Rod lay on the ground like a bar of molten white metal, sizzling on the cold grey dust of the desert. Dragonstooth was held in his right-hand glove, its light extinguished, its metal appearing no more magical than the dead iron of Faran's own weapon.

The line of vampires closed around the priest like a dark fist. Faran could see now what he stared at: there was an area of swirling energy in the dark shadow of the pyramid, a nexus point. He felt a chill coming from it: not a physical cold but an absence in the air, a sense of infinite realms beyond. He was reminded of the shimmering curtain of light that had hung before Marizian's tomb.

The light of the Rod had cast the priest into silhouette, but now Faran noticed that his mask was gone. How curious that after this year of pursuit he would finally see Urthred's true face.

He held out the mace and touched a flange to the priest's neck. Yet still Urthred didn't move.

"Drop the sword," Faran said.

Now it seemed that consciousness returned to the priest, for his body twitched as if he had suddenly come awake. He opened his glove and Dragonstooth fell to the ground with a hollow thump.

"Where is she?" Faran asked.

Urthred's voice came after a few seconds. "Gone, taken by the Doppelgänger."

"Where?"

The priest nodded in front to the shimmering portal. "Into Shades."

Now Urthred pulled his head away from the flange of the mace and finally turned and looked him in the eye, and Faran saw his true face for the first time. The pale blue eyes, the aquiline nose, the high, almost aristocratic forehead, the fine chiseled features.

Faran realised the priest was unaffected by his gaze: his mesmerism too had gone with his blood lust. The strongest had once bowed to his will, but now he was no better than this priest of Reh. The coming of Iss' kingdom had brought him nothing, not even joy at having his old enemy in his power.

Perhaps he no longer desired the priest's death. But Thalassa was still alive, somewhere in the Mirror World. His eyes dropped to the burning Rod. He knew its uses through the ancient text, the mould-eaten, dusty pages of the *Book of Worm*. It was the key to the gates of Shades. He would open it and follow Thalassa. She would be his; he would bring her back from that Shadow World.

He shook his head. What was this madness? Why couldn't he live without her? She was only flesh and blood whatever the *Book of Light* proclaimed. No Lightbringer she: had he not seen her pale, naked flesh shivering in front of him those nights in Thrull? He clenched shut his eyes, remembering. No, she had been more than that, even then; it was he who had not recognised it. She alone of all the others had survived the trips to his throne room month after month. All the others he had drained, but not her: he had been as one who hesitates from drinking the last drop of a rare vintage.

She was an addiction as potent as blood; his lust for life made flesh. She was lost in Shades; as remote a place as death. But he would bring her back.

The Rod was an artefact of fire, inimical to him. The priest would have to use it. Urthred glanced up and their eyes locked once more. There was a flicker of understanding. The priest had guessed what he intended.

Faran gestured to one of the vampires next to him. The creature had taken a halberd off one of the dead warriors in the Great Square. He thrust it forward, pricking Urthred's chest with its blade.

Faran pointed at the Rod. "Pick it up," he ordered Urthred. "Open the way."

"You want to follow her?" Urthred asked. He gestured at the inky black dome of the sky. "Her star has gone out.

Darkness has vanquished the light. Iss has won. Isn't that enough?" He ignored the halberd and the mace and leaned forward so he was only two feet from Faran's face. "What do you want from her? Is it her blood? Or is it something else? Something you lost when you first died?" He took a step closer. "Is it love, Faran Gaton?" He nodded at the vampires congregated around. "Look at them and look at yourself: love cannot be had beyond the grave."

"She will live," Faran hissed. "I will find a way."

"Save the Lightbringer? Strange words coming from you."

"Just pick up the Rod," Faran said through clenched teeth, pushing the flanged edge of the mace deeper into the priest's neck. A line of beaded blood formed where the skin was broken by the pressure. The vampire applied the point of his halberd even harder.

Now a flicker of pain registered on Urthred's face. He bent slowly and picked up the Rod in his right hand, the dazzle of the instrument washing the colour from his face and upper body.

Faran creased his eyes against the light, gesturing for the vampire with the halberd to keep his weapon on Urthred. "No tricks," he growled.

"All right, no tricks, but if we go, let's go alone," Urthred answered.

Faran looked at the waiting vampires. He looked at their pale expressionless faces, their bloodshot eyes, their gums pulled back, their yellow teeth, and all he felt was a sudden disgust for them. Were they a mirror of himself: was he like them? No, he had lived once, unlike these creatures who had only been slaves. He had known love, in Tiré Gand. His heart had once beaten with fire. That was why his desire for Thalassa still lived though the sun had died. He wouldn't come before her with these monstrosities.

He thrust the mace back into his belt and seized the halberd from the vampire. Then he barked a command and the line of undead shambled back.

"Lead on," he said to Urthred, prodding him with the halberd point.

The priest turned and stepped towards the pyramid, holding the Rod two-handed above his head, then swung it down toward the portal. There came a flash of burning light that caused the watching vampires to flinch. When the afterimage had disappeared, Faran saw that the gateway was open. Ghosts flew from the portal like a thick mist, wafting over their heads, up and up towards the heights of the underworld. The dead he had heard wailing all around him since they had arrived in the city. The portal stood open, black emptiness, like a grave. Faran realised that his sight, having been exposed to so much brightness—the dragon's flames and now this supernatural light—was gradually dimming. He was nearly blind.

"Go on," he cried, prodding Urthred forward.

The priest stepped into the area of swirling mist that was the portal, Faran followed him. Darkness washed over him like water over a drowning man. He stumbled on blindly. Even he who never experienced physical privation felt the cold eating his limbs, then a strange sensation of being peeled from the inside out, so his core was his skin and the skin the core. Then came a grey glimmering, and he saw a sudden flare of light from the Rod in front, ropes of mist parted in front of him and he stepped into the Mirror World.

CHAPTER FORTY-ONE

The Palace of Grey

The dazzle of the Rod gradually died away and he saw he stood on a bridge that flew in an arc across space, twisting and corkscrewing from side to side like a snake. The drops to either side were not depths, for depth implied a finite measurement. The gloomy canyons beneath were beyond distant, were as infinite as the sky and space; a dark stain like night lay far, far below in the grey mists. The Abyss.

The priest stood on the bridge, a step in front, the Rod blazing in his left hand. Faran's halberd, still at his back, kept Urthred out of arm's reach. Faran risked looking down again. Their feet were lost in the undulating layer of mist covering the surface of the bridge, pouring over it like water into the Abyss.

Faran's head swam with vertigo and he looked up again. The bridge seemed to stretch on and on but at its end stood a building, many tiered, with grey flying buttresses, rising from an island of mist, its walls hanging over the infinity of space, a hundred pinnacles and towers surmounted by a single spire. The Palace of Grey, the former dwelling place of Lord Iss in Shades.

He turned. The bridge went back for another mile, then ended abruptly, the mist drifting ever onwards over a uniformly flat plateau that blended with the pearl horizon; impossibly far, yet still visible. Its name came into his mind, like a dull toll of a bell filtered through thick fog. The Plains of Grey.

A strange humming filled the air. At first he thought it almost a pleasant sound and his mind wandered for an instant. He remembered, two hundred years before, a terrace in his mansion in Tiré Gand, a balmy afternoon, a row of small white and blue flowers growing out of the cracked moss-covered balcony. A hummingbird had come, with this exact noise, a creature whose wings beat so quickly they seemed invisible and an onlooker would have believed that the blue torso of the tiny creature hovered unaided in midair, its proboscis sucking the nectar from the flower.

For a moment he had forgotten where he was: he forgot the bridge, the Palace of Grey, even the priest himself.

But then consciousness returned: these were no birds of a distant afternoon. There was no pleasure or happiness here, in this damned place. The humming was the moaning of the ghosts who flew past them down the bridge seeking the Mundane World.

Faran turned back to Urthred. They eyed each other silently. The priest glanced from him to the depths on either side, as if he longed to throw him into them. Faran urged him on with the halberd, forcing him to take a step backwards up the bridge. For a second he teetered, before regaining his balance.

"Go on," Faran growled.

Urthred looked down at the layer of mist hiding the bridge, and then up at their destination, so far away. Then he turned and set off, looking neither to left nor right.

Faran followed, feeling for the edge of the bridge with the tip of his boot, yet never finding it. The dark looming depths of the Abyss beckoned on either side, inviting him to slip, to fall into that place from where no soul would ever return.

He shook his head, trying to rid himself of his dread, and prodded Urthred forward again. They ascended the sinuous curve of the bridge over the limitless grey cloud, like climbers on a mountainside, their legs shrouded by spindrift. They may have continued for hours and hours, or only minutes, for time here had no meaning.

But after an indefinite span had elapsed, they saw a figure approaching them, a dark smudge on the undulating grey of the mist on the bridge. Soon details could be made out. The stooped shoulders of a once tall man, the tousled blond head hung low, the battered armour of one of the Legions of Flame. The two halted and waited as the figure came on. It stopped a few steps away and lifted its head. They saw that one side of his head was smashed, with a fresh wound, an eye missing, a jagged pumping wound running down the side of the head, blood falling like rain from the bottom of the cloak into the mist at his feet.

"The Doppelgänger," Faran hissed, flinching back, the halberd levelled at the creature.

But it was as if the spectre in front had heard him, and it shook its head so that a spray of blood turned the mist beneath him pink. Its words came out in the barest of whispers.

"No, Faran Gaton, it is I, the true Jayal. Now I walk this bridge of sighs that joins Shades and the Mortal World." He gestured feebly with his hands. "A path I have visited once before, when Manichee touched me with the Rod and brought me back to what foolish men call life, but which was for me a torment.

"And here I first saw my double flying to me as quickly as I flew at him, and here our souls were joined and then separated once more. So we passed on our different ways in our changed bodies. But now that journey is reversed. Even now my body rots where it should have died seven years ago: upon Thrull field with the bones of my comrades. The Doppelgänger lies up yonder in the Palace of Grey. The plague destroyed him, as I intended. Now I am freed by my death. Freed from you, and freed from the curse."

Urthred hung his head. Jayal turned to him. "Don't pity me, my friend. Think of those you can still help. Thalassa lives a little longer, but she too is infected by the plague.

Hdar is in her blood, as it was in the thousand hearts that he"—he pointed at Faran—"released from the mines. Let your soul be damned."

"It is damned already, Illgill. You cannot curse me further," Faran replied, menacing the ghost with his halberd, but Jayal ignored the blade and turned his solitary eye back to the priest.

"She has only a little time left. She waits for you in the Palace of Grey. Hurry. She is sorry: the light of the earth is dead, she has failed. Worse, you have followed her into Shades and will share her damnation."

"Don't forget I have the Rod: it can take a man from the world to Shades and from death to life."

The ghost smiled thinly. "You remind me, Jayal Illgill, of this?" Then the smile faded. "Don't forget the curse and what you promised me in Lorn. When you have finished with it, bury it deep, friend; somewhere no one will ever find it."

"Let's go on," Faran said, impatient, turning the halberd point on Urthred. But the priest ignored him for the moment, his eyes fixed on Jayal.

"My friend, what will happen to you?" he asked.

The ghost smiled faintly again. "The dead should not return to the Mundane World. Only through the Rod and through magic; magic like Manichee had when he met you in that storm in Thrull. Yet I feel, as ghosts feel; that sweet yearning, just as my twin once did, to return from the nullity of this plane to the Mundane World; to at least see life if not to be part of it. That is why we dead return as ghosts, reversing the journey you just made, through that portal to the world once more: every day more and more, ever since Marizian opened it five thousand years ago.

"I too could return and fly up and join the million other souls that once thronged about the sun like starlings in the autumn gloom, anxious to leave for warmer climes. But now the sun is dead. I have lived long enough in the Mortal World, to wish not to be a ghost in the dark sky forever . . ."

His voice trailed off, and he stared down into the Abyss to one side of the bridge.

"Once as I lay dying on Thrull field I saw this place, the Abyss," he continued. "I saw my dead comrades being sucked past as if they were part of a river, sucked into Hel. They cried for mercy, for redemption from their fates. Aye, some of them were lucky, some were blessed by Reh; their bodies were burned in the carrion pyres—they were given the God's absolution! Their souls flew up to the Hall of the White Rose.

"But the others fell down into that place, the Abyss. Only I remained, caught like a branch in an eddy, on the very edge of that place between Heaven and Hel, neither following them down nor flying up to safety. Then the Rod brought me back to life: but now there is no going back.

"Promise me, Urthred, if day and the kingdom of Reh ever return, go to Thrull. It is deserted now, destroyed by the demon. But the pyramid of skulls still stands. My body lies next to Manichee's head. Burn it according to the rituals so I may go to heaven."

"I will," Urthred replied. "And may Reh have mercy on you."

"My thanks, as in death and in life, you are a good comrade. Farewell, I will go now, wander that far plain. There I will find my father and Manichee and all those others who have no graves, and do not rest."

With those final words he drifted toward the two men. There was no room for them to step to either side to avoid him. Both took a step or two backwards, but he came on relentlessly; then, it seemed he melted through them and out the other side.

They turned to follow his progress. Presently he was lost to view, walking down the bridge to the Plains of Grey.

"My wish is granted: he is truly damned," Faran spat. "Go on," he said, prodding Urthred forward once more.

They set off again over the arcing bridge, their feet disturbing the mist so that like liquid overflowing the brim it fell over its edge and in waves of spindrift fell into the purple depths of Hel.

Urthred spoke, without turning round to face his old opponent. "This is how the world will be, Faran, when your lord is come to earth. The sun has died, and the world, like the fire that burns in every human heart, has burned down to embers." He stared at the grey light of the sky. "A place without fire, desire or life."

Faran stared at the priest's back. He had guessed the secrets of his heart, had seen his despair. He sighed, and the scent of stale air, an old man's breath, full of leather and catarrh, wafted up into his nostrils. "You're wrong. There will still be desire," he said hollowly. "Your passions, priest, are those of the flame; but a flame can only burn itself out, consume itself: the fire carries the seed of its own destruction within it. But those of the Worm are immortal, renewable: all we need is blood to make ourselves new, regenerate ourselves. And through blood we will live forever in Iss' eternal darkness."

Urthred shook his head. "You think your lord cares for you any more than a dung beetle? Will he not raze you from this world when he comes? He has your souls: that is all he cares for. Why should he spare your empty husk?"

Now he stopped and turned. "Look at yourself: your body decays; not like flesh but like a leather mannequin whose sawdust stuffing slowly leaks out. But we of Reh are different; though we burn and are reduced to embers and then grey ashes when we die, the soul is left behind, refined by the fire: it will rise from the ashes and fly to Reh's palace in the sun. But you will never fly. You long ago forfeited your soul to Iss, and when the borrowed life you cling to gives out, you will have nothing left but the darkness of eternity."

"A pretty speech," Faran sneered, "but though time is dead, sands still run: Iss comes in his majesty. Move on."

Urthred turned and resumed the march up the arcing bridge without another word.

The palace had appeared no nearer for the hours they had

journeyed, but now, suddenly, it loomed higher and higher overhead, its walls bathed in a grey light that shimmered and darkened as if invisible clouds passed overhead. But there was no sun or moon to cast them, and it seemed that it was the walls themselves that were made of flickering shadow. A rampway rose ahead into the bowels of the building. Halfway up it lay a figure, facedown. Beyond, under the arch, they saw thousands of grey shapes moving about a courtyard surrounded by high translucent walls.

Faran and Urthred climbed the rampway to where the figure lay. Faran kicked it over, so that it lolled onto its back. The very image of Jayal Illgill, except the perfect features were blotched with the purple and black welts of the plague. But this was not Jayal, it was the Doppelgänger.

"He never made it back to where he came from," Urthred said, looking from the corpse to the palace.

"Perhaps the ghosts don't allow those who have escaped to return," Faran answered, pointing upwards to the archway.

The spirits, noticing their approach, had thronged the gateway of the palace, blocking their way; all that could be seen of them were etiolated faces, necks outstretched as if in an endless silent scream. But they didn't come forward to meet the intruders: some invisible barrier seemed to halt them on the threshold.

Urthred glanced at Faran and he nodded. The priest stepped past the Doppelgänger's corpse, followed by the vampire lord. Now there came a muttering from the spirits. Instinctively, Urthred held up the Rod as they neared them and they melted back from the gate, forming an avenue down which he and Faran passed. The spirits stood hissing to either side.

"He has the Rod . . ."

"Priest of Flame, set us free . . ."

"Let us back into the World of Light . . ."

But the two men ignored them and strode on, looking neither to left nor right. Now angry curses and imprecations followed them.

They passed under a series of arches, then came out into the open again. They were in a vast courtyard, with shadowed arcades and passages on each side. Above them perspectives and distances scrambled together; dark shadows fell across their way from the towers, and they moved through a strange striated light in which the ghosts appeared, then disappeared.

Some sixth sense told Urthred where to go: he led Faran across the space to one of the vaulted corridors. More ghosts waited for them here, whispering, holding out their hands like beggars, wishing for a touch of the light. But he brushed past them.

Now he began to see familiar faces, as if he followed a path of his own memories in which the features of his mentors and tormentors appeared: the faces of the novices and the monks at Forgeholm Monastery, all those hundreds he had met that one night in Thrull, their faces a blur; the people of Goda, and Lorn.

And there, of course, was Manichee, his teacher and his guide. He glided out of the blue-gray shadows. At his approach all the other ghosts shredded away.

Urthred bowed low. "Master . . ." he began. But Manichee lifted up his hand to silence him. "My son, I thought I would never speak to you again. But here you have come to the very realm of the dead, defying even prophecy and fate; and with you you have brought Death." He indicated Faran.

"Ah, master, I have wondered if I am not that dread lord, Death. For whoever I have touched or come near to in the world outside has died. See, their ghosts hover round me like gnats at the end of a summer's day. Only one, one who gave me back my life, lived. The one you told me of that night long ago in Thrull: the Lightbringer."

Manichee nodded sadly. "Aye, I feared that this might happen. Saw how fate would lead you to her, but instead of seeing one who was semi-divine, you would see but a woman. Saw how your heart so long locked away would be sorely tempted by her flesh and her grace, forget your priestly vows. I saw much of what would follow. But not this; that you would follow her into this place."

The ghost looked away, for the first time in life or death unable to meet his pupil's gaze.

"What are you saying?" Urthred asked.

"Ah, I have led you in vain hope and have destroyed you, Urthred. Yes, I came to you in Thrull. I had seen this time when day is no more, only endless night; knew you were the last with powers equal to mine in this whole world, that you and Thalassa alone had a chance to avert the darkness. But I didn't tell you how infinitesimal that chance was. It was not even a hope; it was a thought beyond hope. A thought shading this side of despair. And now my fears have become concrete: the light of the sun is gone."

"But only for a short time, master."

Manichee shook his head. "Men need hope, and while the sun still shone there was hope. Then we needed talk of the Lightbringer. But the world is old: the sun's fires burn down. Iss' triumph would have come whatever, even before this demon-brought darkness."

"Perhaps in millennia from now the darkness would have caught its tail like the serpent consuming itself, and there would be no more light. But not yet. This darkness is a thing of sorcery and conjury only. We will destroy it, send Iss back to his home in the stars," Urthred replied.

Manichee nodded. "Perhaps: perhaps, I despair too soon. Already you have changed destiny. You wear my mantle now, Urthred. You have come further than even I dreamed. Now change the world and the prophecies and the letter of the law. Let the Lightbringer live!"

Now Manichee began to fade as he had done those months before in Thrull. "Thalassa lies within," he whispered, barely audible. "Down the corridor yonder. Hurry, her spirit passes even now!" And with these words the ghost of the Elder vanished into the ether.

Urthred stared at the spot where his master's ghost had been. All that was left was the merest will-o'-the-wisp that then drifted off towards the great curving walls and towers of the palace, like thistledown. He turned in the direction Manichee had indicated. A long corridor stretched ahead, flanked by high walls into which the silver light fell, casting patches of brightness and other areas into total darkness.

He was not meant to have seen Manichee again after Thrull. Those had been his master's words. But he had defied fate, had come into Shades. Now he would defy fate again. Thalassa would live.

He turned. All the other ghosts had disappeared. Only Faran remained. "Lead on," the vampire lord ordered, the halberd once more at Urthred's chest.

He prodded the priest down the empty passageway. Their footsteps were silent on the flagstones. Ahead was a rectangular opening in a high brick wall; as they passed under it, they saw an altar illuminated by a solitary shaft of silver light from a ceiling a hundred feet above.

Thalassa lay upon the altar still dressed in the yak's wool cape from Goda. Purple and black splotches discoloured her face and neck.

Faran urged Urthred on with the halberd. The priest moved forward until he stood over her. Her breath was laboured and harsh.

He turned. Faran was staring down at the dying girl, his leathery features shrunken in on themselves, his eyes barely visible anymore under the creases of his brow. Strangely a tear trickled down the gristly cheek onto the ground. His weapon was completely forgotten.

Then Urthred became aware of another presence: someone had entered the chamber after them. He turned, and his heart froze.

She stood there, as alive and beautiful as she had once been: Thalassa. Gold-brown hair, a pale, high forehead, lightly freckled complexion. No mark of the plague upon it. Her lips slightly apart: surely these were the ones he had kissed, not those of the plague-blighted creature below him?

She was exactly as he remembered her. She wore the diaphanous dress she had been wearing when he had first seen her in the Temple of Sutis. Underneath that her perfect body was veiled yet revealed tantalizingly—just as it had been that first night he had seen her at the dancing in the temple. Everything about her promised life. Everything about the body on the altar promised death.

A spear of ice went through his soul.

"Thalassa," he whispered involuntarily, and took a step towards her, forgetting what lay on the altar behind. Even as his limbs began to move, he saw something strange in those grey eyes: something mocking, challenging, knowing.

"The scarred priest," she said. The voice was like fingernails being dragged over chalkboard. Not her voice, but a caricature; as much her voice as the cackling of a raven to the cooing of a dove.

"Who are you?" he whispered, though he knew.

"Why, I am she, but not she. Approach," she said, pulling back her golden brown hair, revealing one side of her face. "See? Am I not as beautiful as she?" She pushed forward one of her lithesome thighs, running her fingernails over it. "She is frigid, as cold as the stone she lies on, ice between her legs though she pleasured a thousand before you. But I will give you fire, priest, the fire that mirrors your own lusts." She ran her tongue over her lips, in a manner that brought to his mind a cat licking its lips after a meal. And, despite the voice, Reh help him, did he not feel a stirring in his loins? She was close now, her tapered fingernails rising to stroke his chest. He could already feel them through the cloth though she hadn't touched him.

Once more he was back in the Temple of Sutis, before he knew what Thalassa really was. When he thought her just another whore. And just as then naked lust raced through his body.

He flinched back just as the fingers reached his chest.

"Shy, priest?" she mocked him. "But I know your lusts. I see how you struggle. Remember her touch, priest, when she was close to you—but her caresses are nothing like mine: I have a touch that could raise dead flesh and make it beat once more. You thought she loved you, priest, but she only pitied you, lusted for the strange, the anomalous, just as when she lay with the deformed and dying in Thrull. A thousand damp lusts she has enjoyed. Think of it, priest. How many times she has lain with those with plague: the very thing that consumes her now. Perhaps gods and justice exist."

"You are not her," Urthred said, gritting his teeth, but despite his words, he glanced back. The body was still, motionless upon the slab. But the blotches had now covered every bare inch of skin, destroying all vestiges of beauty.

"She is dead and corrupt," Thalassa's shadow said. "What pleasure is there in the grave? Only he, Faran Gaton, can enjoy corpses cooled by the earth, the bed of worms between their legs, the dead blood like tar instead of raging torrents in their veins. Look at me. I am here. I am as good as her. That other half that dwells here, the other half that is in all of us. Your double is here too, priest. He is near. He comes. Do you not scent him in the air? A creature of madness, a slave of unbridled lust as you believe yourself to be all cool reason. Embrace me quickly. Only if you give way to your lusts and diminish his thereby can you save yourself."

But all this time Urthred's eyes had never left Thalassa's body on the altar. She was now utterly still; not a movement of her chest. Dead. Yet, however marked with the plague, she was lovelier than this ranting harpy. The light still seemed to glimmer through her mottled skin as it had in the Lightbringer's shrine, as it had that day in Ravenspur when they together had found his mother's grave under the mountain. Now the world was black outside, and with her gone all hope was dead, and his love too.

But then: a miracle. He saw her chest rise and fall. She was still alive, but only just. Perhaps the world was still held in balance, poised between light and an endless dark. He had thought Reh had abandoned him and the Flame, but there was still hope. He remembered who he was and why he was here.

The Rod still glowed in his band. The Rod—the source of the curse and the means of ending it. The instrument of deliverance for Thalassa, for the world, from the evil that stood in front of him.

"No!" he cried. With an abrupt movement, he raised it suddenly above Thalassa's body on the altar.

There was a flare of light. The Doppelgänger's face suddenly cast into the glare passed in a millisecond from Thalassa's beauty into a staring white mask of rage and horror, but Urthred had barely time to take in the transformed features before he touched the Rod to Thalassa's chest.

A flash of light, like a lightning strike. He heard Faran curse and where the Doppelgänger had stood, a high-pitched scream. But all was white and leached of colour. Gradually forms returned. He was staring at Thalassa's body on the slab below. He saw her move. She was alive! As the afterimage of the flash receded, and the spots in front of his eyes cleared, he saw the plague marks had gone.

"Thalassa!" he cried. He threw down the Rod, and slid his gloved hands under her back and lifted her upright as gently as he could.

"Where am I?" she said groggily.

"In Shades."

"Shades?" she repeated.

"I'm going to get you out," he said. Before he could continue, he saw her eyes suddenly focus on something behind him. He whirled round. The Doppelgänger stood, arms reaching out to them, but now she had Thalassa's old body: mottled arms, purple and crimson, the veins upstanding, each inch of exposed flesh covered with the plague boils. He flinched back, pulling Thalassa from the altar.

The Doppelgänger tried to follow, but she only took a step before she staggered and fell to the ground, struggling like a broken-backed insect, unable to move.

Now there was only Faran. Urthred snatched up the Rod from the ground and searched the shifting shadows for the vampire lord.

He stood a little way off, turned slightly away from them. The halberd lay on the floor, and he had drawn his mace from his belt. He groped in front of him with his free hand. His eyes had been damaged before they had even entered

Shades, but now the orbs were a dead white, like ash after a fire; destroyed by the flash of light from the Rod.

But then he took a great breath of air and turned to face them. He had scented them.

Urthred backed away. He noticed something had changed. Fire had returned to his veins. His powers had returned. The Lightbringer was alive once more, the star shone in the world outside, the darkness was reversed. And Faran had recovered his blood lust. The Undead Lord took a step towards them, his lips pulled back into a savage grimace.

Urthred held the Rod in front of him. Faran stopped when he heard its sizzling fire. "I have the Rod," Urthred cried. "Come no further lest you are burned."

"It has already wrought enough mischief, priest," Faran answered. "But now it must end. Do you think I fear its flame?" Another step and then he threw himself forward over the intervening space.

Urthred thrust the Rod up between them, trying to parry him, but the force of Faran's dive drove him back so that he fell heavily on his back, the vampire lord's teeth snapping but inches from his nose. Only the Rod held between their chests gave him enough leverage to keep Faran's teeth off him. He smelt sizzling leather and saw that the Rod was burning through Faran's armour.

Faran snapped again, even closer. Urthred jerked his head to one side, and the teeth just missed his ear, but something strange was happening to Faran's face. The leathery cheeks seemed to be shrinking in on themselves, as if the dead matter were being drawn from them, leaving only a hollow, empty mask behind.

Urthred thrust up, and the vampire lord, who had seemed so solid a moment before, fell to one side as if he weighed nothing. Urthred rolled away and scrambled to his feet.

Faran lay below him: his battered leather armour burned right through where it had touched the Rod. Within, his chest and abdomen smouldered with a charring black fire. Half of the cavity was already no more than grey ashes, his yellow backbone revealed deep in the terrible gash. But despite the wound, his lips still moved in the shrunken, leathery face, as if he was trying to speak.

Thalassa stood next to Urthred staring down in horror. He put his free arm around her to comfort her. Somehow Faran scented her over the burning stench of his own flesh and turned his dead-white eyes on her.

"A hundred nights, Thalassa, you could have been mine," he managed to pant. Urthred felt her shiver.

"The hundred nights have gone, Faran Gaton," she replied unsteadily.

"Aye, like a flower that sheds its petals, one by one," he whispered.

Then his back arched and his entire body, which had merely smouldered before, erupted in a sheet of blue-yellow flame. Within two seconds it had shrunk first to a black tarry mummy, then to a length of feathery ash. It caught a fugitive breeze and floated up for a second, then broke into a thousand parts and drifted away.

Urthred and Thalassa stared at the remains of their bitter enemy. Gone in a second. How many months had his shadow fallen over their lives? How many thousands had died because of him and his blood lust? Yet as they looked at one another they felt a strange pity: for under that monster's skin, the vestiges of a human being had once or twice been glimpsed; the shadow of the man that had existed before.

Urthred turned away and stared around him. Gone were the walls of the Palace of Grey, leaving only the empty grey vistas on either side and the bridge over the Gulf of Hel.

There was no north or west, south or east in this place, but where he imagined the North Pole to be there burned the single star, growing and growing in magnitude until it blazed like a sun.

The plains glimmered under the influence of the rays. And there at the end of the bridge that seemed suddenly very near stood the portal back into the Mundane World.

CHAPTER FORTY-TWO

The Light that Never Dies

Slowly, with an anguished groaning of the cogs and levers that articulated and drove his body, the Man of Bronze came alive again. Another death, another awakening. He saw the damp-stained walls of a tomb, a jade sarcophagus at its middle. Ahead of him, in the fresco on the wall, he saw the desert painting. The star had reappeared in the sky at the centre of the picture. He remembered staring at it before he slept: the nexus point was behind it.

His mind whirred: How long had he slept? How many generations of man had passed? Another five thousand years, as had gone before Marizian came and dug him from the desert where he was buried?

Or the four thousand he had spent in the First Father's Tomb?

Memory returned, like the rapid opening of shuttered windows when the light floods in. Iskiard; the great temple; the descent into the underworld, following the Lightbringer. Then he knew: the time of his sleeping had been much shorter, but a blink of an eye.

In front, he saw a shimmering gateway: a nexus point

through onto another plane. He went forward and the walls of the tomb vanished. He passed through the gateway with a sizzling of energy that played like an electric-blue waterfall off his armour. A grey desert stretched away to the horizon. The Lightbringer was near.

His iron sabbatons threw up the silver sand of the desert. The red beams of his eyes scoured over the dunes; he saw the pyramid ahead, and just over the horizon he glimpsed in his mind another glimmering portal: the gateway to Shades.

He crested the rise of the dune. In front of the base of the pyramid there were forty vampires ranged in a semicircle around two figures: Thalassa and Urthred. The sword Dragonstooth burned on the ground in front of them; the priest held the Rod of the Shadows in his right hand.

As the Talos watched, the vampires surged forward. It looked as if the two humans would be overwhelmed, but then the priest swung the Rod in a bright arc, causing a semicircle of fire to erupt around them. It hung like a frozen swathe of flame in midair. Some of the vampires blundered into it, and immediately they erupted like resin torches, spinning to the ground where they were reduced to tarry puddles. The others fell back in momentary confusion.

Now Urthred lunged forward and snatched Dragonstooth from the ground, and brought it up so that he now held both weapons: one coppery red, the other blue-white.

The ring of fire began to die; the vampires ran forward, dodging past the one or two of their comrades' bodies that still burned. The Man of Bronze began striding down the slope towards the battle.

The priest clashed his two weapons together in a cross. There was a great buzz of energy and the horizon lit up, fiery balls of energy erupting from the contact point, flying in all directions, striking down a dozen more of the undead. The others threw themselves at him.

The priest fought like a madman, cutting left and right with his two weapons, but he was borne backwards; he overbalanced and fell to the ground, the Rod dropping from his hand. Thalassa snatched it up where it had fallen as Urthred parried the bite of one of the vampires with the sword.

The Talos picked out the area of ground in front of Thalassa and Urthred and opened his eyes wide. Fierce ruby beams shot from them and landed by the vampires' feet. The tiny amount of water vapor in the ground boiled and red-hot steam exploded upwards into the undead. They danced a mad dance in a ring, their dried skin attacked by their twin enemies, water and fire; their desiccated flesh sloughing off.

Then the Man of Bronze reached them, flinging the few survivors to left and right like rag dolls. The last ones stumbled away into the endless grey desert. He watched them until they had become distant pinpricks. Without blood they would perish out there. If anyone ever ventured to this desolate spot again in the future, they might be found, desiccated husks, sleeping the second sleep of the blood deprived.

For a moment they stood amongst the smoking corpses: the Lightbringer, the Herald and Marizian's three great magical items: the Rod of the Shadows, Dragonstooth and the Man of Bronze. Joined at last under the gleaming star. The *Book of Light* had been right. When the three were reunited once more, the darkness would be defeated.

"The star shines once more upon the Mortal World, and Faran Gaton is dead," Urthred said.

The Man of Bronze's neck gears groaned as he nodded. "Aye, it shines. But there is more to do. The sun is still lost behind the demon's cloud—and still the ghosts leave this plane to cover its face. Look!" He turned the twin beams of his eyes onto the gleaming portal at the base of the black pyramid. From it, like steam exposed by bright sunlight, they saw spirit forms flowing out and then, as if suddenly caught by a strong air current, they accelerated, flying quickly over the desert towards the gateway to the underworld. "The sun still dies. Iss still travels to earth from the stars."

"What must be done?" Thalassa asked.

"First, the Rod of the Shadows. It is the key to Shades,

stolen from here by Marizian. Return it where it came. Throw it through the gate, and may it never see the light of the Mortal World again."

"Will it be safe there?"

"It will lie there until another accursed man, in another accursed time, who learns too much of the secrets of the gods and the secret roadways that lie between the planes, finds a way to Shades and brings it once more from the Mirror World. Then man will suffer again. For believe me, there will be one in every cycle of history who does as Marizian did, and a million others who suffer for the actions of that one man.

"But not until then, in many millennia. Let humans sleep until then in their beds of down, wrapped in their vain dreams. Throw the Rod into Shades and return the light of the sun."

Thalassa looked from the Rod to Urthred, suddenly hesitant. It would be her act that would finally reverse what Marizian, the great magician, had started. Was this the final, irreversible step? After this would she ever have peace? Would she not become something more than she was now—for she still did not think of herself as the Lightbringer—: the very mythological being, the legend that she herself had denied being?

She wanted none of that destiny that was now undeniably hers. There must be some place in this world, perhaps somewhere in the rolling downland of Surrenland, where a man and a woman could go and live out their years, forgotten by mankind, forgetting themselves and the events that had overtaken them. Surrenland! She conjured pictures of whitewashed houses nestling in a valley, orchard trees bowed with fruit, green meadows on which horses gamboled. Urthred could learn to tend a farm, reap the harvest in late summer and plough the fields in the autumn. Together they would live out their years in anonymity.

They had the sword, Dragonstooth: Urthred knew its magic. He could carry them anywhere in the world after she shut up the mouth of Shades. She knew that the priest, as scarred as she by the past, would want nothing better than to forget his magic and his vows and be with her in peace.

And when they were safe on that farm in Surrenland, he would renounce his magic and bury Dragonstooth where it would never be found again.

But she knew fate had something else in store—they were never going to Surrenland.

Urthred was looking at her, with those frank blue eyes. Alanda had known it, that one day it would come down to this. When the greatest threat was over, Thalassa must forsake what she was, a living breathing person who had found love. She must become what the prophecies expected of her. And his eyes told her that he saw the same: there was a sad acceptance in them.

"You and I are not finished," she said to him. "Whatever follows, we will always be together."

"Make no promises now," Urthred replied. "Only later."

She would have spoken again, but there was nothing more to say. She lifted the Rod of the Shadows over her head. Instantly its light, the same light that had caused the deaths of a thousand thousand souls, seemed at last to be tamed. She raised it, to the star that was named after her, that shone even in this forgotten dimension.

"Let Shades be forever closed," she cried.

And with that she hurled it, end over end, into the shimmering portal at the base of the black pyramid. Another incandescent flash, of a thousand suns colliding it seemed, darkness followed by ripples of light, which fled in waves over the endless wasteland all around. Then, slowly, the even light of the desert returned. And when Urthred looked at where the portal had been, it was gone, vanished like a pinprick into the air.

He heard a low moaning all around. Those ghosts that a moment before had flown away over the desert fell slowly like distant rain showers to the glimmering sand, down and down.

"It is done," Thalassa breathed.

After a few moments of silence she spoke again. "What time is it in the world outside?" she asked.

"It would be nearly dawn if the sun still shone," the Man of Bronze replied, his voice echoing from his great helm.

"You who see all things, what do you see?" she asked.

Instantly the ruby lances of his eyes shot forth over the desert dunes, bending out of sight over the horizon. How far they travelled she could not tell, but instantly it was as if the Man of Bronze had seen all that went on in the world outside and he spoke again. "As I have said, the Athanor still cover the sky. Iss still comes. The Worm is not dead. A battle rages in Tiré Gand. Those of Reh against Iss. The battle goes badly for the Flame: their only hope is the coming of the dawn."

"Tiré Gand. Half a world away," she mused, staring at Dragonstooth, which Urthred still held. "Then we must go there."

Urthred looked at her, a question in his eyes. It was not too late to pull back. She put steel in her voice. "You have the magic, Urthred. Take us to Tiré Gand."

He nodded slowly, then lifted his head to the grey sky. "In Thrull it was dawn: Reh shone upon me, and the magic came. But here there is no dawn."

It was the Talos who spoke. "Then find the same magic in your heart, priest, for there the fire burns that causes all things to move, all things to grow, all things to live: that is where you have found the true Reh, and he the true you."

Urthred turned to Thalassa. "Amen to that," he murmured. Thalassa had stepped very close to him; he could feel her breath upon his neck. She leaned in close to him, her voice low in his ear.

"I'll always be with you," she whispered.

"And I with you," he said, lifting the sword.

He braced himself, his feet apart, holding the sword two-handed above his head. "Let us go to Tiré Gand," he said, staring at the one star burning in the sky.

CHAPTER FORTY-THREE

The Last Star at Dawn

Tiré Gand. After the starlight died in the vesting chamber there was utter blackness. Each of the men with Fazad and Gurn knew that they had only seconds left. Each composed a last thought to take into eternity. They felt the dead breath of the Purple Knights close by in the darkness; the smell of mildew and long pent air vented slowly from their great helms.

But their enemies didn't attack with their weapons. They had no need to. Their words came across the short space: strange, seductive words telling the humans that they wanted their blood to drink, not to shed. Not the iron of the battle but words so soft that even the hardest heart began to melt. Words of pity, offering them eternal life—if they were to surrender. Gurn ordered his men to stay where they were, but the hypnotic words were too much for some: they heard the shuffle of feet as one and then another of the men broke from the circle.

Fazad had never taken his eyes off the point where the star had beamed through the great glass dome of the observatory before it had been extinguished. He stared at it with a total fixity, fighting the seductive words of the vampires. If they wanted his blood, they would have to come and get it. His hand tightened on his sword. This darkness was absolute; was this what blindness was like? But he had heard of a darkness so dark that it turned to white before the observer's eyes. Maybe that optical trick was happening now, for suddenly the utter darkness of the ceiling brightened dramatically. It was as if the star had been but a candle blown nearly to the point of extinguishing by a gust of wind. Then, as when a draft of air has gone, it flamed back to life, burning if anything even more strongly than it had before.

Its light grew and grew in magnitude until it seared through the glass dome of the vesting house a thousand times more brightly than it had burned before. The Purple Knights were right in front of the few remaining Galastrians; the ones who had fallen spell to the vampires' mesmerism were behind them, kneeling on the tiled floor, their heads bowed, their necks exposed. Some of the Purple Knights had taken off their helms to drink from them, and their faces were a terrible sight: hardened to the consistency of black lacquer paint overlaid by a hundred layers of dark varnish; black teeth interspersed with gold. The oldest of the old who had lived in this half life a thousand years or more.

But the sudden dazzle made all the undead flinch back. In the light they seemed vulnerable where they had appeared invulnerable before. A surge of hope shot through Fazad, and he leapt to his feet. The Galastrians in the circle around him did likewise. Then they threw themselves forward.

They had only mortal weapons, not ones of fire as they had fought with before. But they had desperation. Some of their blows found the gaps in the knights' armour, wounding the creatures' dead flesh, but no blood flowed from it, for it had dried a long time before, at the time of their deaths, hundreds of years earlier.

The knights were bundled backwards by the sheer press of the living bodies in front of them. The Galastrians kneeling on the tiles suddenly came to their senses, and grappled their enemies with their bare hands.

Fazad was in the front rank, his sword flashing left and right at the undead in front, though he knew it did no good.

Ahead was one of those who had removed its helmet, its face more skull than flesh: popping eyes, bulging from their sockets, the nose fallen into its cavity, its teeth exposed in a lipless mouth. The vampire struck at him with its mace and he only just had time to parry. The knight was twice his strength. The blow ran down his blade and up his arm, his jaw and teeth ground together by the force of it. He was thrown from the line of struggling figures, the vampire leaping through the gap behind him, but then Gurn's axe blade whirled and the creature's head flew from its body; black ichor splashed into Fazad's eyes.

He wiped his glove over them, feeling them stinging from the corrupt liquid. The headless torso of the vampire blundered on, smashing into the wall covered by the cloaks and then falling in a tangled heap of vestments to the ground, where it struggled to disentangle itself from them. One of the soldiers had managed to light a torch and threw it down upon the cloaks. The dry wool caught light and thick choking smoke filled the room as the vampire ignited. Fazad snatched a torch from the wall and lit it from the pyre. He whirled it in an arc as another of the legionaries advanced on him, the flame causing his adversary to take a backwards step.

The fire held the vampires for the moment, but Fazad knew his men couldn't last long. There were but a handful of them left, and more and more of the undead crowded the room from the square outside.

The flames of the torch began to die. The vampire leapt forward and batted it from Fazad's hand, forcing him back to the corner of the room. Gurn was by his shoulder. Yet Fazad noticed there was something strange in the light now the torch was gone; he tried to register what it was as he feinted to the left and the right, dodging the snapping teeth and mace of his opponent.

Then he realised what it was. Grey light. Not the light of the star but a more general ambience, growing and growing, filling the dark corners of the chamber, causing the vampires to stop, to look around them uncertainly: even those crouched feeding over the bodies of the fallen Galastrians looked up, their chins running with blood.

"It is the dawn!" the seneschal cried.

He was right. It was getting lighter. Fazad stared up at the dome glass above them.

"Dawn!" Gurn exclaimed again and threw himself forward once more, the soldiers still standing following him. The vampires who had been feeding got up, red smears over their pale lips, looking around them with the dazed appearance of half-sated beasts rising from their prey, unable to defend themselves, buckling as the Galastrian swords landed on their heads, shearing away skin and bone.

They began backing away under the onslaught, doglike growls echoing from behind the great helms of those who still wore them, retreating to the doorway leading to the Great Square.

Fazad had time to look up at the glass dome again. Now he saw it was no dawn that was breaking over them. The light grew and grew, as if the star now fell towards them, a blazing comet flaming through the darkness, leaving a fiery trail behind. Closer and closer until the whole dome over their heads was filled with a molten gold, as bright as the sun. Steam began to rise off the undead's armour as their flesh dissolved in the light.

Now they fled, fighting each other to get through the doorway, while outside in the Great Square the massed ranks of the undead ran like shadows across the cemetery, under the yew trees, towards the entrance of the pyramid. But it was like bright day in the yard and only a few made it more than a matter of yards before their armour fell empty, the mist spilling out of them. The Galastrians watched from the door, too stunned by the reversal of fortune even to cheer.

Fazad stepped over the bodies choking the doorway into the fresh air. The square and the trees were alive with orange light. He looked up. The star seemed to fill the sky; it fell, like a flaring torch, sparks and geysers of flame shooting far and wide in the darkness. And it fell, it seemed, straight towards him.

In Goda, the snows had overreached the frozen eaves, and the village was buried. Tunnels had been carved through it, connecting one house with another. None of the inhabitants had seen the earth or the sky for more than three months; their world was now confined to the inside of their houses and the walls of white snow and ice outside. Of all the stories of the bitter winters Garadas' ancestors had passed down, none surely compared with this.

He and Ostman only had returned. Perhaps they had got lost in their journey through the planes, or perhaps they feared returning to the world of men. For it was only after the star had died in the sky and the dawn was defeated that they walked down the mountain from the Lightbringer's shrine. At first the people had thought them ghosts, and fled from them. But Garadas had gone to his home and, like a stranger, had knocked on his door and his wife Idora had taken one look at his lined, snow-ravaged face and cried out to their daughter Imuni to come, for her father had returned. But even then, when the girl had come and stared curiously at him, he didn't open his mouth to reassure her: it was as if he was too numb to speak. Instead he went past and sat in his favorite chair and didn't stir for the next two days, merely staring at the fire in the grate.

It was the same with Ostman. Only gradually did the people hear of the strange manner of their return and the relatives of those who had gone with them learn of their bereavement.

Many cursed the headman, cursed him for their loss and for the loss of the sun, and for the whole course of events that had occurred since the Lightbringer had visited their village.

But others forgave him, placing their gnarled hands upon his as he stared at the earthen floor of his house, too ashamed to look up: they told him not to worry, that the sun would return, that his part in the great adventure would not be forgotten, that he was a hero.

But as the lightless hours dragged on, hope and supplies ran down. Fuel and food got lower and lower.

Finally the few sticks of firewood dwindled to nothing and the survivors gathered here in the headman's house, even those who had cursed him, forgetting their hatred for the sake of companionship and body warmth in their final days. Items of furniture—cribs, chairs and tables and then beds—were broken up and thrown on the fire, yet still it felt as though a heart of ice had settled in that room.

The swathed figures of the survivors sent out great billows of steam at every breath. The steam circled upwards to the circular hole in the roof that served as the chimney. No words were spoken, for words would use energy that none of them had anymore.

Perhaps it was only Garadas' daughter Imuni, the Lightbringer's handmaiden, who kept any faith, staring up at the aperture in the ceiling, half-veiled by the smoke that poured back down into the room with every gust of the blizzard outside.

It was quiet in the room apart from the whistling of the wind, so everyone still conscious started when the girl suddenly cried out.

"What is it?" Garadas asked, suddenly sprung from the reverie into which he had slipped over the last few days.

But now Imuni was on her feet and he shuffled over to her, his fur cloak wrapped tightly round him like a mummy's cocoon. "Look!" she said, pointing at the ceiling. He followed the direction of her finger, through the coils of smoke. Beyond he saw the star that had been their only light for the last several months, blazing now, moving across the sky like a comet towards the eastern horizon.

The world began to spin crazily in front of Urthred as he held Dragonstooth before him and uttered a prayer to Reh. He prayed that once more he would become one with the dragons of the god-time, as he had four times before; that the God would give him wings to fly through space. Flame seemed to erupt through his being: the air in front of the sword began to spin, like the mouth of a whirlpool, and he, Thalassa and the Man of Bronze were drawn into it. Once more he flew, following the glowing cross of the sword through the heart of the sun.

He opened his eyes. He was high in the air, higher even than when he had flown with the dragons, caught in a fiery sphere with Thalassa and the Talos. The world spread out below them. The Niasseh range, Shandering Plain to their left, the Lake of Lorn circled by its emerald forest, the curve of the horizon lost in the darkness.

Dark shapes loomed in front of them in the air, holding the black canvas of night stretched tight from the east to the west, hiding the sun. The Athanor.

But they were no match for the incandescence of the comet that seared through their midst, their wings withered like scorched moths, and the creatures plummeted downwards, dead, to left and right, the fabric of the night tearing apart as they fell.

And through the rents of the dark sky Urthred saw over the eastern mountain ranges the sun rising in a fiery or-ange ball. Its rays struck the fiery sphere in which they flew, irradiating the air with an intense red glow, and the fire surrounding them seemed to pick up extra fierceness, as more and more of the inky blanket of the night was ripped apart.

On they flew, into the growing day. The plain of Thrull to their right and the Fire Mountains, the prison of his youth, the snowcapped peaks glinting in the light of the comet. And in front he saw the high moors of Ossia. Towards which they fell with giddy speed. Below them the clouds opened and he saw the dun-coloured uplands and the dark towers of that hated place, Tiré Gand, its buildings spread like a stain over its seven hills. Here and there he saw windows reflecting an orange gleam, as the comet was reflected back upon them. They were falling fast. He felt his face stretching with the

force of their descent and from his mouth there came a cry
that even he did not hear, such was the roaring in his ears.

A moment of sudden deceleration, his vision blacked out
for a second. Then he felt solid ground underfoot.

CHAPTER FORTY-FOUR

To Valeda

His eyes sprang open, as they had that day in Goda when they had first arrived in the darkness of the Lightbringer's shrine. He stood next to Thalassa. They were in a great square shaded by yews and punctuated by gravestones. The Man of Bronze towered thirty feet over them. A great pyramid rose up to the north, its gates ajar, and shadowy presences milled briefly within, trying to escape the light: the undead.

A ring of dying fire surrounded them and the earth was scorched and blackened: the remains of the comet that had brought them. The fire had set light to some of the yew trees: smoke rose up into the air, twisting around the upper reaches of the buildings overhanging the square. They stood in the middle of a battlefield. Corpses littered the earth, dark pools of blood soaking into fallen orange and red Flame standards. Here and there, broken-backed vampires vainly crawled away to the shadows, trying to escape the coming light of the sun that high above he could see bathing the upland moors and the dark wizards' towers on top of them.

There was a small group of soldiers on the western side of the square. Their armour, what was left of it, was embossed with the red and gold lacquer of Reh; each of them looked near death: pallid, unshaven, their faces black with dirt and soot.

All this he saw in a split second. The grey walls of the temple were still dark, but above them it was as if the fabric of the night continued to peel away admitting the red bars of dawn and its golden light. The black edges of the night flew away to all the cardinal points, as if pulled there by invisible cords. Blue sky appeared and then, for the first time in months, in the east, newly risen over the high moors, the face of the rising sun, stronger than any dawn Urthred had ever seen. It finally penetrated the square. Its beams shot down and sparkled on the damp high-peaked roofs of the lower town and the waters of the circling river.

Screams echoed from the temple precincts as the undead were caught in its beams, and from the shattered gates there leaked a thick mist from the vampires' vaporised bodies. The cries continued for a few seconds, then an eerie quiet settled over the place.

He heard a bird sing, far away. Like the songbird long ago in Goda when they had awoken in the Lightbringer's shrine. The song of the nightingale, just as it had been there. But here it sang at dawn. How did it come to be here? Had it been lost in the endless night and alighted here in the most cursed of all places? But now its song, like hope, filled the air.

He turned back to the surviving soldiers. At their head stood a boy, about thirteen years old with a bloodstained sword in his hand. Next to him was a grey-haired, one-armed man of about fifty.

The two of them slowly bent their knees and knelt on the cobblestones, bowing their heads. With a rustle of cloaks and a creak of armour joints, their men followed suit.

Silence, save for the bird that sang on and on, as the Galastrians waited for them to speak. Thalassa stepped forward. "Rise up," she said. "The Second Dawn has come. We are all equal under the sun; each man who has fought for the Flame is a king in the sight of Reh."

But the boy shook his head, refusing to stand; staring

steadfastly at the cobblestones. "We are not worthy: you are the Lightbringer. Your star gave us hope when all had abandoned it."

"What is your name?" Thalassa asked.

"I am Fazad."

"Then, Fazad. I, the Lightbringer, command you and your men to stand." They did so reluctantly, with a rustle and clank of armour. Thalassa nodded her head in approval. "Good," she said. "Now tell me where you're from."

Finally Fazad raised his eyes to meet hers. "I am of the Falarn family, once of Thrull. These men are all that remain of the army of Galastra."

"Thrull?" she asked. For a moment she was tempted to say that she, too, had come from there. But she reined herself in, the words unspoken. She was not that person anymore. "How did you get here?" she asked instead.

"My lady, it is a long story, and begins with the night that Thrull was destroyed. A night of portents . . ."

And so, as the sun rose over them, imparting some warmth to the square, he told her his story. How strange it was to hear from a third party of how Jayal had arrived at Skerrib's Inn, and how he had asked for Thalassa Eaglestone by name, and how, as the dawn finally broke, Fazad had ridden out across the marshes and saw the fiery comet ascending into the sky that, unbeknownst to him, had been Dragonstooth taking her and Urthred, and Alanda and Jayal, to the north at the beginning of their quest . . . Her mind spun away, lost in the maze of coincidence and fate.

Fazad continued his story even as her mind wandered: she barely heard the boy's account of his long ride on Cloud to Bardun, through Surrenland to Perricod and then over the frozen sea to Galastra.

"And where is Cloud?" she asked.

Fazad looked back at the vesting chamber. The light had penetrated its gloom and they saw the horse lying on his side at its centre.

"He died just as the star did. He was a creature of the gods, not of this world. He spoke to me not in a human tongue, but directly to my mind. He told me that the last of the Illgills was dead—and with the passing of his master's family, he too must die."

Her mind flashed back to those happy days before the battle of Thrull: the stables on the Silver Way, Jayal's proud father, helping his son into Cloud's saddle. Even then no one was sure how old the horse had been. It had lived through many generations of their family.

That day the gelding had carried Jayal round in complex dressage patterns, the young man smiling down at her as each maneuver was accomplished, the pattern left in the arena sand almost geometric such was the perfection of the horse and rider. Even Baron Illgill had permitted a small smile to flicker over his normally stern features. Now both the Illgills were dead—Cloud too.

The men had by now raised their heads and were looking at her curiously. She straightened her back. Her white cloak glowed in the mounting light, her golden brown hair whipping out on the breeze. The sun was getting higher and higher and it was becoming warm in the square, an unfamiliar sensation after months of icy bitterness. She wondered what season it would have been when there had been seasons. The autumn. Nearly a year had passed since she had left Thrull.

"Where are the rest of your men?" she asked Fazad.

He pointed at the corpses in the square. "Some died here. But more never made it this far."

Thalassa saw the hunting horn at Gurn's belt. "Sound the horn, seneschal," she commanded.

He applied it to his lips and blew lustily, but no answering call came from below: they waited an hour but no survivors climbed up to the square. The rest of the human army had been wiped out. Perhaps some of the elves still lived: once more invisible in the sun as they had been for so many millennia, perhaps they even now travelled away from the city, back to their forest home.

When it came again, her voice was light and ringing, like a flute playing on the edge of the blustering wind so that it carried far and wide. "The Worm has been defeated. The sun shines once more; shines as we have never known it. The seasons will return with their plenitude, the crops will ripen, the fruit will burden the branch until it touches the greensward. The bird you hear singing will multiply and its song will fill the world. The ice that holds the seas and the ports will be gone and ships will cross the blue oceans blown by gentle breezes; trade and prosperity will follow. The cities will be rebuilt, all but one." She gestured at the dark buildings surrounding the square. "This accursed place, Tiré Gand. It will be razed forever and its ruins ploughed into the marshes and the hills."

Urthred felt a shiver down his spine. With the sun burning off her golden brown hair, her face pale and intense, she seemed transformed, an avenging spirit. What had happened to Thrull would be re-enacted here, in Tiré Gand.

She continued: "Reh's temples will be reerected. Mankind will heal the wounds of these years. The glory of the time of the gods will return, the time that they called the Golden Age." There was a cheer from the surviving soldiers, and once more they knelt.

"I give you my service and my army's, such as it is," Fazad said, kneeling too. "We will follow you, until you command all the lands of the world," he added reverentially.

She smiled thinly—suddenly the look of exultation passed from her face, and her shoulders sagged; a shadow of doubt came over her face that the kneeling soldiers could not see.

She turned to Urthred, and there was such an expression of mute appeal in her look that it was difficult for him not to reach out to her, to touch her, to tell her to come close, that her duty was done: that he would harness the light of the risen sun and use Dragonstooth to take them to that secret place she dreamed of. But he knew she had made up her mind: the Worm must be erased forever from the earth.

She turned abruptly back to Fazad. "I am not the one who will wield power on this earth."

It was now the old seneschal who spoke. "I am but an old

soldier. But I ask, since the Illgills, Queen Zalia of Galastra, and Sain, Governor of Perricod, are all dead, and the Emperor disappeared two hundred years ago, who will rule for the Flame?"

"You are right: each land stands empty of a king. And in the olden days it was the emperor who was the kingmaker. We must go to Valeda. Perhaps the Emperor's descendants still live, waiting for the sun to be reborn." She turned to Urthred. "We will need Dragonstooth one more time."

He nodded, feeling her slipping away once more.

"Let's find a high place where the magic of the sword will be most efficacious." She continued, gesturing at the Talos. He lifted his head, and grinding the stone slabs under his feet, strode to the gates of the temple. Grasping one in each fist, he tore them down, casting them aside as if they were no more than feathers. They fell over the curtain wall to either side, down into the lower city, toppling over and over their axes almost in slow motion. The echo of their fall rang from the hills and walls like twin claps of thunder; dust rose up to cover the face of the sun.

When all was silent again, Thalassa swept into the shadow of the inner courtyard, the Godan cloak glowing in the dark. The rest of them followed, their weapons at the ready, seeking vampires in the shadows. The temple pyramid rose up in front, a deep shaft cut into its centre leading down into the crypts. Shadowy figures moved there but the Man of Bronze's eyes opened and a ruby blast of light shot down its length: like moths caught in the flames, the undead whirled round and then were ash, their remains swirling about the corridor.

"Now we must separate," she said to the Man of Bronze. "You know what you must do—leave not a stone standing."

He inclined his massive head. "I will destroy this city, then I will return to Lorn, and seek the Forge where I was born, and there I will wait through the aeons until the world turns dark again and I am needed once more."

"Farewell, then," she answered, then turned and hastened towards the pyramid. She ignored the deep shaft leading down into the underworld: instead she began to climb the shallow steps towards the summit two hundred feet above.

Urthred and the surviving Galastrians followed, up and up until the city fell away below them. It took them a few minutes to gain the summit, which was surmounted by a blue glass dome sparkling in the sunlight. Thalassa stopped, putting out a hand for balance on the dome, for the breeze at this height was quite fierce. Inside the dome there was a faint haze of mist and several crumpled purple cloaks, brocaded with silk hems and precious stones sown into the rich fabric, lay on its wooden floor. Perhaps they had belonged to the undead Elders of the city, caught here in the observatory by the sudden appearance of the comet and the dawn,

Fazad and his men formed a ring round the summit. Below, the Man of Bronze stood where they had left him in the courtyard. Thalassa raised a hand in farewell, and he did the same. Urthred held the sword aloft: its point caught the rays of the sun and blazed like phosphorescent fire.

Now all that could be heard was the soughing of the wind coming off the high moors and the twittering of the bird again, still invisible against the burning disc of the sun, but filling the crystal blue of the sky with its song.

"A moment, Urthred," she said softly. Her eyes travelled over the marshes to one of the gloomy mansions on the far side of the River Furx.

"What is it?" he asked.

"Faran Gaton's palace," she answered.

He followed the direction of her stare. Even in the warm sun, the building seemed shrouded in gloom, its walls hung with a nightmare of ivy, its mullioned windows like dark eyes, creepers trailing from its turrets. A weeping willow spread its shadow halfway over the river, its sad leaves dragging in the sluggish flow. The place to which he had promised her he would one day bring her back as his blood slave, when he was ruler of Tiré Gand and all of Ossia.

"I will build Reh's temple on the site of Faran Gaton's mansion," she declared, "where that monster was born and lived who brought the world to grief. Let the priests of

Flame come and pray there for all those who have been slain by the Worm, or who succumbed to the false promises of the Life in Death."

"It will be done," cried Fazad and the other Galastrians.

She let out a deep sigh, as if releasing an evil trapped within her. "The sun rises to its zenith. Ready the sword. Let us go to Valeda."

"To Valeda!" came the echo.

And they were gone in a flash of white light.

A VALEDICTION

Sunset in Valeda

The world is not as it once was. Valeda is different now: an oasis in a desert. The golden sun falls aslant the towers, arcades and flowering gardens; a riot of colour, the blue fountains, silent for all the years of the Emperor's exile, frothing in their basins!

Valeda: I never thought I would see your hidden treasures and secret gardens—but then, those many years ago, I did.

The last chapter: do I grow weary of the infinite magic of the spheres? Perhaps. I will not describe that third and last journey that Dragonstooth took us on, quicker than the blink of an eye, apart from in the scantiest detail: over the moors to the high red cliffs where Ossia ends and the high country of Attar, where Valeda is situated, begins.

We travelled many leagues, then alighted upon the dun steppe; sere grass stretched as far as we could see to a horizon on every side unmitigated by tree, or even a cloud in the sky—which now shaded towards evening, but still burned hotter and stronger than the sun had ever burned before.

In front of us stood the palace where the Emperor had retired two hundred years before. It was an eerie sight. Red stone walls stretched five furlongs to either side.

Beyond the walls were a hundred conical-shaped towers, built crudely of unrendered stones and red plasterwork. Not the smooth towers of Tiré Gand or Thrull or Iskiard. The highest was a long way away. It had a glinting obsidian summit and we saw strange objects protruding from its height, pointed at the sky. Telescopes. The tower where the astrologers had retired at the Emperor's orders to observe the sun. In front of it stood great wooden doors, reinforced with bronze, painted red, now peeling and blistered, and divided into a hundred panels.

A hundred leather scroll cases were nailed by spear heads to the panels: these had been cracked and blackened by the elements over the years. But most of the messages were still safe in their leather scrolls; some of the cases still had gaily coloured streamers attached, blowing in the wind, whipping back and forth like snakes.

Some of the messengers who had come had died waiting for the doors to open and a servant to take down their scrolls. The flat beige of the steppe was broken in several places by tent poles, the canvas that had once stretched over them long since gone, and beside them piles of white bones, one or two still held together by fluttering rags.

A great iron clapper, a hundredweight, that would take a man two hands to lift and let fall, was mounted on the wall to the left of the gate.

As our eyes adjusted to the glare we saw, beyond, rising into the blue sky, the columns of light that history writes of, like white chalk marks, still following the paths of the gods' steeds when they departed the earth ten thousand years ago. A great circle had taken us back to the top of the world, on a latitude nearly level with Iskiard.

The wind blustered and suddenly the heat was gone and the sun was sinking to the west. The cold cut keenly, reminding us that though the sun shone, our constant companion of but a day ago, ice, was still not far away.

The seneschal ordered one of the soldiers forward to the gate. The man strained his back, lifting the clapper off its striking plate, and then when it was at right angles he let it fall. Its dull thud echoed flatly around the walls and over the steppes like the clap of doom, but no answering cry came from within. We waited while the wind whipped a dust devil or two over the dead grass. Silence and a weight on the heart: futility in the air. We all knew the Emperor was dead. Had been dead most of the two hundred years since he had quit the inhabited lands. Why had we come?

So we might have stood until the same fate overcame us. It was Thalassa who made the first move, stepping forward, approaching the doors with their porcupining of rusted spear heads. I followed close behind. An iron handle stood in the centre of each door. How many times had they been tried by the dead petitioners in the wasteland around us? The blueing of the iron had been quite worn away.

She reached forward and grasped one of the rings and turned it, and the gate, which had not been opened for two hundred years, swung back as if it had been oiled and re-hung that day. By now, the Galastrians seemed inured to such miracles. None of them uttered a word, but merely followed her into the palace. There was no one within. A garden stood in front of us, but there was not a leaf that was green in it. All was dried and dead: giant palms, dead white leaves rustling in the wind; the moss brown around the silent, empty fountain; the flowers, withered and dun, yet all preserved in the dry air as a ghostly reminder of the verdant place it once was. Beyond, massive arches led into the shadows.

Thalassa looked behind and then glided under the arches. We followed. On either side were shadowy rooms full of dust and termite-eaten furniture, then, at the end of that passage, another dead garden; and so the pattern was repeated over and over: passage and gardens, interspersed with plazas at the centre of which stood conical towers. The palace was a huge labyrinth. We headed in the direction of the high observatory.

How many weary hours passed? Night fell and we slept, and then dawn came. We moved on, and not a living thing did we see all that time, not even an insect. All was sterile, dead. We reached the final corridor: fifty yards long, hung with rotted tapestries, a once ruby-red carpet now turned so white with dust that only a ghostly pink remained, each constituent thread of its weave revealed.

Here at last we found the first of the palace's inhabitants. A line of kneeling skeletons, a hundred either side of the passage still wearing faded scarlet cloaks now white with age and dust. The Emperor's servants: not one had broken from his place even in death, though one or two had toppled to the side. We stepped over their bones. In front stood a double door, the imperial seal, interlinked dragon and serpent device, over the centre, and the handprints of the servants who had died outside set into the wax, as fresh as if it were yesterday.

We broke open the sealed gates to find that final mystery: the centuries' silence broken. We saw the court asleep, in their chairs either side of the long hall, their mummified faces ashen with dust. At the end stood the throne with the dead Emperor upon it, preserved from the winds and the cold of the high altitude, his skin as dry as the dust outside. And all around the throne I beheld the heaped gold of the generations, and the carved screens, and jewelery lying in open caskets, a mirage of gold and amethyst and emerald and ruby: it was like a dream.

The Emperor was dead. In that spot, standing next to his bones, Thalassa anointed Fazad the Emperor of all the known lands, and Gurn his chamberlain. She would have had me High Priest, but I shook my head: I had had enough of "priest" for a while.

No man would linger for long in that place. First I buried Dragonstooth there in Valeda where no man would ever find it again. Then, that very night, leaving all else as we had found it, we set out for the western lands. We went on foot, for now all urgency had gone.

And that is the end of my story, or nearly. I will hurry the rest, for I hear the monks going to vespers in the courtyard below, and you, my scribe, Kereb, must join them.

Never again did men call her Thalassa: in the histories of that time, they call her the Lightbringer only. What she once was—a courtesan and Faran's plaything—is also forgotten:

the victors rewrite the histories of every war. So it is with that of the Wars of the Flame.

Some of the history books recounting those days are in the library here in Forgeholm, written by the new scholars of our age, men I have never met. I sometimes wonder how they came to the knowledge of those times, for I did not see them fighting by my shoulder in the streets of Thrull, or in the Nations of the Night, or in Iskiard or in Ossia when Tiré Gand finally fell.

As I have said, their words are lies. They have written with the Elders of the temple at their shoulders, censoring their every curlicued *i*. They speak of the Lightbringer as the betrothed of Jayal Illgill, son of Baron Illgill, Hearth Knight. It is more fitting that she is portrayed thus than as the amour of a celibate priest of Reh!

Their accounts for the main continue thus: Jayal returned soon after the battle of Thrull, recognised her as the heroine who would save the Elect of Reh, and vowing to protect her honour, chastely took her with him to the north. There he died tragically in Iskiard. She alone entered Shades, died only to be reborn again, and conquered the darkness.

As I say, the histories do not mention my name. In their accounts I am nothing more than a shadowy figure, the Herald, a lowly priest of Reh, a mere servant of the Lightbringer. None refer to the love we shared, for our acolytes are taught that priests do not need the comforts of the flesh. Did I not myself once teach this doctrine with zeal? Learned under the blows of my tutors in this very place, this Forgeholm?

So there is the irony: after I set out into the world from this tower, I changed, but the world did not. Even after the bitter wars of religion, when we saw what the Worm could do, what did we of Reh do in return? Worse than they visited on us in Thrull and Perricod and Imblewick. The cities of the Worm were destroyed and their inhabitants rounded up and enslaved. They were made to work on the great rebuilding of the Flame temples around the Empire. Thousands died of hunger and disease, and still do so to this day.

As I have said, I lost my zeal, but more fanatics came in my place, as water will rise in a well however many times you dip into it.

I said good-bye to Thalassa in Ossia. I had barely seen her the few weeks before we got to the place where we parted. By then our army had thronged to several thousand strong. The Wolf King, now the Emperor, rode west, back to Surrenland and Galastra. More and more flocked to his side every day, many of whom had been serving the Worm but a few days before.

I cannot name the spot where we left each other: that land is a treeless place of moors and deep valleys where the Worm has mined the heart of the earth and left it heaped in spoils, where towns and villages are named in the strange tongue of the High Priests of Tiré Gand. We parted at an anonymous muddy crossroads, as a dank curtain of rain fell from an autumn sky. My way lay due north, hers to the west.

Perhaps there was a tear in her eye when we parted: I do not know. For by then she seemed a stranger to me, surrounded by strangers. Each minute of the day they petitioned her, seeking miracles and wise words. She was never alone.

I travelled north back to the lands I knew.

For the second time I passed under Superstition Mountain and into the great bowl of marshes that surrounds Thrull as the winter rains fell heavy and drear, forcing the marsh waters up almost to the level of the causeway. And there I found Jayal's remains lying on the summit of the pyramid of skulls. I sat with my friend, and as I mourned, I saw those strange creatures that I had first met with Seresh in the underworld, the leech gatherers, moving over the marshes and the distant cliffs. They had come into their inheritance: the rock of Thrull was theirs again, as it had been before Marizian came. Now no longer did they catch leeches, but bones, bones of all the dead of Reh. Through them and through divination I discovered those of Manichee and Alanda's husband, Theodric, of Seresh, Count Durian, Furtal and the many others I had a debt to. I put them back together, piece by piece, all I could find. It took me two years to find all of them, but I had time.

Then, one dawn, when the autumn pinched the air once more, the leech gatherers and I carried the bones to the top of the shattered mountain and began building a pyre. It was dusk by the time we had finished and the sun in sullen red majesty fell towards the Astardian Sea beyond the Fire Mountains.

I conjured a ball of flame as angry as that sunset, as angry as my heart: and it took the last of the Illgills with it up into the sky to the Hall of the White Rose, and with him the remains of my master Manichee and all the rest I saved. May their souls rest; and all those I couldn't find, forgive me where you wander Shades. Reh will shrive you at his fiery second coming.

I watched the flames for many hours. When I stirred again it was midnight and the leech gatherers were gone. I never saw them again. A white ghost moved over the plains behind me, like one of the will-o'-the-wisps. Cloud. I heard his neigh as once more he pawed on the causeway, seeking his young master. Rest now, I called: *he* is at rest, gone to Heaven.

In the spring of the next year I travelled on over the Palisades to Goda, where Garadas and the others greeted me. Simple blessed folk. They asked me news of Thalassa, and I told them what she had become and how the entire Empire knelt before her, and they nodded as if they truly understood these things, but I knew that suddenly she seemed as remote as the statue in the shrine had been before her arrival in the mountains those three years before.

Another summer came and I went on to Ravenspur and opened my mother's tomb and laid fresh flowers by her grave. That winter I lived in a hut by the side of Lorn, and there in the bare woods I saw the pitiful figure of Nemoc pass, afraid it seemed of the very shadows: certainly too afraid to approach me. Each night when the moon hung full over the lake I watched for the gateway that led to Lorn, the burial place of my father. It never reappeared.

And when the winter had passed I came here, to Forge-holm. A few priests remained, some faces I recognised from my departure four years before. I think they were as amazed to see me alive as I was to find myself back here. But where else could I go? I had no other home.

Word didn't take long to reach the lowlands, that Urthred, priest of Flame, had returned to Forgeholm. A mes-senger came from the Elders in the new High Temple in Per-ricod. The letter named me Abbot, told me of all the work that was needed to restore Forgeholm to its old status, and rescinded my travel privileges until the work was done. In short I became a prisoner: head jailer in the place where I was imprisoned.

Well, I never intended to leave. I had seen enough wan-dering to last ten lifetimes. Besides, I had a mission, to make the lives of the young monks and acolytes of Forgeholm as unlike my time as a novitiate as possible.

So I have remained in the tower, and the years have passed. But quickly or slowly I cannot tell—who counts? Only Reh's infinite majesty rules in these mountains, not time. He is in the shadows on the buttresses and the cliffs, his face is the driving cloud that comes off the top of the Old Father in a plume, his eye burns in the sky, his soul is the eagle riding the thermals. So the days have passed: the noon and dusk of my life.

I hear the lands of the Empire prosper. There are festivals of light in every land. And every summer solstice, the largest of them is held in Galastra: the ports of Surrenland are thronged with pilgrims wishing to cross the Astardian Sea. They flock to see the Lightbringer—she appears on the bal-cony of Zalia's White Tower, before crowds of a hundred thousand or more.

Yet in the winter months, when the festivals of light are ended and the harvest is brought in, she leaves the island and travels east.

So now it is night in Forgeholm. The summer draws to its end, yet the stones of the piazza outside still hold the heat of the sun. The scribe, Kereb, is gone at last. I rise and take my cane. Tip, tap, on the marble floors. I make my way to the open doorway that gives onto the balcony. Beyond, when I had sight, I looked down the dizzying pass that leads to the plains of Surren and to the distant patchwork fields. There, like a chalk mark on its endless plain, the road to the west disappears into the heat haze towards the sea and the cerulean blue of the sky.

Though the danger is many years past, I hear the watchmen in the monastery's towers; at every lighting during this and every night the guards sing out to their comrades the time, telling that all is well. I listen now, a minute or two passes, then I hear their voices a dozen strong, a ripple, an echo as one takes up the cry of the next until like a ring of sound it echoes from every compass point of the monastery.

Already it is Tenebrae, the darkest time!

Alone, always alone. I seek for her, not with my eyes, but with my inner mind.

At the beginning of the summer she travelled around the Empire as the festivals dictate, passing through Ossia into Thrulland and Surrenland, and then in midsummer over the seas to Galastra. Many of our friends were gathered in Imblewick, but not I: I am a prisoner. To the people of those lands, I no longer exist.

Now it is summer's end: as when I summoned the dragons from the fire of my blood, so now I summon an image of her. She too is old, yet still that light shines through her as if a lantern burned within.

No one owns the light, my friends: it shines impartially upon all of us. I do not own her—what she gives is given as the sun lends necessary light and heat to all things that live; so she gives to all of her people so they may have hope; even in the darkest night when the spirit is lowered like a guttering flame and it seems that the shadows hold ancient evils.

I, too, she shined upon, and I have grown. Inside, life has blossomed: she has not neglected me, nor forgotten.

That is my hope, that is what I live for. So though it is dark and my eyes stare sightlessly over the mountains, in my inner eye I see her—she is not far away, hurrying through the night on that chalk-white road over the plains, with her retinue and a thousand lamps ablaze. By dawn she will be in Forgeholm, and tomorrow night, once more, she will be in my arms!

CODA

Nemoc

Under the sun of four dozen summers, the forest had put on some green again, covering the fallen trunks so that at the beginning of the spring, a delicate emerald haze hovered over the devastated wilderness. The Way was lost that he had once trod—the Way that joined this world with an immortal paradise.

He sat in a hut made of salvaged wood by the lake. A heat haze came off the water's surface. For a brief period every few years he returned, the time of year depending on where his travels had taken him. This year it was the summer. He lay back, enjoying the warm sun, yet still his heart was sad, knowing that soon he would have to go on his travels again.

When he wasn't at the lake, Nemoc wandered the world, sleeping in haystacks and barns, in pigsties and kennels. Animals were his only friends: the dogs never barked when he came into the towns and villages like a ghost, nor did the cockerels crow; the cows shuffled sideways to give him room to lie down in their stalls. Mice used to come and sleep in the folds of his cloak.

He travelled through the nights, past isolated farmhouses and villages, doing as his master had told him. When he saw a light he would rap upon the doors and windowpanes of the cottages and houses, hoping to find one who would listen to his tale, the story of the end of Lorn. But always the labourers and farmers took him for a begging leper, with his hideous face and his rags: all sent him packing into the night with blows. His body became even more hunched through its many wounds. The mortal world weighed on him. His bones ached as they had never ached in Lorn. There he had been immortal, but here he felt the bitter pinch of mortality. So after each period of futile wandering, some lasting several years, he returned here, to the lakeside, the nearest he would ever get to returning to Lorn.

He rarely left his hut during the day. The only sounds were the birds singing in the trees and the waves lapping the lakeshore. Only one man had ever come back to this spot: his master's son. He had come fifty years before, shortly after Nemoc's first trip through that bitter winter that never ended, when the sun had been eclipsed for many days and was then reborn. Urthred, the child that Nemoc had abandoned under Ravenspur. He saw that Urthred was cured, that he wore his true face, yet still a mask of sadness hung there. He would have gone and spoken to him of his father, the Watcher, lost in Lorn, but his guilt was too great. He set off once more, this time to the south, to the Ormorican desert, and didn't return for years.

Now he was old and knew he wouldn't live beyond his next trip. Where fifty years before Urthred and Jayal had knelt at the edge of the road that slipped into the lake, he himself now knelt and studied his face, and shuddered at what he saw. It was like running wax, one eye sunken out of sight into the folds, the other red and rheumy, the skin as wrinkled as a bloodhound's.

Through the passing years, a strange cloud could be seen on clear days, dust grey, rising in a column far to the east. He had passed near its source on his journeys: Tiré Gand. The air in the upper atmosphere caught the smoke and drove it across the skies and when it blew it his way, fine particles of dust fell out of the sky like grey snowflakes.

But this year the cloud had abruptly disappeared.

Late one night, when the moon was nearly full, and

Nemoc once more roamed the lakeside knowing he must soon leave and go on his final journey, he noticed the glint of armour high up on the peak of Ravenspur. He saw an explosion of flame and felt the earth tremble faintly beneath his feet. Louder and louder, stronger and stronger, came the vibrations until the birds flew in panic from the trees and the whole forest shook. Only one creature could make such a noise. The Talos was returning.

Nemoc stood by the lakeside, his head bowed. Trees fell in the forest, and in front where he stared at the full moon rising, the lake surface shivered. Nemoc turned to confront the giant. With a final crash of undergrowth, there he stood, his breath hollow in his metal chest. His ruby eyes were raised to the sky. Nemoc remained standing, wondering what the Man of Bronze would do. The moments passed in silence: it seemed the Talos was waiting for the moon to reach its zenith.

Slowly it reached its height. And then, a miracle. A golden light curved away under the lake's surface, and the Way and the thousand lamps that led to Lorn stood revealed for the first time in fifty years. At its end Nemoc saw the immortal city standing as it once had, its buildings intact, Erewon's palace atop its mount, under the light of the full moon in an endless summer night.

"Come, the Way is open," the Man of Bronze suddenly said, the ruby beam of his gaze finally falling on Nemoc. "The world is healed, Tiré Gand razed to the ground. You are forgiven. Time may carry us back as well as forward."

Nemoc bowed his head. "I must stay—I made a vow long ago to tell the tale of Lorn to all who would hear."

"The Watcher lives again, in a new incarnation, and waits for us in Lorn. His sons are with Reh. No one listens to you, Opener of the Way; they pass you where you hide during the day in the hedgerows and haystacks, carrying bushels of corn and laughing. And at night they return home, singing, in their laden carts. They don't care for your tales of the dark times. We are but myths, myths that must sleep for a little while."

"A little while?"

The Man of Bronze stared up at the moon. "In the eyes of the gods a thousand years is but a twinkle of an eye, a hundred thousand but a short sleep. Come, you have suffered enough, return to the immortal land where Reh's servants wait for his return. Once more you will be the Opener of the Way, and when the circle is closed and humans need you, a thousand years from now, or a hundred thousand, you and I will come as we did before."

So saying, he stepped forward onto the Way where it disappeared into the lake and began to sink below its level. Nemoc stared after him, the golden glint of his armour shining beneath the dark glass of the waters, and then up at the moon.

Soon it would be too late: the gateway would close. Mortality or immortality? He stretched forward a leg and it too disappeared beneath the surface and touched the Way. And once more he travelled the road to Lorn.